MW00974527

THE MUSSORGSKY RIDDLE

To Joan,
Can you solve
the Riddle?

DARIN KENNEDY

A Division of **Whampa, LLC**
P.O. Box 2160
Reston, VA 20195
Tel/Fax: 800-998-2509
http://curiosityquills.com

Cover Art by **Polina Sapershteyn**
http://www.polinas-portfolio.com

Author Photograph by **Michael Church Photography**

ISBN 978-1-62007-806-8 (ebook)
ISBN 978-1-62007-807-5 (paperback)
ISBN 978-1-62007-808-2 (hardcover)

LIBRETTO

To everyone who believed, this one's for you.

My music must be an artistic reproduction of human speech
in all its finest shades. That is, the sounds of human speech,
as the external manifestations of thought and feeling must,
without exaggeration or violence, become true, accurate music.
Modest Petrovich Mussorgsky

Lead me from tortured dreams, childhood themes of nights alone
Wipe away endless years, childhood tears as dry as stone
Greg Lake

One wants to tell a story, like Scheherazade, in order not to die.
It's one of the oldest urges in mankind.
It's a way of stalling death.
Carlos Fuentes

I

Overture

Freshly turned earth. Ammonia.

The alternating aromas fill my senses as I take the first Charlotte exit off I-77 and forge my way through the rain toward the cloud-obscured cluster of skyscrapers in the distance. Death and despair hang over the city like the leaden sky that has been my only companion for the last hour. I peer through the deluge, my rapid breathing in time with the staccato rhythm of my windshield wipers, and contemplate turning around.

Have I done the right thing coming here?

The tinny drone of my GPS guides me through the clogged maze of streets, the hint of ammonia growing stronger with each passing minute. When I finally arrive at the clinic, the odor becomes so overpowering, I nearly retch. I take a moment to clear my thoughts the way my mother taught me before rushing through the downpour and inside. Cool, sterile air fills my lungs as the receptionist motions me to meet her at the door to her left.

"Are you Mira Tejedor?" she asks.

I nod and head for the frosted glass door leading to the back. One last wave of nausea ripples through me as I step through the doorway and follow her to an office at the end of the hall. The sickening ammonia stench fades with each step, though no time passes before another scent fills the gap.

Part of me wishes I'd awake tomorrow with only the five senses God afforded the rest of humanity.

But my wish is a fool's wish.

I am, after all, my mother's daughter.

My grandmother always knew when it was going to rain. More accurate than any weatherman, people outside our family usually guessed the arthritis gnarling her fingers gave her this particular insight. The truth is far stranger.

The women in my family all possess certain talents that set us apart. With Grandma, it was the weather. With Mom, truths, half-truths, and lies. And me? Emotions. I can sense happiness like the average person smells fresh-baked apple pie.

The faint scent of roses drifting across my consciousness, for instance, suggests the receptionist's hint of a smile is genuine. Still, the barely veiled disapproval in her gaze tells me all I need to know.

Like so many before, she thinks I'm a fraud.

Or worse, insane.

You'd think I'd be used to this by now.

"You can wait in here, Ms. Tejedor." Studying me over her zebra-striped reading glasses, she keeps her eyes on mine as she backs out of the room. "Dr. Archer is finishing up with his one o'clock. Shouldn't be but a few more minutes."

"Thank you, umm…" Her ID is flipped around backward. May be unintentional, but it wouldn't be the first time a person tried to see if the "psychic" could guess their name.

"Agnes. My name is Agnes." Her cheeks flush. "Can I get you a water or something?"

"Sure."

She disappears into the hall only to return a moment later with a bottled water complete with folded napkin. A pleasant pine fragrance lights up my mind.

A woman who shows up for work in teddy bear scrubs should probably get the benefit of the doubt.

"Thanks, Agnes. I'll make myself comfortable till the good doctor gets freed up."

"Not too comfortable." She straightens the papers in the desk inbox. "Dr. Archer is pretty particular about his office."

As she pulls the door closed, I hang my compact umbrella on the rack by the door, slip off my lime-green peacoat, and take a look around.

Clearly a man's space, the slab of polished cherry that serves as his desk appears large enough to land a plane. The air smells of old books, leather, and aftershave. The delicate sounds of a string quartet echo from the high-end stereo system in the corner. The quiet strains compete with the crescendoing rain that beats the roof like a thousand snare drums.

The polished brass nameplate on the desk gleams with his name in script letters.

Dr. Thomas Archer.

Sounds like some hot neurosurgeon from *Days of Our Lives.*

To the untrained eye, the office likely appears cluttered, but I recognize organized chaos when I see it. Every book and piece of paper is no doubt exactly where the good Dr. Archer wishes it to be. Diplomas, licenses, and awards fill two of the walls, each triple matted with matching frames and hung with immaculate precision.

Perhaps the good doctor suffers from a bit of OCD himself.

My pocket buzzes. A missed call on my cell phone. Mom's number. I try to call her back a couple of times but the reception in the office is for crap. I'd be lying if I didn't admit a part of me is relieved. Yet again, she's keeping Isabella while I'm on assignment and I'm not quite up for one of my mother's patented guilt trips at the moment.

Continuing my inspection of the office, I pull an old, leather-bound book from the shelf and try to decipher the title.

"*Die Traumdeutung.*" Though trilingual in English, Spanish, and Italian for the better part of my years on the planet, any attempt at German ties my tongue in knots. I flip through the first few pages and discover the work appears to be an original from 1899 and printed in the original tongue. Several spots throughout the book have been marked with scraps of colored paper.

I let out a laugh. "Must be a real page turner."

"Freud's book on the interpretation of dreams."

Smooth as chocolate mousse, the baritone voice sends a shiver down my spine as the tang of sweat after a long day's work plays across my consciousness.

"Groundbreaking work in its time, though it comes across a bit dated these days."

Leaning in the doorway, a man dressed in a gray blazer and dark slacks regards me with a genial smile. Like Agnes, however, his steely blue eyes tell a different story. Just shy of disdain, the professional dismissal in his gaze is all too familiar.

"Ms. Tejedor, I assume?"

"That would be me." I close the book and slide it back into its space on the shelf. "And you must be Dr. Archer."

"Batting a thousand so far. A little demonstration of the old 'extra sensory perception'?" He steps into the room and brushes his temple like some carnival mind reader.

I force a smile. "Sorry to disappoint. I recognized you from your website." That much is true. Though his official photo must be a little out of date, the years have been kind to him. A few years older than me, he's mid-thirties, forty tops. He's taller than I would have guessed, and even better looking than his picture. "Not to mention, this is your office."

"Fair enough."

He gives me a quick but firm handshake, steps behind his aircraft carrier of a desk, and drapes his jacket across his leather swivel throne. I'm not sure if it's the brush of his broad shoulders or the hint of cologne as he passes me that breaks my concentration, but it takes a couple blinks and a deep breath to refocus on why I'm here.

"I wasn't sure we'd have the pleasure of your company today," he says, "what with all the storms between here and D.C."

With that voice of his, it's clear Archer has found the right vocation. There's also little doubt about what he's trying to say.

"It was I-85 pretty much the whole way." I offer him the most genuine smile I can muster. "Rain or no rain, it's a pretty easy drive. Would've been here an hour ago, but traffic was backed up for miles a little north of here. Someplace called Concord Mills?"

He lets out a chuckle. "With all the highway construction there at the bypass, I'm not surprised." He inhales deeply through his nose and any joviality vacates his features. "Look, I appreciate the fact you've come a long way, and in less than perfect conditions, but…" He glances at his shoes and then back at me. "May I be frank, Ms. Tejedor?"

I set my jaw. "I'd expect nothing less."

"How do I say this?" His eyes go up and to the right, as if he's trying to remember a word that won't quite come. "Can you tell me what it is you hope to accomplish here?"

And there it is. The kiss of death. If six years of this gig have taught me nothing else, it's once you identify yourself as a "psychic," the absolute best you can hope for is a healthy dose of skepticism. I can count on one hand the number of times I've shown up for a job and been met with anything even remotely resembling acceptance, and that includes the clients who paid good money for me to be there.

Most people assume you're either a con or a lunatic. The average cop won't give you the time of day and the few who will won't stick up for you in front of their buddies. The clergy I've worked with are always too busy trying to save my soul to listen to anything someone like me might have to say. Worst of all, however, are the doctors. Like they're fighting to keep their spot at the top of the moral food chain.

Regarding people like me, the head shrinkers lead the pack.

Archer rubs at his right eye as a sympathetic twinge of pain blossoms above mine. Three minutes in my presence and he's developing a headache. An auspicious beginning.

"Caroline emailed me a few days ago. Said she'd asked you to come today, but—"

"With all due respect, Dr. Archer, Ms. Faircloth all but begged me on the phone to drive down and meet her family today. In fact, she paid a full week in advance to ensure she'd have my undivided attention. I woke up a little after five to get here on time. Spent eight hours on the highway dodging rain and hail and a whole slew of idiots who don't know how to drive in either. All the road construction put me behind an hour, so I skipped lunch to make it here before two. Trust me. I'm not going anywhere."

Archer studies me like some kind of museum exhibit.

Or, more likely, a prospective patient.

"Look." I hold my hands up before me in mock surrender. "You and me, we're on the same side here. I just want to help the boy."

Archer grabs a medical chart the size of a small encyclopedia from his desk and holds it before him like some kind of sacred text. "I've taken care of Anthony for the better part of four years, Ms. Tejedor. I have no doubt your intentions are good but trust that I have some idea about what's best for him and his family."

Something akin to the smell of black pepper permeates my senses. Skeptical. Defensive. Almost hostile. My sigh becomes a chuckle.

Why did I think this time would be easier than all the others?

"...and that doesn't even take into account all the privacy issues involved with you joining us in session."

Crap. I zoned out for part of the good doctor's rant, and he knows it. The peppery smell assaulting me now reeks of vinegar. Before he was simply defensive. Now he's mad.

"I believe Ms. Faircloth is focused on bigger issues right now than maintaining medical confidentiality. From what she told me, her son hasn't spoken a word in weeks despite the best efforts of everyone involved." My head tilts to one side. "No offense, but it sounds to me like you could use a little help." The hint of condescension in my tone turns even my stomach.

Archer bristles and his face turns a shade of scarlet. "You're staying, then?"

"As of this moment I'm officially on the clock." A glance down at my battered wristwatch, a vintage Cartier and the nicest thing my grandmother ever owned, reveals a few minutes remain before the scheduled appointment. "They've got both of us for an hour. I'll do my best to stay out of your way, as long as you return the courtesy."

His face shifts, almost imperceptibly. "You honestly believe you can help the boy?"

Huh. A legitimate question. Will wonders never cease?

"I won't know till I try."

Neither of us speaks for a moment, the only sound in the room the hammering rain.

"Florida State." I motion to one of his immaculately hung diplomas on the wall. "I applied to that program back in the day."

"You were on track for a PhD?"

"Didn't agree with me." I bite my lip. "As you can imagine, they were less than impressed with some of the extras I brought to the table." He doesn't respond. Maybe a less contentious topic. "You got sick of the 'Sunshine State'?"

"I've only been in Charlotte eight years now but my time in Gainesville already feels like ancient history." A wistful smile breaks through his pensive stare. "It's funny. I don't feel thirty-seven."

I return his smile. "When I was still in middle school, I asked my dad when he started feeling his age."

"What did he say?"

"As I recall, he looked me in the eye and said, 'Not yet.'" My father's quiet laugh and broad smile trickle through my memory. "The last few years, I've begun to understand what he meant."

"Sounds like a wise man."

"He was."

Archer glances over at me. "Just putting this out there. If all of this gets a little over your head, there's no shame in bowing out. This case is a tough one, a bit beyond a lost set of keys or a missing dog."

"And once again my reputation precedes me." I lean across Archer's desk and fix him with a no-nonsense stare. "Trust me. I'm capable of a lot more than lost and found."

"Oh, I know all about what you're capable of. When Caroline mentioned you might be coming today, I did some light reading on one Mira Tejedor. Not too much out there, but what I did find was fascinating, particularly the business with the kidnapping in Fredericksburg last summer. I'm not sure how you kept your face off CNN, but it was pretty clear the police would never have found that little girl without you."

A thousand invisible spiders make their way up my spine and march across my scalp. "So, you *are* familiar with my work."

Archer's dour facade cracks. "Sarah… I forget her last name. How is she?"

The rain pelts against the glass of the office's lone window. "Last time I checked in, Sarah was doing fine. As fine as she's going to be, at least." My hands tremble despite my best efforts to keep them still. "When I think of what she went through…"

Two Julys back, a girl named Sarah Goode was taken from her front yard at three o'clock on a Friday afternoon, two days before her tenth birthday. The animal who took her managed to keep her hidden for thirteen days before the Fredericksburg Police located her, albeit with a quiet assist from yours truly. He left her locked up in the attic of a decrepit old shack in the woods with no food and barely enough water to survive. And that doesn't even take into account what he did to her.

But there's more.

I never told anyone, not even her parents, that Sarah possesses more than a touch of psychic potential herself. Without her reaching for me as I reached for her, I doubt I would have ever found her. Still, her talent made the scars of the ordeal run all the deeper. Bad enough having to deal with your own emotions in such a place, but to feel what he felt. His glee, his lust, his madness. To be inside the head of the bastard when he climbed on top of you…

Stop. Enough of that. It's been fifteen months.

"Her kidnapper was denied bond and is still awaiting trial." I brush a tear from the corner of my eye. "I suspect when the trial comes around, they'll call me to testify."

"How did you find her? The papers said the police had all but given her up for—" Before he can finish, Agnes pokes her head into the office.

"Dr. Archer. The Faircloth family is here."

"Thank you, Agnes." Archer stand and slips back into his gray blazer. "Shall we?"

Archer stops me in the hall.

"Before we go in there, at least let me give you some background. The whole situation is pretty complicated."

"Actually, if it's all right with you, I'd rather meet Ms. Faircloth and Anthony cold. I know most of the basics from talking with her on the phone and too much advance information tends to muddy the waters, so to speak." My lips pull into a smile. "If I have any questions, I'll be sure and let you know."

"Fine." As he closes the door to his office, he shakes his head and chuckles. "Whatever spins your crystal ball."

Archer stops at the front desk and reviews the onscreen schedule with Agnes. Time to give the good doctor the Tejedor once-over. The whole sixth sense thing has proven more than useful over the years, but part of being good at what I do involves paying as much, if not more, attention to the other five senses.

Let's see. Shoes shined to a high luster, shirt pressed with a touch of starch, pants with a crease so sharp it could slice vegetables. Either he's married and his wife is cool with the no ring thing or he's on a first name basis with a good dry cleaner. He clearly spends time in the gym. Wears a bit of product in his hair. Nails trimmed but not manicured. Good. Mom always said to never trust a man with nails nicer than yours.

I catch Archer's eye. His smirk suggests he's been half-watching me take inventory. I jerk my eyes away and allow my gaze to wander out into the sparsely populated waiting room where two sets of eyes are locked on me like laser beams. The first pair belongs to a sullen young man who glares at me with something just this side of contempt. The second pair of eyes, however, could not be filled with more wonder. A girl with wavy red hair, seven or eight at most, stares at me as if she were looking at an angel.

"Those two?"

"Anthony's brother and sister." Archer turns his back on the window so the kids can't tell they're the topic of conversation. "Jason's a senior in high school. Plays defensive tackle on the football team and comes off a bit gruff. Rachel, on the other hand, is a sweetheart. Usually pretty quiet. Not Anthony quiet, mind you, just a little shy."

I chance a wave at the girl, but am met with only that same star-struck stare. And something else. Something just below the surface. Something desperate.

"Ready?" Archer asks as the acrid smell plays across my senses.

I tear my gaze away from Rachel Faircloth's forlorn eyes. "Ready."

"All right." Archer takes a few steps down an adjacent hallway before stopping at a closed door. He rests his fingers on the handle, and looks back at me. "Last chance to bail."

"You're not scaring me, you know."

"Just making sure you're committed."

I raise an eyebrow. "Why, Dr. Archer, was that a joke?"

"Perhaps." A mischievous grin flashes across his features as he opens the door and steps inside.

II

Promenade

"Good morning, Caroline." Archer's voice shifts into a pleasant lilt. "Glad you could make it in today. It's coming down in buckets."

"Took us over an hour." The weariness in the woman's voice punctuates the waves of fatigue emanating from the room. A musty mothball scent like that wafting off the dresses in my grandmother's attic plays across my senses. "There was a big wreck on 77. Honda Civic meets tractor-trailer. You can probably guess who won."

"I'm impressed you got here," Archer says. "Over half my morning clients called in to cancel." His voice grows quiet as he shifts into therapist mode. "How is Anthony?"

"The same." She lets out a sigh. "He's always the same."

"I see." Archer glances back at me through the open doorway. "I understand you've requested a visitor join us today?"

"She's here?" Ms. Faircloth's voice swells with hope as the dank aroma of the room shifts to rosemary and lilac.

"She is." Archer nods curtly and motions for me to enter.

Dappled light filters through the leaves outside the rain-spattered window and mixes with the cold fluorescence of the room to reveal walls painted the pastel blue-gray of an overcast sky. The royal-blue shag carpet is plush and clean, though worn in spots. An unmolested box of toys sits in the corner and against the far wall rests another bookcase filled with books, these more Dr. Seuss than Dr. Freud. Three chairs and a couch form an incomplete oval around a short table containing a half-completed jigsaw puzzle. On one end of the couch, a woman and a boy sit huddled close together, the coolness of the room made worse by their half-drenched clothes.

Ms. Faircloth appears just west of forty. Her clothes speak of money, though the dark roots at the base of her hair and the dusky circles under her eyes hint at busy days and sleepless nights. Next to her sits a boy who has to be Anthony. In the throes of puberty, his thick black hair lies mussed to the point of being almost stylish. A pair of rectangular wire glasses rests crooked on the bridge of his nose and the wisp of hair on his upper lip suggests he has yet to begin shaving. He stares at the wall before him. His head bobs to a slow rhythm apparently only he can hear.

"Good morning, Ms. Faircloth. I'm Mira Tejedor. We spoke on the phone."

"Ms. Tejedor," she says. "I wasn't sure you'd come."

"You sounded desperate. How could I refuse?"

Archer's jaw clenches. "If Ms. Tejedor is to stay and participate during our session today, we should discuss some ground rules. I must admit involving someone with her particular skill set lies outside my normal comfort level. I'm curious. What do you hope to gain from her participation in Anthony's care?"

Ms. Faircloth chokes back a sob. "Dr. Archer, you know my family better than anyone and even you admit nothing we've done has helped Anthony get better. If there's a chance Ms. Tejedor can help us understand what's happened to him, maybe even get through to him somehow, it's worth it to me." Her attention shifts to me. "Before we get started, Ms. Tejedor, there's a few things you need to know." She clears her throat. "To start with, Anthony has never been like other kids."

I offer her my most comforting smile. "That's what you said on the phone."

"He's pretty quiet most of the time, painfully awkward in social situations, and has been known to drop into full on temper tantrums when he doesn't get his way. His grades are all over the place, but he's a good kid."

"I get that." I glance in Archer's direction. His disapproving stare is tempered with curiosity. "Has anyone ever been able to put their finger on what exactly is going on with him?"

Caroline lets out a pained sigh. "Over the years, my son has been diagnosed with high-functioning autism, Asperger's, learning disability. Early on, the doctors even toyed with a diagnosis of mild mental retardation, though Dr. Archer assures me his IQ measures significantly higher than either of his siblings and that none of these diagnoses quite fit. I've had him in therapy since he was very young and he's come a long way."

Her pain washes over me, a cavalcade of scents and sensations. "I'm sensing a but here."

She motions to Anthony's undulating form. "This is not my child. When I talk to him, he doesn't respond. He won't eat unless you force-feed him. And it's getting worse. For the last few days, he won't even walk. My older son, Jason, had to carry him in from the car."

"I see."

"We've been to a dozen doctors in the last few weeks, done every blood test, x-ray, and scan they've recommended, and not one of them can tell me what's wrong." Her voice cracks. "Help him, Ms. Tejedor. Please."

"I'll do everything in my power." I sit next to her. "And please, call me Mira."

"Thank you, Mira." She offers a trembling hand. "Caroline."

She attempts a smile and I take her hand. Her fingers are cold as icicles.

"Dr. Archer has been kind enough to allow me to sit in on today's session." I try to sound confident, though truth be told, Archer isn't the only one working outside their comfort zone. "This is his show. I'm only here to help if I can."

"Okay." Archer sits in the chair across the table. "This is our fifth session since Anthony's behavior began to change and from what you're saying, he's only getting worse."

"You have no idea." Caroline rubs her eyes. "A week ago he'd still come to meals when he got hungry. Now he just sits in his room and rocks. For God's sake, I've had to put him back in diapers." She turns to me. "I wait on him hand and foot every day, catering to whatever he needs, and he barely even notices I'm there."

I lean in. "He ignores you?"

"More like he can't even tell I'm there." Caroline shakes her head. "Unless I try to touch him, that is."

"What happens then?"

Caroline lets out another sigh and her gaze drops to her lap. "Here. Let me show you." She wraps an arm around her son and his slow bobbing stops. For a moment it appears she has put him at ease. The truth is far less comforting.

It starts in his hands. His fingers ball into fists, his knuckles white. He stiffens as if in pain and his face pales as a bead of sweat forms between his thick eyebrows. I focus, trying to get a read on what Anthony's going through, but all that comes across is a jumble of conflicting emotions, many of which are no doubt coming from his mother.

Caroline pulls away. "Anthony was never big on physical contact, but he's never been like this. If anyone touches him now, especially me, it's like you're twisting a knife in his back." Caroline rises from the couch and walks to the window. "No one can give me any answers and I can't even hug my own son without making him worse."

Outside, the river birches sway in the gusty wind of the October storm. A curious mingling of emotions wafts off Caroline. The overpowering cayenne smell of frustration. The pungent aroma of guilt. The acrid scent of despair that always reminds me of raw onions.

Caroline stands at the window for another moment before returning to the couch. "It doesn't help Jason's never home. Between football practice and all of his friends, I barely see him anymore. Then there's Rachel. She's never been all that big a talker with anyone but Anthony. Since he stopped speaking, she mainly stays in her room." Caroline's gaze drops to her lap. "A house full of kids and I'm still alone."

Archer grabs the box of tissues from the table and offers it to her. "It's an awful lot to take on, Caroline. We're doing the best we can here, but there's only so much we can do in this setting."

Caroline's cheeks flush crimson. "No one is putting my son in an institution. I've taken care of him every single day for thirteen and a half years and nobody's going to take him away from me now."

Archer takes a step back. "After all the time we've spent in this room trying to help Anthony be a functional part of your family, surely you don't think I want to take him away from you. I'm just trying to figure out the best way to help him." He glances in my direction before returning his attention to Caroline. "Same as you."

"Anthony has already spent five days in the hospital this month and we have nothing to show for it." She turns her attention again on me. "Twice now they've pumped him full of dye for head to toe CT and MRI scans that didn't tell us anything. They've taken like half a gallon of his blood and every single test came back normal. The best pediatric neurologist in town put him in a bed and stuck wires all over his scalp looking for some kind of seizure activity and nothing." Her eyes narrow. "Imagine if it were your child, Ms. Tejedor."

As if I could stop myself. Since I first entered the room, Isabella's face has been dancing at the edge of my mind. A moment later, my phone starts to buzz again. I silence it before resting a comforting hand on Caroline's leg.

"I can't begin to imagine what you've gone through the last few weeks, but I promise to do everything in my power to help. If Dr. Archer is in agreement, I've seen and heard enough to get started."

"Now, wait just a minute." Archer's eyes dance between Caroline and me. "We haven't even discussed what it is you plan to do."

"Whatever is hurting Anthony is in here." I pass a hand in front of the boy's face. "Not out here. In his condition, he can't tell us what's wrong with him. Maybe if I meet him halfway, we can start to get some answers."

"Please," Caroline says to Archer. "Let her try."

Archer's gaze passes back and forth between Caroline and me. "All right, all right. Whatever it is you're going to do, go ahead and do it." His voice grows quiet. "Just be careful. The boy's pretty fragile."

"Thank you." I motion to Caroline. "Now, if you'll give me a hand."

Anthony's mother and I help him into a reclining position on the couch. He stiffens briefly at our touch, but eventually relaxes. His hazel eyes stare dreamily at the drop ceiling for a moment before drifting shut.

I move a chair to the end of the couch, rest my elbows on the cushioned arm, and look into Caroline's frightened eyes. "Now, let's see if I can get some impression of what's going on inside your boy's mind."

"Do your best," Caroline says. "That's all I ask."

I give her a quick nod and lean over the boy. "Hello, Anthony. My name is Mira. You're going to feel my fingers in your hair."

I study Anthony's pensive yet peaceful expression and take in every aspect of his upside-down face. With his hand across his mouth, Archer looks on. His expression vacillates between exasperation and amusement as I massage the boy's temples.

"Try to relax, Anthony." My body begins to rock, the gentle back and forth motion in time with the boy's strange bobbing. "You're safe here. No one can hurt you."

"Hmmph," Archer mutters under his breath. "Hypnotism. Haven't seen this before."

I shoot Archer a stern glance and return my attention to Anthony. "Listen to the sound of my voice, Anthony. Only the sound of my voice."

A pungent odor not unlike that of rotten eggs drifts across my consciousness.

"I'm getting something." My voice comes out as a whisper though the rocking of my body becomes more pronounced with each passing second. "He's afloat in a sea of emotion. Anxiety, sadness, but most of all, fear." I glance up at Caroline and do my best to ignore Archer's quiet sigh. "Any idea why Anthony might be afraid? Anything you can think of?"

Caroline considers the question. "Nothing at home I'm aware of. I mean, there's always school, I suppose."

"He doesn't get along with the other kids?"

"Even on his best days, Anthony always had trouble navigating social situations. That's been one of the focuses of his therapy since we started with Dr. Archer. He's been bullied in the past, but at the latest parent-teacher conference, they said he was doing pretty well this year. Between his teachers looking out for him and Jason being a defensive tackle on the football team, I figured he was all right."

"What about his father?"

Archer bows his head and massages the bridge of his nose as Caroline looks away.

"William died two years ago," she says.

"Oh." My cheeks grow warm. "I'm so sorry. I didn't—"

An odd sound grabs my attention. Just above the level of perception, the strange rhythm grows louder with every beat. I focus my attention on the unmistakable sound and the reason Anthony and I were rocking in unison suddenly becomes apparent.

The sound is music.

Played on piano, the strain is simple and pretty, though unfamiliar to me. Thirteen notes repeated over. And over. And over.

A strange thought dawns on me.

"What if Anthony is… stuck?"

"Stuck?" Caroline and Archer ask together.

"Like a scratched record, unable to get to the next section. Whatever has happened to him, his mind can't get past it." I hum along with the repeating piano notes, the short melody already burned into my memory.

"No." All color drains from Caroline's cheeks. "That's not possible."

"What is it?" Archer asks.

"That song." Caroline dabs at her eyes. "It's Anthony's favorite."

"I believe it. The tune is coming off him like radio waves." My cheeks grow hot with a mix of embarrassment and pride as the smug expression on Archer's face evaporates.

"You hear music?" Archer asks. "Coming from Anthony?"

"As plain as I can hear you." I mirror Archer's previous brush of the temple and smile. "Just a different set of ears."

"Can you hear anything else?" Caroline hovers over Anthony's still form, her face a storm of mixed emotions.

"Nothing but the music so far, but give it a few more seconds. It feels like I'm about to round a—"

Before I can complete the thought a maelstrom of color envelopes me. Vivid and bright, muted and pastel, light and dark, the entire spectrum flies at me, a tidal wave of prismatic light. If there's a place rainbows go when they die, it's here. Everything and everyone fades away in the flood of color and I am alone.

"Dr. Archer?" A trace of fear invades my voice. "Caroline?" Before I can say another word, the strange music begins to crescendo.

"Can anyone hear me?" The only answer is yet another repetition of the thirteen-note strain, the notes mocking in their intonation. The colors swirling about my head spin faster and faster as the sulfur smell of fear still fills my senses. A wave of nausea passes through my body and nearly doubles me over.

In the years since I first discovered my talent, I've faced more than my fair share of the bizarre and unexplained, but this is different from anything I've experienced before. Trapped like a prehistoric animal in a tar pit and helpless to free myself, my every effort at escape only draws me in deeper. Wherever it is Anthony's stuck, he's not alone anymore.

The run of thirteen notes grows louder and faster with each repetition. The previously pleasant melody descends into an ear-splitting cacophony. I clench my eyes shut and clutch at my ears, though my eyelids and hands do little to stem the overwhelming assault on my senses.

"Please," I whisper. "Stop."

The deafening melody pounds at me with physical force. My heart races like a hummingbird's as my mind flirts with sweet unconsciousness. My arms fall to my sides and I collapse to what should be the shag carpet of Dr. Archer's exam room. As I lie there amid the onslaught of light, sound, and smell, a realization sweeps across me. Before my thoughts fade into oblivion, I stare up into the swirling mass of color and speak. "It's okay. You can stop now."

The music halts for the briefest of moments, as if awaiting my next words.

"I hear you… Anthony."

III

Scheherazade

No sooner do the words leave my lips than the barrage of light and sound stops. The sudden silence is somehow worse. Before I can take a breath, a burst of brilliance like a thousand flashbulbs firing at once blinds me. With ears still ringing from the auditory onslaught, I rub at my eyes as my vision adjusts to the muted luminescence of another place entirely.

An enormous hallway stretches out before me, the sheer opulence of the space reminding me of pictures from the Louvre. The way before me is clear, though the passage to my rear is blocked by a pair of ten-foot high doors fashioned of dark oak. A lock the size of my head hangs between them. Won't be leaving that way.

"*Dios mío*," I mutter, channeling my mother.

If even God can hear me in this place.

Its walls alabaster white with mahogany trim, the hall's hardwood floor is laid in an intricate herringbone parquet pattern of alternating oak and rosewood. Above my head, the vaulted ceiling is decorated with a fresco reminiscent of the Sistine Chapel's, though the style of the painter appears far more Dalí than Michelangelo. Also, where David's sculptor found his inspiration in the many stories of the Bible, the tortured images that fill the ceiling of this place are all stolen from classical mythology, the entire surface an anthropologist's acid dream.

Directly above me, Leda's rape by the Zeus-swan fills my vision. Just adjacent, the three Fates continue their eternal task of spinning, measuring and cutting the thread of life, the product of their work resolving into a misshapen infant's umbilical cord. Prometheus, chained to the rock with the eagle's head buried in his flayed abdomen, lies in agony above the gigantic door that blocks my escape. The Titan's gaze follows me as I venture farther down the hallway and an additional picture comes into view. Persephone rests on one knee in the darkness, her fist clutched around the crimson pomegranate that remands her to Hades for half the year.

Guess that minor in Classics isn't looking like such a waste of time and money anymore, now is it, Mom?

If my theory about this place is right, two things are very clear.

Anthony Faircloth has an intimate knowledge of world mythology.

And he's not too big on subtlety.

As I proceed down the hallway, the images above me grow more and more bizarre, even as the scenes they depict become less and less familiar. In one, a spider climbs into the sky with a bound python caught between its front legs. In another, a bearded man wears a black T-shirt with a white lightning bolt like the Gatorade logo and holds aloft what appears to be a glowing baseball bat. The largest portrays a half-dead Norse warrior standing atop a fractured rainbow. A multitude of slain enemies lie at his feet. The scantily clad women that graced the covers of my brother's old *Heavy Metal* collection would look right at home next to Odin or Thor or whoever the hell Leif Erikson on steroids is supposed to be.

"Have you come to weave me a tale?" The whispered voice seems to come from nowhere and everywhere at once. "Of lovers and dangers and unrequited passion?"

"Anthony?" I work to keep the tremor from my voice. I fail.

"I know your secret," the voice continues. "You hope to lull me with your honeyed words and clever plots."

I've spoken with others mind-to-mind on numerous occasions in the past, a unique experience each time, to be sure. I've never been addressed this way before.

"Who said that?" There's no sign of anyone else along the great hall. "Show yourself."

"In due time, Scheherazade." A low chuckle fills the hall. "We will meet soon enough, I fear."

"Wait." My pulse begins to race. "Where am I? What is this place?"

The voice doesn't speak again, the only answer a quiet titter that echoes down from the vaulted ceiling. I hold my breath, hoping for any clue that might help me escape this place, but an oppressive silence, unnatural in its fullness, fills the air.

Neither masculine nor feminine, the whispered voice could represent an ally, but my money's on adversary.

"Won't figure it out standing here," I mutter. "Time to move."

As I continue my slow progress down the vast hallway, a name echoes across my psyche.

Scheherazade.

The voice called me Scheherazade.

Above my head, a fresco of the gorgon Medusa swirls into a blob of muted colors that eventually resolves into a more familiar image. A woman in white lies prone among ornate silk pillows at the feet of a man dressed in royal robes and a turban. Her eyes wide and arms raised, she appears to be telling him something of great importance. Though he looks on her with stern eyes, his hand resting on an intricately jeweled dagger, the man hangs on her every word. A familiar scene.

My father, the right-brained one in my parent's marriage, insisted I get a firm grounding in classic literature. As a result, we spent my eleventh winter reading Scheherazade's tales. A bad case of pneumonia kept me in bed for a month and a half, but Papi's baritone voice reading *One Thousand and One Arabian Nights* helped pass those particular forty-nine Brooklyn nights without pre-teen Mira having a nervous breakdown.

God, I miss him.

My addled mind sifts through the story. Stung by the infidelity of his latest wife, the sultan marries a new virgin each day, only to execute her the following morning and marry again. This continues for years until he meets the beguiling Scheherazade who staves off her execution each night with one compelling story after another. Never finishing a tale the same day she starts nor completing one story without starting another, she postpones her fate for one thousand and one nights and eventually the changed Sultan grants her a pardon and she becomes his favored wife.

"I don't know what you think you know about me, but I am no Scheherazade." My shouts echo in the empty space. "Release me from this place."

Answered again with silence, I jump as an ornate mirror materializes on the wall to my right. The woman staring back at me is a stranger. Me, and yet not me. So focused was I on my bizarre surroundings, it hadn't occurred to me I might have changed as well.

Taller and darker than me, her raven hair extends well past her waist and hangs in loose, yet intricate, braids. Statuesque and classically beautiful, the woman stands wrapped in a green sarong, the same color as a coat hanging in an office a million miles from here. From the blood-red ruby adorning her forehead to the gold bracelets encircling her wrists to the bejeweled dagger hanging at her side, she is clothed in opulence. Her eyes, lined with thick strokes of dark pencil, study me with fear and awe.

"Scheherazade, eh?" A glance down reveals the selfsame clothes and jewelry draped across a body I barely recognize. So entranced am I by my strange new frame, I almost miss the flicker of movement in the mirror.

Behind me. A flash of brown.

I spin around, the dagger in my hand before I can form another thought, only to face an empty alcove.

An alcove that wasn't there before.

The painting hung at the rear of the space wobbles as if it's been hit by a passing runner. I rush inside to confront whomever or whatever is responsible, but there's no one there.

And that's not the only oddity.

Taller than it is wide, the full-length painting portrays a forest scene. Well rendered in oil, the picture contains nothing of particular interest. Clearly a portrait, it would appear the subject of the piece is missing. My gaze drifts above the frame and comes to rest on an elegant placard bearing a single word inscribed in plain block letters.

GNOMUS

Like a gnome? Mom used to have that coffee table book with all the little bearded men in their blue coats and red cone hats. At one point I had the entire thing memorized, it's pages filled with pictures of tiny bearded men with their plump wives and small children, frolicking with rabbits and squirrels and avoiding the nasty trolls with their matted hair and dripping noses.

My ears pick up the sound of small feet running in the hall. I poke my head out of the alcove and spot another flash of brown. And something strange. The hallway has changed, the long straight space now interspersed with an alternating series of alcoves like the one in which I stand. Each opens beneath a curved arch and is lit from within.

The music returns, a symphonic arrangement of the same melody from before. The piano replaced by the smooth tones of a trumpet, a full orchestral accompaniment kicks in as the piece finally gets past those initial thirteen notes. The music swells till it fills the space, though compared to the high-decibel assault from before, the sound is barely a whisper.

I creep down the hallway, the bejeweled blade hidden in the folds of the green sarong, and step into the next alcove. Another oil, the painting depicts a decrepit old castle. Its battlements lay in various states of ruin and its massive drawbridge hangs loose like a broken jaw. Before the castle stands a brightly colored troubadour playing an instrument resembling a short silver saxophone. The placard above the painting contains three words in Italian, each written in tall block letters.

IL VECCHIO CASTELLO

The Old Castle. Not a real stretch there, though what “Medieval Kenny G” and his castle have to do with a woodland scene and a disappearing gnome is lost on me. Far different from the Edith Hamilton revue from the ceiling, these paintings likely represent the first real clues to where the hell I am and more importantly, what makes Anthony tick.

I steel myself before stepping back into the hall to head for the next alcove. My little friend in brown doesn’t make a third appearance, though the melody returns yet again, almost as if it’s the tour guide for this strange museum. My ears still ringing from their previous onslaught, the notes are strangely comforting this time.

The next space, not surprisingly, holds a third painting. This one’s motif different from the others, the watercolor piece depicts an avenue in what appears to be a French garden. The yard swarms with children. Running, quarreling, playing. I'm about to turn and leave when I spot him.

At the far right edge of the painting, a diminutive Anthony stands alone and watches as the world passes him by. Oblivious to all the other children, he stares off into space. Above a starched white button-down shirt, a pair of archaic spectacles sits askew on his face much like the glasses of the comatose boy lying in Archer's office.

Above this painting, the placard displays a single word inscribed in elegant script.

TUILERIES

My gaze drifts back to the painting before me and locks with the forlorn eyes of the Anthony within. Staring out at me in desperation, he appears every bit the prisoner. We stand, neither of us moving an inch for what seems an eternity until his attention shifts to something across my shoulder. His expression descends into something like disgust.

I whirl about and find I'm not alone.

A misshapen man no more than two feet tall peers at me from the arched doorway. His skin appears brown, though it's unclear if from dirt, pigment, or both. On his head rests a forked cone of animal hide with bells at either end. His worn leather boots are covered in mud while his rough clothing is replete with buckles of all shapes and sizes. He twirls his mossy beard absently, his thickened fingernails like tree bark.

"Who are you?" His voice the groan of trees bowing in a hurricane, the gnome drags a grimy sleeve across his runny nose. "What are you doing here?"

"I'm not sure." I shift my body, ensuring the dagger remains hidden from view, and offer him a pleasant smile. The gesture isn't reciprocated.

"You don't belong here. I know the Exhibition inside and out. You aren't part of it."

"I'm a visitor."

"We don't get visitors here."

"I beg to differ." I perform a subtle curtsy. "Unless you believe me a figment of your imagination."

The gnome snorts. "All right. We have a visitor. What is it you want?"

"You're from the painting, aren't you? The one down the hall."

A quizzical look crosses his face. "Why do you ask such things?"

"It is my nature to ask such questions." I search for any way to connect with this strange creature, and then, in a flash, it comes to me. "I am called Scheherazade."

The gnome stares at me in awe. "The Scheherazade?"

I work to keep any hint of confusion from my features. "The same."

He scratches the side of his head. Dried bits of mud fall from his scalp to the hardwood floor, a scalp that has a grain not unlike the wood that frames his picture.

"Tunny."

"Pardon?"

"My name. Tunny."

"You're from the painting. The sign said *Gnomus*."

He squints at me. His nose crinkles as if he smells something foul. "Perhaps."

"What are you doing out here then, among the… Exhibition, I believe you called it?"

"We *are* the Exhibition, and don't you forget it." He huffs and shoots up the hallway toward his alcove. "You're the intruder here."

I slip the dagger into its scabbard and give chase. Catching the gnome, however, is harder than anticipated. How can a creature with such short legs move so quickly?

"I'm sorry, Tunny. I meant no offense."

"No one ever means offense," he shouts as he scrambles away. "Yet that's all they ever do. Offend, offend, offend."

He steps into the alcove with the woodland scene and a scuffing sound fills the air. I sprint up the hallway and arrive at his alcove in time to find him halfway into his painting, struggling to get his other foot up and over the bottom of the frame.

"Wait." I rush to his side. "I need your help."

"My help?" He lets out something between a snort and a laugh. "You, fair Scheherazade, an angel among swine, desire my help?"

"I didn't come here of my own free will and I can't leave. Did you not see the door?"

"The door with the enormous lock?" He lets out another phlegm-laden chuckle as he finishes hoisting himself into the woodland scene. "What do you think keeps us all here?"

"You can't leave?"

"Of course not. We are the Exhibition." He snorts. "And people say gnomes are thick."

I try a different tack. "What if others wanted to visit the Exhibition? You know, see the art? Why would you put all of this behind a locked door?"

"You would have to ask *her*."

Jackpot. "And who might that be, Tunny?"

"Silence, gnome." The voice from before echoes throughout the space from nowhere in particular. Its grating tone sends my skin crawling. "You have already said far too much."

The exasperation on Tunny's face evaporates, replaced by wide-eyed terror.

"My apologies, Mistress."

"Be warned. Speak out of turn again, and you will face the consequences." The voice grows quiet. "And as for you, weaver of tales, I know who you are and what you have come to do."

"Who are you?" I shout. "What have you done to Anthony?"

"Ah, fair Scheherazade. I recommend you silence your questions and leave now, lest you become another of our fine exhibits."

"You really should listen to her." Tunny trembles within his mahogany frame. "She rarely speaks in jest."

"I'll leave as soon as she shows me the way, though I'm not sure why I should fear anyone who won't show their face."

A screeching cackle fills the room. "You don't want to see my face, Scheherazade."

The sound of tumblers falling into place echoes from the main hall. I crane my head out of Tunny's alcove and catch my breath as the lock holding closed the massive oak doors falls to the floor with a thunderous crash. The door to the left creaks open and before I can so much as summon a thought, the hallway fills with a forceful wind.

"Fare thee well, Scheherazade," comes the strange voice as the gale rips at my hair and sarong. "Do not return here, or you may encounter more than barred doors and whipping winds."

"I'm truly sorry about this." Offering an apologetic shrug, Tunny goes still in the foreground of the beautiful landscape, his wooden form effectively invisible against the forest backdrop.

The blasting wind steals my answer even as it flings me up the hall. I fly at the doorway like a piece of straw in a cyclone, the massive oak doors open just wide enough for me to fly through and into the kaleidoscope of light and sound. The last thing I see before I lose consciousness is the enormous door, surrounded in a nimbus of light, slamming shut behind me.

IV

Fugue

Thank God," whispers a woman's voice. "She's coming around."
My eyes open on a damp washcloth draped across my face and any attempt to raise my hand and pull away the cool rag meets with utter failure. My limbs have apparently gone on strike. I inhale to speak and the effort nearly sends me back to dreamland.

A place I'm no longer certain I wish to visit.

"Mira? Can you hear me?" A man's voice. Familiar.

"Dr. Archer?" My voice comes out like a toad's. That is if said toad had just been punched in the throat.

"Welcome back." The skeptical sarcasm in his tone gone, the good doctor's baritone soothes the static in my mind. "Are you all right?"

My second try at pulling the washcloth from my face meets with more success. I blink a few times but the drop ceiling above my head remains a distant white blur. Archer hovers over me while Agnes and Caroline move in and out of the edge of my vision. My hand trails to my side. They've moved me to the couch while Anthony sits on a high-back chair across the room, continuing to bob to a song I now know all too well.

"What happened?"

"We were going to ask you the same thing," Archer says. "One second you were talking to us and the next you cut off mid-sentence and slumped to the floor."

"You mumbled quite a bit." Caroline leans over me, absently gnawing at her knuckle. "Almost like we were hearing one side of a conversation."

The experience floods my mind, parts of it as clear as a movie I've seen a hundred times, other parts a jumble of barely coherent images. Scenes of the immense hall and its many alcoves stand seared into my mind's eye while the music plays across my senses as if it were being broadcast directly into my mind. Another glance at Anthony's bobbing form leads me to wonder if that might not, in fact, be the case.

I sit up, my biggest mistake of the day thus far. Agnes grabs the wastebasket in the corner and shoves it in my lap just before whatever remains of my breakfast makes a violent return appearance. Caroline drapes the cool washcloth across the back of my neck. It helps. A little.

A couple minutes pass before I attempt to move again. My feet touch the floor and the room slows its spinning. At Archer's subtle nod, Agnes returns to her station, closing the door behind her as she leaves. He and Caroline hover over me as if I'm a house of cards about to fall while Anthony couldn't be more oblivious to my presence.

Caroline breaks the silence. "I don't understand. You heard the music. Anthony's music. Then you went away. What happened to you?"

"You've hit it on the head, Caroline." I rub at my temples in an effort to banish the dull ache growing in my head. "Strange as it sounds, every fiber of my being is screaming I actually did go away." A quick glance in Archer's direction reveals a new curiosity in his eyes. "I know what you're going to say, Dr. Archer, but unless I'm mistaken, I just took a trip inside Anthony's mind."

"His mind?"

"I went somewhere. A strange place. Like a museum. There was music, art, and… a gnome. Tell me, Caroline, does the name Tunny mean anything to you?"

"Tunny?" Caroline's eyes grow wide. "That's what Rachel called Anthony when she was a toddler."

"Well, there's a little man made of wood calling himself Tunny running around in the gray matter between your son's ears. And he's not alone in there." Another memory washes across my mind. A laugh that could freeze water. A voice that even now makes my heart skip a beat.

"I remember a door. A locked door. No way in. No way out."

"A door?" Caroline asks.

Archer steps in. "A locked door could represent many things. Like a mental block or a repressed memory."

"But even with Anthony all locked up, you still got in." Caroline's gaze fixes on me. "That means something, right?"

Another flash. "The gnome." Tunny's exasperated face flashes across my memory. "He had a name for the place. 'The Exhibition.' Ring any bells?"

"A gnome, walking around an 'Exhibition,' you say?" Caroline's gaze shot to Archer. "Do you have it?"

Her surprise is mirrored in Archer's eyes. "It's right here."

Archer reaches into the large file he brought from the office and retrieves a child's sketchpad. He flips through it for a few seconds. His eyes flash when he finds the picture he wants me to see.

"Did your little brown man look like this?"

With tremulous fingers, I take the pad of paper. My vision blurred, I hold the drawing close to my face so I can see the image clearly. What I find there is impossible.

Tunny, rendered in pencil and colored with brown and tan crayon, gazes out at me from the crisp, white paper. Though the art itself is a little rough around the edges, the likeness is unmistakable. The tree moss beard. Skin like mahogany. The gnome's piercing eyes.

"The very same." I turn to Caroline. "You say Rachel used to call her brother Tunny when she was young?"

"It was one of her first words. They were inseparable back then."

I flip the sketchpad around so Archer can see the picture. "I'm not the psychologist here, but assuming you believe a word I'm saying, what do you make of this?"

"That's a pretty big assumption." Archer cracks his neck. "Though what you're saying makes sense in a weird sort of way."

Caroline glances at Archer. "What do you mean?"

Archer sighs. "A lot is going on here that's way beyond anything I understand, so before I start, a few caveats."

Here it comes.

Archer takes Caroline's hand. "Let's assume Ms. Tejedor can actually do what she says and this isn't all just some hallucination or, God forbid, some twisted game she's playing."

My neck gets hot and I try without success to stand. "Now, you hold on just a minute."

"My apologies, Ms. Tejedor, but today's events notwithstanding, this is all a lot to take in. I'm just laying out a theory."

"Very well." Weakened by my journey abroad, my attempt to cross my arms and come off indignant ends with my hands barely making it to my lap. "Go on," I mutter.

"Let's also assume this Exhibition you claim to have visited is indeed some figment of Anthony's imagination. As I conceptualize it, everything you encountered there would in some capacity be an extension of Anthony's consciousness."

"And that would mean what, exactly?" Caroline asks.

"That Anthony has stepped back from himself and assumed another face. He's never been particularly skilled at social nuance despite our best efforts over the years. Perhaps, deep down, he sees himself as a repugnant little gnome."

"Are you saying my son is like the woman in that *Sybil* movie? The one with all the different personalities?"

"Perhaps," Archer says. "I don't put much stock in what Hollywood and popular media call multiple personality disorder, though I have worked with more than my fair share of dissociative patients in my time. I've long suspected aspects of such a disorder were complicating Anthony's case and if any of what Ms. Tejedor says is true…"

"There was someone else there." My voice sounds a bit closer to normal, though it's still taking all I've got simply to sit up straight.

"You said before the gnome wasn't alone." Archer's eyes narrow. "I can't believe I'm about to ask this, but who else did you meet?"

"A voice that came from everywhere and nowhere at once. Very angry with Tunny, and none too pleased with me invading their turf. Tunny was gruff, but non-threatening. This other presence, not so much."

"Fascinating." Archer laughs nervously. "You pull Anthony's favorite piece of music out of thin air, describe in detail a picture you've never seen, then have a one-on-one conversation with my patient's id and superego. Maybe you should be the psychologist."

"Cut Mira some slack, Thomas. She's accomplished more in ten minutes than we have in weeks. Look." She gestures to the chair where

Anthony sits. He's dozed off, his head pitched backward like it might fall off. For the first time since I first laid eyes on him, he is still. The worried furrow of his brow, smooth.

I tilt my head to one side and put on my best smile. "What do you think, Dr. Archer? Do we work together on this or do we each go it alone and hope for the best?"

As if either of us was the deciding vote. We both turn to Caroline and for the second time that day, the scent of cut roses washes over me, a mirror of the hopeful expectation in her eyes.

Archer holds out his hand and offers a subtle bow. "Welcome to the team, Ms. Tejedor."

It's early evening before Archer lets me leave. The good doctor insists on observing me for the afternoon after the episode with Anthony. After a couple much-needed catnaps and a quick perusal of the array of psychology journals in his office, however, I'm ready to go. Agnes' admonishment about Archer's particular nature compels me to put each magazine back exactly where I found it, though I do make a point to leave one in the stack upside down as a reminder of my presence. Compared to the piles of bills, papers, and magazines that typically rule any space of mine, the meticulous order of his office is almost comical.

It's close to half past six when I arrive at the Blake Hotel in downtown Charlotte, or 'Uptown' as Agnes corrected me just before helping me into my car. Considering how this situation is unfolding, my initial plan to get in a little shopping in on Saturday and drive back on Sunday already looks like wishful thinking. The setting sun blinds me as I make the last turn into the parking deck, and I jump despite myself as my pocket buzzes for the first time in hours.

I flip the radio off and pull out my phone. The name on the screen is no surprise.

"Hey, Mom." I've tried to stay quiet since early afternoon, hoping the rest would relieve my inexplicably strained voice. Apparently, that was a bit too much to hope for. I still sound like one of my vocal cords was replaced with rusted barbed wire. "I tried to call you back before."

"Mira? I can barely hear you. We must have a bad connection."

"No, it's just me. I'm… coming down with something."

"I tried to call you this afternoon. Twice."

My neck gets hot. "I couldn't pick up. I was in the middle of meeting my new client."

"I know you're busy, but I wouldn't have called if it wasn't important."

Hotter. "But Mom, I just said—"

"Are you sitting down?"

"Haven't even gotten out of the car." I steer one-handed into the narrowest spot imaginable and slide the gear shift into park. "What is it?"

"Dominic's in town for the week."

"Dominic?" Good God. I leave town for one day and my ex decides to pay a visit. I swear sometimes it's like he's tapped my phone. "Fantastic. Does Isabella know?"

"Yes. He called earlier and—"

"Let me speak to her."

"But, Mira. You might want to—"

"Isabella, Mom. Just put her on."

"All right." Mom shouts for Isabella as I head for the parking deck elevator. "Here she is." The ire in Mom's tone comes through loud and clear despite her best efforts.

Then, my favorite voice in the world.

"Hello?" Isabella's voice sounds like it's about to bubble over with excitement. "Mami?"

"Hi, sweetheart." I step off the elevator and enter the hotel atrium. "How are things?"

"I'm great. Nana took me out to the movies and the mall. We got cookies at the food court."

"That sounds great, honey." I find a couch in the center of the room and collapse into the inviting cushions.

"Will you be home for dinner, Mami?"

"Honey, I'm down in North Carolina. Remember what we talked about yesterday?"

"I remember." She takes a slurp of something no doubt full of high-fructose corn syrup. "Did you help the boy? He sounds so sad."

"I'm trying, honey. I just got here, but his mami and I are doing everything we can."

"I miss you, Mami."

"I miss you too, sweetheart."

"Me and Nana are having fun. She makes me milkshakes." She takes an excited breath. "Did she tell you?"

"Tell me what?" As much as it's going to hurt, I have to let her say it.

"Daddy's come home for a visit."

"Really?" I try to keep the bite from my tone. "Did he come by to see you?"

"No, but he called before. We talked for a long time." Isabella takes another breath, as do I. "Do you think he'll stay this time?"

"We'll have to talk about that another time, sweetheart. Hopefully this job won't take too long and then we'll be together again and can figure all this out."

"Well, umm, Daddy wants to come by tomorrow. He said we could go to the mall, maybe get me that new video game with the ponies. Is that okay?"

My heart freezes. Dominic hasn't set foot within a hundred miles of our home in over six months, and the second I leave town for work, he's there to swoop in and play Superman with a Visa. It's a damn conspiracy.

"As long as Nana knows where you are at all times and can get in touch with your dad if she needs to reach you, I guess that would be all right."

I pull the phone away from my ear in preparation for the inevitable squeal.

I'm not disappointed.

"Thank you, Mami," she squeals. "I love you. I love you. I love you."

I swallow hard and do my best to keep my voice even. "I love you too, sweetheart. Can you put Nana back on?"

"Okay." The click of Isabella's shoes on the tile in Mom's kitchen echoes across the line as she skips into the next room. Unbidden tears well at the corners of my eyes at the excitement in her voice as she tells my mother fifty times I agreed she could have a meal with the reigning world champion of absentee fathers. I collect myself as Isabella passes her the phone.

"Mira?" Though Mom is quick to temper, she's also quick to cool.

One of the things I love about her. "Are you okay?" Before I can answer, she asks, "What do you want me to do?"

"Be firm with Dom. Same rules as last time. No big presents. No cash. And he needs to follow through with anything he promises her. I swear, if he breaks Isabella's heart again when I'm not there to put the pieces back together, I'll hunt him down and kill him myself."

Mom chuckles. "Don't worry, honey. I'll make sure he toes the line."

"A heads-up. Things here appear a lot more complicated than I anticipated."

She sighs. "How long this time?"

"A week." My whisper echoes on the line. "Maybe two."

Mom doesn't say a word, but the sound of a door closing says it all.

"It's important, Mom."

"It's always important, Mira. Do you have any idea how many days you've been away from home in the last year alone? How much your daughter misses you when you're gone?"

"This boy needs me."

"Your girl needs you. She practiced weeks for that dance recital last month."

"You think I wanted to miss that?" Hang on, Mira. Keep the volume down. "In case you're forgetting, Mom, I helped the police catch a serial rapist that night. Don't I get any credit for that?"

"From me, dear? Of course. But do you think Isabella understands?"

"She understands quite a bit. In fact, sometimes I wish she didn't understand so much." I pull in a deep breath. "Anyway, this one is different. No cops. No one lost or missing. This Anthony kid just stopped talking, walking, or doing much of anything a couple of weeks back and it looks like I may be the only one who can help him." An image of Anthony's worried face filters across my mind's eye. "Would you turn your back?"

Mom lets out an encore of her trademark world-weary sigh. "Of course not, Mira. Let me take care of Isabella while you get out there and save the world." A sharp intake of air. "Again."

"Thanks, Mom." Though her words are harsh, it's the best I'll get tonight from one Rosa Tejedor. "For everything."

"Good night, Mira."

My breath catches at the sudden silence from the other end.

"Good night." I press the end button and head for the hotel desk. For once in my life, check-in is a breeze and one short elevator trip later, I'm in my suite and collapsing on a king-size bed that feels like it was custom made for my aching back. One silver lining of this particular job, my retainer from Ms. Faircloth has allowed more than my usual motel accommodations.

Near the top floor of the Blake Hotel, the window in my suite looks out on a fifty-story building resembling an enormous martini glass. Lit up like a pink and blue Christmas tree, columns of light decorate the skyscraper's every angle. Exhausted, I flip on the tube, change into my pajamas, and rummage through the desk for the room service menu. My order for the night is salmon with risotto, a well-deserved glass of wine, and what better be some passable chocolate mousse. Desperate for any distraction from my rumbling stomach while I wait, I flip channels till I find the local news. Just past the bottom of the hour, the anchors are reviewing the big stories of the day.

"…the daughter of Stuart and Margaret Wagner, whose home in Myers Park has become a shrine to the missing high school junior. As we enter the fourth week since Julianna's disappearance, hope dims this favorite of her teachers and peers will be found alive."

The story cuts to an interview with a portly police officer. With just the right amount of gravitas, a female voice from off camera asks, "Any news in the search for Julianna Wagner?"

"Our team is following up on various leads." The officer's stern eyes offer little in the way of reassurance. "We're aware the situation looks bleak, but Charlotte Police Department has not given up on bringing Miss Wagner home safe and sound."

I've heard all this before. A few weeks into a missing persons case, the focus shifts from rescue to recovery. This guy talks a good game, but you don't need to be a psychic to see what's written all over his face.

The news begins to run pictures of the missing girl. Seventeen and blonde, fair skin, gorgeous smile. They transition into how everyone loved her and follow with a message from the parents to any potential abductors, video of the candlelight vigil at her school, and numerous interviews with friends, family, and teachers.

It's a story I've seen a hundred times.

Wait.

That last picture.

A photo of Julianna and a date standing below a cluster of blue and white balloons. In an off the shoulder red dress and a pair of heels that probably cost half my rent, she stands next to a boy in a tux. A boy with a familiar face.

Jason Faircloth.

I cradle my face in my hands. My last words to my mother echo in my mind.

"No cops, eh, Mira?" I mutter.

For a bunch of missing persons, they sure don't seem to have any trouble finding me.

V

Gnomus

I spend most of the weekend in my suite at the Blake, rising from my king-size oasis only to eat or take advantage of the room's oversize whirlpool tub. The "Do Not Disturb" in the room's keycard slot keeps housekeeping away and other than room service or my few calls home to check on Isabella, I don't speak to another living soul for two days.

My sojourn through Anthony Faircloth's mind took more out of me than I realized. For that and a hundred other reasons, the logical side of my brain screams to leave. To cut bait and run.

But if I don't help this kid, who will?

By Monday morning, I'm finally recovered and head for one of the local parks for a jog. The burn through my thighs and calves helps to clear my mind. Two trains of thought vie for supremacy as I start my fifth lap around the miniature lake: Anthony Faircloth's strange malady and this Julianna Wagner girl the news channels can't seem to stop talking about. Not to mention the undeniable feeling the answer to the first is somehow wrapped up in the second.

I arrive at Archer's office a few minutes before two for our follow-up session. I'm not certain if he considers what happened with Anthony a breakthrough, but he agreed to give up his lone administrative time this week to be a part of the next step. The doctor in him no doubt wants to supervise every aspect of his patient's care, but if I were putting money down in Vegas, I'd bet his sudden change of tune has a lot more to do with him wanting to watch the show.

In that way, the good Dr. Archer is just like everybody else.

As we settle into his office and wait for the Faircloth family to arrive, I break the uncomfortable silence with a question.

"What do you know about Julianna Wagner?"

"Julianna Wagner?" He raises an eyebrow. "What do *you* know about her?"

"Only what they're saying on the news. Pretty sad case, don't you think?"

"Why do you ask?" Archer maintains a steely facade as he tries to play off the suspicion in his voice, though the whiff of spoiled milk at the back of my mind is a dead giveaway.

"It's just… one of the pictures the news keeps putting on the screen shows her with Anthony's brother at a formal." I lean in. "Were Julianna and Jason Faircloth dating?"

"At one point." Archer runs his fingers through his thick hair. "Caroline told me they broke up a little over a month ago. Didn't say why. At the time I figured it was just your garden variety high school drama." He rubs his brow. "Boy, was I wrong."

Scenes from last night's various newscasts flicker through my memory. "Julianna has been missing for how long? Just under a month?"

His eyes drift closed in concentration. "She was last seen by a couple of friends in the stands at her school's football game three weeks back. No one remembers seeing her there after halftime and she never made it home that night."

I bite my lower lip, half afraid to ask the next question. "Isn't that about the time Anthony began to have issues?"

Archer's mouth turns up in a grim smile. "You're quick, Ms. Tejedor. Everything with Anthony started the next day."

"This Julianna girl dates Anthony's brother for months, becomes a part of his life, and then one day after she disappears without a trace, his brain decides to take a sabbatical?"

"I know." Archer raises his shoulders in a subtle shrug. "Seems like there should be a connection, but to the best of my knowledge no one has even told Anthony she's missing."

"Were they close?" I ask. "Julianna and Anthony?"

"As Caroline tells it, Julianna and Anthony got along just fine. In fact, sometimes she and Jason let him tag along when they'd go out for a movie he might like. You know, give their mother a night off every once in a while."

"Any way he might know what happened to her? Something like that could push anyone over the edge, especially someone as fragile as Anthony."

Archer shakes his head. "Anthony was sick the night Julianna vanished. From what I understand the whole family was cooped up that weekend with some kind of stomach bug. None of them left the house that night and everything with Anthony started the next morning, long before anything about Julianna's disappearance hit the news."

A question burns in my gut. "What about Jason? Any chance he's hiding something?"

"Unlikely. The police questioned him the day after her disappearance and as you've seen, he's not sitting in a jail cell." Archer walks to the window and peers between the blinds. "I've known Jason for as long as I've been caring for Anthony. He may be a bit on the moody side, but he's a good kid."

"Of course." I join him at the window and inspect the few feet of fractured asphalt that bridge the gap between his building and the next. "What were he and Julianna like?"

"I only saw them together once. It was Jason's eighteenth birthday party, right at the end of summer. Caroline invited me to drop by for a bite of cake and some punch. One thing that day was pretty clear. When he's with Julianna, Jason is a different person." Archer returns to his chair and leans back, a wistful grin on his face. "As best as I remember, that party is the one time I've ever actually seen the boy smile."

"I've been doing this a long time, Dr. Archer." Rounding the desk, I return to my chair and rest both elbows on his plateau of cherry. "Not casting any aspersions, but anyone can put on a smile for the world."

"A bit more cynical than I'd expect from someone like you." Archer studies me for a moment. "All I'm saying is, he was as in love as any young man I've ever seen."

Archer's comment stings more than it should. "Even though they had broken up, Jason must have taken it hard. Any chance he let it slip to Anthony that Julianna was missing?"

"Anything is possible, I suppose, but I doubt it. As long as I've been working with the Faircloth family, Jason has always seen himself as Anthony's protector. He'd be the last person to tell Anthony anything that would cause him pain. From what I understand, he'd already kept the breakup from him."

"But maybe Anthony asked him—"

Agnes pokes her head in the door.

"Dr. Archer. Ms. Tejedor. The Faircloth family has arrived."

"We'll be right there." Archer fixes me with a no-nonsense look. "Listen. Caroline is dealing with more than enough right now with Anthony. I'd appreciate if you left any discussion of Jason and Julianna out of this."

"Of course." My hands rise, palms out in surrender. "Like I said, this is your show."

"If only." Archer rises from his seat and gets the door. "Shall we?"

Archer leads me down the hall to the same room we used on Friday. Caroline sits waiting on the couch. Anthony appears to have dozed off.

"Hello, Caroline." I manage to keep a pleasant lilt in my voice.

She looks up at me with a grim smile. "Wasn't sure if you'd come back."

"What can I say? I'm a glutton for punishment." I sit in the armchair opposite her. "How is Anthony?"

"Better. He fed himself a bit yesterday and even slept straight through the night twice in a row. First time in weeks."

"Sounds promising."

Caroline's eyes drop. "I would have agreed with you right up till four o'clock this morning when he woke up screaming."

Archer and I share a concerned glance.

"Screaming?" I rest a hand on her shoulder.

"The word 'no.' Over and over. Like the devil himself was climbing up the foot of his bed and clawing at his toes."

What can I possibly say? "At least he said something." Ooh. Not that.

Caroline's looks up at me, her exhausted gaze colored with a hint of derision. "Pardon me if I'm not encouraged by the striking development." She rubs her eyes with balled fists. "Sorry. Just because Anthony managed to get a bit of sleep doesn't mean I did."

Archer steps in. "Remember what I told you, Caroline. If you don't take care of yourself, you won't have the strength to care for Anthony or the rest of your family. They need you right now." He takes her hand. "They need their mother."

"I know, Thomas. I just can't seem to nod off when I lay down at night. Too many thoughts." Her face turns a shade paler. "Not to mention the nightmares."

"One of the psychiatrists on our staff may be able to prescribe something to help you."

"Enough about me." Caroline pulls herself together, brushing the tears and fatigue from her face as she turns to face me. "Can we get started?"

"By all means." I turn to Archer who studies me with a contemplative gaze.

"Ms. Tejedor," he says, "if you will humor me, I have an idea. A safeguard."

My knight in shining armor. "In that case, I'm all ears."

"As part of my practice, I perform hypnosis from time to time. What you and Anthony do in some ways mimics a trance state, so some of the same rules may apply."

"I don't understand your concern, then. I've always heard hypnosis can't hurt you."

"That's not what I'm talking about. From what you've told me, you were forcibly expelled from Anthony's mind last time. If you can be kicked out—"

"Then logically, I could also be kept." The sound of the tumblers from the massive lock in Anthony's mind echoes through my thoughts. "What do you suggest?"

"If you will allow me, I can place a post-hypnotic command in your thoughts. A word, for instance, that will trigger your mind to awake and break away from Anthony's in the event of an emergency. What do you think?"

Though I'm not the biggest fan of letting anyone muck with my thoughts, I give him a simple nod. "Let's do it."

Archer turns down the lights and sits in front of me. He bobs a small flashlight before my face, his soothing voice washing away any concern. My entire body relaxes, my eyes refuse to stay open. Then, a moment later, I'm back, more rested than I've felt in weeks and helping Caroline position Anthony on the couch before beginning anew the ritual that three days before sent me careening into the boy's mind.

"Hello, Anthony. Remember me?"

As I stare down into his vacant brown eyes, my heart begins to pound, though I'd never admit it to Archer or Caroline. The last time we danced this dance, a malevolent force the likes of which I've never felt forced me from the boy's mind. If Archer is right, that force is Anthony himself, or at least some particularly nasty part of him. Regardless, the boy's mind is nothing but one big ambush and I'm about to stroll back in. Unarmed. And alone.

Fantastic.

I stand alone in the Exhibition hallway, staring up at the massive wooden doors at the end of the hall. The lock securing them is twice as big as its predecessor and metal spikes the size of my forearm pierce the wood at even intervals, stabbing into the stone at the threshold as if a giant has nailed the doors shut from outside.

Looks like somebody doesn't want company.

Assuming, of course, the doors are barred to keep people out.

Turning, I lean back and rest my shoulders against the smooth oak door. The hallway stands unchanged from my previous visit. The nine alcoves, alternating left and right every few paces, await me, each likely opening on another painting from Anthony's vivid imagination. A single glance up reveals the ceiling has undergone a dramatic change. Where before the frescoes there comprised a pastiche of classical mythology, now the arched ceiling contains a smattering of scenes no doubt from some of Anthony's favorite movies.

There are the classics. Mark Hamill in desert gear staring across the sand at a binary sun. Keanu Reaves decked out in black and dodging a hail of bullets atop a skyscraper. Uma Thurman in a yellow motorcycle jumpsuit facing an army of masked men in suits.

Then there are others I don't recognize. Sean Connery lecturing some guy with long hair and intense eyes, both of them dressed like they're heading to the Renaissance Fair. An oddly coifed man in a bow tie and a tweed jacket standing in the door of a wooden phone booth painted a deep blue. A white stallion racing up the side of a skyscraper as a thunderstorm rages.

Good God. What did I do to end up at the mercy of *this* kid's imagination?

"Why did you come back?"

Though the voice is familiar, I nearly jump out of my skin. Coming to just above my left knee, a certain brown-skinned gnome stares up at me in awe. One of the bells on his forked hat grazes the middle of my thigh through the green silk of the sarong.

"Hello, Tunny."

"You shouldn't have come back," he says. "She's going to be very angry."

"Who is going to be angry, Tunny?"

Tunny stares at me for a moment before beginning to shake, his head swaying back and forth like Anthony's did in Archer's office on Friday. "You shouldn't have come back."

"Here I am. What is this 'she' going to do about it?"

"Last time, she merely sent you away and no doubt considered that a kindness." He lowers his head and stares up at me through his bushy eyebrows. "She is not one for kindnesses."

I half expect the menacing voice of the Exhibition's keeper to echo down from above and am strangely disappointed at the silence that follows.

"So, I'm an intruder and 'Lucy in the Sky with Diamonds' is the guard dog. I get that. What I don't get is why you're so afraid."

"The Exhibition is hers to run. The rest of us remain here wholly at her leave. No one crosses her. No one."

"And why is that? Tunny, who are you talking about?"

"Please don't push, fair Scheherazade. We don't speak her name. Bad things happen when anyone speaks her name."

"Then bring her here." The haughty words of an Arabian princess pour from my mouth. "I would speak with this woman who engenders such fear."

Tunny laughs, though a hint of fear undercuts the mirth in his voice. "You can't be serious. We all go well out of our way to avoid any encounter with her." He takes me by the hand. "In fact, if you're going to insist on staying, we need to get you out of sight. Come. You can stay in the forest with me until you return to… wherever it is you come from."

Tunny leads me toward the alcove that holds his woodland painting. After a careful survey of the space, he steps forward and begins a frantic scramble across the bottom of the frame. Hiding my amused smile behind a cupped hand, I hold back a laugh and join him by the painting.

"Here." I stoop and interlace my fingers. "Let me give you a hand." With just enough of a boost to allow him to leap into the forest beyond the canvas, Tunny is on his way. His small figure moving within the confines of an oil painting reminds me of where I am—an odd dreamscape somewhere between Anthony Faircloth's slightly too-big ears. As my brain attempts to reconcile Tunny's fluid movements within the unchanging realm of oil, he shouts out of the picture at me.

"Well? Are you coming?"

I brush the back of my hand across the painting, the texture of oil on canvas as real as anything I could imagine. "I can't. The way is blocked. What do I do?"

Tunny snorts. "Climb. Jump. Step. Just get in here. You look a bit vulnerable out there."

Though my every sense screams at the absurdity, I raise a foot and take a fateful first step. The surface of the painting passes around the tip of my sandal-clad foot like a warm waterfall. My foot finds purchase on the other side, the crunch of dried leaves beneath my sole indistinguishable from reality. Another step and I'm standing amid an old forest, composed of broad strokes of grays and browns, and countless dabs of green.

The smell of fresh earth permeates my senses. In a blink, my body redistributes its dimensions to fit the few square feet of canvas, the latest in what seems an endless run of miracles. An invisible orchestra springs to life as cello and brass and viola and woodwind all intermingle to tell the story of the awkward little gnome. Runs of oafish playfulness intersperse with an occasionally beautiful melody, all building to a huge fall followed by a brass run that sets my heart to racing.

"Tunny?" The little gnome is nowhere to be found. "Where are you?"

"Here." Standing perfectly still at the base of a large oak, Tunny's brown skin and grimy hair blend in with the surrounding bark and moss. He flashes me a wicked grin, his yellow teeth like petrified wood. "I may not be much to look at, but in these woods, I can vanish in an instant."

I let out a laugh. "You clearly have the home court advantage."

Tunny joins me for a few seconds before his face draws down to its previous sobriety.

"You never answered me before," he says. "Why in the name of the Creator did you return here? Sent away as you were, I can't imagine anyone daring to show their face in these halls again."

I offer him a subtle curtsy. "As you can see, I'm not just anyone."

"And no one but you has ever come here anyway. What is it you want?"

"I'm looking for someone."

"Who is it you seek?"

"A boy, Tunny. A very special boy."

He studies the ground at his feet. "No boys here. Does this person you seek have a name?"

I take a deep breath. "His name is Anthony."

Tunny turns and begins to burrow at the base of the tree. "Don't know any Anthony, though I'm probably not the one to ask. Mostly, I know these woods and not much else."

"I've seen him here."

"Where?" A momentary stiffness overtakes Tunny's wooden spine.

"In *Tuileries*."

The gnome stops burrowing and glances across his shoulder. "You can forget about him, then. If he's in *Tuileries*, he's lost to you forever. Like all the other children there."

"Can't say I agree with you on that, Tunny. I believe I can save him. In fact, I may be the only one who can."

Tunny spins and sits on a gnarled root. "What makes this boy so special, anyway?"

At last. Contact.

"His mother sent me from a land far away to bring her boy home. There is no one more special to her."

He stares at the forest floor. "She must miss him very much."

"You have no idea." Tunny's befuddled gaze suggests I've taken this line of questioning as far as I should for the time being. My gaze wanders back to where we entered the gnome's forest and my brain attempts to reconcile the sight of the rectangular hole in space floating there as well as the dimly lit hallway beyond that beckons for our return.

I rest a hand on Tunny's shoulder. "Tell me about this place. Everything you know about your Exhibition."

"What would you care to know, fair Scheherazade?"

I smile at the compliment. "For starters, you stand day after day here amid this woodland scene. Down the hall, a musician plays a silver horn before a ruined castle. Another few steps away, a crowd of children plays among the French garden. Why these paintings? What's the common thread?" I kneel, bringing myself eye to eye with the gnome. "Why does this place exist?"

Tunny stares at his boot-clad feet as he contemplates my question. "I simply exist, like all the others. There is no why."

"The troubadour by the castle, the children playing in the garden. Are they free to roam like you? Do you ever speak to them?"

"Oh no," he stammers. "She doesn't allow us to speak. We each stay in our spaces and leave the others alone. It's the law."

"Her law?"

Tunny lets out an impatient huff. "Who else's law would it be?"

"Who are you referring to? And why do you all live in such fear?"

His eyes slide shut. "Once we trusted. Once we loved. Then came the betrayal and the pain that accompanied it. She keeps us from ever feeling that pain again."

"What do you mean? Betrayal?"

"Stupid, stupid gnome." The malevolent voice from my first trip to the Exhibition echoes through the forest. "What did I tell you about talking to her?"

Tunny begins to shake in his mud-caked boots.

He isn't alone.

"I'm s-s-sorry, Mistress. She returned despite your warning and it's been so long since I had anyone to talk to and—"

"Silence. I have been most generous, leaving you to your little woodland oasis, even giving you the run of the Exhibition when the others are quiet, and this is how you repay me. Deliberate disobedience. Have you forgotten what you are?"

Tunny falls to his knees and stretches his stubby arms to the sky. "Forgive me, Mistress. I merely wished to—"

"You, more than anyone, should know the penalty for such disobedience."

"Leave him alone," I shout as the sky above the forest canopy grows dark. "He's done nothing wrong."

"You were not given permission to speak, Scheherazade. Keep your tongue. I know full well the poison in your honeyed words."

The bile rises in my throat. "For an invisible voice in the sky, you seem awfully full of yourself. Are you afraid Tunny and others will discover the Wizard of Oz is just an old man hiding behind a curtain?"

Tunny's eyes grow wide. "By the Creator, don't antagonize her." His wooden teeth set to chattering. "You have no idea what lengths she'll take to defend her honor. Take back what you said. Please, take it back."

"It's too late for that, little gnome. Her words, be they brave or foolish, cannot be unspoken." A pair of squinting yellow eyes appears in the clouds gathering above our heads. "You desire my presence, Lady Scheherazade? So be it."

From the pink and gray oils of the darkening sky shoots a streak of lightning, a long jagged fork of white and gold. A tongue of fire envelops a tree to our right in broad strokes of bright orange and gold. The unseen painter adds more and more color to Tunny's home within the frame, and before I can say another word, the entire forest is ablaze.

"God, Tunny. I'm so sorry." Another lightning bolt strikes mere feet from where we're standing. "We've got to get out of here."

As I sprint for the hole in space leading back to the Exhibition, no footsteps follow me. I shoot a glance back and find Tunny curled into a fetal position at the base of a low shrub that has just begun to burn.

"I disobeyed," he whimpers. "I disobeyed and now I must pay the price."

"Don't listen to her, Tunny. Listen to me. You did nothing wrong. Come with me and we'll find somewhere safe."

Refusing to move, he mutters again, "I disobeyed."

The flames continue to build around us. The invisible painter erases every color but orange and black from the canvas. Though my pounding heart and panicked mind demand I run for the exit, I turn back. Crouching at Tunny's side, I whisper in his ear. "I'm sorry, but I can't do this without you. You're coming with me."

Before he can argue, I scoop the gnome from the charred ground and sprint for the hall, dodging tree after dripping tree as the conflagration rages all around us. Thick smoke burns my nostrils and clogs whatever passes for lungs in this place. My arms grow weaker with every step and I nearly drop Tunny as I duck beneath a jet of flame that appears meant for my head.

"Hang on, Tunny," I get out between gasps. "We're almost—" My words are cut off by the crack of splitting wood.

An ancient oak, half the diameter of my car, snaps just above head level and falls across our path. Encircled in flames, the strange heat of the dream inferno scorches my skin. A different song invades my thoughts, an old favorite by Johnny Cash. It plays in my head as I cast about for any avenue of escape. Then, so quiet I barely hear it, Tunny mutters the last line, the ominous four words ironically chilling me to the core.

"*The ring of fire.*"

After five years of psychology studies, not to mention my fair share of extracurricular research, I've read multiple papers detailing what happens if you die in your own dream. Now, for the first time in thirty-one years, I entertain a different question.

What happens if you die in someone else's?

VI

The Old Castle

"Leave me." The gnome's scream echoes in my ear. "Save yourself, fair Scheherazade."

"Not happening." I pace like a caged animal as Tunny squirms in my fatigued arms. A blackened branch falls from high in one of the trees and bashes my shoulder, driving me to my knees and setting my sarong aflame. Holding back a howl of agony, I scramble for a clue to how to save us from the approaching inferno. The resounding thud as another tree falls a few feet to my rear jars loose a memory.

Abnormal psych. My first and last year of grad school. Professor Frye's thick Boston accent echoes through my thoughts.

"Ms. Tejedor. You seem to be up on the reading for the day. Please define for the class a lucid dream."

This person I haven't been in years blushes as she stands before the class. "A lucid dream is one where the dreamer is aware they're dreaming."

"Go on." I would have never guessed that nine years later the memory of Edwin Frye's voice would bring such comfort.

"Often the dreamer finds they can exert some control at least over their own participation in the dream environment. Research has shown people discovering answers to questions long sought, outrunning imagined pursuers, even flying."

"Precisely." The voice shifts from memory to an audible, intimate whisper. "Now, unless you wish to burn in an imagined forest as you wander a mind not your own, perhaps some practical application of your hard-won knowledge is in order."

My eyes narrow as I back up the few steps remaining in the rapidly shrinking glade, mutter a short prayer, and make a run for the fallen tree. I wait till the last possible instant to leap, and…

My foot catches on a crooked branch covered in orange coals, sending searing pain up my leg. How anything can feel so real in a place like this is beyond me, but the sheer agony erases any doubt about the capacity of Anthony's psychotic art gallery to kill.

The moment before impact, I grip Tunny's small form and twist to one side. The pair of us hit the forest floor like the proverbial sack of potatoes and Tunny's shoulder drives the air from my lungs. Our momentum sends us sprawling and we end up in a pile before the opening leading back to the Exhibition. I hurl Tunny through the hole in space and try to rise only to find my leg entangled in the gnarled roots of the forest floor.

Like fingers of wood rather than bone and sinew, they grow tighter and tighter about my calf till my foot goes numb. I rip the jewel-encrusted dagger from its scabbard and slash at the roots binding me, but to no avail. My vision clouds with pain and my battle to remain conscious begins to go badly. Just before the agony becomes greater than I can stand, a blob of brown slips the blade from my limp fingers and goes to work on my bonds. Flash after flash of silver lessens the crushing force surrounding my leg until it releases altogether.

Coarse fingers encircle my wrists. These fingers, woody like the ones holding my leg before, possess a kindness the roots did not. Dragging my limp form across the forest floor, the roughened hands lift me and push me out of the painting and onto the parquet floor of the hall.

I lie there for what feels an eternity, catching my breath. At a second thud, I use every ounce of will to raise my head from the floor. Beneath the painting, Tunny lies on one side, the dagger gleaming in his hand. His breathing, much like mine, is interrupted by fit after fit of coughing, the clean air of the Exhibition despoiled by the smoke wafting off our charred clothing. A glance at my leg reveals an open ankle wound framed with charred, blistered skin and denuded skin all along the calf. The burn throbs in time with the music as the haunting thirteen-note melody begins anew with mocking insistence.

"Tunny." I use my last ounce of strength to sit up. "You saved me."

The gnome rolls to a standing position, walks over to me, and returns the dagger. On his face, a sheepish grin. "You saved me first."

"Then I suppose we saved each other."

"You think you can escape me so easily, storyteller? Gnome?" The voice echoes down from above, the timbre like a cello played with a bow of barbed wire. "Do you forget who rules this place?"

"Quickly." Tunny leaps to his feet and runs out of the alcove into the hall proper. "Follow me, Lady Scheherazade.'

"Where are you taking me?"

"To a place she can't find us." Tunny sprints as fast as his short legs will take him toward the next alcove. He's halfway across the hall before I can take my first painful step. The melody of the hall floods the room from every direction, the tempo accelerated to breakneck speed as I hobble after Tunny. I nearly fall twice crossing the wide hallway, catching myself in the alcove doorway as I join the gnome before the second painting.

The Old Castle. Just as I remember it. Well, almost. The troubadour still stands before the castle of old stone with its cracked parapets and ruined drawbridge. He has ceased playing his silver horn and instead stands with his arms crossed, studying us with an impassive stare.

"Run all you want, little gnome," the voice from above booms. "There is nowhere here you can hide from me. You were warned not to trust the storyteller and your betrayal has already cost you your home. Continue on this path and I assure you that will be far from the biggest price you pay this day."

From the hallway without, a crash echoes as if from far away, closely followed by a reverberating thud. Another crash, another thud, back and forth, like the ticking of some impossibly huge clock.

Crash. Thud.

Louder and closer with every repetition.

Crash. Thud.

My heart threatens to burst from my chest.

Crash. Thud.

The tree-bark brown in Tunny's cheeks blanches to a color more resembling sweet caramel as he whispers, "She is coming."

"Then what are you waiting for, gnome? An engraved invitation?"

This new voice comes from the painting. The accent is vaguely British, the tone haughty and patronizing. By the castle entrance, the troubadour's arm is lifted in a beckoning wave, his expression somewhere between bored and annoyed.

I crouch next to Tunny and whisper in his ear. "Do you trust him?"

Tunny glances across his shoulder and waggles his thumb back toward the hallway. "More than I trust her."

The gnome's panicked gaze grows wider with each crescendoing crash. Whatever or whoever is after us is getting closer every second. But Tunny's helpless stare is rooted in a much simpler issue. Unlike *Gnomus*, an oversized portrait that stretches nearly to the floor, *The Old Castle* is a landscape and the bottom extent of the frame rests just out of his diminutive grasp.

"I'll never be able to reach…"

Before he can say another word, I clutch his coarse-fiber collar and one of the many buckles covering his brown coat and shove him through the canvas. He lands on the other side, rolls down a steep bank and disappears from view.

"Tunny," I shout. "Are you all right?"

"Hurry, Scheherazade," Tunny's disjointed voice screams. "She is upon us."

I stare at the painting before me. Slightly wider than it is tall, the painting's lower extent sits just above my navel. Given time, I could clamber across, but if I wasn't all the way through when the keeper of the Exhibition arrived…

Crash. Thud.

Just outside the alcove.

Another memory is jarred loose.

Coach Douglas from my one ill-fated year of track in high school.

"Make the jump," she always said with that ever-present insistence in her voice. "The landing will take care of itself."

Though the thought of taking a running jump at a perfectly good wall somehow fails to excite me, I step back to the mouth of the alcove and sheathe my weapon. I rebel against an overwhelming compulsion to sneak a glance out into the hallway and instead make a mad dash at the painting. The distance is too short and my run is at best a hobble, but technique honed by hundreds of high bar jumps somehow prevails.

One moment, I'm shivering in the cool air and muted light of the Exhibition and the next I'm rolling down a grassy embankment beneath a midday sun. Still picking up speed when I reach the bottom, I nearly flatten my nose against a dark piece of slate. A survey of the area reveals the rock is merely one of hundreds of oblong hunks of stone forming a walkway leading to the castle in the distance.

There on the cool ground of a boy's imagination, I allow myself a moment to gather my wits and survey this strange body I possess for injury. So quiet it fades into the background like the babbling of a brook or the chirping of crickets, a pleasant melody fills the air. A solemn tune, the melody wanders back and forth between woodwinds and strings. The music has nearly lulled me to sleep when the momentary interlude is interrupted by the crack of a branch above my head.

I sit up and whip my head to the right. The troubadour is creeping toward me, sword drawn. He's somehow familiar, though I can't place where I've seen his face before. My hand drifts down to the dagger at my side, but before I can so much as utter a word of challenge, Tunny charges from the underbrush. Though the troubadour is three times his height, Tunny's attack takes the gaily-clad stranger by surprise and brings the two of them to ground. Far more agile than my diminutive friend, however, the man in blue and white stripes rolls with the fall, springs to his feet, and levels his gleaming foil at Tunny's brown throat.

"You dare touch me, filthy gnome." The disdain in the troubadour's voice hits Tunny like a physical blow. "Give me one reason I shouldn't split you for firewood."

"Stay away from him." I rush to Tunny's side. Instinct kicks in yet again and the dagger finds its way to my hand. "He means you no harm."

"Indeed? And who, may I ask, is imposing upon whose home?" He brings his foil up across his chest.

"But you invited us in." Tunny's voice comes out as a high whine.

"Better than having you stare at me from the hall. The very height of rudeness."

"Forgive us, troubadour." I lean forward in a careful bow, not taking my eyes off the man in blue. "The gnome and I seek sanctuary from the mistress of the Exhibition."

His face pales at my words. "So, the gnome's clumsy cavorting has finally angered the witch. Can't say I'm surprised. But who are you, milady, to come to the assistance of such a creature?"

"Don't you recognize her?" Tunny squeaks from the ground, the sharp point at his throat forgotten for the moment.

"Should I?"

"This is the renowned Scheherazade."

A loose stone falls from one of the castle's many parapets and is swallowed by the murky moat below.

The troubadour eyes me with a crooked smile. "Really? Tell me, noble Scheherazade. What brings you to our Exhibition?"

"She's looking for someone," Tunny says.

"Aren't we all?" The troubadour puts away his foil and helps Tunny to his feet. "Pathetic gnome."

Tunny hangs his head as the troubadour turns to face me.

"Who do you seek that has so angered she who rules the hall?"

"His name is Anthony." I attempt a smile. "Perhaps you've heard of him."

"Can't say I have. Very few visitors here at the castle." He lets out a caustic laugh. "The last few didn't fare so well."

"The last few? Who are they? What happened to them?"

"Now, now, fair Scheherazade. Just because you are a teller of tales doesn't mean I plan to flap my lips about everyone who has passed my way."

"Fair enough, troubadour, though I can't imagine why you would bring them up if you had no intention of discussing them."

"Hm." The troubadour glances over at Tunny and raises an eyebrow. "She's clever, this one."

"You know my name." I sheathe the dagger. "What should I call you, sir troubadour?"

"I have entertained for many years under many names, milady, but you may call me Modesto."

"Funny. You don't strike me as the modest type."

He laughs. "Ah, you wound me, fair Scheherazade, though I must admit you are even more beguiling than I was led to believe."

"And who has spoken to you of me?"

"The Prince. When last we spoke, he said we might cross paths."

I glance at Tunny. He gives me only the subtlest of shrugs.

Turning back to Modesto, I ask, "Does this prince have a name?"

"He is known as the Kalendar Prince, and as his name would connote, he visits the Exhibition every week like clockwork. Twice, if things are amiss."

"And you've seen this… Kalendar Prince?"

The troubadour scratches his chin and looks off into space. "Not in so many glances, but all of us know him, his deep voice, his soothing words."

"He speaks to us from the sky, like the Mistress." Tunny's gaze drops. "But he's nothing like *her*."

I peer at Modesto. "This man visits you each week, but you haven't seen him."

"He is a good man and I understand his skill with the bow is without compare. Still, there is nothing he can do to help us now."

"Why?" Neither of them answers. "Why can't he help you? What is different?"

"Juliet," Tunny whispers. "Since she vanished, the Mistress has—"

"Quiet, gnome." Modesto's affable tone turns harsh. "Do not speak that name here."

"Juliet?" I ask. "Who is she?"

"And now you as well." Modesto's eyes grow wide with rage and fear. "Foolish woman. Would you bring the witch? Do not repeat that name again or—"

Another crash rends the air, followed by a thud that shakes the ground beneath us. Back and forth, the two sounds repeat again and again from the portal leading back to the Exhibition.

"Now you've done it," Modesto snarls. "Quickly. To the castle."

"We're invited to the castle?" Tunny's face turns up in an expression of disbelief.

Modesto groans and inclines his head toward the drawbridge in the distance. "You'd best move those stumps you call legs before she catches you and plants you outside her hut."

The three of us flee up the stony path to the castle. Modesto negotiates the dilapidated drawbridge with ease, leaving Tunny and me to fend for ourselves. I offer to carry Tunny across, but at Modesto's quiet snicker, he refuses and sets off on his own with me close behind. We're nearly across when Tunny's stump-like legs send him plunging toward the murky depths below. I dive forward, catch him by his mossy beard, and haul him back up.

"Careful." I pull him close and leap across the gap in the bridge. "I need you alive."

"You… need me?"

"Come along, stubby," Modesto says. "There will be plenty of time to let your heart go pitter-patter once we're safe inside."

I rush inside and set Tunny on a stone outcropping as Modesto grabs a rusted old crank.

"The bridge," he cries. "It won't budge."

I sprint to his side and together we somehow get the crank to turn. The alternating crash and thud from the hallway grows more earsplitting with each repetition. The top of the bridge crosses my line of sight as our pursuer arrives at the portal. I catch a glimpse of an enormous club striking the ground and the tip of what must be a long, hooked nose before the battered wood blocks my view and slams shut.

Modesto lies prostrate on the floor, panting as if he'd run a marathon. My pumping lungs ache to join him, but I remain standing, mostly for Tunny's sake.

"Safe for the moment," Modesto says once he reclaims his breath. "That is, if we can all agree to avoid invoking certain names." He glances at Tunny, though he reserves the majority of his glare for me.

"A different topic, then." I motion to the frightened gnome across the room. "Tunny lives alone in in a wooded paradise, or at least he did before his home was destroyed, while you live here alone in an old castle. Does any of this make sense to either of you?"

The gnome and the troubadour stare at each other, my question apparently far beyond anything they've ever considered before.

"Of course I live in the forest," Tunny says, yellow tears forming at the corners of his eyes. "Or, I suppose, lived."

"And yet here you stand in this grand castle, the guest of our new friend here, the two of you separated only by a few steps in an art gallery. Haven't the two of you ever gotten lonely? Perhaps dropped by the other's home for a visit?"

"We are discouraged from speaking to each other," Modesto says, "or venturing beyond our own individual realms, though the gnome has been known to skirt up and down the main hall from time to time."

"It doesn't have to be that way. I'm guessing if the two of you sat down and talked, you might find you have a lot in common."

Tunny beams at Modesto, his hopeful gaze answered with a disgusted sneer.

"Befriend the little freak of nature, you say? Your words are powerful indeed, fair Scheherazade, but surely you jest."

Tunny's expression descends into a disgruntled pout. "Same goes for me."

I let out a sigh. "Then at least pretend you like each other as long as I'm here."

"Very well." Modesto nods in Tunny's direction.

"Agreed." The gnome shoves his hands in his pockets.

"Modesto, this is your castle?"

"Every stone."

"And are we safe here?" I peer back at the closed drawbridge. "Will that door keep out your so-called Mistress?"

"But of course." He surveys the interior of the structure, a proud smile breaking upon his face. "This old castle may not look like much, but she's solid."

A monstrous force strikes the raised drawbridge and buckles one of the central beams. Tunny leaps to one side and narrowly avoids being crushed by a hail of stones.

"Solid as a block of Swiss cheese." Tunny sprints away as fast as his short legs will carry him.

Crestfallen, Modesto grips me by the arm. "Come, Scheherazade. She will be upon us in no time." As he leads me toward the rear of the castle, we pass a stone stairwell leading downward into darkness.

"Where does that lead?" I ask as we rush past.

"The Catacombs, but no one goes there. It's—"

A shriek erupts from beyond the drawbridge door. A second strike bows the bridge leaving two of the three timbers just shy of splintered.

Tunny spins around and points a stubby finger at Modesto. "You berate us for saying names and then invoke the Catacombs in the presence of the Exhibition's mistress. Now who is the fool?"

"Quiet, gnome," Modesto shouts as he drags me deeper into the castle.

"Where are we going?" Before either can answer, the drawbridge shatters inward as if struck by a bomb. Through the dust, a figure emerges. At the apex of the arched doorway, a roughly human form sits atop a tapering cylinder, a giant cudgel in one hand and a gnarled branch terminating in broom bristles in the other. I have but a moment to take in the sight before Modesto drags me around a corner.

"You dare try to look the witch in the eye?" he shouts. "Are you trying to die today?"

We sprint down a hallway decorated with rich tapestries all in a various states of disrepair. Tunny leads us by several lengths, though his short strides allow us to catch up to him as the alternating crash and thud begins again in earnest.

"This way," Tunny says as he darts down a hallway to the left.

"Like you know you're way around *my* home." Modesto sneers and heads the opposite way.

Tunny stops in his tracks and looks back at me. One shared glance is all it takes to convince us to follow the brightly clothed troubadour. We catch up to Modesto at a double door at the far end of a long, narrow passage, all of us winded.

"This doorway better not be locked," Tunny shouts above the crashes echoing down the hall behind us. "I can hear her grinding ever closer."

"Of course it's not locked." Modesto draws the door open, his face an unabashed sneer.

"No," Tunny squeaks. "It's not."

My heart sinks as Modesto turns to face the doorway. His smug air evaporates like a snowflake over an open flame as he discovers what Tunny and I already know.

The massive double doorway opens onto a stone wall.

Tunny moans. "Now look what you've led us to."

"It's not me," Modesto shouts. "It's her." We all turn to our rear. There, so close her rancid breath turns my stomach, our pursuer awaits.

More wrinkled and bent than any living person I've seen, the ancient hag sits perched atop a tall stone cup. In one hand, she carries an enormous wooden club with a rounded tip that rests on the granite floor. The combination reminiscent of the old mortar and pestle Mom would drag out for all her "from scratch" recipes, my mind recoils at the thought of what 'ingredients' the hag would be grinding to need implements of such size. In her opposite hand, the witch carries a broom that swishes back and forth behind her as if of its own accord. Her clothing ramshackle at best, the tattered gray housedress has been repaired over and over until it is more patch than original cloth. The mop atop her head seems as much grime and dirt as hair.

"You were warned, Scheherazade." She stares down her long crooked nose. Spittle flies from between her sharp iron teeth. "You are not welcome here."

"What have you done with Anthony?" I cross my arms before me in an attempt to control the tremor in my hands.

The witch smiles, as horrid an expression as I've ever seen. "I'm the one that asks the questions in this place, storyteller." The mortar tilts forward and the old hag drags it closer, using the pestle like a paddle on a stone lake. Behind her, the broom in her opposite hand sweeps back and forth like a dog's wagging tail, erasing any evidence of her passing.

"What do you want from me?"

"I thought that quite obvious. I want you gone from here."

"But they need me." I gesture toward Tunny and Modesto. "Hell, all of you need me."

Tunny gasps at my words, but puts up his little fists in a gesture of defiance. Modesto pulls his foil from his sheath and assumes a defensive stance. I rest my fingers on the jewel-encrusted hilt of the dagger at my side and wait to see who makes the first move.

The witch laughs as she reaches into a bag tied at her side. "Children, children. This fight is over before it even begins." She brings a gnarled hand to her foul mouth and blows a cloud of silver-gray dust into Modesto's face.

"Sleep, troubadour." The music that filled the space when I first arrived in Modesto's picture swells back to life. The weapon drops from Modesto's fingers, his eyes growing heavier with each passing second.

"Scheherazade," he whispers as he falls to the floor, his skull nearly colliding with Tunny's on the way down. Before anyone can say another word, he begins to snore.

"And you, little gnome." She stares down her hawk like nose at Tunny. "Dance."

Tunny stares at her defiantly, but within seconds, his foot begins to tap. The song that played throughout his forest home begins to echo through the hall, and soon he is moving and cavorting in time with the strange undulating tune. He goggles at me frantically, unable to control his own limbs or even speak, moving in place as if on strings.

"Leave us." The witch waves a wizened hand and Tunny twirls up the hall and around the corner, leaving me alone with the Modesto's sleeping form and the cackling crone.

"They weren't much to begin with, but it appears your friends have left you quite stranded, Lady Scheherazade. Whatever shall you do now?"

"I'm not afraid of you, witch."

"Of course you are, dear. A lone woman, armed with only a tiny blade, facing an old witch in an abandoned castle, and her two defenders, such as they are, incapacitated. You're brave, but you're no fool."

She's right. I tell myself a thousand times everything in this place is nothing but a figment of Anthony's imagination, but it doesn't stop me from trembling.

"Perhaps," I say, "but I know something you don't."

"And what would that be, dear?"

"No matter what you might do to me, you won't hurt them."

"Perhaps, Scheherazade, and perhaps not. Regardless, your half-chewed morsel of supposition won't save you."

"Who said I needed saving?" I chance one last glance at Modesto's sleeping form and utter the safe word Archer drilled into my head with a bit of hypnosis just before this most recent jaunt into Anthony's mind.

"Coda."

The witch dives at me, her clawed hand snatching only air as we fade from each other's perception. The castle dissolves around me into flashes of prismatic light, the witch an oddly shaped shadow quickly swallowed by the surrounding light.

"No..." Her screams fade into nothingness as the maelstrom of light slowly dims.

Chilled to the bone, I awake clammy and disoriented.

"Mira?" Caroline Faircloth's concerned voice, as if from across a crowded room.

"She's coming to." Archer's rich baritone. Thank God. I'm back.

A hand at my throat. Choking me.

No. Just checking my pulse.

"Still beating?" My voice little better than a whisper, I work again to focus my eyes. A sweep with my fingers reveals they've left me resting on the shag carpet this time. Archer and Caroline look down on me, her gaze relieved while his is filled with concern.

And something else.

The faint scent of hyacinths fills my mind.

"Mira." Archer runs the back of his fingers down my cheek. "Can you hear me?"

"Why, Dr. Archer, I didn't know you cared." I do my best to sit up. Not happening.

"Take it easy, Ms. Tejedor. You're still coming to."

"Aw, don't back down now, Doc. If we're going to get all touchy-feely, Mira's fine."

He clears his throat. "Fine, Mira. Now, hold still and give yourself a minute."

Archer tries to sound tough, but the heady aroma of flowers that continues to grow in my mind tells a different story. This sudden resurgence of my olfactory "emotion detector" draws attention to something I hadn't noticed before. When I travel Anthony's mind, the sixth sense I've possessed since puberty apparently takes a back seat. I have yet to miss it there, but out here in the real world, such a loss would be akin to losing an arm or going deaf.

Neither of which I'm particularly eager to experience.

I peer around for a clock. "How long was I gone?"

"Over an hour," Caroline says. "Much longer than before. We were beginning to worry you might not wake up." She helps me sit up and props me against the couch.

"It's not as bad this time," I croak, "though I won't be running any races tomorrow." I catch a glimpse of Anthony's bobbing head out of the corner of my eye. "How's Anthony?"

"No change from before," Archer says, "though for a while there, you both acted like you were having the mother of all nightmares."

"That would make more sense than you know." I cover my mouth and let out something between a yawn and a cough. "One thing is clear, though. I've got a lot more research to do before I go in there again." My eyes slide shut. "I need you both to tell me everything you know about this *Pictures at an Exhibition*."

VII

ACCELERANDO

It doesn't take a psychic to pick up on the fog of despair hanging over the Faircloth home. The lawn is well above ankle length, the plants are all wilted from lack of water, and dust-laden spider webs decorate the windows on the front porch. One of the door numbers is broken, leaving their 574 address a simple 5/4. The doorbell doesn't make a sound so I grasp the brass knocker and give it a couple taps. Caroline doesn't keep me waiting long.

"Good morning, Mira." The weariness in Caroline's voice mirrors my own exhaustion. "Have you eaten?"

"I grabbed some breakfast on the way over, but thanks." Her offer is polite, but there's an edge there. Definitely picking up on some manure among the roses today.

"I was expecting you hours ago."

"I was expecting to be awake hours ago. My second sojourn through your son's mental playground took a lot more out of me than I expected. Slept right through the alarm and three phone calls from home. If it weren't for the housekeeping staff at the Blake, I might still be out."

"I can only imagine." The irritation wafting off Caroline ebbs a bit. "Can I at least offer you something to drink?"

"Anything with double the recommended dose of caffeine should do the trick."

"I have just the thing." Caroline gives me a knowing smile and heads for the kitchen. "Make yourself at home."

I step into the living room and catch a pair of eyes beneath red curls ducking behind a doorway at the far end of the room.

"It's all right, Rachel." I sit on the couch. "I don't bite."

The girl pops her head around the corner. "You're Miss Mira. The one who's trying to help Anthony."

"That's me." I pat the cushion next to me. "You want to sit down?"

She glances in the direction her mother went before stealing over to join me by the couch. "Mama told me to stay in my room."

"It's okay. I don't think she'll mind you talking to me." An odd combination of scents filters through my mind. The usual twin tangs of trepidation and curiosity flirt with my senses, but under it all, something subtler vies for my attention. The same subtle something I sensed when I first laid eyes on Rachel Faircloth in Archer's office.

"You miss your brother, don't you?"

She sits next to me and looks up at me with an innocence I had already left behind by the time I reached her age. "Can you really help him? Bring him back so we can play?"

"I'll do my best." My bottom lip trembles. "Promise."

Rachel looks me up and down as if taking my measure. 'Shake on it?" She smiles and holds out her right hand.

I let out a chuckle. "I'll even pinky swear if it makes you feel better."

"Rachel?" Caroline stands in the kitchen doorway holding a tray with a pair of coffee mugs. "I thought I told you to stay in your room."

"But, Mama, I just wanted to talk to Miss Mira."

"Well, now you've talked to her. Back to your room."

"Don't worry, Caroline." I pat Rachel's knee. "She's not bothering me."

Caroline dons a long-suffering smile, though her not-so-subtle glare and the reek of vinegar attacking my senses suggests she and Rachel have danced this dance before.

"Go on, Rachel. The grown-ups need to talk."

"Yes, Mama." Rachel rises from the couch and trudges across the room. She chances one last glance in my direction before vanishing down the hall. As the sound of Rachel's door closing echoes through the space, Caroline rests the tray on the coffee table and joins me on the couch.

"She really wasn't bothering me, you know. She's precious, and understandably worried about her brother."

Caroline's shoulders fall as if she were a balloon and someone let the air out.

"Don't you think I know that? She and Anthony have been inseparable since she was old enough to crawl after him. Now she's all alone."

"Any friends at school?"

"A few. As you said, Rachel is a sweet kid. She gets along with everybody, adults and children alike, but what she and Anthony share is special. Their bond is like nothing I've ever seen in a brother and sister. It's like they know what the other is thinking before they even speak."

Then it clicks. That scent of desperation. Where I've sensed it before.

Sarah Goode.

Burgeoning psychic talent mixed with utter despair.

After the last few days, Anthony's abilities have become all but a foregone conclusion, but suddenly the bond between him and Rachel makes a lot of sense.

I glance around the room. "Do you have it?"

"It's right here." She goes to the bookshelf, pulls down an old LP, and hands me the record.

The cover shows an old edifice with a trio of arches and a bell tower holding three large bells beneath a Russian dome. A crowd of people, both on foot and horseback, huddle at the base of the structure beneath a sky of blue and lavender clouds. Written across the top is *Phase 4 Stereo - Mussorgsky/Stokowski - Pictures at an Exhibition - Leopold Stokowski - New Philharmonia Orchestra.*

"This is it? Anthony's favorite?"

Caroline chuckles. "We bought him several versions on CD and a couple others on vinyl but he likes this one the best. Says the vinyl sounds more real. Truth is, this was the first one he heard, and Anthony tends to stick with what he knows. He's worn out two copies of this one already."

"Thank God for eBay. You know, it's funny. I played flute in band all through high school, but I've never even heard of this piece." I flip the album over and peruse the titles of the various movements.

"Gnomus," I mutter. "The Old Castle." My stomach churns. "Tuileries."

Welcome to the Exhibition.

Caroline rubs at her temple. "You really believe this music has something to do with what's happened to Anthony?"

"You tell me." I run my finger along the words on the back of the album sleeve. "I spent the better part of yesterday talking to a gnome and a troubadour inside an old castle while a witch chased me through a psychotic art gallery." I scan the titles for the identity of the witch, but find nothing other than perhaps "The Catacombs" that would lead in that direction. Didn't Modesto mention something about such a place?

Great, Mira. Now you're referencing conversations you've had with figments of a child's imagination.

I point to a title on the album cover. "The only other picture I've seen in Anthony's Exhibition is this *Tuileries* one."

"Was it a garden?" Caroline asks.

"Yes, though the painting focused on a crowd of children playing under the watchful eye of their teacher. They looked… French."

"Well, that makes sense. The Tuileries Garden was built on the site of the destroyed Tuileries Palace in Paris. The original picture on which Mussorgsky based the piece was of children playing there." Noting the confusion in my gaze, Caroline smiles and gestures toward the door leading to the bedrooms. "Professor Anthony has taught me many things."

Yesterday's jaunt through Anthony's mind. The forlorn face staring out at me from the sea of children. "I'm guessing this is one of his favorites."

"He loves them all, but he dances with Rachel when "Tuileries" comes up. Quite the little lady and gentleman. They even bow and curtsy."

"The *Tuileries* picture in the Exhibition." I take Caroline's hand. "I saw Anthony there."

Her brow knits into a wrinkled W. "And the other pictures? You said the gnome's name was Tunny. That's got to be my son somehow. And the troubadour? Anthony loves music. You heard what Dr. Archer said. They're all Anthony."

Across Caroline's shoulder, a current family portrait catches my eye.

Another revelation.

"Not necessarily."

"What do you mean?"

As we wandered the castle yesterday, I didn't recognize the constant frown, the petulant stare. Like Anthony's interpretation of me as Scheherazade, his characteristics are magnified, distorted, but faced with photographic evidence, there's no ignoring the obvious.

"The troubadour. It's Jason."

She raises an eyebrow. "You're serious?"

"With a British accent and perhaps a bit sharper of tongue, but it was your son."

"Sharper of tongue?" Caroline's shakes her head and smiles. "You don't know Jason."

"If what Archer says is true, both Tunny and the troubadour represent Anthony in one way or another. Of course he'd want to populate his fantasy world with people he trusted, respected, maybe even loved."

"But a witch? I can see a friendly gnome, a musician, a crowd of children, but a monster at the end of the hall?"

"Kids Anthony's age often fear a boogeyman under their bed or in their closet. Perhaps the witch represents that fear." At Caroline's unimpressed stare, I add, "What do you bet Dr. Archer already has a theory about this witch?"

Despite the situation, Caroline laughs. "Not taking that one."

Is this what cancer surgeons go through? Like me, they explore their patients and take out parts that used to be functional but have spiraled out of control.

But what to save? What to cut out?

And how would I even do any of those things in the first place?

"Another strange thing. All the characters along the Exhibition know me as Scheherazade. My dad read me *1,001 Arabian Nights* when I was a kid, but what does that have to do with—"

Before I can finish my question, Caroline pulls another record from the shelf.

"Now there's no doubt you've visited my son's mind." She drops the album in my lap. "Our fourth copy of this one."

Scheherazade, Sir Thomas Beecham with The Royal Philharmonic, the cover done in pastel yellow, blue, and hot pink. The Sultan stands at the center, scimitar in hand, while Scheherazade reclines on a bed beckoning. Not sure how to feel about a thirteen-year-old thinking of me in such a way, but a lot of things make sense.

I hold up the two records. "Can I borrow these?"

"I have both on CD. You may have an easier time listening to those." She steps into the next room and returns with two discs. "I keep these on hand for emergencies."

"Anthony probably doesn't deal well with record skips."

She hands me the discs. "You're learning."

I peruse the pair of cases. *Pictures at an Exhibition* displays a pencil and watercolor sketch of "The Hut on Fowl's Legs," the next to last movement of the piece, while the *Scheherazade* disc is decorated with another picture of the beautiful Arabian storyteller, this time dressed in white and dancing in a field of flowers. I flip this second one over and study the list of movements. A now familiar title, "The Kalendar Prince," jumps out at me, followed by the less comforting "The Ship Breaks Against a Cliff Surmounted by a Bronze Warrior."

A quiet groan escapes my lips. "Does Anthony like any pieces of music that don't have titles that could get me killed?"

Caroline laughs. "Plenty, but nothing like his obsession with these two. Throw in a little Tchaikovsky and Stravinsky for good measure, though, and you pretty much have my boy covered. Anytime he's drawing, writing, or reading, which are pretty much all he does, he's got something classical playing. Almost always Russian."

I shake my head and let out a quiet chuckle. "What's the deal with Anthony and Russian composers anyway? He's a thirteen-year-old kid. Shouldn't he be into comic books and *Star Wars*?"

"Oh, he likes that stuff too, but as you've found out the hard way, Anthony's anything but your average thirteen-year-old. The classical music, though? That's all Bill. He was the right-brained one in our marriage. He was researching Slavic composers for his thesis when Anthony was still in the womb. When he was a baby, that was the music that would lull him to sleep, and as soon as he was old enough to talk, Mussorgsky or one of his friends was what he asked for." A mischievous grin peeks through the fatigue in Caroline's eyes. "Bill always joked that when the doctors said 'autistic,' Anthony thought they said 'artistic' and went with it.'"

"I can tell you from our last couple of sessions, his education is pretty complete. I'm guessing his taste in movies and books tends toward the fantastic."

"You have no idea. My boy is all over any movie with broadswords and magic wands and will read any surface with writing on it as long as it's about gods or superheroes. He's devoured two library's worth of books on mythology and is hungry for more. The kid can quote Edith Hamilton line and verse. Better than his teachers, in fact."

"Sounds about right. His mind is pretty much wallpapered with the stuff. And not the pretty stories either."

"That's my Anthony. When it comes to stories, the more tragic, the better." Caroline's sad smile fades. "Now he's the tragedy."

"We're going to help him, Caroline. I give you my word."

"Mira, I have to ask you something and I want the truth."

Her lips purse as a hint of sour milk tickles my brain. I know what she's about to ask.

"Shoot."

"You've never done anything like this before, have you?"

I pause to consider my words. "To be honest, no. Usually when I bring my talents to bear for my clients, I deal more in impressions, feelings, hunches. I find things. Sometimes I find people. But have I ever been pulled into someone's mind and dealt with their inner demons on such an intimate level? No. Let me assure you, though. If I can't find Anthony in there, no one can."

"No one." She looks away. "That's what I'm afraid of."

The click of a deadbolt turning followed by the quiet creak of a door sounds from the foyer. A moment later, Jason Faircloth saunters into the room. He takes one look at me and his lip turns up in a snarl.

"What's she doing here?"

"Mind that mouth of yours," Caroline says. "Ms. Tejedor is here at my request. She needed a few additional pieces of information to help your brother."

"Come on, Mom. You're still buying all this crap? Psychic powers? Magical art galleries filled with gnomes and witches? It's a fairy tale." His glare shifts to me. "An expensive fairy tale."

Caroline steps between us. "We've already had this discussion. If you're going to stand here and be rude to our guest, then you can just go on to your room."

"It's all right, Jason." I step past Caroline, palms up in surrender. "If I were in your shoes, I doubt I'd believe me either."

"What's your angle, anyway?" His eyes narrow, the vinegar and pepper coming off him so strong I gag. "You don't know us."

"That's enough." Caroline turns to me, her cheeks pink with embarrassment. "I'm sorry, Mira. My son has a lot going on these days."

"I'm aware of that." I lock gazes with Jason. "I know about Julianna."

He jumps as if struck by a cattle prod. "How do you know about that?"

"Oh, don't worry. I didn't read your mind or anything." I raise a mischievous eyebrow. "I mean, that would be a fairy tale, right?" At his confused stare, I add, "I saw the story on the news. They showed a picture of you two at prom and I put two and two together. Any news—"

Jason puts his hand in my face, cutting me off as he gives his mother a glare that would strip paint. "Look, Mom. You can pay this fraud to play street corner psychic with Anthony till we're broke for all I care, but we are not discussing Julianna."

I rest a hand on his shoulder. "I'm sorry. I didn't mean to cause a—"

He brushes my hand away and leans in close. Anger wafts off him in palpable waves. "What part of 'I'm not talking to you' did you not understand? God, for someone who claims to be psychic, you're pretty fucking dense." Before I can even formulate a response, he turns on his heels and heads for his room.

"Jason Faircloth. You come back here and apologize." Caroline almost knocks me over as she storms after her son. A slamming door knocks a picture off the wall.

Caroline engages in a one sided argument through Jason's door for a bit before quitting and knocking on a different door. Soon, a girl's gentle sobbing alternates with a mother's whispers.

I'm guessing this isn't the first time Rachel has had to listen to a fight around this place.

A few minutes later, Caroline returns, her face red and eyes swollen.

"I'm sorry, Caroline. I didn't mean to upset Jason. I was just trying to connect with him."

Caroline sighs. "Actually, that went about as well as any interaction I've had with him the last few weeks. Since Julianna went missing, he's been nothing but a big bundle of nerves. I know they were broken up and everything, but I'm not sure if that's made it better or worse. I give him as much space as he needs, but it's not been easy. None of this has."

"What's your take on what happened to her?"

"It's hard to know what to think but it doesn't sound good. An attractive high school senior disappears halfway through a football game and her car is still in the parking lot the next day? Not the most promising start to an investigation."

"Didn't someone at the game miss her? I mean, she is on the cheerleading squad, right?"

"Actually, as I understand it, she was taking a break from cheering this year to pursue other interests. She spent the first half with some friends from drama club and no one saw her again after halftime. Even the police are stumped. To tell you the truth, I honestly don't know whether they've been interviewing Jason as a witness or a suspect."

"Dr. Archer told me she and Jason were pretty serious for a while."

"They dated for eight months. The picture they keep showing on the news is from Jason's junior prom last April." Caroline's gaze grows distant. "When they were together, he was as happy as I've ever seen him."

"Any idea why they broke up?"

"As Jason tells it, that was all her. Hit him out of the blue. She told him they needed to take a break. That they were getting too serious, too fast." She shakes her head. "She broke the poor boy's heart."

The slight hint of distance in her tone hits me as strange. "Caroline. It's probably none of my business, but may I ask a personal question?"

Caroline eyes me cautiously. "You answered mine."

"Jason isn't yours, is he?"

Her eyes drop. She's been asked this question before. "I love that boy as if he were my own, but technically I'm his stepmother. When I married Anthony and Rachel's father, Jason was part of the deal. A welcome part of the deal, to be clear. Don't let him fool you with all his macho bullshit. He's a good kid, and his bark is worse than his bite."

"Is he always so… angry?"

"These days, yes. But I really can't blame him. He was two when Bill and I started seeing each other and turned three the week before we got married. He was always a sweet child and grew up into this smart, funny, athletic young man. Losing his father changed him in so many ways. The only person able to bring him out of his shell since was Julianna and now she's gone as well." Caroline looks away. "If only Bill was still here. He'd know what to do."

I touch her shoulder. "The loss is still pretty raw?"

She looks back at me, her eyes red. "Shouldn't be. It's been over three years since Bill died." Her hands ball into fists. "Doesn't stop it from feeling like yesterday."

"If it's not too personal, can you tell me what happened?"

Caroline shakes her head as if she still can't believe it, though I have no doubt she's told the story a thousand times. "The kids were all out of school for the week and we had the car packed for Orlando. It was going to be Anthony and Rachel's first trip to Disney World. The four of us were sitting down for dinner, waiting for Bill to get home from work, when we got the call. Heart attack." Caroline chokes back a tear. "It's not fair. Bill was forty-one years old, never smoked a day, and other than an undying passion for Italian cuisine, had no real vices. Hell, he even ran a marathon the year before."

"God, Caroline." I take her hand. "I'm so sorry."

"Bill was so good with the kids. He and Jason did all the sports stuff. You know, Panthers games, throwing around the baseball, and all that. But the way Bill had with Anthony, now that was something to see. Music, movies, books. Those two communicated on levels I never quite understood and probably never will."

I gesture to the collection of records occupying three of the built in shelves across the room. "I take it your husband was the music aficionado."

"That's an understatement. The only classical music I knew before I met Bill was classic rock. I never really got into it, but Bill and Anthony? They'd fill the room with chairs and conduct an invisible orchestra." She lets out a pained sigh. "Funny thing? Anthony knew. Came and climbed in my lap half an hour before the call. I didn't know why. I guess with everything that's going on now, that kind of makes sense, right?"

More than she knows. I squeeze her fingers. "He sounds like a great guy."

"The best, and now he's gone, leaving me with a stepson who won't spend five minutes in the same room with me, a little girl pining for her lost brother, and poor Anthony. Sometimes I think if one more thing happens—"

The phone rings. Caroline steps across the room and picks up the receiver. Her face grows pale.

"I understand. We'll… be right there."

She hangs up the phone.

"Who was that?" I ask.

"The police," she whispers. "They want to talk to Jason again."

VIII

Da Capo

"He's been back there for well over an hour."

Caroline paces our corner of the police station waiting area for what must be the thousandth time. She has yet to wear a groove in the tile, but this end of the room is going to need another coat of wax. The sharp bite of chlorine etches into my consciousness as her anxiety starts to boil over. I have no desire to spend the afternoon in a muggy waiting room, but I was there when she took the call and there was no way I was leaving the poor woman to sit and stew down here by herself.

Like Dad always used to say.

In for a penny, in for a pound.

"It's a police station, Caroline, not a torture chamber. I'm sure Jason is fine."

Truth is, I'd trade places with him in a hot second. The skinhead across the room has been eyeing me like a starving cannibal for at least half an hour. Thank God for handcuffs.

"Julianna's been missing for almost a month," Caroline says. "In that time, the police have brought both Jason and me in for questioning. They've assured me neither of us is a suspect, but here we are going on an hour and a half at the police station. Looks like they had more than just a 'couple' of questions."

"He's not under arrest." I take her arm. "That's something."

"Not yet, at least. The papers and the news keep turning up the volume. Beautiful girl. Loved by everyone. Missing for weeks. Everyone in this city expects the worst and wonders if their child is going to be next. You better believe the cops are looking for someone to pin this whole thing on."

"And you think that someone is Jason."

"I know my son. He'd as soon hit me as lay a finger on Julianna. I know his reputation at school though. Only takes a couple of fights on the football field to label you as hot-tempered. Jason was at home sick with me the night Julianna disappeared, but if the torches and pitchforks come out, God only knows what might happen."

"I still don't believe they won't let you be present for the questioning."

"He's eighteen. Not a minor anymore. Not to mention my hothead of a son didn't want to wait for the lawyer. After this all went down, I got in touch with a local defense attorney, but Jason keeps saying, 'I'm not a suspect,' almost like he's trying to convince himself that's the truth." She shoots a glance at the door leading to the rest of the station. "Not even out of high school and they're probably back there grilling him like he's a convicted felon."

"You don't know that, Caroline. Maybe they just—"

"I appreciate your efforts, Mira, but you know as well as I do why the police bring someone back for questioning. They're trying to catch Jason in a lie."

"I'm sorry." I stare down at my nails, the faint scars at my wrists from another time, anything to avoid Caroline's frantic gaze. "I'm just trying to help."

She flops down in the chair next to mine and buries her face in her hands. "I know, I know. I just can't take this waiting. Things have been rough lately, but Jason's still my son. Just the thought of him back there…"

My angst over Isabella being wined and dined for a few days by her absent jerk of a father suddenly seems a bit petty. Of Caroline's kids, one lies in all but a comatose state, another is being interrogated in a murder case, and the third is spending her fourth day in a row with neighbors while her mother tries to piece their shattered life back together. And none of them will ever see their father again, at least not in this world.

Dominic's face fills my mind's eye. His devilish smile. His ever-present stubble. The sparkle in his eye when he's with Isabella.

The way he used to look at me like I was the only other person on the planet.

Then the part that always burns.

I wasn't even the only other person in the city.

The door at the far end of the room opens. A pair of detectives escort Jason back into the waiting room. He looks none the worse for wear, though his swollen eyes reveal a tender side he likely doesn't let many people see.

"Jason," Caroline whispers, trying to keep the insistence out of her voice. "Come here, honey." She opens her arms, and in what seems an uncharacteristic move, her sullen son pulls his mother into a tight embrace.

"An hour and a half," Caroline mutters as she glares across Jason's shoulder at the two detectives. "Unbelievable."

"Everything's okay, Mom." Jason rubs his eyes with the heels of his hands. "It's over. They're not after me."

"That's what they say." Caroline glances in my direction. "That's what they always say."

As Caroline comforts her son as only a mother can, the two detectives who questioned him mill about the room trying to appear busy. Both dressed in the perfunctory dark suits of their trade, the pair are otherwise a study in opposites. Tall and gaunt, the one in front appears to be the senior of the two. Falling on one side or the other of fifty, his sparse red hair is trimmed close to his pale scalp. His pockmarked face reminds me of a book on lunar geography I bought for Isabella last Christmas. The lines around his mouth are not those of a man who smiles very often.

While Detective Sea of Tranquility all but leers at the sobbing teenager, his partner steps across the room and examines a bulletin board filled with wanted posters. He's probably already committed the various photographs to memory, but I respect his effort at giving a mother and son a moment of privacy. Unlike his associate whose bony frame isn't suited for coat and tie, this man fills out his navy blue suit like an ex-linebacker. I study him in profile as he studies one mug shot after another. Strong chin. Steady gaze.

Knowing smirk.

Shit. Caught looking twice in one week. Time to brush up on the whole subtlety thing.

He smiles at me out of the corner of his eye, his even white teeth set off by his dark skin. He glances in my direction, a rare kindness in his brown eyes. Curious, I open myself up to feel the room and there it is, cutting through the angst, worry, and fear.

A hint of lilac.

He inclines his head and at my subtle nod, heads my way. The smile and the floral bouquet flowing from his thoughts leave me thinking he's going to ask me out for drinks. Instead, the first words out of his mouth make me wish I already had one or two under my belt.

"Ms. Tejedor, may I speak with you?" His voice a deep bass, a subtle hint of Boston invades an otherwise pleasant Southern accent. He's not from around here, but he's been in town a while.

My hand makes its way to my hip. "Do I know you? How do you know my name?"

Then it hits me. Jason.

"Don't worry." Again with the smile. "I'm good with faces. Recognized you from all the hullabaloo surrounding that kidnapping case in Virginia last year. Good job, by the way. That girl owes you her life."

A believer. What do you know?

I follow him to a corner of the room. "Thank you, Detective…?"

"Sterling. Calvin Sterling. Don't be angry with the kid. I was pretty sure who you were when I first laid eyes on you. After a bit of resistance, Jason confirmed you were, in fact, Mira Tejedor, psychic extraordinaire from Virginia. You might want to be careful. Kid seems to have a bit of a crush."

Heat rises in my cheeks. "If by crush, you mean he hates my guts, possibly. Otherwise, you've got me."

His gaze takes on a slightly more serious set. "You're in town working with the Faircloth family?"

"I'm on retainer with the family for the next few days. What about it?"

Footsteps approach from behind us. The high-pitched nasal voice that follows raises the hair on my neck.

"I believe my partner here is hoping you can read some tea leaves and help us catch a murderer." Unlike Sterling, "Detective Skin and Bones" doesn't even make an effort at civility. All business, this one. Though a part of me recoils, I do respect the straightforward approach. In a world filled with artifice, even a jerk like this gets a few points for being a straight shooter.

Sterling steps between us, his brow furrowed as if he were trying to figure out how to build a bridge across the Grand Canyon. "Ms. Tejedor, this is my partner, Mitch Bolger."

I extend a hand and try to keep the ice from my tone. "Pleasure."

Bolger grips my hand like a vise. "Just a handshake for now, Ms. Tejedor, but if all goes well, maybe I'll let you read my palm later." I half expect to hear the crack of knuckles or maybe the snapping of a bone, but I somehow manage to keep the pain from my face.

"Mitch," Sterling whispers, his winning smile gone as if it were never there. "Break the lady's hand and they're going to stick you behind a desk for a month." So quiet, I barely hear it, Sterling adds, "Again."

"Hey." Bolger releases my hand and turns his palms up in an innocent shrug. "Just making nice with the pretty psychic lady, Cal, like you asked."

Sterling lets out a frustrated sigh. "Please excuse my partner, Ms. Tejedor. He doesn't have quite as open a mind about these things as some of us."

I tilt my head to one side, trying to stay focused as the blood flows back into my fingers. "What things?"

He hesitates, apparently taken aback by the question. "I assumed Ms. Faircloth brought you to town to help search for the Wagner girl. I'm sure you're aware Julianna Wagner was dating Mr. Faircloth until a month or so before her disappearance. We—" At Bolger's not so subtle cough, Sterling makes a quick course correction. "All right, *I* was hoping you might be willing to share if you came up with anything. Perhaps even help us out with our investigation." The peppery scent wafting off Bolger stifles me, made all the worse by the stupid smirk plastered across his face.

"I'd love to help, but I'm not here to find Julianna Wagner." I motion to Jason and Caroline. "Ms. Faircloth asked me to come here and help her son."

Bolger lets out a half chuckle. "And why exactly does lover boy there need your kind of help?"

In my heels, I'm eye-to-eye with Bolger, and more than capable of delivering him my most withering glare. "Not that it's any of your business, but I'm not here for Jason, either."

"Then who?" Sterling asks. "Wait, the kid brother?"

Caroline strides over and interposes herself between us. "Detective Sterling, I think you've monopolized enough of our time for one day. Ms. Tejedor is here at my request to work with Anthony in matters not related in any way to your case. I'm not sure exactly what you think you're doing, but I'd appreciate it if you'd let her be."

Sterling puffs up his chest. "Ms. Tejedor?"

"I don't know what to tell you guys. I'm sorry, but I wasn't even aware of the missing persons case until I arrived in town."

Over a year has passed since I've watched the news regularly. Ever since I found Sarah Goode chained to a urine soaked mattress covered in her own feces, I've tried to scrub the image from my mind and can't bear to watch anything that reminds me of that particular time. I pray at some point a day will pass without imagining it had been Isabella instead.

A synapse fires in my mind. "On the other hand, Caroline, even you've wondered about the timing of Anthony's symptoms."

"Symptoms?" Sterling asks. "Is the boy sick?"

"You could say that." I turn back to Caroline. "Archer and I were talking. All of the stuff with Anthony started the day after Julianna disappeared. I know it's a long shot, but maybe working with the police may help shed some light on what's going on with him."

God, did I just say that? I swore I wouldn't do this again, but my every instinct screams this is the way to go.

Sterling bites his lip as he waits for Caroline's answer. A part of me wonders why he seems so eager to involve me in the case. Suppose I'll have to tease that one out later.

"Maybe you're right," Caroline says eventually. "As long as Anthony remains your top priority, I don't have any problem with you working with the police."

"Then that's the way it's going to be."

"As for Jason," Bolger interrupts, "he's free to go."

Sterling steps in. "We appreciate you and your stepson's continued cooperation. We'll let you know if we have any other questions."

"I'm quite certain you will, though any further question and answer sessions and he's going to have both me and a lawyer present, understand?" Caroline takes Jason by the arm and heads for the door. "And don't try playing divide and conquer with me, Detective. Jason's every bit as much my son as Anthony."

Quite the mother lioness, Caroline. I recognize a bit of myself in her no nonsense stare.

"You'll help us, Ms. Tejedor?" Sterling asks.

"I'm busy today, but I should be available early tomorrow afternoon."

"All right," Sterling says. "What do you need?"

"All the files you have on the case, every scrap of physical evidence, and a quiet room where I can have some privacy."

"Done. We'll be looking for you around one?"

"One it is."

The satisfaction on Sterling's face is wiped away by a derisive snort from Bolger as he retreats to the bowels of the office. "Don't forget your crystal ball," he grunts before disappearing behind the door.

"Sorry about Mitch," Sterling says. "He's like that on days that end in 'y'."

"No problem. I've heard worse." I cast Bolger's taunt from my mind and slide into my best long-suffering smile. "Now that I think about it, it might help if I could interview the Wagner family as well. Do you think they'd be willing to meet with me?"

His eyes slide shut as he considers my request. The musty smell of old books fills the space. Here's where the rubber meets the road.

"I'll see what I can do," he says.

"Thanks." I head for the exit where Jason holds the door for us. "See you both at Dr. Archer's office?"

"He fit us in at four." Caroline checks her watch. "We'll have to hurry."

"Ms. Tejedor," Sterling catches me before I walk out the door. "One last thing. What if I need to get in touch with you?"

"Just think pleasant thoughts." I place my card on a table by the door. "I'll come running."

IX

Bridges

My efforts to focus as I prepare to enter Anthony Faircloth's mind a third time break like ocean waves against black rock as my conversation with Isabella from last night replays in my mind.

"Mami," she asks, "when are you coming home?" Her words leave a dull ache in my chest.

"Like I told you, sweetheart. When I'm done."

"Are you still helping the boy?"

"I'm trying, honey. I'm trying." Bracing myself, I ask the question she's waiting for. "Did you see your father today?"

Her quiet squeal speaks volumes. "We went for ice cream and then to the aquarium. I got to see all the fish. We fed the starfish and sea urchins. I even petted a baby shark."

"That's great, honey." Through clenched teeth, I somehow maintain a pleasant lilt to my voice. "I'm glad you had a good time."

"If you get home before Daddy leaves, maybe we can all go together. They even have a whole tank full of Nemo fish, just like the movie."

"Maybe, sweetheart. We'll have to see."

As the memory of my daughter's not so subtle plea begins to cycle again, I take a deep cleansing breath, open my eyes, and meet Caroline's gaze across her son's subtly rocking body.

"All right, Caroline." I rest my fingertips at Anthony's temples. "I'm ready to begin."

"This should be good," Jason mutters loud enough to make sure I hear. He insisted on joining us in the room today, reportedly to look out for Anthony, but like Archer on his first time, he's likely just curious. I catch Archer's gaze and take comfort in the fact the dismissal I once found there has been replaced in part with expectation, excitement, and perhaps even a hint of admiration, though there's little hope he'd ever admit the last.

"Don't forget," Archer says, "If you get stuck or feel you're in danger, just say the magic word."

I offer a quick salute. "Worked like a charm last time."

"I'm serious. Everything I've read about dreams, which is as close to what's happening here as I can venture to guess, states a dream cannot kill you. Like I've told you, though, this is light-years beyond anything I've encountered before."

"Like I'm not making this up as I go. Just watch my back and make sure I keep breathing." I shift my attention to Jason. "Thanks for coming today. I know you have trouble believing what we're doing is anything more than a bunch of smoke and mirrors. Please understand I wouldn't be here if I didn't think I could help Anthony."

"Can you all just get on with it? It's almost Anthony's dinner time." Resentment flows off him, the aroma one of my least favorites—burned popcorn.

Caroline swats Jason's leg. "Have you already forgotten our chat from yesterday? Mira is here to help your brother, and as of an hour ago, she's working on your case as well. Now, show her some respect."

"Great." Jason's nails dig into the upholstery. "Bad enough she's got you all snowed. Now she'll be wasting the police's time, too."

Caroline's brow furrows, but she appears more concerned than angry. "I'd think you of all people would be glad she was helping, for your brother's sake if nothing else."

"She's been here for days and Anthony isn't a lick better. You said so yourself. Now you want me to pretend she can find Julianna when the cops have already tried just so you can feel like you're doing something?"

Caroline's face goes crimson as heat rises in my own cheeks. I agreed to let Jason come back with us as a gesture of goodwill, but that may have been a mistake. Still, though my standard policy is not to let any negative energy in the room when I'm working, it's a necessary evil if I'm going to win Jason over to my side. He may refuse to be told anything he doesn't want to hear, but perhaps he can be shown.

"Desperate times call for desperate measures, Jason." A waft of licorice joins the burned popcorn. "Bear with me and I think you'll see—"

My words catch in my throat as the "Promenade" theme erupts in my mind. Before I can utter another sound, reality is washed away by a tsunami of prismatic light. I fall for what seems like forever, squeezing my eyes shut to block out the barrage of brilliance and holding my hands over my ears against the percussive strike of thirteen notes already scarred on my soul. The light and sound eventually taper to nothingness and I open my eyes to find myself again in the hallway of the Exhibition.

The ceiling has changed again, filled with scenes of a rock concert from before my time and definitely before Anthony's. Unlike the usual still frescoes, the ceiling's images move, reminding me of the IMAX theater in DC where Isabella and I saw that movie about the penguins a few years back. Somewhere between ABBA and Pink Floyd, the trio of rock musicians include a bare-chested keyboardist dressed in a blue and silver jumpsuit, a bass player dressed in the finest paisley polyester of the early seventies, and a drummer decked out in what looks like purple velour pajamas.

Their version of "Promenade," played on organ, is easy on the ears, but as the music shifts into their rendition of the song from Tunny's portrait, the volume shakes my teeth. Louder and louder it grows, and just when I can't take another note, the music stops and the bassist breaks into song, his voice smooth and soothing even as his lyrics of tortured dreams and childhood tears threaten to break my heart.

"Enough, Anthony," I shout above the singer's voice. "Stop it. Come out and talk to me."

The bassist's vocals cut off mid-word even as the ceiling goes dark. As with my last trip to the Exhibition, the silence is somehow worse than the assault of sound.

"Anthony?" My voice echoes in the stillness. "Are you there?"

"You must be special," says a familiar rough voice. "It's been some time since The Sage and his minstrels entertained us from above."

From the alcove of *The Old Castle*, Tunny's brown face peers out at me. The sound of a familiar saxophone fills the void left by the silenced Sage as somewhere the troubadour's talented fingers and lips coax note after note from his silver horn.

Tunny's voice becomes a low whisper. "Modesto plays to cover your steps. Hurry and join us before she notices you."

I rush to the alcove to find Tunny already climbing into Modesto's painting via a knotted rope no doubt hung there by the diminutive gnome.

"I've been staying here since the witch destroyed my forest," he says. "The stone floor of the castle sucks the warmth from my bones, but having a roof over my head and someone to talk to has been quite a nice change."

"Better than talking to yourself, I suppose." I smile despite myself. "So, Modesto lets you stay in the castle with him?"

"He was a bit sullen about it at first, but he's actually quite decent once you get to know him." Tunny gets both feet onto the ground on the other side of the frame and turns to give me a hand. "Come, Scheherazade. We've been quiet, but the Mistress, she is clever."

I perk my ears for the telltale crash and thud of the witch's mortar and pestle but no sound other than the slow melody of Modesto's realm fills the air. I take my time and with as much grace as a woman can muster in a full-length sarong, climb into the painting. I'm almost through when the scabbard hanging from my belt catches on the frame and sends me sprawling. A quick grab at Tunny's rope saves me and the only thing hurt when my butt hits the ground is my pride. I stand and brush the dirt from the green cloth draped about my legs.

"Where is Modesto?" The notes of his horn filter through the space, but the troubadour is nowhere to be seen.

"Up there." Tunny points to the castle's highest parapet and there, one foot propped up on a crumbling stone, stands the blue and white clad troubadour.

"Greetings, Lady Scheherazade."

"Greetings, Modesto." Even more dashing than I remember, the troubadour clearly represents an idealized version of Anthony's older brother. This smiling fellow, however, represents a side of Jason Faircloth I haven't seen.

"Come up," he shouts. "We have much to discuss, and I would hear a tale if you are willing."

"Very well." I take Tunny's hand, a gesture that sends a shiver through the gnome's brown body, and step toward the castle. The repaired drawbridge stands half-closed, the dark moat hiding God knows what beneath its turbid surface. "Perhaps it will be easier if you lower the bridge."

The strains of music cease as Modesto disappears from view. A few moments later, the sound of a loud crank fills the air and the rattle of chains rings out as the bridge lowers, revealing Modesto standing at the castle's mouth.

"Welcome, Scheherazade. I have prepared a table." He shoots Tunny a glance. "Even brought out the high chair."

"Hmmph." Tunny strides past the gaily-dressed troubadour, brushing Modesto's white and blue striped pants with his dirty arm and leaving a smear of brown. "High chair, indeed."

We sit at the table and sup on the humble fare of Modesto's home. The troubadour busies himself seeing to our needs as Tunny informs me of the situation back at the *Gnomus* forest. With every tree charred, if not burned to the blackened forest floor, the wildlife has fled and nothing of import remains. The plant life surrounding the castle, conversely, has grown more lush and full since my last visit here.

"It seems Tunny has brought a bit of the forest with him." The flash of pride on Tunny's face lasts but a second.

"Indeed." Modesto sneers in Tunny's direction. "The little gnome leaves so much ripe filth everywhere he sits, the plants have no choice but to grow."

Tunny's initial snarl at the caustic remark fades into a chuckle that shakes his round belly. "A little green was exactly what this place needed."

I laugh as well. "You've enacted some repairs since my last visit, Modesto."

He sets a glass of water before me and offers a slight bow. "The bridge is functional once again. After the mishap with our friend from the end of the hall, I thought having a defensible space would be preferable."

"Can't say I disagree." I glance back down the hall and mentally retrace our steps back to the giant door. "But can it hold against… her?"

"If the bridge with all the reinforcements I have added cannot withstand her pestle, then nothing will."

"A toast, then." Tunny seizes his glass and raises it above his head. "To Modesto."

We raise our glasses and drink. Though a part of me understands the entire scenario is merely a series of images flashing across a boy's mind, it doesn't change the sensations or the experience. The cool spring water coursing down my throat. The smooth glass on my fingers. The plush cushion beneath me. As real as the place where Caroline, Jason, and Archer no doubt look over Anthony and me with matched trepidation and wonder, this dream world borne from a catatonic boy's imagination is truly a marvel.

"Both of you." I lower my glass. "I have a favor to ask."

Tunny lowers his head, staring at me through bushy eyebrows as Modesto cocks his head to one side.

"And what would that be, fair Scheherazade?" Modesto asks.

"The boy, Anthony. I saw him before on my first visit to your gallery. I was wondering if you would help me."

Tunny and Modesto share a concerned glance.

"Are you certain you wish to pursue this child further?" Modesto peers at me askew, his eyebrow raised. "I believe the witch will be quite cross if you continue in this matter."

"I don't know." I glance around the room unconcerned. "She hasn't bothered us yet today."

"She burned my forest to the ground." Tunny rises from the table and paces the floor. "And destroyed the drawbridge of this very castle on your last visit. Would you bring destruction on all of us?" He comes to a stop at my feet and looks up at me pathetically. "More importantly, aren't we enough for you?"

My hand goes to my mouth. "I'm sorry, Tunny. I didn't mean to insinuate you weren't important. However, I've come here with one purpose and one purpose only. To bring Anthony Faircloth home."

At the mention of Anthony's full name, both Tunny and Modesto look away. The troubadour's contrite gaze returns first, followed a moment later by the gnome's brown eyes.

"We'll do as you ask Scheherazade." Modesto smiles.

Tunny tugs at my sarong. "But first, a story."

X

Tuileries

I stand before another painting. The fine script on the placard above the frame marks this canvas as *Tuileries*. The ink forming the letters runs as if still wet. All the children within the painting, save Anthony, have moved since my previous viewing and the once lovely French garden, beautifully portrayed in watercolor, now lies trampled beneath their many feet. There, at the center of it all stands Anthony, staring out of the painting at me as before, his body still beneath his starched white shirt, his pale face emotionless. As before, his glasses sit askew. My every instinct screams to leap into the painting and straighten them, muss his hair, and show him he isn't alone in the ocean of children, but one simple fact keeps me on this side of the canvas.

He and the other children are no longer alone.

Near the right edge of the painting stands a woman in a full-length dress the color of a pale buttercup and decorated with translucent blue and pink flowers in chains. Her blonde hair pulled back into a tight bun and away from her stern face, she is every bit the schoolmarm of this piece. She tries not to let on she's noticed me, but I've caught more than one sidelong glance from her position against a gnarled fruit tree. Unlike my initial encounters with Tunny and Modesto, she's made no overtures for me to enter her space or communicated in any way. I steel myself for what I fear will be more a confrontation than an introduction.

But first, as promised, a story.

I turn to face my two companions. Truly an odd couple, both Tunny and Modesto stare unmoving at the boy in the painting. Their expressions shift from reverence to trepidation as the children within resume their destructive dance.

"All right, you two. Time for your story." At my words, a harmonious woodwind melody fills the space, followed by a violin solo. The first note, pure and high, remains for a breathtaking moment before the unseen instrument arpeggiates down and up the scale before returning to the original note. It's not from Mussorgsky's piece, but I recognize it nonetheless.

It's Scheherazade's theme, from the Rimsky-Korsakov piece. In his composition, the violin signifies when the Sultan's wife is spinning a tale. My cue to begin.

"Once upon a time…" I stumble, uncertain whether the rapt attention of gnome and troubadour is helping or hurting my concentration. "I'm sorry. Let me start again. Once upon a time, there was a boy named Anthony—"

Tunny grunts and points at the *Tuileries* painting in disgust. "The story is about the Anthony kid? I want to hear about knights and damsels and monsters, not some stupid boy." The gnome crosses his mud-covered arms and looks away, focusing his attention anywhere but on me or the painting before him.

"Quiet, gnome," Modesto says. "Do not interrupt the greatest storyteller in history." He turns to me and offers a regretful shrug. "Accept my apologies for my rude little friend, fair lady. Please, continue."

"Thank you, Modesto." I have to remind myself that behind the troubadour's handsome eyes lies the mind of an addled thirteen-year-old boy. "Okay. Story time. Once upon a time, there was a boy named Anthony. Anthony was special, like no other boy in the world."

"Special," Tunny snorts. "That's the word kids use when all the grownups are around."

Modesto raps him on the skull. "Quiet, I said."

"Please, don't hit him." I stoop before Tunny and lift his chin until he meets my gaze. "It's all right, Tunny. I'm not trying to upset you. It's just a story, and there is a point. Is that all right?"

Abashed, Tunny nods and looks up at Modesto. "Sorry."

At Modesto's brisk nod, I continue. "Anthony lived in faraway place known as Charlotte, the largest city in a land called the Carolinas. The people there built glowing buildings that scraped the sky and great roads that led into and out of the city's heart like concrete veins and arteries. The pulse of the city was its people, and there were plenty of them—rich, poor, black, white, good, evil, and everything in-between. Anthony, however, was different from all of them, for he knew something the others didn't."

I pause, waiting to see which of them will speak first.

"Well?" Tunny asks after a few seconds. "What was it? What did he know?"

"Something Modesto already understands. The power of music."

Modesto puffs up his chest and clutches his horn tight even as Tunny crosses his arms and lets out another "Hmmph."

I turn and gesture to the painting. "See how he stands there. All the other children run and cavort around him, but he just stands there. Watching. Waiting."

"Waiting for what?" Tunny asks.

"Waiting for someone who understands him." I kneel before the gnome. "Have you ever felt alone? Ignored? Like no one cared to even look at you?"

Tunny stares down at the dirt beneath his dark fingernails. "What do you think?" A single tear, yellow like pine sap, courses down his mud-encrusted cheek. "Look at me."

"And you, Modesto. As a troubadour, an artist beyond reproach, you understand the power inherent in the right song played at the right moment."

Modesto puffs up. "Seems a fair assessment."

"Not everyone appreciates music like you do. The way love can be captured in the correct lyric or joy with just the right melding of melody, harmony, and rhythm. Such a gift, in the presence of those without such understanding, could leave you horribly alone, don't you think?"

Modesto nods. "More than you know."

I gesture again at the painting. "Then help me rescue the boy. He stands alone in a garden filled with children who can't understand him like we three can."

"But he stands right there. What help could you possibly require?"

"I agree. My task would appear to be, pardon the expression, child's play. Do you believe for a moment, however, that it will be easy for me to retrieve him?"

"Perhaps not," Modesto says, the usual swagger in his voice absent. "What would you have us do?"

"For starters, do you remember the music that played when we strolled down the hall?"

His eyes narrow in concentration. "I do."

"Can you replicate it?"

The troubadour sits on a wooden stool and brings the horn to his lips. The "Promenade" theme echoes in the small space, the smooth tones of Modesto's silver saxophone far removed from the blaring brass from before. A glance back at the painting reveals Anthony is closer.

No more than a step, but closer.

He hears us.

"Keep playing, Modesto. I'm going to go get him." I turn to Tunny. "Any sign of the witch, come and get me."

"Of course." He steps to the mouth of the *Tuileries* alcove and sets his feet shoulder-width apart. "She won't get past me."

I pat his split leather hat and turn back to face the painting. The children have continued to circulate like a slow hurricane with Anthony at the eye of the storm. His mouth agape, the boy appears for all the world like the figure from *The Scream.* The buttercup-garbed schoolmarm still leans against the tree, though she no longer hides behind any pretense and watches me warily.

"Here goes nothing." I touch the surface of the picture and the style of the art shifts from near transparent washes of watercolor pigment to brilliant photorealism. Every bent blade of grass, broken flower, and cracked branch suggested before by the stroke of an unseen brush now appears as real as the park back home where I take Isabella on weekends.

The children have destroyed this place.

I grasp both sides of the frame and prepare to step through, only to be pulled headfirst into the painting and flooded with every emotion conceivable. The innermost feelings of the mob of children hits me like a tidal wave and in seconds, I'm drowning in sensation. Fear. Isolation.

Frustration. Each child suffers more than the one before. Out in the regular world, this sense is a boon, helping me understand the world in ways only a few people on the planet can. Its absence here in the Exhibition has presented a challenge, though its overpowering resurgence may well now be the end of me.

Without warning, stabbing pain clenches my stomach. I double over and retch as agony rips through my body. Between waves of nausea, a simple truth dawns on me.

All of these children and their tumultuous emotions are, in fact, extensions of one consciousness. The suffering of a single child. Magnified a thousand times.

"Anthony," I shout as the crippling pain in my midsection eases. "Anthony Faircloth."

As bad in its own way as the kaleidoscope of light that hits me with each sojourn into Anthony's mind, the emotional maelstrom only intensifies at my words and brings me to my knees. The children continue their circling of the garden, though I have replaced Anthony as the focus of their bizarre dance. Within seconds, I'm surrounded.

"Anthony Faircloth," I shout again. "Stop this and come to me. Your mother has sent me to find you."

The children stop, the few directly in front of me parting to reveal Anthony's trembling form. He stands at the center of the garden, the flowers at his feet the only ones left unbroken. No more than twenty feet away, he may as well be a mile.

His gaze flicks in the direction of the schoolmarm, his bespectacled eyes filled with fear at her dispassionate gaze. Beneath her disinterested facade, however, she clearly is taking my measure even as I take hers.

"The boy's name is Antoine." The words that flow from her mouth are flavored with a thick French accent. "Go along and play with the rest of the class, young man." She pushes him away from me and into the mob of children. "I will deal with this… person."

A war plays out across the boy's features. He shifts his feet, about to run to me, when the schoolmarm's open hand becomes a pointed finger.

"Stay away from her, Antoine. Remember what your mother taught you about talking to strangers?"

The boy deflates, his crisp features devolving into a wash of watercolor pink even as the schoolmarm sharpens like a camera image coming into focus. She strides in my direction, the children parting around her as if she were Moses crossing the Red Sea, until she stands directly over me. The blue and pink train of flowers adorning her dress brushes my nose.

"And who might you be, stranger?"

"I am called Scheherazade. And who, may I ask, are you to speak so to this boy?"

"I am Antoine's teacher, Madame Versailles. I watch over him as he plays with the other children and keep him safe. No one touches him here." She kneels before me, bringing her nose close to my face, and locks her steely gaze onto mine. "No one."

The whirlwind of emotions abates for the briefest of moments and I get my feet beneath me. "He must trust you explicitly, then."

Versailles smiles. "I'm all but family. Ask his mother. She'll tell you."

"Why do you keep him here, then? Surrounded by all these children, and yet so alone. Don't you see how cruel all of this is?"

Doubt crosses her features, banished a moment later by a mask of cold determination.

"Before this place existed, the other children did anything but leave him alone. Do you know how many lockers Antoine has been thrown into? Dumpsters? Walls? They hit him with their textbooks and book bags and fists and feet. His school, his neighborhood, even his home is a gauntlet he has had to survive each and every day of his life. Here, no one bothers him, or for that matter, even notices him."

"I would argue this fate is no improvement." Fighting off waves of pain, I struggle to my feet. "To be ignored is far worse torture."

"Like you would know. You've never been ignored in your life. Look at yourself. Perfectly coiffed hair, dark brown eyes, immaculate olive complexion. You claim to understand anything about what this boy has seen and experienced?"

We both turn in time to see Antoine pick a large gob of wax out of his ear canal and wipe it on his shirt.

"He used to eat it, you know." She smiles at me like a predator. "I taught him different."

"Wow." My lips turn up in kind. "He's come so far."

"Enough with this." She squints at me. "Why have you come here?"

"As I said before, Anthony's mother sent me to retrieve him." I clutch my stomach as another wave of pain passes through me. "I'm not leaving without him."

"His name" she hisses, "is Antoine."

"Po-tay-to, po-tah-to," I grunt. "He's still coming with me."

"It seems we are at cross purposes, then." Madame Versailles' eyes begin to glow, the blue of her irises scintillating yellow as if afire. "Children, please escort Lady Scheherazade back to the hallway of the Exhibition." A pleasant melody of alternating flute, oboe, and strings fills the air. What follows, however, is anything but pleasant.

The dozens of watercolor children wandering the garden all stop and turn to face me. Their eyes, glowing with the same golden phosphorescence as their teacher's, pierce me with their cold cruelty. As one, they rush me, their little faces turned up in snarls like rabid animals, their teeth gleaming in the light cast from each other's radiant gazes.

Before I can slip the dagger from its jeweled scabbard, the first wave collides with my legs and forces me to the ground while the second grabs my arms and holds me still. The vinegar of their anger, however, overpowers the other ambient emotions and for the first time since I entered *Tuileries*, my mind is free.

"Hold her." An apple appears in Versailles' hand. She takes a bite as she stares down at me without an ounce of pity in her gaze. I crane my head to the side and catch a glimpse of Anthony. He stares at me from the same spot as before, his eyes sorrowful behind his crooked glasses.

"Anthony… Antoine," I groan. "Help me."

He pauses for the briefest of moments and takes a step in my direction when a rough voice rings out.

"Off of her," Tunny shouts as he tears one of the children from my shoulders. "Leave the Lady Scheherazade be, you brats." Tunny may not be much to look at, but seeing him in action, it's clear those tiny brown fists pack a wallop.

"Careful, gnome." Another welcome voice, Modesto holds his silver horn above his head and away from the sea of small hands that would no doubt love to tear it apart. "Wouldn't want to hurt the children, now would we?"

The shock of Tunny's initial attack spent, the next line of children closes on the three of us. Tunny lowers himself into a wrestler's crouch, the heels of his boots scraping against my rib cage, and again raises his fists.

"I'm warning the lot of you. Lay another finger on Lady Scheherazade and you'll pay."

Versailles raises her hand and turns her index finger in a slow spiral. "Encircle them, children. Show your teacher how much you love her." She looks down on Tunny with utter disdain. "Try as you might, you can't hold off all of them, little gnome."

"He won't have to." Modesto puts the instrument to his lips and begins to play, the melody overpowering that of Madame Versailles. The tune slow and familiar, the notes of the main theme from "The Old Castle" fill the air. As he continues to play, the lights in the children's eyes fade and they begin to mill about the garden as they did before. Even the few still holding my legs let go and join the others in their aimless wandering.

"You've brought a Pied Piper with you." Versailles' face turns down into a scowl. "We'll see how effective he is without his precious instrument."

She dives at Modesto even as Tunny leaps between them in an effort to stave off her attack. I scramble to my feet and survey the situation. Surrounded by a mob of directionless children, Versailles, Tunny, and Modesto grapple over the troubadour's horn. I inhale to scream when a voice I've never heard before takes the words from my lips.

"Stop fighting!" The merest hint of a French accent colors Antoine's squeaky voice as he rushes to my side, grabs my hand, and squeezes. "You've got to stop them. Now."

"Why, Antoine?" I don't understand his insistence. "What's going to happen?"

"They're going to bring her." Antoine's eyes squeeze shut as terror continues to color his every feature. "They're going to bring her here."

"She won't come here." Versailles shoots Antoine and me an incredulous glare. "She wouldn't dare."

"Oh really?" The voice booms down from above as a single orchestral hit shakes the space.

"Oh no." The fear that stabs my heart is mirrored on every face in the garden and none more so than in the wide-eyed gape of Madame Versailles.

"No," she says. "It's impossible."

A couplet follows, then the rolling melody of the witch.

"She's coming," I rush over and grab Versailles by the shoulders. "Stop this senseless fighting and help us save the children. I can get Antoine to safety, but not if you and all the other children are against us."

"None of these children matter," the teacher says. "You know as well as I they are mere figments of the boy's mind."

I lock gazes with the furious schoolteacher. "As are you, Madame Versailles."

"I exist only to care for Antoine. The rest of these children can rot."

"Fine." I push my anger down and turn to Modesto. "You're our resident Pied Piper. Think you can get them all to the castle?"

Modesto raises an incredulous eyebrow, as if I've asked him to achieve world peace, before throwing me a wink. "I can try."

Versailles steps away from the troubadour and he resumes his song, albeit with a faster tempo. The haunting melody washes over the children, and in seconds, all but Antoine have gathered around Modesto's dancing form. Turning, he steps out of the painting and into the hallway beyond and one by one, the children follow, leaving only Tunny, Madame Versailles, Antoine, and me in the garden.

As the witch's melody continues to crescendo, Versailles glares at me with smoldering hatred. "So, Lady Scheherazade. Mere days as a part of the Exhibition and now you're the hero of the piece? Who do you think kept Antoine safe before you came along? Kept his soul intact as the entire world did its level best to tear him down?" Her chin falls to her chest. If I didn't know better, I would swear she was crying. "Now you're trying to take him from me."

The music continues to grow louder. Time is short.

"Perhaps you do care about the boy, but keeping him a prisoner and keeping him safe are two different things. Now, I'm freeing Antoine from this place. Please don't try to stop me."

"And what of me?" she asks. "Would you leave me to the witch?"

"Your fate is your own decision." The fact that, on some level, I'm arguing with Anthony over whether he's going to let himself come with me or not sends a twinge of pain through my head. "You are, of course, more than welcome to join us."

"And leave the garden?" Her eyes flash with fear. "But… *Tuileries* is my home."

"Then make a new home with us." I offer a conciliatory smile. "Antoine could use such a fierce and determined advocate."

She actually considers my words. A miracle. "Where do you plan to take him?"

"A safe place. At least as safe as I've found among the Exhibition."

She glances down at Antoine and another emotion that seems foreign on her face appears.

Compassion.

"Is this what you want? To go with the storyteller?"

He doesn't answer, his frightened gaze shooting back and forth from Madame Versailles to me. Through the hammering music, the sound of the pounding pestle and scraping mortar grows louder with each measure.

"Antoine," I whisper. "She's almost here. We can keep you safe, but you're going to have to come now."

After a momentary pause, he nods and looks up into his teacher's tear-filled eyes. "Please come with us."

I lock eyes with Versailles. "Make your call. We're leaving now."

She stoops before Antoine. "I'm sorry, my child. I cannot leave this place. It's the only home I've ever known. Now, go with Lady Scheherazade. She will keep you safe."

"But, Madame Versailles. I—"

"Go, Antoine."

I rest a hand on her shoulder. "Are you sure about this?"

"It's clear. He doesn't need me anymore. Not with you here." She turns her back on the portal leading to the Exhibition. "I will hold her as long as I am able."

"Thank you." I scoop Antoine up and sprint for the open face of the painting, the dim light of the Exhibition hall just steps away. Antoine fights the entire way. We dive out into the hallway and I chance one quick glance back.

At the picture's horizon, a black dot in the distance grows into the familiar form of the witch hunched atop her stone mortar. From within the painting, Madame Versailles gives me one last look, her eyes filled with determination, before turning to face her fate. Her feet set shoulder width apart, her hands ball into fists and before I can think another thought, the canvas crumples inward as if squashed by invisible hands.

XI

Bydło

"No!" Antoine screams. "Madame Versailles!"

I leap for the hall with Antoine's struggling form draped across my shoulder and run for the alcove of *The Old Castle.* Barely halfway across the parquet floor when the witch's theme begins anew, I curse myself for believing Versailles' sacrifice would slow the witch for even a second. Everything here is governed by one set of laws only–the limits of a boy's imagination.

"Hurry." Modesto pops his head out of the alcove. "She is coming."

We're halfway across the great hall when the floor beneath me splits open and catches my foot. The momentum of the fall sends me careening headfirst into the floor as a sickening crack splits the air. Antoine flies from my arms and hurtles into the wall by Modesto's alcove. White-hot agony shoots up my leg, wrenching a scream from the depths of my soul. A glance down my body reveals my ankle bent at an angle I would have once considered impossible.

"Lady Scheherazade," Modesto shouts, his eyes wide with fear. "You must come now."

"It's too late," I whisper through gritted teeth. "She is nearly upon us." Holding back a second scream, I lock gazes with the panicking troubadour. "Take Antoine. Hide him in the castle. He should be safe there until my return."

Until my return. Pretty big assumption.

Modesto stares at me, impotent.

"Now, Modesto." My words cut through the space and even through the mounting melody of the witch. "Get him out of here."

Another second and a decision plays out across the troubadour's features. He steps out of his alcove, scoops Antoine up from the ground, and disappears back inside to where his painting and castle reside, leaving me alone. The various themes of "Promenade," "The Old Castle," and the witch all battle for supremacy, louder and louder and louder. Then, there is silence.

Face down, bloodied, and mere steps from safety, I await the witch. Her foul presence creeps along my other senses long before I see her. Turning my head to the side, I spit out a mouthful of blood-tinged phlegm before turning my eyes on my pursuer. Crouched atop her stone mortar like some dark bird of prey, the witch glares at me. The pestle rests easily in one gnarled hand while the ever-swishing broom continues to pass back and forth behind her like a wagging tail.

"Oh, Scheherazade. You must be so proud. You have gathered the gnome, the troubadour, and the young monsieur. How you convinced the fine Madame Versailles to allow the boy to leave her fine home is beyond me. Still so far to go, though, and the irony is you don't even know what it is you're here to accomplish."

"Then why don't you tell me, oh wise and omnipotent Baba Yaga?"

She starts at the utterance of her proper name, likely the first time it has been spoken above a whisper in this space in a very long time.

"You… dare?"

"Yours is but a name like any other, witch. The others fear you, but I know where you come from. What you want. Who you really are."

Yaga's mouth turns up in a repulsive grin, her rusted iron teeth glistening with foul saliva. "You know many things, storyteller, but you do not know everything. That dagger you fiddle with beneath your emerald robes, for instance. Do you truly believe its blade is meant for me?"

She pounds the pestle into the ground and the crack that holds me fast opens a bit, releasing my injured foot.

"Stop this," I shout, trying to keep the fear from my voice. "I mean you and your Exhibition no harm. I've merely come to help a boy who needs me."

Yaga, atop her mortar, floats in my direction, the rhythmic swishing of the broom a distinct counter point to the echoing thunks of the pestle striking the ground. As she reaches my crippled form, the mortar upends itself until she hangs beneath it like a bunch of dried grapes dangling from a severed vine. Directly above me, she cranes her neck till we are nose to bulbous nose. She opens her gaping maw and from between her metallic teeth comes breath so fetid, my stomach threatens to rebel.

"I cannot fathom why you continue to invade my domain, fair Scheherazade, but if you've come here to learn, then I shall be your teacher." She rights her mortar and raises the pestle above her head, hesitating for an excruciating moment before bringing it crashing back down. I clench my eyes shut in anticipation of impact, but the wooden club strikes the floor rather than my skull. With a roar like an avalanche, the crack in the floor splits open, forming a chasm that swallows me whole before I can mutter the magical word Archer taught me.

I fall for what feels like forever, the darkness punctuated by rays of blinding light that somehow find my eyes even when my lids are closed. The word "coda" passes my lips no less than a dozen times before I face the fact it's not going to work this time.

Just as I can learn, so apparently can the witch.

As the last remnant of conscious thought threatens to leave me, the falling stops. I open my eyes on a new landscape. Somewhere between the lush vegetation of Tunny's home and the cold stone of Modesto's castle, this new place stretches out before me in all directions, a bucolic masterpiece crafted in muted pastels.

A road unfolds before me. To my left, a split-rail fence borders a large grassy field while the forest to my right blocks whatever is around the next curve. A plodding piano dirge echoes in the distance. A snort to my rear prompts me to spin around where I find a pair of oxen pulling a wooden cart in my direction.

Atop the cart, a man roughly my age dressed in a forest green shirt and a burgundy vest drives the oxen. The music grows louder as the oxen get closer, their legs and hooves moving in time with the lumbering music as the man guides the pair of bulls with an expert hand. As they pull up alongside me, he brings them to a halt with a flick of a long tasseled stick.

"Ho, there. And who might you be?" His accent is Polish, but not difficult to understand.

"What is this place?" I ask.

"My property, milady, and I shall ask the questions here. Now, who are you and why do you trespass on this section of road?"

I search for any answer that makes sense. "I am called Scheherazade. I was sent to this place against my will and I am lost."

"I must disagree." The trepidation rushing through my mind dissipates as his face breaks into a toothy grin. "I'd say you've been found." He removes a box of tools from the seat next to him and pats the space. "Climb on up. I don't make a habit of biting, unless I get quite hungry."

"But my ankle. It's…"

The pain. It's gone. A quick glance down my body reveals a pristine ankle, as if it were never injured. I spring to my feet and put all my weight on that side. Still nothing. Another miracle.

At the man's insistent waving, I climb up onto the cart and join him. It's clear the seat is meant for one as my body presses against the man's well-muscled arm. We share a quick glance, his slate-gray eyes harboring a strange intelligence for a man who drives an oxcart. Then again, this man is Anthony. As are the oxen. Tunny. Modesto. Antoine.

Baba Yaga.

"My apologies for trespassing. As I told you, it wasn't my decision to come here."

"No apologies necessary, and please excuse my brusque manner before. Dark times have fallen and people roam these parts who cannot be trusted."

I raise an eyebrow. "And how do you know you can trust me?"

"Oh, I have a sense about such things. Would you care to join me back at my home? Perhaps a drink to quench your thirst before we try to find your way back to where you were before?"

"Of course." This must be what Alice felt before she sat for tea with the Mad Hatter. "You are most… generous."

He flicks his wrist and the tassel on the end of the stick pops the air with a sharp crack. The oxen resume their trudging march forward, accompanied by the crescendoing dirge from before.

He smiles at me with no pretense. "I am Hartmann."

I return his smile, and do my best to keep any concern from my eyes. "A pleasure to meet you, Hartmann. Pardon, but I must ask. Is your house far? I have many things to accomplish, and my time here is short."

"Fear not, Lady Scheherazade. My home lies around the next bend."

Pastel rows of corn beyond the fence to our left stretch as far as the eye can see. I can all but picture the artist with her crayons putting down each individual stalk with a flick of her wrist. "Hartmann, is this a farm?"

He gazes out across the field and seems surprised by the neat rows of stalks he finds there. "Hm. I suppose it is."

"You did say this was your property, didn't you?"

"Indeed. This land is mine to protect and keep watch over."

"But you don't know what your well-plowed acres are used for?"

Hartmann's face grows a shade of crimson. "There's no need to be argumentative."

I hold my tongue for a moment, unclear as to what I've said that's upset him.

"I'm sorry. It's just that—"

"We've arrived." Hartmann brings the cart to a halt at the side of the road and climbs down. "Are you coming?" he asks as he rounds the curve in the road and disappears.

"Wait," I shout. "I don't know where I'm going." I climb down from the cart and race around the bend after him. The sight that awaits me there is the strangest yet.

At the end of a cobbled walkway stands a two-story cabin fashioned of wood and stone. With its old slate roof, burgundy storm shutters the color of Hartmann's vest, and stonework porch, the house is nothing special, save one simple detail.

The entire structure is upside down.

The house's rocky foundation turned upward to face the sky like some bizarre flower, the front door sits some thirty feet in the air. I can't imagine the woven rope doormat lying on the stoop gets much use at all.

I catch up to Hartmann. "You live here?"

"Indeed."

"But, the whole thing is upside down."

"Upside down, and all mine. My humble abode may seem a bit unconventional, but what can I say? I rarely have to mop the floor."

I let out a chuckle at that last bit. "There is that, I suppose, but how do you… sit?"

Hartmann's face breaks into a broad smile. "Come inside, I'll show you."

He leads me up the cobblestone walkway, bemoaning all the way the poor state of his yard, and stops before a tall second story window converted into a door.

"Please excuse the lack of housekeeping." He slides open the makeshift doorway. "It's not often I have house guests."

I step inside and a wave of motion sickness threatens to overtake me. All done in bright pastel colors, the curtains hang upwards, defying gravity. Chairs, tables, and rugs rest on what has become a hardwood ceiling. An entire sink of water hangs precipitously above my head, filled with suds and a stack of dishes. I stumble with vertigo, a sensation not helped by the inverted chandelier I seize to steady myself.

"How do you live this way?" I point to the floor above my head. "Has your life always been like this?"

Hartmann adopts a thoughtful, if emotionless expression. "It's odd. One day everything was right side up and the following morning I had to climb out of bed and scale down the wall to get out of the house." He motions to the kitchen above our heads. "May I interest you in some tea?"

I giggle despite myself. "That would be lovely."

Without a second thought, he turns and walks up the wall, his body parallel to the horizon showing through the window. He continues in this fashion until he reaches the floor above our heads and then, as if gravity were a mere suggestion in this place, he steps off and into his kitchen.

Hanging upside down from what is technically the floor, he flashes me a quick smile and waves me up. "Come along. It's not as hard as it looks."

With some coaxing, he convinces me to climb up the wall and join him at a small table by the window. My brain has difficulty coping with the sideways gravity, but by the time I catch up to him, everything seems to sort itself out. In fact, as long as I don't look out the window, sitting upside down in this upended house seems practically normal.

"The question of the hour, milady." He goes to his cupboard and pulls down a pair of teacups and matching saucers. "Do you drink Earl Grey?"

Hartmann pours me a cup of piping hot tea and we sit together, each enjoying the brief silence. Though the blood rushes to my head a bit, my hair stays about my shoulders and my sarong about my knees, both obeying the strange physics of Hartmann's home.

I finish my tea and set down the ornately decorated teacup. "The person who sent me implied I was to learn something from my visit. Other than you and this house and the forest and fields, is there anything else here to see?"

Hartmann scratches his chin. "Only me, the house, the fields, and my oxen."

"Visitors, then? A gnome? Troubadour? Perhaps a child?"

The porcelain cup falls from his suddenly trembling fingers, defying our current treaty with gravity, and shatters on the ceiling above our heads.

"There are no children here. Why do you ask such a thing?"

Whoa. Hit a nerve. I look away from Hartmann's perturbed eyes and notice something strange in the field beyond the window.

"A question. The oxen. Do they usually work the fields without your hand to guide them?" I lead the Cart Man to the window. Outside, his pair of yoked oxen now pull a large plow across a field of low crops.

Shock washes across Hartmann's face. "What are they doing there?"

He darts down the wall, diving out the second story window before I can say a word.

"Hartmann," I shout as I rush toward the door-window. "What is it?" I step out the window and find Hartmann standing a few feet from his house on this side of the split rail fence surrounding his property.

"Who put my oxen in that field?" he whispers. "They're not supposed to plow there."

The plodding dirge returns, though a full orchestra has taken over for the simple piano from before. The music grows louder and louder as the oxen pull the plow toward the center of the field.

"Get away from there," Hartmann screams, followed by a barely audible whisper. "Some things should remain buried."

He scales the fence and sprints across the field. The oxen keep moving despite their master's shouts. I tense to pursue Hartmann, but before I can take a second step, a root juts out of the ground and encircles my ankle. My excruciating lesson from the Exhibition hall still fresh, I roll with the fall and come up facing the Hartmann's strange home. Amid the house's uprooted foundation, a pair of yellow eyes stares down at me. Baba Yaga rests atop her stone mortar, though not a note or beat of her theme betrays her presence. Even the gentle swishing of her broom has halted. My hand instinctively goes to the dagger at my hip.

Do you truly believe its blade is meant for me?

Her taunting words echo in my mind as the witch brings one gnarled finger to her cracked lips and shakes her head from side to side. She points back across the field at Hartmann's rushing form. I glance away for half a second, and when I look back at the house, the witch is gone.

I rise from the ground, rush the fence, and leap into the field beyond. The crop, a thick wooden vine that tangles my feet, bears fruit resembling bunches of grapes that stare up at me like a thousand bruised eyeballs. Hartmann charges the oxen from the front, brandishing his whip stick before him. The deafening melody stops as the oxen halt in their tracks. Hartmann draws close to the oxen and as I catch up to him, he is working to unhook them from the plow.

"Not this field," he repeats over and over, oblivious to my presence. "Never this field."

"What is it, Hartmann?"

"Return to the house, Scheherazade. This is no place for a woman."

"What has happened? What is it about this field?"

"To the house," he shouts across his shoulder as he struggles with the yoke on the oxen to my left. "I'll come for you in a few minutes."

"Very well." I'm about to leave when I see it. Just beyond the blade of the plow.

Jutting from the ground like some morbid signpost, a hand points to the sky, the blood-covered fingers wrapped around of all things, a silver pen.

"There's a body."

"There's a body," Hartmann repeats, his tone mocking. "Of course there's a body. Why do you think I don't want the oxen to plow here?"

"Do you know who it is?"

"It doesn't matter. Now, return to the house while I clean up this mess."

"I'm not leaving until I find out who is buried here." I rush around the oxen and fall to the ground beside the upraised hand. Hartmann moves to stop me but the ice in my eyes convinces him to keep his distance. Alternating between the dagger's edge and my manicured nails, I dig till my fingers are as bloody as the corpse's. Knowing what I'm going to see before I get there, my raw fingers find the shock of blonde hair, confirming my worst suspicions. I brush the moist soil away and look down on a face I've only ever seen before in photographs or on a television screen.

The face of Julianna Wagner.

I gasp a full lung of air and open my eyes back in Archer's office. Drenched in sweat, I glance around the room, my bleary eyes refusing to focus. Three faces look down on me. Archer's steel-blue gaze, filled with concern, is the first to resolve out of the backlit fluorescent blur. Caroline holds a damp washcloth in her hand, while Agnes holds a cell phone in her trembling fingers.

"Hold on, Agnes." Archer's baritone anchors me in this reality. "I think she's okay."

Agnes adjusts her reading glasses and slips the phone into her pocket.

"How bad was it?" Though not as rough as the first couple of times, my voice still comes out like the mewling of a half-drowned cat.

Archer helps me back to the couch. "You fell to the floor. At first it was like the other times, but there at the end, it looked like you were having some kind of seizure."

Caroline touches my shoulder. "We were about to call 9-1-1."

Panic fills my chest. I seize Archer's wrist. "Don't do that. Don't ever do that."

"What? Why?"

"Once I've gone in, don't let them take me away. No matter what happens." I turn my head to face Caroline. "If I'm in there and you separate me from Anthony, I might not be able to find my way back."

"Like we're letting you do this again." Archer crosses his arms. "Absolutely out of the question."

"Oh, I'm going back in there."

As Archer and I continue to argue, I catch Jason's gaze. He's doing his best to play it cool, but the stunned shock in his eyes says it all. Like his mother and even the skeptical Dr. Archer, he's become a believer. A few minutes later, as he and Archer help me to my feet, Jason mutters, "That was unbelievable." The skeptical black pepper scent from before is gone, replaced with an aroma reminiscent of fresh brewed coffee. "You're for real."

"Did you…" Caroline considers her words. "…learn anything? Anything that will help?"

"I got a few answers and confirmed a couple things I already suspected." I stretch, the muscles of my back, chest and arms aching like I just pumped iron for a day or two. "Before my next trip through the Exhibition, though, I'm going to need to pay a visit to Anthony's school."

XII

SEGUE

I pull into the lot behind the police station a few minutes late. After my harrowing tour of Anthony's mental playground yesterday afternoon, I could hardly open my eyes this morning. I had planned to enjoy a relaxing brunch around eleven to center myself before the interview. As it stands, I barely got out of my room by noon. I park next to a white Cadillac Escalade with a flyer in the window sporting a picture of Julianna with contact information and a reward.

Looks like the Wagners beat me here.

Detective Sterling meets me at the front desk.

"Ms. Tejedor. Thanks for coming."

"Sorry I'm late. The roads in Charlotte change names about every four blocks."

"You think Charlotte's bad? I lived in Atlanta for a couple of years. Didn't know you could name every road in a city after a peach tree."

The same floral bouquet wafts across my consciousness. Nice to know he actually wants me involved. "Are the Wagners here?"

"Just arrived a few minutes ago. They're… eager to meet you."

"Dramatic pauses are a dead giveaway, Detective Sterling."

He raises an eyebrow. "I suppose I shouldn't try to pull anything over on someone with your resumé."

"Let me guess. One or both of them isn't too crazy about bringing in someone with my particular skill set."

"Two for two. Mrs. Wagner has been chomping at the bit to talk to you since we called last night. Mr. Wagner, on the other hand, has been less than enthusiastic."

"Don't worry." I straighten my blazer. "I've worked tough rooms before."

Sterling directs me back to one of those interrogation rooms you see in all the cop television shows. If only it was the first time I'd set foot in one of those.

Or even the twenty-first.

Detective Bolger is there, hanging off the corner of the table. To his left sit a couple plucked from a high society magazine. Tanned and trim, Mr. Wagner leans back in the straight-backed metal chair. His eyes do a half roll as our gazes meet before his face slides into a practiced smile. Mrs. Wagner, conversely, stares at me with a look of desperation that mirrors Caroline Faircloth's expression from five days before. Two mothers, both clutching at straws in an effort to save their children, neither of whom I'm sure I can help.

Different though their reactions are, the double dose of raw onion is a testimony to the Wagners' shared torment.

"Ms. Tejedor." Mr. Wagner rises from his seat and extends a hand. "Thank you for coming. I'm Stuart Wagner and this is my wife, Margaret."

Mrs. Wagner offers a cautious smile, but keeps her silence.

I shake Mr. Wagner's hand. "Detective Sterling asked me to come by this afternoon and see if I could add anything to the case." Mr. Wagner sits back down and I take the seat opposite him at the table. "Is it all right if we go ahead and get started?"

"No offense, Ms. Tejedor, but I'd like you to answer a few questions before we agree to your involvement."

Pretty standard response. As the skeptical hint of black pepper works its way into the mix, I have to work to keep the frustration from my face.

Sterling sits down next to me. "Ms. Tejedor has agreed to work with us on your daughter's case, but as involving someone with her talents lies a bit outside of our normal procedure, we'll only proceed as you are comfortable."

"Don't worry, Detective Sterling. I'll be more than happy to answer any questions Mr. Wagner might have."

Julianna's father leans back in his chair. "Before we lay out all our dirty laundry to a complete stranger, I was wondering if you'd perhaps review your credentials. After Detective Sterling here got in touch with us last night, I did some research online. I know all about the case you worked in Virginia last year, and what I read was encouraging. Still, it's a lot to swallow. What sets you apart from a carnival palm reader or those 900-number people on TV that tell you whatever you want to hear to keep you on the phone?"

I lean across the table, interlacing my fingers as I put on my business face. "What sets me apart is I get results."

"Now, honey," Margaret Wagner says. "Ms. Tejedor drove all the way here just to meet with us. Let's give her a chance to speak."

Far from placated, Mr. Wagner crosses his arms and lets out a not so subtle grunt. The black pepper stench doubles in intensity.

"Please excuse my husband, Ms. Tejedor. We've both been beside ourselves since Julianna disappeared. He doesn't want me to get my hopes up."

I grip her hand. "I'm afraid I have to echo that sentiment. I'll do the best I can to help, but Julianna has been missing for three weeks. Statistics show—"

She jerks her hand away. "Don't talk to me about statistics. You found that girl in Virginia. Now find my daughter."

"Fine." This is going to be a banner afternoon. "Let's get started."

The Wagners and I spend the next half hour discussing their daughter. Everything I learn about her makes me like the girl more, even as the sinking feeling there's nothing anyone can do grows in my mind. An honor student and captain of the cheerleading squad, Julianna also held the lead in the school play the last two years and even volunteers at a local soup kitchen every other weekend. All that, and somehow she's managed to pull it all off without the entire school hating her guts. A pang of jealousy stabs at my gut like the tip of a rapier.

Jealousy of a seventeen-year-old girl who is most likely dead in a shallow grave off a back road in rural North Carolina.

That's great, Mira. Just great.

The Wagners touch briefly on Julianna's relationship with Jason Faircloth. In an effort to maintain the Faircloths' confidentiality, I fight the urge to delve further. The image of their daughter's pale face staring up at me from the dark soil of Hartmann's farm, however, will not leave my mind. No matter what anyone says or does, it's only a matter of time till these two mysteries collide.

The discussion turns when we get to the night of the disappearance. As Archer said, the last anyone saw Julianna was during the football game the last Friday of September. She apparently went to fetch something from her car just before the second half and never came back. Detective Sterling assures me they've searched the school grounds top to bottom and haven't recovered anything of interest. Bolger hands me transcripts of Julianna's incoming and outgoing texts from that night. The reason why they brought Jason Faircloth in a second time practically leaps off the page.

I know it's been a while, but can you meet me at half time? You know the place. –J

The text, sent from Jason's number, is answered with a simple "*K*" and a winky face. Pretty damning evidence, other than the fact Jason claims his phone went missing two days before the game, not to mention his relatively airtight alibi. Not surprisingly, the longer the conversation surrounds the eldest of the Faircloth brood, the more it seems a gasket in Stuart Wagner's head is about to blow.

"Mr. Wagner, if I may ask, why does talking about Jason Faircloth make you so angry? He was stuck at home with a stomach bug the night your daughter disappeared and according to Detective Sterling, isn't even under suspicion at this time."

"I don't give a shit where that kid says he was or anything about his phone going missing. The evidence is right there in black and white and no one will do a damn thing about it."

"Calm down, Mr. Wagner," Sterling says. "We've already brought Jason Faircloth in for questioning twice and he was cooperative on both occasions. His story checks out. His mother was with him at his house all the way across town not ten minutes from the time Julianna was last seen. Not to mention the cell tower where that text originated is all the way up in the University area, a good forty minutes from the Faircloth home. I know you're frustrated, but the boy is no longer a suspect."

"I know, I know." Mr. Wagner pounds the table. "My only daughter has been missing for a month and the best we've got are some dead end cell phone transcripts and 'Miss Cleo' from Virginia here. Pardon me if I'm just a little upset."

Detective Bolger, who has remained atypically quiet throughout the interview, steps in.

"That's enough for today." He sees the Wagners to the door. "We'll let you know if we develop any new leads."

Mrs. Wagner flashes me one last desperate look. "Don't judge us, Ms. Tejedor. Stuart and I are doing the best we can. Please, if there's anything you can do, help them find our daughter."

I offer a simple nod. "I'll do everything I can. Promise."

Bolger escorts them from the room, leaving me alone with Sterling.

"That went well." I can tell from Sterling's half smile he's trying to be funny.

"Actually, it went very well, aside from the fact Mr. Wagner doesn't think I could find a cheeseburger at McDonalds."

"Like Mrs. Wagner said, they're both under a lot of stress. Since Julianna disappeared, everything's fallen apart. He can't keep up with his law practice. His clients are pulling out left and right. His wife won't stop crying. Bad news all around."

"I'm not here to cause them more pain."

"And they know that." He rises from his seat. "Do you have a few minutes to review some additional information about the case?"

"I wanted to get to the other stuff today, but we'll have to do it tomorrow afternoon. I have an important appointment across town." I glance down at my grandmother's watch and let out a frustrated laugh. "And it looks like I'm going to be late for that one too."

I arrive at Anthony's school near the end of the day and navigate a sea of minivans and SUV's before finding a parking space in the far visitor's lot. Afraid I'll miss Anthony's teacher, I jog up the sidewalk, stopping momentarily to inspect a makeshift memorial by the front door. Several yards in diameter, the mound of notes, mementos, photos, flowers, and half-burned candles surrounds a tripod with a picture of Julianna Wagner in full cheerleader regalia. Half a dozen students stand staring at the photograph, their expressions frozen somewhere between shock and sorrow. A sharp balsamic tang fills my senses and I head for the school before the overpowering wave of teenage grief gives me a headache.

As I enter the school, I'm struck by a quality rarely found in high schools.

The quiet.

I've attended livelier funerals.

A clump of students drifts past like extras from a zombie movie. The janitor, a few years past his prime and no doubt a few pounds heavier, mans his mop, the melancholy whistle escaping his pursed lips the soundtrack for the depressing scene. The entire place reeks of mothballs and old scotch, my brain's weirdo shorthand for mourning.

"Can I help you, miss?" Hunched over his mop and bucket, the janitor stares at me with his one good eye while the other appears to take in a bulletin board on the wall to my right. "You a parent?" He winks at me with the good eye. "Or maybe someone's older sister?"

I sniff the air. He's a flirt all right, but nothing more sinister below the surface as best I can tell. "Actually, I'm here on business. I need to speak to one of the teachers. Ms. Veronica Sayles?"

He gestures to the hallway directly behind me. "Office is that way. They can probably help you more than me."

"Thanks."

As I turn to leave, a barely audible whisper hits my ears. "Careful turning over rocks. You never know what you might find underneath."

I spin and catch him staring at me with his lopsided gaze. "Excuse me. What did you say?"

"Nothing worth repeating, ma'am." And with that, he turns away and resumes mopping the floor outside the cafeteria. I fight the urge to question him further and instead head for the office as he suggested.

I've gone three steps down the hall when the bell rings, dismissing school for the day. Children pour from rooms like ants and rush past me. I wait for the river of adolescent hormones to ebb and head for the office.

As I step through the door, a woman in an out-of-season sweater glances up from a heated phone conversation and motions to a spiral bound notebook resting on the counter. "Visitors Sign In Please" is printed across the cover. Grabbing a pen, I flip through the pages until I find an open line and sign in.

"May I help you?" The woman cups her hand over the phone's mouthpiece.

"I'm looking for Ms. Sayles. Ninth grade."

"Are you a parent or family of a student?"

"Actually, no. I'm here on business."

"Ms. Sayles might be a while." She gestures to a complex looking spreadsheet hanging on the wall. "She's got bus duty every afternoon this week."

"And where is that?"

"Oh, you don't want to go out there, honey. Those bus fumes could choke an elephant."

"What would you suggest, then? It's important I talk to her today."

"You can wait in her classroom, I suppose. Not sure if she goes to her car straight from the buses or not, though."

"That will be fine." Following the woman's directions, I head back out into the hall and hang a left. The crowd of children has dissipated, leaving but a few stragglers. I wander the hallways, doing my best to remember the series of lefts, rights, and stairs.

Funny how all high schools look the same. The dilapidated lockers. The scuffed floors that never seem to come clean. The ubiquitous water stained ceiling tiles at every turn. Isabella will be navigating halls like this in just a few short years. My heart shrinks with dread.

I come to Sayles' room and a familiar scent works its way through my mind. It's the pungent aroma I picked up off Anthony and to a lesser degree, Rachel. It only makes sense. Until three weeks ago, this was Anthony's classroom.

I step into the empty room and flip on the lights. A bulletin board filled with student's stories and projects catches my eye. Anthony's all but jumps out at me from across the room and I move closer to examine it further. A good five times thicker than any other project on the board, the cover sports a pencil sketch of the witch who chased me from Anthony's mind just twenty-four hours ago. Perched atop her ancient mortar, she holds the pestle before her and grins with that pit of iron blades she calls a mouth. Even sketched in No. 2 pencil, those opaque eyes send a shudder through me.

Unable to face even the two-dimensional version of the witch, I turn my gaze away only to find Madame Versailles from the *Tuileries* garden staring back at me from a frame atop the filing cabinet by the teacher's desk. Dressed in the dark robes of a graduation ceremony, she appears to be accepting some sort of award. The open smile on her face in sharp contrast to the sardonic grin her dreamscape doppelganger wore in Anthony's Exhibition, the woman in the photograph is simply beautiful, the last word I would have used to describe Antoine's teacher in the *Tuileries* picture.

Washing over me like a balmy wind before a thunderstorm, a wave of frustration approaches from hallway. The clacking of heels echoes in the hallway grows louder with every step till a woman I've only met before in a boy's mind strides past me and into the room. Her hair pulled back into a tight ponytail, she doesn't notice me as she grabs an eraser and starts to clear her whiteboard.

"Excuse me," I ask. "Ms. Sayles?"

She jumps at the sound of my voice and spins to face me. "Can I help you?"

"You're Veronica Sayles, Anthony Faircloth's teacher?"

"That's me." Her brow furrows. "Is Anthony all right?"

"Depends on your definition of all right."

"He hasn't been in school for the last month." The color runs from her face. "Tell me he hasn't taken a turn for the worse."

"No. He's stable, more or less." We meet in the middle of the room, her grip firm as she shakes my hand. "My name is Mira Tejedor. I'm here at Caroline Faircloth's request. I'm a consultant, working with Anthony's doctors as we get to the bottom of what's ailing him."

"You know, his last day in class was one of his best. I'm sure Caroline's told you Anthony's not like the other kids."

"She has, though I didn't need her to tell me Anthony is special."

"That Friday was the day the kids presented their short stories. Part of our recent push to reincorporate the arts into our curriculum. I remember Anthony's well. What it lacked in grammar and structure was more than made up for in sheer imagination."

My mouth turns up in an undoubtedly knowing grin. "Do tell."

"As good as any action movie I've seen. Knights. Maidens. Dragons. Witches. The requirement was for five pages. What Anthony turned in would qualify as a novella."

"From what I know about Anthony, that's not surprising." A scent like fresh-baked bread drifts through my consciousness, lending a genuine flavor to her concern.

Sayles pulls a tissue from the box on her desk and dabs at the corner of her eye. "You know, for all his oddities, the kid's kind of a genius. His Asperger's, or whatever his therapist is calling it this week, is definitely a two-edged sword, though. He placed out of two grades in elementary school, putting him far ahead of others his age, but that's left him stuck in a class where everyone is two years older than him. From an academic standpoint, he was more than holding his own, but I've seen fourth graders that can outmaneuver him in social circles. I used to thank God every day his brother was on the football team. Probably the only thing that's saved him from his fair share of poundings."

"One constant in high school." I raise an eyebrow. "Kids are cruel."

"Truth." She sits atop one of the student desks and motions for me to join her. "So, Ms. Tejedor. How can I help you?"

"Honestly, I'm here gathering information. I thought talking to his teacher might shed some light. I assume Caroline told you he's not talking."

"Last I heard, he hadn't said a word since the night when everything went to hell."

A new scent plays against the pleasant bakery aroma from before. Faint, like the chlorine smell of an indoor swimming pool.

"And what night is that?"

"The night when Julianna Wagner went missing," she says. "She and Anthony were close, you know."

"I know she used to date Anthony's brother, but I hadn't heard anything about her relationship with Anthony."

"Caroline never wanted to hear it, but I suspect a lot of what Anthony's going through has to do with Julianna's disappearance. She may have been Jason's girlfriend, but I can tell you which of the Faircloth boys was the most smitten with the beautiful Miss Wagner."

Sayles retrieves the ream of paper covered with Baba Yaga's menacing grimace from the bulletin board. She flips through what looks like a hundred pages of single space type broken up occasionally by one of Anthony's intricate pencil sketches and finds what she's looking for about halfway through the manuscript. A hand-written scrawl appears beneath the expertly rendered drawing of the girl pictured on the memorial in front of the school.

"The Fair Juliet." A pang goes through my chest. "Do I even have to ask who the Romeo of this little fairy tale might be?"

Sayles lets out a quiet chuckle. "Would you believe, a diminutive and underappreciated knight named Antonio?"

I take Anthony's fantasy manifesto and flip through the pages. It's like a sketched tour of the boy's mind.

I would know.

"Poor kid."

"I've been teaching for six years now," she says. "Seen a lot of hopeless crushes between students. This one was the most hopeless by far."

"Did she ever see this?"

"I never showed it to her, though it wouldn't surprise me if Anthony let her read it. Like I said before, his social boundaries were never too concrete. Can't say I blame him, though. Everybody loved Julianna."

"You don't think they'll find her?"

"You've seen the news. The girl's been missing over three weeks. You know how these things turn out."

The hint of chlorine from before swells. The whole school reeks of it. Julianna Wagner's disappearance has left the whole place a big pit of anxiety.

"They don't always end badly." Sarah Goode's face flashes across my memory, as vivid and sharp as if I pulled her out of that attic an hour ago instead of a year. "You can't lose hope."

"That's all that's holding this place together," she says. "Hope." Her eyes drop. "If she was taken, it was right off the school grounds with people everywhere, surrounded by all her friends. I used to feel safe here at the school. Now I sprint to my car if I have to leave after normal hours."

"I'm sure the police are doing everything they can. I saw a patrol car out front as I pulled into the parking lot."

The roll of her eyes speaks volumes. "I feel safer already."

"Mind if I borrow Anthony's story? And anything else he's written?"

"Anything to help my favorite little guy." She hands me the fifty or so stapled pages. "Just curious, you don't strike me as medical. Are you some kind of P.I.?"

"More or less." I hand her my card.

"Mira Tejedor, Paranormal investigator." She glances up at me, her eyebrows arched into a sideways question mark. "Should I ask?"

"Maybe next time." I head for the door. "My number is on the card. Give me a call if you think of any information that might help."

As I walk up the hall toward the office, I contrast Veronica Sayles with her counterpart in the Exhibition.

How did the kind woman I just met get translated into the stern schoolmarm from Anthony's *Tuileries*?

Hmm. I suppose I haven't seen her teach.

I'm nearly out the front door of the school when the wall-eyed janitor catches my gaze one last time. His eccentric stare and crooked smile send a shiver up my spine.

"Find what you were looking for?" he asks.

I hold up Anthony's story. "Time will tell."

"In that case, good luck." The janitor chuckles. "You know what they say. Yesterday's answers are often tomorrow's questions."

"I suppose they do." And with that, I turn and walk as briskly as I can for my car. I feel the janitor's eye on me the entire way, but don't dare look back.

Once I've rounded the corner, my mind downshifts out of fight or flight mode and returns instead to the strange symmetry developing between Anthony's case and the circumstances surrounding Julianna's disappearance. As I sat with the girl's parents earlier, it seemed I was agreeing to a second case. After my talk with Sayles, it's clearer than ever the two cases are merely two sides of the same coin.

Tomorrow's questions indeed.

XIII

Ballet of the Unhatched Chicks

"What do I have to say to convince you this is a bad idea?" Archer's eyes burn with intensity.

"I get closer every time. Closer to the answers we need." I pray he and Caroline don't hear the tremor in my voice. "I have to go back."

Caroline looks up from Anthony's sleeping face. Tired hope flashes across her eyes even as Archer's exasperation boils over.

"You don't have to do anything. The first couple of times left you so exhausted you could barely move and the last time sent you into a seizure." Archer looks away. "I'm not sure I can continue to condone this. There must be other ways of looking into Anthony's problem."

"Like these?" I pick up the dictionary-sized file of Anthony's work up to this point. "The answers aren't in all these tests." I brush my hand across Anthony's forehead. "They're in here. You know it. You've seen what I can do, what I can learn."

Archer lowers his head. "Doesn't change the fact I don't want to sit here and watch you kill yourself trying to be a hero."

Caroline places a hand on my shoulder. "I appreciate everything you're doing, Mira, but Thomas is right. You didn't see what happened to you the last time. It was more than just a seizure. You looked almost… possessed."

Jason, who has stood uncharacteristically silent in the corner since their arrival, catches my eye before turning his attention back to the swaying branches outside.

I close my eyes and rub at my temples, my head aching from the sulfuric fear wafting off the three of them. To be honest, there's nothing I'd like more than to never have to set a metaphysical foot inside Anthony Faircloth's mind again.

Two things, however, spur me on.

The sad eyes that stared out at me from *Tuileries* and a promise I made to Isabella.

"Find the boy," she said, "like you found Sarah." Then the part that made me cry. "You can do it, Mami."

The thought of returning home and facing Isabella having failed is unbearable.

"I appreciate what you two are trying to do, but I'm making progress here and I'm not stopping now. I've made it out safely three times before and I'll make it out again." I turn to Caroline. "You know in your heart this is working. But I need you to believe in me. In Anthony. Can you do that?"

Caroline doesn't say a word as she lays Anthony down on the couch as we've done three times before. She pulls a chair around for me and as I take my seat at her child's head, she rests a hand on each of my shoulders and whispers into my ear.

"You look after my boy, Mira Tejedor, and I'll look after you."

The "Promenade" theme is different this time. Not the harsh piano assault from my first adventure in Anthony's mind, nor the rich brass from my second and third. This time, muted woodwinds and strings fill the air, their tone and meter mournful. All in a different key than the previous iterations, it's clearly some sort of hint I'm supposed to understand. In some ways, this cat and mouse with Anthony reminds me of Sarah Goode's kidnapper and the games he played with the police. Anthony maintains an air of mystery while doling out clue after clue, all but begging me to decipher the strange puzzle his mind has become even as he changes the rules at every turn.

Unhampered by witches, gnomes or the other denizens of the

Exhibition, I pass the alcoves of the various pictures I've already visited and head for the next along the hallway. I consider stopping by the castle to check in on Tunny, Modesto, and Antoine until the ridiculousness of the idea dawns on me. As real as all this seems, the Exhibition is not an actual place and the "people" I count among my "friends" here are not real. This realization, along with memories of all the different ways this place has tried to kill me, quickens my steps.

The next alcove is different from the others. The space is dim, the ambient light that fills all the other alcoves replaced with a pair of candelabras, one on either side of the full-length frame. Bathed in the flickering light, the picture surprises me as well, both in its medium and its subject matter. Rather than the elegant oils, watercolors and pastels of the other masterworks, a detailed pen and ink sketch with a few flashes of color fills the frame of this piece. In it, a trio of young girls dance arm in arm.

Ballerinas all, the dancers stand arrayed in the strangest costumes I've ever seen. With beaks upon their noses, their heads and arms are covered in yellow down while their legs are costumed to appear like bird legs. The strangest facet of the ensemble, however, is the large unbroken egg surrounding each of their bodies. I step into the alcove to inspect the drawing further. Below the candelabra to the right of the frame, a placard contains five words written in tiny script.

BALLET OF THE UNHATCHED CHICKS

No sooner do I read the words than a quick melody of woodwinds and strings erupts in the space. The pen and ink girls in their hatchling costumes begin to dance across the paper's smooth surface. With flawless technique, the three of them move *en pointe* in perfect step as the space within the frame opens up and a third dimension comes into play. The music evokes the sound of chirping birds and bumbling chicks making their way around their nest. The pleasant tune fills the space for over a minute before stopping, the sudden silence leaving the trio of girls frozen in place.

I touch the picture, expecting the surface of the intricate drawing to fall away and allow me inside as the others have before. This time, however, art remains intact, the thin paper forming an impervious barrier to the world beyond.

"*Ballet of the Unhatched Chicks*," I mutter. "Where did this Mussorgsky guy come up with this stuff?"

"I come and watch them dance from time to time."

The voice, though startling, is not altogether unexpected. I spin around and lower my eyes.

"Hello, Tunny."

"Why are you here watching the canaries dance?"

"They're canaries?" I ask.

"Canary chicks. Or at least girls dressed as canary chicks." Tunny smiles, his teeth like petrified wood. "Contrary to what Modesto would say, I'm not completely without sense."

"You two are on a first name basis, then?"

"He hates it when I call him that." Tunny hangs his head. "Truth be told, I'm pretty sure he hates it when I call him anything at all."

"I don't know about that." I remember how Jason looked over Anthony's still form the day before. "Under all the bluster, I suspect he likes you more than he'd care to admit."

Tunny raises a mossy eyebrow. "You think?"

I turn back to the picture. "You said you come and watch them dance, but their dance lasts not much longer than a minute. What if you want to see the rest?"

"That's all there is." Tunny answers. "The ballet is quite short and the chicks dance but once with each visit."

"We have to leave if we want them to dance again?"

"Come. I'll show you."

Tunny takes my hand and the two of us saunter back up the hall. We pass a painting called *Bydło* where two yoked oxen plow the fields surrounding a house that rests on its roof, its frame hanging crooked on its section of wall. The crumpled canvas of *Tuileries* lies undisturbed on the parquet floor of its alcove. *The Old Castle* still hangs in its place, though the drawbridge remains up and the edifice secure as I requested of Modesto at my last visit. We pass the alcove where the charred frame of the *Gnomus* painting rests.

Tunny looks up at me wistfully. "It's hard not having a home."

"I'm sorry, Tunny. I can only imagine. But, what about the castle?"

"It's fine, I suppose. Modesto spends all his time trying to help Antoine talk and doesn't even look at me anymore except to tell me to 'get out from underfoot' or nonsense like that." He kicks at an imaginary rock, and studies the floor. "I'd rather spend time out here in this lonely hallway than listen to that guff."

"Don't be so hard on him, Tunny. Or yourself, for that matter."

Tunny looks up at me, and his face breaks into a half smile. "All right."

"My daughter used to do ballet, you know." Isabella's last recital from over a year ago flashes across my mind. How proud she was and how much she enjoyed losing herself in all the pirouettes and spins. "I miss seeing her dance. She enjoyed it so much."

"Why did she stop?" Tunny asks. "Is she all right?"

"Oh, it's nothing like that. Our family had… other priorities."

Tunny snorts. "We've been gone long enough." He pulls me back toward the alcove that houses the *Ballet.* The moment we arrive and step through the arch, the music begins anew, the woodwinds chirping like a nest of baby birds. The trio of egg-clad ballerinas begins a similar but different dance from their previous performance, each separating from the others yet all three twirling in unison. Somehow, they manage not to fall despite their clumsy costumes.

"I need to get in there, Tunny." I glance down at my little friend. "Can you help me?"

"You must enter before the song is over." He touches the paper's surface, his squat digit penetrating the plane as if he were reaching through a flowing sheet of honey.

Taking Tunny's lead, I dive through the surface of the sketched piece of art. As with everything in this strange ballet, the experience is different from with the other paintings. I stare down at my hands. Unlike the other works of art, where I retained my basic form, my limbs and torso have been reduced to pen and scrawled color, much like the three ballerinas. My clothing has shifted as well, the intricate green sarong I've worn since my first voyage into Anthony's mind replaced with a red ballet costume trimmed with black lace. The tutu about my waist fans out like a set of dark wings, keeping with the feathered motif of the *Ballet of the Unhatched Chicks.* More than anything, the sudden absence of the dagger's heft at my hip leaves me feeling naked.

Before I can take a breath, the chirping music begins again and I'm up on my toes, dancing in step with the trio of hatchling dancers as if I were a marionette on strings.

"Tunny," I shout, glimpsing my gnome friend time and again in the brief seconds the fervent dance allows me to look in his direction. "Help me."

Tunny's lips move, his arms flailing frantically, but I can't hear a word he's saying. The music picks up, and my body launches into a succession of pirouettes that ends with me frozen with one leg thrust in the air and the other holding me aloft *en pointe*. "*Arabesque pose*," comes Isabella's voice from the depths of my memory.

Strangely appropriate for someone who goes by the name Scheherazade.

The trio of hatchling dancers stand similarly frozen and stare at each other. Like me, it appears their eyes are the only parts of their bodies under their control. The two girls on the outside of the trio appear bored, even complacent in their held poses, but the girl in the center gapes at me, her green eyes filled with terror. Familiar green eyes. I fight to force my lips open, to speak, to make my tongue move even a millimeter.

"R—"

Her eyes grow wide.

"Ra—"

Almost there.

"Rachel." As the word leaves my lips, my body goes limp, the invisible strings controlling my body cut. I fall to the floor, my teeth snapping down on my tongue as my chin hits the unforgiving wood. My body attempts to cry out in pain, but no sound comes, at least not from me.

"Dear, dear, Scheherazade. There is no Rachel here." The witch's voice emanates from every corner of the space. "The girl's name is Trilby, and she has no need of you or your poison tongue."

"Trilby." My tongue freed, I push the words from my mouth. "And why do you keep her this way, witch? Forced to dance for all eternity for your amusement?"

"Young ballerinas need discipline, wouldn't you agree?" A raspy cackle fills the space.

I force my gaze from the floor and look up at Trilby, her lips quivering beneath the prosthetic beak, her trembling green eyes awash with tears.

"Not like this."

Trilby, her body frozen mid-contortion, begins to hyperventilate.

"Please," I grunt. "She can barely breathe."

"She'll be the better for it later."

"But you know the truth, don't you?" The Jupiter-like gravity on my limbs lets up, at least a little. "This girl isn't Trilby, or even Rachel for that matter. She's—"

"Silence." Any joviality in the witch's tone vanishes. "You believe you can talk your way out of every trouble that comes your way, Scheherazade, but your stories will not help you in this place."

My body rises to its feet yet again, my unseen puppeteer apparently ready to put me through my paces anew.

"Now," the guttural voice commands. "Dance."

I'm on my toes in an instant, arms stretched to the sky, my fingers flirting with each other above my head. The chirping music of the ballet begins again and my body spins in answer. I cavort to the left and the right as the three hatchling ballerinas surround me in a close circle.

"What are you trying to prove?" The music accelerates and my body answers. "You reign over the Exhibition with jaws of iron, claiming your actions protect these priceless pieces of art, but you enslave or destroy anyone who stands in your way."

"And your way is better?" Her derisive tone cuts across the playful tune. "Love the boy enough and he'll return from wherever his mind has gone? Is that it?"

There it is. I made her say it.

"Love *who* enough, witch?"

The music falters and whatever force animates my limbs releases me.

"Well played, Scheherazade," the witch mutters. "I suppose your honeyed words can beguile even me."

"You speak of Anthony, don't you, Baba Yaga? Anthony Faircloth, son of Caroline and William and brother of Jason and Rachel. Even in this place, where his sister dances for your amusement, it's still all about Anthony."

The music slows, growing discordant before falling into a random succession of notes and beats. The room goes silent and for the second time in as many minutes, I fall to the ground like a discarded toy.

"Do not speak such names here." The witch grows quiet. "You will upset the balance."

One of the two dancers flanking Trilby falls unconscious at the green-eyed dancer's feet.

"Anthony…" Trilby disengages from the other dancer. "That name makes me sad."

"Do not listen to her, Trilby," the witch says. "This is your stage. This is where you dance. That is what makes you happy, is it not?"

"Where I dance." The ballerina raises her head to the pen-sketched rafters and addresses the booming voice. "And who do I dance for, witch? You?" She points a shaking finger at me. "Her?"

In a swirl of gray and thunder, Baba Yaga appears in the air above us, the bottom of her mortar concealing all but her wiry arms, the pestle and ever-swishing broom gripped in her bony hands. The stone bowl comes to rest between Trilby and my motionless form.

"Have I not taken care of you, little girl? Kept you safe? Provided you the company of the finest dancers imaginable? Are you not happy?"

I fight to speak. "Perhaps she yearns for the one thing you cannot offer her here."

The witch spins and turns her cold yellow eyes on me.

"And what would that be?"

"Freedom." The whispered word falls from Trilby's lips even as the unhatched egg surrounding her torso shatters, revealing a svelte dancer's form wrapped in white. Her body molts, the yellow down and beak falling away revealing Rachel's auburn curls and freckled cheeks.

"Trilby," the witch whispers. "Don't."

"My time on this stage is done." Trilby turns to me, her expression uncannily like that of the girl who looked in on me from the hallway at her home yesterday. "Will you take me to Anthony?"

"Of course." In the face of Trilby's defiance, the strength returns to my limbs.

I rise from the hardwood floor.

"You will never leave this place," the witch grumbles, to me or Trilby I can't be sure. "I will not allow it."

The fallen ballerina comes to her knees and wraps her lithe arms around Trilby's legs as the one still standing leaps at her shoulders. The pair wrestles her to the ground and holds her there as the witch's mortar floats over to her side.

"Do you now see, little girl?"

Trilby stares back in defiance, her eyes darkening like an approaching storm. "In your forest among the Steppes, you may reign, witch, but this is my ballet. My home." Her body rises from the wooden stage, the pair of other dancers hanging off her like so much dead weight. The girl floats in the air before the witch and in a blink the other two dancers vanish, absorbed into Trilby's form. Her clothing shifts, her raiment transforming from white to an ensemble mirroring mine, the black lace atop the ruby red a stark contrast to the yellow fluff that covered her moments before.

A foreign expression flashes across the witch's face. Is it… sadness?

"So," the witch hisses. "You would choose the storyteller over me." She spins and glares out into the Exhibition where Tunny still waits, his wooden visage a mix of fear and confusion.

"All of you have betrayed me in one way or another." The mortar tilts to one side until the witch is again nose-to-nose with me, a closeness I'd hoped never to experience again. "Take the girl, then. The boy, the gnome, the troubadour. Take them all. Still I will deny you the answer you seek. That revelation rests in my realm, and you dare not go there." She gestures toward the frame and the hallway beyond where Tunny looks on, his mouth agape. "Unlike the gnome, the girl understands her place in her work of art, as do I. Farewell, Scheherazade. Pray we do not meet again."

Before Trilby or I can say a word, the witch spins the pestle above her head like some sort of archaic propeller and the mortar rises into the air, passing through the ephemeral ceiling above our heads. The moment she vanishes, my limbs are my own again. I rise from the sketched wood of the stage and brush off my pencil and ink form.

"So, Scheherazade," Trilby says. "Where do we go from here?"

"I don't know." A quiet chuckle passes my lips. "Seems like all the children are grown up."

"Why, storyteller?" Her gaze takes on a puzzled cast. "Are you projecting?"

"Perhaps." I catch movement from the corner of my eye, Tunny waving to me from beyond the frame hanging in space. "I suppose my friend the gnome will have to leave and return so we can dance out of this place." I motion for Tunny to take a walk. For the first time, Trilby and I are alone.

"There is something I must tell you." I grapple with the words. "You are no more Trilby than I am Scheherazade. This place is—"

Rachel places one finger to her lips and shakes her head, not dissimilar from the way the witch directed me from atop Hartmann's house.

"Time for that later, Scheherazade. This day has had quite enough revelations already."

I nod even as Tunny comes back into view. The music begins again, and though it's the same music from before, the lilting chirps fill my heart with gladness for the first time since setting foot in the *Ballet.* Rachel spins on one foot and performs a *grand jeté* toward the hanging frame. I follow, our steps in sync as if rehearsed a thousand times. As she leaps through the frame and out onto the hallway, she glances back and mouths the words, "Thank you."

As I pass the frame, I'm again surrounded in prismatic light, the music of "Promenade" buffeting my form for what seems like days.

Then, there is silence.

XIV

Operetta

"Mira? Can you hear me? Mira?"

The sound of Archer's voice serves as a calming anchor as I return to reality. My eyes struggle to focus, the twin fluorescent bulbs above my head burning across my vision like a rectangular blue-white sun. His fingers warm on my wrist as he checks my pulse, he looks down on me with his usual mix of concern and exasperation.

"Ah," I mutter, "saved again by the Kalendar Prince."

"What was that?" he asks.

I bring my other hand across to meet his. "Nothing worth mentioning."

"Welcome back, Mira." Caroline's eyes fill with teary hope. "Did you find any sign of Anthony in there this time?"

"Give her a second, Mom." Jason's voice sounds from somewhere to my right. "Looks like another rough landing."

"It's all right." I start to sit up but think better of it. Every muscle in my body sings with pain as if I've just run a marathon. "I'll be okay in a minute."

"You sure? Your pulse has been in the 150s for at least half an hour." Archer rests my hand across my belly. "At least you didn't seize this time."

Agnes steps into the room with a bottle of water. "Something for your throat," she mutters. Refusing to look me in the eye, she crosses herself before leaving the room.

Archer gives me a moment before asking, "What happened in there?"

"Remember the troubadour from *The Old Castle* and how he's the spitting image of Jason?" Archer and Caroline both nod, while Jason looks on dumbfounded. "Now there's a ballerina named Trilby that could be Rachel's twin."

"His brother and sister. They're like guards or something?" Caroline hangs her head and rubs at the bridge of her nose. "I had no idea he felt that way."

"I don't think Trilby and Modesto serve necessarily as keepers, Caroline. Like every character of the Exhibition, they are no more than aspects of Anthony, facets of a greater whole. Like Archer said, Tunny is most likely how he sees himself, while Modesto, all confident, good-looking, and musical, represents the man he would like to be."

"And this Antoine, the one that looks just like Anthony." Caroline asks. "Who is he?"

"I can tell you that one," Jason says. "All alone in a crowd, nothing to say and no one paying attention to him? I've seen Anthony at school. That particular slice of his made up Exhibition isn't so made up."

"That leaves the schoolmarm, the Cart Man, and the witch," Archer says.

"And this Trilby character," Caroline adds.

"I have no idea what Trilby represents." A throbbing pain flares to life above my left eye. "I'll tell you this, though. She's stronger than the witch."

"Now, there's a surprise." Jason chuckles. "Girl's got more spunk than the rest of us put together."

Caroline laughs as well. "You've seen how well she listens to me. I can tell her to do something twenty times and she still treats it like a suggestion."

It occurs to me the youngest of the Faircloths wasn't sitting in the waiting room when I arrived. "Where is Rachel today?"

"With a babysitter. Our neighbors' daughter, Shelby, watches her from time to time." Her gaze drops to the floor. "The last couple of times here really upset her, so we decided to leave her at home today."

Caroline's cell phone rings. She pulls it from her purse and reads the screen. Her brow furrows.

"Funny. That's Shelby calling now." She taps the screen twice and puts the phone to her ear.

"Hello?" Caroline's eyes grow wide. "Yes. I understand. Just calm down. What's wrong with her?" Her face goes pale. "We'll be right there."

Caroline ends the call and gathers her things.

"What is it?" My second attempt at sitting up is more successful. "Is it Rachel?"

"She's unconscious," Caroline whispers. "Shelby found her in the yard." She turns to Archer. "Sorry, Thomas. We've got to go."

"Wait, Caroline." I force myself to my feet, as clumsy as a toddler taking their first steps. "I'm in no shape to drive, but I'm coming with you."

Sprawled on the neighbors' loveseat, Rachel Faircloth stares at the ceiling. Her pale face drips with sweat despite the cool rag resting across her forehead.

"You didn't see her fall?" Caroline stands at Rachel's head, glaring at Shelby who is at best sixteen and about to hyperventilate. With her hands on her hips and her no-nonsense tone, Caroline looks and sounds every bit like a district attorney cross-examining a murder suspect. Jason stands in the corner, sullen, his few glances at the girl filled with misplaced anger and blame. Guilt wafts off the poor girl, the odor reminiscent of a sweaty locker room.

"I'm sorry, Ms. Faircloth. She went outside to play. I was taking her some water because I thought she might be thirsty. She was only out of my sight for a few minutes."

"And she looked fine?"

"Same as when you dropped her off." Shelby wipes a tear from her cheek. "I swear."

Caroline looks up at Jason. "Honey, can you go take Anthony inside? He's going to suffocate if we leave him in the car much longer."

"Are you sure, Mom?" He glances over at Rachel. "What about—"

"Your sister is going to be fine. I'll let you know if anything changes. Now, go check on Anthony. Oh, and flip on the crock pot so the roast beef can start to cook."

Jason nods and turns for the door, his accusing gaze flitting across Shelby before he lets himself out.

As Caroline inhales to continue her inquisition, I step into the breach.

"Shelby, can you tell me what you saw when you found Rachel?"

She looks up at me through swollen eyes. "She was lying on the ground, pale, hardly breathing." Her voice cracks. "Her lips were blue."

"Did she say anything?"

"Not at first."

Caroline leans in. "What do you mean 'not at first'?"

"Right before I called you, she woke up. For just a second, but she was awake. It was really strange."

"Strange?" I ask. "How, exactly?"

"One second, she's lying there pale as a ghost. Then, all of a sudden, she sits up, raises her arms above her head, and says 'Thank you' before falling back to the grass." Shelby glances over at Rachel's still form. "She's been like this ever since, but this is nothing compared to when I first found her."

I sit by Rachel on the couch. Running the back of my fingers down her cheek, I lean in and whisper in her ear.

"Rachel, can you hear me?"

She doesn't respond, at least not with her lips. An echo of melody drifts across my consciousness.

The chirping notes of the *Ballet of the Unhatched Chicks*.

"Rachel?" I lean in closer. "Trilby?"

At the mention of the second name, Rachel turns and looks me straight in the eye.

"Schehera–"

I put a finger to my lips, hushing Rachel as Shelby and Caroline rush to our side.

"Rachel." Shelby tries to keep her voice calm, though the relief in her voice comes through loud and clear. "Thank God."

I glance up at the girl, feeling her emotions cool with every passing second. "Shelby, will you excuse us, please?"

"But—"

"I'm pretty sure I know what's going on here. You didn't do anything wrong, but I need to discuss it with Caroline in private."

Her eyes flit from mine to Rachel and back. "She's going to be okay?"

"She's going to be fine." I take Shelby's hand. "In no small part thanks to you."

Shelby leans in, kisses Rachel on the forehead, and whispers, "Feel better."

Rachel's eyes flutter, but she remains silent.

Shelby steps into the next room and I ease the door shut behind her.

"Caroline, I have something to tell you, and you're not going to like it."

"This has something to do with Anthony." Caroline completes my thought. "Doesn't it?"

"Yes, but—"

"It's spreading," she says, "whatever's happened to him. It's coming for Rachel now."

"Stay calm." I sit back down by Rachel's head and stroke her hair. "I think it's more likely that Anthony reached out to her, the way he has with me. You said he and Rachel were close, right?"

"As close as any brother and sister I've ever seen. Anthony may be an odd kid but Rachel couldn't love the boy more if she tried. Don't let her size fool you. The last kid who picked on Anthony with her around left with a bloody nose."

"Mommy?" At Rachel's whisper, Caroline drops to her knees and grasps her daughter by the shoulders.

"I'm here, honey. Are you okay?"

"Where's Anthony? He was just here."

"He's at home, Rachel. It's just you, me and Ms. Tejedor."

"But, I was just talking to him. Him and Miss Mira."

Caroline pulls Rachel into a tight embrace and shoots me an accusing glance. "It was just a dream, honey. Just a dream."

"If only that were true." I take Rachel's trembling hand in mine and gaze into her green eyes even as Caroline's glare bores into me. "Rachel, do you remember anything? Anything at all?"

Her eyes lose focus as the melody of the ballet again fills my senses. "I think I was dreaming, but the dream became a nightmare. There was dancing and music. You were there, Miss Mira. You and Tunny." Her cheeks flush a bit. "I mean Anthony."

"Oh my God." Caroline gasps. "Rachel is Trilby."

I give Caroline a curt nod as I gently stroke Rachel's hand. "What else do you remember?"

"There was a bad person there." Rachel's bottom lip begins to tremble. "A witch." A jolt of remembrance flashes across her face. Her eyes focus on mine. "She tried to hurt you."

"I'm fine, Rachel. I'm fine." I brush my thumb across her damp cheek. "You saved me, remember?"

"I guess so." She turns her head to look at Caroline. "I'm tired, Mommy. Can I take a nap?"

"Of course, honey. Of course." As if in a daze, Caroline pulls a fleece throw blanket from a basket in the corner and wraps it around Rachel's body. In moments, the girl is asleep and Caroline turns on me.

"What the hell is going on here, Mira?" She keeps her voice low, but the anger pouring out of her is palpable. "As if Anthony wasn't bad enough, now my daughter is getting sucked into this thing too?"

"It would appear that unlike the other characters in the Exhibition, Trilby in some strange way is Rachel, or at least connected to her intimately."

Caroline thinks for a moment. "Why Rachel, though? You say this Modesto character is the spitting image of Jason, yet you've crossed his path multiple times in the Exhibition, and nothing bad has happened to Jason out in the real world."

"I'm sorry, Caroline. I wish I could tell you more. This is all uncharted territory for me." I glance over at Rachel's still form. "I do have a theory, though."

"I'm all ears."

"Anthony has chosen to populate his mind with familiar images and faces, like the gnome from his sketchpad, his siblings, even his teacher, Ms. Sayles."

"I think we've already established that pretty well." Caroline strokes Rachel's cheek. "What makes Rachel different?"

I take a deep breath. "I have to tell you something."

"This is the part I'm not going to like, isn't it?"

"When I first encountered your family, I sensed something familiar. Something I've only sensed in a few others in all my years on the planet."

"What are you trying to say, Mira?"

"I believe Anthony is like me." I wait for the information to sink in. "Rachel, too."

Caroline's eyes slide closed as she slumps into a chair. Her hands tremble in her lap. "Actually, that makes a lot of sense. The way they've always been so close. I always thought it was uncanny how they always seemed to know when the other was sad or upset or alone."

"I've suspected Anthony possessed talents similar to mine since the first time he drew me in. I've come in contact with hundreds of minds over the years, but never one that pulled me in like Anthony. Your boy is very special."

"Special." She says the word as if it's a curse. "And Rachel?"

"Her abilities are nowhere nearly as developed as Anthony's, but the potential is there."

"And when you met this Trilby person, she was Rachel, wandering Anthony's mind the same as you do?"

"Yes and no. When I interact with Anthony, there is an intention there to help him and I know what's happening. That may be why I keep my own identity even as Anthony translates me into his vision of the Lady Scheherazade. With Rachel, I think his talent pulls her essence into the Exhibition and she becomes just another character in his mind. The fact Trilby is more than a figment of Anthony's imagination may explain why she can stand up to the witch when no one else can. Still, whoever or whatever the witch represents in Anthony's mind, it's something strong."

"She's going to be all right, isn't she?"

I massage my still aching scalp. "You've seen what happens to me when I travel the Exhibition. Rachel may be small, but she's tough. Both of us should be fine in a few hours."

Caroline sighs, and for the moment appears at least somewhat relieved. "So, what now?"

"There's something about this whole situation I'm not getting. A connection that doesn't make any sense." I rise from the couch. "Would it be all right if I talked to Jason?"

I let myself into the Faircloth home. As I step into the family room, the hair on my neck stands on end, though it's not the chilly temperature from the air conditioning that fires my nerves. Frustration, guilt, and shame, all wrapped up in a bright red bow of anger, are to blame for that.

"What are you doing here?" Jason stands in the doorway leading to the back of the house. "Where's Mom?"

"She'll be along soon."

He hangs from the doorframe, his adolescent biceps bulging as he does half a pull up. "How's Rachel?"

"Still waking up, but she talked to us. Looks like she's going to be fine"

"Good." He lets go of the door face and drops to the floor. "I got Anthony all tucked in. That's usually my job anyway, at least when Mom's busy."

"You take good care of your brother."

Jason looks away. "Ms. Tejedor. I have a question."

"Ask away."

"You read minds, right? Anybody's mind."

"Not read, per se, but my ability gives me a pretty good sense of what's going on with people." The acrid smell of onion filling the room spikes. "Why do you ask?"

"The cops think I killed Julianna, or at least know what happened to her. You know it and I know it. They've brought me in twice now only to ask me the same questions they've already asked a dozen times." He bites his lower lip and swallows. "No matter what happened before, I love Julianna. I would never hurt her. Not in a million years."

"What are you asking me, Jason?"

"Read my mind. Tell them the truth." His voice cracks. "Tell them I didn't do it."

I shake my head. "Even if I could do what you're asking, I'm not sure they'd believe me."

"You could try. I'm not perfect, not by a long shot, but I'm no liar and I'm not a murderer."

"You want me to touch your mind. Do you know what you're asking?"

"I'm asking you to help me. That's what you came here to do, isn't it? Help us?"

I lead him over to the couch and take a seat opposite, the coffee table between us.

"Have you talked to your mother about this?"

Jason's stare bores through me. "I'm old enough to decide what's best for me."

"That may be true, but I'm not sure how your mother would feel about me mucking around in your head. You're the only one of her three children so far untouched by all this."

"My ex-girlfriend's been missing for three weeks, my brother's comatose, my sister just had a seizure, my mother's about to fall apart, and the police want to send me to the chair. Don't talk to me about 'untouched'."

"I'm sorry, Jason. I didn't mean to imply—"

"I don't need you to be sorry, Ms. Tejedor. I need you to help me."

Jason and I lock gazes, the insistence in his stare wearing at my resolve until there's not a doubt in my mind what I have to do.

"All right. Rest here on the couch, like we did with Anthony before." I help him get into position. "Be right back." I pull a chair in from the dining room and take a seat at his head.

"I believe you, you know." I brush the hair from his eyes. "Not to mention I don't know too many cold blooded killers who are eager to have a psychic around."

"You're about the only one that does. The whole school is talking about me behind my back. Julianna's friends, the guys on the team, everybody. I've even caught Mom watching me out of the corner of her eye sometimes." He looks away. "What do you do when your own mother doesn't believe in you anymore?"

"She believes in you, Jason. I can feel it when she's around you. She's a bit preoccupied with Anthony and Rachel right now, but never doubt your mother loves you."

Jason rubs at his neck, nervous. "Can we just get on with this? I know it's my idea, but the thought of having someone poke around in my head is freaking me out a little."

"As well it should, but don't worry. I'm a trained professional." I give him a quick wink. "Are you ready?"

He stares up at me, his upside down face filled with anxiety. "As ready as I'll ever be."

"Then just relax and let me do the driving."

Jason closes his eyes and tries to unwind but he still winces as I cup his head in my hands.

"It's okay, Jason. Just take some deep breaths and listen to the sound of my voice."

It takes a few minutes, but he eventually manages to let go of his anxiety and drifts into that halfway state between dream and wakefulness. Once he's ready, I open the part of my mind I have to keep closed when I'm in a crowded room, the part that lets me truly listen. At first, the same storm of emotions from before hits me like an ocean wave, but as I simultaneously focus and let go, Jason's thoughts come into focus. Unlike the mousetrap of Anthony's mind, Jason's is like most I've encountered over the years, an obstacle course punctuated by images that play across my mind's eye like a thousand different movies at once. Some memories, no more than flashes, flit by like ghosts while others take center stage, demanding my full attention.

Jason's hands behind the wheel as he negotiates a busy freeway.

A rainy football field, the score tied at ten on a dilapidated old scoreboard.

The back of Anthony's head and Rachel in profile in the front seat of a roller coaster. Their delighted squeals fill the air as they crest a rickety climb and fly down the scaffolded hill.

Julianna Wagner's face so close, I can almost feel her skin, her breaths coming faster and faster as the image leaves her eyes and goes to her bare neck.

A much younger and much happier Caroline, walking with an ice cream cake topped with seven lit candles as a crowd of young children sing.

A man sitting and laughing with Julianna. About my age. Reasonably good looking.

Slate-gray eyes.

Though dressed in clothes more befitting the modern day this time, I'd recognize the man's face anywhere.

It's Hartmann the Cart Man.

"Jason? Can you hear me?"

The man in the vision holds a wineglass, as does Julianna. He offers Jason a glass filled with what I'm guessing isn't Cheerwine, but Jason waves it off.

"Talk to me. What are we seeing?"

"How are you doing this, Ms. Tejedor?" Jason's voice echoes through this recreated place. "I can hear you, and not just with my ears."

"A part of me is in inside your mind and communication is a bit more direct. Now, tell me. What are we seeing?"

"A party. The one after Julianna's recital last spring."

The man with Julianna tells a joke as she takes a sip of her drink, nearly causing her to snort it out her nose as she doubles over laughing. As his hand goes to her knee, anger rises in this Jason's mind, his eyes growing cold and distant. The smell of alcohol grows in the space.

"You don't like him much, do you?"

"Of course I do." The bitterness in Jason's every word is palpable. "Everybody does."

"Who is he?"

The aroma of open wine bottles roiling across my consciousness grows sour.

"Julianna's music teacher. Tutors her in voice a couple nights a week."

The underlying anger in this place goes from a slow simmer to boiling.

"You don't like him being around Julianna."

"Would you?"

"What's his name?"

"I'm sorry." Jason's voice in my mind grows pensive, distant. "I'm so sorry."

"Jason. His name. What is it?"

A moment of silence stretches for what seems like hours as the man and Julianna get closer.

His hand on her knee.

Her hand on his arm.

"You can tell me, Jason." I bring my internal voice down to a whisper. "I understand."

"His name is Glenn," Jason whispers into my mind. "Glenn Hartman."

XV

Dissonante

"What the hell do you think you're doing?" Caroline's voice rips me from Jason's mind as angry vinegar washes all other emotion from the room. Standing in the doorway to the foyer with a still woozy Rachel by her side, her stare could melt an iceberg. "I leave you alone for fifteen minutes and you go screwing with my son's head?"

"Stop it, Mom." Too groggy to sit up, Jason turns his head in Caroline's direction. "I asked Mira to help me—"

"I'm not talking to you right now, Jason."

I shake my head from side to side, working to bring myself back to reality. "I'm sorry, Caroline. I was just trying to—"

"You were trying to help. That's what you're going to say." She rushes to Jason's side and helps him sit up. "My family has had about all the help we can take. Anthony's all but comatose and Rachel is still recovering from the backwash of your latest efforts. Did you really believe I would approve of this?"

"It's not like that. Please, let me explain."

"This has all been a big mistake." Caroline shakes her head and pulls Rachel tight to her hip. "I'm sorry, but I think you should leave."

Heat rises in my cheeks. "You begged me to come here and now you're sending me away, right when I'm starting to put the pieces together?"

"Don't worry, Mira. You'll be paid."

I pull back as if I've been slapped. "That's not what this is about. At least listen to—"

"I asked you here to help Anthony. That's it."

"Stop yelling at her, Mom," Jason says. "Mira didn't even want to do it. I begged her to help me find out what happened to Julianna."

"And those gorgeous eyes of hers had nothing to do with it."

Jason grabs a set of keys from the coffee table and heads for the door. "I'm not going to stand here and listen to this shit."

"Don't you walk away when I'm talking to you," Caroline shouts.

Jason slams the front door behind him, leaving Caroline and me staring at each other. Rachel peers out at me from behind her mother.

"Listen, Caroline. Jason is stressed out. He asked me to take a peek into his mind, try to find a clue that might help him refute all the accusations being leveled against him."

"With all due respect, Ms. Tejedor, this is my house and these are my children. You've overstepped our arrangement and I would appreciate it if you would leave. Now."

"What happened with Rachel isn't my fault, you know. She and Anthony are very special. They're going to need help with—"

"You think I don't know my children are special?" I choke on the vinegar and cayenne coming off Caroline.

"No. *Special.* Like me. I'll go for now, but understand I'm not leaving town till I've done what I came to do."

"You do what you have to do, and I'll do the same." She finally meets my gaze, her anger tempered with sadness and desperation. "I know you mean well, but it's all too much." She buries her face in her hands. "Too much."

"I'll let myself out." I gather my things and head for the door. "Give me a call when you're ready to talk."

The sting of Caroline's angry words is still present as the cab drops me back off at Archer's office. I hop in my car and return to the Blake, waving weakly at the front desk clerk as I head for the elevators. No sooner do the doors open on my floor than my phone rings.

"Hello?"

"Mami?"

"Hi, sweetheart. How are you?"

"I'm fine. Me and Nana are baking cookies."

"That sounds like fun."

"I miss you, Mami. When are you coming home?"

"Soon." The gnawing sensation in my belly climbs into my chest. "I'm not done here in Charlotte, but I'm getting there."

"Are we still going to go to the beach? You promised we'd go see the ocean one more time before it got too cold this year."

Girl's got a memory like a hard drive. "Of course. When I get back, we'll make plans to head down to Virginia Beach. We can check out the Navy ships just like we talked about."

"Nana wants to talk to you."

As I wait for Mom to pick up, I let myself into my room and fall back on the bed.

"Hello, Mira," comes my mother's voice a few seconds later.

"Hey, Mom."

"How are things going with the Faircloth family?"

"Um… they're going fine." I honestly don't know how to respond to her question. For days, Mom has been irritated every time we've spoken and now she sounds almost jubilant. "I feel like I'm making some progress, though I hit a bit of a roadblock today."

"Do you need to talk about it?"

"All right, who are you and what have you done with my mother?"

"Just trying to be supportive. I didn't like the way our last conversation went and I thought maybe if I cut you some slack—"

A chuckle escapes my lips. "What's his name, Mom?"

"What are you talking about?"

"Is it that Stavros guy from the supermarket? He finally asked you out, didn't he?"

She laughs. "Maybe." Even a state away, I feel the heat of my mother's blush. "Took him a few weeks to get up the nerve to talk to me about something other than cuts of salmon."

"It's about time."

"I'm glad you feel that way, Mira. I still miss your father terribly, but Stavros is sweet and it gets pretty lonely up here, especially when you're out of town."

"I'll be home soon. Just need to finish up here."

"And you think you're getting close?"

"Closer every day. I really stepped in it with Caroline earlier, but I think I can recover."

"Good luck. Call me if you need me, though Stavros might be coming by later for a visit."

"Hold on. How's Isabella?" My jaw clenches. "What did her father buy her today?"

"About that." I sense my mother's telltale sigh coming a good second before it comes. "There's been a development."

My stomach does its best impersonation of a pretzel. "Go ahead."

"Dominic isn't exactly here… alone."

"What do you mean?"

"I mean he's not *alone.*"

My mother's words begin to sink in. Like toilet water into my favorite rug. "It's her, isn't it?"

"I'm sorry, honey. I wasn't going to tell you till you got home, but Dominic asked today if it would be okay to introduce Autumn to Isabella."

"Let me get this straight." I shoot out of the bed and go to the window. "He cheats on me for a year with this bitch and now he wants to bring her into my daughter's life?"

"She's wearing a ring, Mira."

"He married her?"

"Engaged. Dominic says they're planning the wedding for New Year's Eve."

The blood rushes from my head and I rest my hand on the windowsill to keep myself from falling. "Happy fucking holidays," I mutter.

"She flew in today. I just found out a few hours ago." Mom's voice grows quiet. "I'm so sorry, honey."

Mom talks me down for the next few minutes, and by the end of the conversation, I'm no longer considering a ten-hour drive to kick a hole in Dominic's skull. She hangs up so she can help Isabella with her bath and I flip on the television for background noise and crash on the gravity well the hotel staff calls a bed.

As I cruise through channel after channel of uninspired reality show drivel, my subconscious does everything to keep from thinking about my daughter spending one moment with the woman who tore our family apart. Not surprisingly, my thoughts drift to Anthony Faircloth and as my mind continues to wander, the strange connections between the boy and me begin to pop up like dandelions in the front yard.

The psychic thing notwithstanding, the parallels are compelling. Like me, he's a middle child. We both lost our fathers early, both been through more than our fair share of tragedy, and neither of us seem likely to cut the cord to our mothers anytime soon.

Another ring of my cell phone jolts me out of my misery and back to the present. It's a local number, but not one I recognize. I click the answer button.

"Hello?"

"Ms. Tejedor? It's Veronica Sayles."

"Ms. Sayles." I don't have to be psychic to pick up the urgency in her voice. "Good to hear from you. Is everything all right?"

"You said to call with anything that might help Anthony."

"What have you got?"

"Can you meet me? I'd rather not discuss it over the phone."

"Sure. Can you suggest a quiet bar not too far from Uptown? It's been quite a night."

I pull in at Copland's around seven. Storm clouds gather in the darkening sky to the west and as the first raindrops hit my windshield, I sprint inside and grab a seat at the bar.

The management has gone to a great deal of trouble arranging the bottles along the wall according to the colors of the rainbow. Reminiscent of my initial fall into the Exhibition, my eyes keep finding their way back to the prismatic arrangement of liquor splayed before me. The "Promenade" theme echoes through my mind, louder with each passing second. Fortunately, I'm not kept waiting for long.

"Ms. Tejedor." Sayles sits next to me and rests her purse on the bar. "Thanks for meeting me. I hope I haven't kept you long."

"I just arrived myself. Can I get you a drink?"

"Allow me." She signals the bartender, a tall, thin man with graying temples and a close-cropped goatee.

"What'll it be, ladies?"

"I'll have a cosmo, and my friend will have a…" Sayles glances over at me.

"House red, please."

Sayles pivots in her stool as the bartender turns to the rainbow bar to prepare our drinks. "I appreciate you meeting me on such short notice."

"Of course. Anything to help Anthony."

The bartender hands us our drinks as the sky opens up overhead. We have to all but shout to hear each other above the pounding rain, neither of which does wonders for the pounding behind my eyes.

"What brings you out on a night like this?" I ask.

She glances around, as if she's afraid she'll be overheard. "It may not be anything, but do you remember when we talked about how Anthony's problems all started around the time Julianna Wagner vanished?"

"I do. In fact, I've already been in contact with the police."

"They've brought you in on the case?"

"Not exactly. Just trying to determine if anything about Julianna's disappearance could be contributing to Anthony's condition."

"In that case, I may have something you want to see." Her gaze drops to her lap. "I found something and I'm not sure what to do with it."

I take a sip from my drink. "And that would be?"

"Evidence that Julianna was involved with someone."

"The police are more than aware Julianna was seeing Anthony's brother, Jason. They've already dragged him down to the station twice, and if it wasn't for an ironclad alibi, he'd be in some pretty hot water."

"That's not what I'm talking about." Her eyes take on a wistful cast. "From what I've heard, Jason and Julianna were *that* high school couple, right up to the minute she dumped him. Good-looking. Popular. First string varsity tackle and co-captain of the cheerleading squad. The stuff of rock ballads."

"Jason says she broke up with him because she thought they were getting too serious."

"But what if that's not all there was to it?" She leans in close. "The media seems obsessed with pinning everything on the jilted ex-boyfriend, but if there was someone else…"

I lean in close and lower my voice. "What did you find?"

She rummages in her purse and pulls out a folded note. "Julianna's history teacher keeps a drawer for all the cell phones, iPods, and notes confiscated from the students. I was filling in for her this afternoon during my planning period and caught a girl texting in class. I sent her to the office and opened the drawer to deposit the phone when I noticed this folded up piece of paper with Julianna's initials written on the flap. Since we had been talking about the case, I got suspicious and took a look." She hands me the carefully folded sheet of paper. "Read it."

I open the note. Scrawled on the back of a flier for the school play is a simple message.

J–

After school. Far end of the parking lot. Looks like rain, but as always, my car is warm and dry. Dinner tonight?

–H

My breath catches in my throat as a musky scent hits my senses like a runaway semi. Whoever scribbled this message had one thing on their mind.

"You're sure this is hers?"

"No, but there are only so many JWs in the school. What do you think?" Sayles searches my eyes. As with our last conversation, a faint hint of chlorine colors her words. "What if the police are questioning the wrong guy?"

"If we could confirm Julianna was seeing more than one person, it would certainly take the heat off Jason." Trying to keep any trace of my own suspicions from my face, I ask, "Any idea who 'H' might be?"

"Someone old enough to drive, I suppose. There are three hundred students in the graduating class and a similar number in the junior and sophomore classes. Probably a good fifty or sixty guys with an H in their name, assuming it's not a nickname." I rest my glass on the bar. "And assuming it's a guy."

Sayles looks at me quizzically. "Paranormal investigator, huh?" She raises an eyebrow and smiles. "I'm guessing your train of thought pretty much starts outside the box. The Faircloth family has a winner in you."

"That remains to be seen." I bite my lip. "Question. Have you ever seen Julianna hanging around with anyone else?"

"Sorry. I didn't know her all that well. I've only been teaching at this school for a little over a year and the juniors and seniors hardly ever set foot on the ninth grade hall."

"What about afterschool activities? You know, ball games, cheerleading?" The last image I gleaned from Jason's mind makes an encore appearance. "The music department?"

Her eye twitches. "She was on the cheerleading squad and I believe she was supposed to be one of the leads in the school play. Other than that, like I said, I didn't know her all that well."

The chlorine odor swells in my mind. I've obviously pushed too hard, though I still have to fight the urge to ask her about Glenn Hartman. The likely identity of the mysterious "H" at the end of the note isn't so mysterious with the insider information I'm privy to, but I decide not to tip that particular card. Now, if only I can convince Detective Sterling and his oh-so-pleasant partner to get a warrant based on my interaction with an imagined Cart Man, a hazy memory filtered through the consciousness of a jealous ex-boyfriend, and a found high school love letter.

"I'm curious about something." My fingers trail along the paper resting between us. "Why didn't you take this note to the police?"

"My main goal is to help Anthony and his family. Kid's got enough hurdles to jump without his brother ending up behind bars. You can take the note to the cops if you want, but I wanted you to see it first."

I fold the note and slide it into my purse. "Anything else?"

"Off the record?"

"I'm no reporter, but sure."

"The police aren't the only ones suspicious of Jason Faircloth. Students and teachers alike have been giving him a wide berth for weeks. Everyone just wants to put this whole thing behind them, and they're looking for someone to blame." She takes the last sip of her drink. "Look out for your client, Ms. Tejedor. You may be the only one who is."

I finish off my glass of wine and reach for my wallet as Sayles produces a twenty from her purse and hands it to the bartender.

"Don't worry. I've got this."

"Thank you, Ms. Sayles."

"Please, call me Veronica."

"All right, Veronica. Call me if you find out anything else of interest. I'll be in touch."

She heads for the ladies room as I make my way out of the bar and to the covered valet stand. Even in the short sprint to my car, I'm half-drenched. I swear under my breath for leaving my raincoat and umbrella at the hotel. I pull the door closed and shiver.

"Lady Scheherazade?"

I nearly leap out of my skin. My eyes dart to my right and there in the passenger seat sits Tunny. His brown eyes tired and hopeless, he looks at me as a drowning man looks at a life preserver.

"Tunny?"

"Don't abandon us, Scheherazade. You're the only one who knows. The only one who understands. Please help us."

"Help you? How?" I blink, and when my eyes open again, the gnome is gone.

XVI

Nocturne

I dial the first nine digits half a dozen times before I finally get up the nerve to let the call go through. The phone rings several times before someone answers, the voice confident, though a bit put out.

"Hello?" The deep Boston-Charlotte hybrid accent comes through loud and clear.

"Detective Sterling?"

"This is Sterling. Who is this?"

"Mira Tejedor. I'm guessing you remember me."

A sharp intake of air comes across the line. "Must say, I'm surprised. Day I've had, I've been thinking anything but pleasant thoughts."

Wow. Good memory. "Do you have a minute?"

"Actually, I'm finally headed home after sixteen hours of paperwork hell. Can this wait?"

"You'll want to hear this. I may have uncovered another suspect in the Wagner case."

Sterling's voice goes quiet. "Where are you?"

Fifteen minutes later, Detective Sterling trudges into the lobby of the Blake, the clear fatigue on his face made all the more evident by the scent of stale bread wafting off him. I catch his eye and motion him over to my table in the hotel's deserted dining area.

"Ms. Tejedor." There's an edge to his voice, but I'm certain he wouldn't have come if he didn't think what I had to say had value. A cop who trusts my instincts. What a concept.

"Detective Sterling. Thank you for coming."

"You said it was important."

"I've got a lead. It's a little strange, but if you'll bear with me, I'll try to explain."

"I'm listening."

I spend the better part of half an hour detailing for Detective Sterling my work with Anthony. I touch on each of my experiences in the Exhibition, the progress made with each encounter, my run-ins with the witch, and eventually get around to my time with Hartmann the Cart Man. The incredulity on his face when I'm finished is colored with no small measure of curiosity, his peppery skepticism barely perceptible in the mix of emotions floating through the room.

"Assuming I believe any of what you're saying, let me make sure I understand. This Hartmann character you encountered in Anthony Faircloth's mind had Julianna Wagner's body buried in the field by his house, and his team of oxen plowed her out of the ground?"

"At the direction of a witch standing atop an upside-down house. Yes."

The fact Sterling didn't get up and leave ten minutes ago speaks volumes.

"And you think somehow this man is the murderer." Sterling leans in. "You know, out here in the real world."

"There's something I haven't told you. I sort of have a second witness as well."

"I'm not going to like this, am I?"

"Jason was pretty upset today. He asked me to touch his mind like I did his brother's, find anything that might help prove his innocence."

Sterling's lips form a thin line. "And you couldn't turn the boy down."

"He's desperate, Detective Sterling. He doesn't know what else to do."

"And did you find anything?"

I hesitate for a moment before pulling the paper Veronica Sayles gave me from my purse.

"You tell me. I was talking to one of Anthony's teachers about the case and she gave me this note she found. She knew I was trying to help the Faircloth family and thought it might help."

"What is it?" He takes the paper and unfolds it. His eyes squint as he reads the scrawled handwriting. "The note is signed 'H.' Who do you think that could be?"

"Most of what I saw in Jason's mind was like a kaleidoscope view of his life, but one scene in particular stood out. Kind of like a replay during a football game, if that makes any sense."

Sterling pulls in close. "Tell me exactly what you saw."

I close my eyes and summon up the image. "Jason was at a party with Julianna and a bunch of other kids from their school. Everyone was drinking and having a good time."

"And?" His voice grows insistent. "What does that have to do with anything?"

"There was a man there with them, one of their teachers." I pause, considering my next words. "Jason gave me his name. Glenn Hartman."

Sterling's eyes slip closed. "Glenn Hartman is Julianna Wagner's music teacher. He was doing some voice tutoring for her a couple nights a week over the last few months. Bolger and I interviewed him a few days into the investigation."

My heart sinks into my stomach. "If what I saw was accurate, he was tutoring her in subjects other than voice."

"Interesting." Sterling rises from the table and reaches for his phone. I grab his arm and motion for him to sit back down.

"Hold on. Don't go off all half-cocked. I'm more than confident in my abilities and I know what I saw, but don't go arresting anyone with no more proof than a couple of psychic impressions from two brothers' minds."

"You don't understand, Ms. Tejedor. Glenn Hartman is already a person of interest. We've brought him in more than once despite the fact his record's pretty much spotless. Bolger had a feeling about him, but nothing we came up with would stick." Sterling strokes his chin, the corners of his mouth turned down in a thoughtful frown. "Regardless of the source, Mitch is going to like this news."

I meet Sterling's gaze with a sheepish grin. "Bolger doesn't like me very much, does he?"

His grimace of concentration curls into a smile. "Bolger doesn't like anybody very much."

He excuses himself and steps into the lobby to call his partner. Even from across the room, it's clear from Sterling's body language that Bolger is less than impressed with the source of the new information on the case. After a few minutes, Sterling strides back over and rests his phone on the center of the table.

"Bolger wants to talk to you. Is it all right if I put him on speaker?"

I shrug and motion to the phone. Sterling presses a button.

"…more stupid psychic shit. How in the hell am I supposed to—"

"Mitch," Sterling says, "You're on speaker. Ms. Tejedor is right here."

"Oh." Bolger goes quiet. Briefly. "So, Ms. Tejedor. You think we're after the wrong guy."

"I can't be certain of anything, Detective Bolger. I told your partner what I saw. No more. No less."

"And you expect me to walk down to the magistrate and get a warrant based on some psychic acid trip? Are you fucking crazy?"

"Watch your language, Mitch," Sterling says. "Remember, Mira's on our side."

First name basis. Interesting. Unfortunately, I'm not the only one who catches the slip.

"Oh, so now it's Mira. Well, fuck me. Let's pin a badge to her chest and give her a weapon and a patrol cruiser."

"Detective Bolger." I try to keep my voice even, though he's pushing one of my hottest buttons. "I understand it's a bit of a stretch to accept, but—"

"A bit of a stretch?" Bolger yells through the phone. "Watching soccer every time the fucking World Cup comes around so I know what the hell everybody is talking about is a bit of a stretch. Changing an investigation based on you playing "Psychic Picture Pages" with the Faircloth kid's retard brother, that's a fucking mile."

I keep the bile out of my voice. Barely. "You can ask Jason yourself if you like, Detective. It's his memory I'm citing, or at least his perception of what happened."

The line goes silent for all of a second. "You want us to bring the Faircloth boy in for questioning again? I got no problem with that. As I showed you, the last text sent to Miss Wagner came from his cell phone. I'm curious, though. What's your beef with Glenn Hartman?"

"I've never met the man." I glance at Sterling and shake my head, my lips turned up in a half grin. "Outside of Anthony Faircloth's head, that is."

Even through the phone line, the explosions going off in Bolger's head are almost audible. I imagine his gaunt cheeks turning as red as ripe pomegranate. Sterling does his best to maintain his grim facade, but the pleasant smell of fresh baked pound cake suggests he's enjoying this more than he's letting on.

"We'll make the call in the morning." Bolger's monotone says more than any angry outburst. "Feel free to let Mr. Faircloth know we'll be in touch."

"Glad to." I wink at Sterling. "Thanks."

"I'm not doing this for you, Ms. Tejedor," Bolger adds. "Trust me." The line goes dead.

Sterling slips his phone back into his jeans pocket. "Sorry about that. Mitch has been a little on edge lately. He and his wife separated a couple months back and the fifteen hour days working this case aren't helping the situation."

"You mean his personality isn't always quite so… 'sparkling'?"

Sterling shakes his head. "Bolger's a good man. Not much for thinking outside the box, but a good man."

"And what about you, Detective? What have you got waiting at home?" The momentary look of incredulity that passes his features has me wishing the words back into my mouth. "I'm sorry. I was just making—"

"It's all right, Mira." His face breaks into a smile. "Umm. Let's see. Half a pizza in the fridge and Season 2 of The Wire on DVD. You?"

"I'm ashamed to say I'm already on a first name basis with the staff at the Wendy's around the corner from the Blake. How many bowls of chili do you think a person can eat in one week?"

"Seriously?" Sterling laughs, a deep throaty sound. "All the places to eat in this town and you're giving Wendy's repeat business?"

I rub at my temple and smile. "I've been kind of busy."

"Do you like Indian?" he asks.

"I'd drink a tikka masala milkshake if they made such a thing."

"There's a little place on East that's pretty popular. Any interest in comparing notes on the case tomorrow night over some tandoori chicken?"

My cheeks grow warm. "Believe it or not, my social calendar is remarkably open."

"Swing by here and grab you after work?"

"Sure." I flash my best smile, even as my stomach ties itself in a knot. "Seven work for you?"

"Seven." He rises from the table. "See you then."

I fall back on my bed, the queasy feeling at my core intermingling with the warm ache of sheer exhaustion. I start the tub, getting the water to that perfect temperature just shy of scalding. Wandering to the mirror, I pull my top over my head and run my hands down my face.

"What have you got waiting at home, Detective Sterling?" Mira in the mirror asks me with a disapproving stare. "God, what an idiot."

I wait for the tub to get half full and slip out of my skirt and underclothes. Stepping into the water, an image of a lobster being dropped into a boiling pot flits across my mind's eye. I bite my lip and surrender myself to the bath's steaming embrace. The stress of the day melts away as the water rises inch by delicious inch. When it threatens to spill over onto the floor, I turn off the faucet with my foot and slide my shoulders down the side of the tub till my earlobes just touch the surface. My eyes grow heavy and a moment later, I jerk awake as my nose goes under. I snort the water from my nostrils and pull my head above the water.

"Not a good day to drown, Mira." I grab a towel from the rack above me, roll it into a tight pillow and put it behind my neck. "Just a few more minutes, then back to work."

My yoga instructor always ends class with deep breathing exercises, always a welcome finish to what on her more sadistic days are basically hour-long torture sessions. Her voice echoes through my mind as I close my eyes, inhale as deeply as I can, and allow the steamy air to work its wonders.

Breathe in.

An image of Sterling's even smile.

Breathe out.

Julianna's body, half unburied in Hartmann's field.

In.

Thomas Archer looking down on me as I come to from my latest venture into Anthony's mind.

Out.

A minute passes. Or is it an hour? A century? I struggle to open my eyes, but it's like they've been stapled shut. I fight to move and can't so much as wiggle a finger. My liquid cocoon goes lukewarm, then cold, then ice. I scream, and with a gasp, my eyes finally open.

The scene that greets my eyes is anything but a tiled bathroom at the Blake.

The room is dim, the walls covered with rich red wallpaper decorated with golden monkeys dancing madly hand in hand. A high-backed chair to my right is covered in burgundy velvet, its dark walnut feet carved into the paws of some great beast. To my left, a leather chaise stretches out in unabashed invitation. Multiple shelves of leather-bound volumes fill three of the walls, while the fourth opens onto a hallway lit by a flickering gaslight just visible from where I lay. I rise from the Persian rug dressed in the green sarong of Scheherazade the storyteller.

"Hello?" I take a step toward the hallway. "Is anyone here?"

Murmurs echo from beyond the doorway, an argument between two men. The first voice reverberates with rich bass while the second is a nasal whine that raises the hairs on my neck. Both are strangely familiar. Neither returns my shout as the argument rages on. With each step toward the door, the heated words become all the more distinct, as do the identities of the two men.

I step into the hallway and find myself standing between bizarre versions of Sterling and Bolger. Their faces unmistakable, their attire reminds me of something from an old black-and-white movie.

Bolger stands in a threadbare suit. A dark russet coat with holes at the elbows hangs off his skeletal frame. Orange pants stained with dirt and sweat cover his legs and his leather boots appear ready to fall apart.

Sterling, on the other hand, is dressed immaculately. A fine waistcoat rests across his broad shoulders, the fabric a fine silk dyed a deep purple so rich it appears black. His boots, unlike Bolger's, are flawless and polished to a high shine.

Each of them wears a Jewish yarmulke, driving home the reason I couldn't understand them before.

They were speaking, or more accurately, shouting in Yiddish.

Their argument forgotten for the moment, the two men turn toward me from opposite ends of the hallway and together in perfect English ask, "And who might you be?"

XVII

Samuel Goldenberg and Schmuÿle

Déjà vu. When you're a psychic, it's all but cliché.

For what already feels like the hundredth time, I offer the dreamscape versions of Sterling and Bolger my standard greeting. "I am the Lady Scheherazade. And you are?"

"A bit presumptuous, wouldn't you say, inquiring that of us?" Dream-Bolger raises an eyebrow at me. "After all, you are standing in our home."

"*Our* home, is it?" Dream-Sterling crosses his arms and scowls. "Brilliant." His gaze slips down to the half-drawn dagger at my side. "You may put away your weapon. You won't be needing it here."

"Do not let her divide us," Dream-Bolger whispers as he returns his gaze to me. "I know of you, Lady Scheherazade. Would you care to tell us what you're doing here, or should the two of us continue on to the drawing room and wait upon you to regale us with one of your lies?"

"Wait, Schmuÿle," Dream-Sterling says. "I know of this Scheherazade as well. From the others along the wooden way. The musician spoke highly of her."

"Modesto?" I ask. "You know Modesto?"

"A most ironic name, don't you think? I've never met a prouder man in my existence." His eyes shift in the direction of the man he calls Schmuÿle. "Present company excluded, of course."

Schmuÿle laughs. "As if you're the model of humility. Hang another piece of famous art on the wall and they're going to turn this place into a museum." He glances in the direction of the hall. "Which, considering what waits outside our door, is more than a bit ironic itself."

"So." A twinge of fear grips my heart, followed by cold certainty. "This *is* the Exhibition." I glance at Schmuÿle before turning my attention back on the spitting image of the man who in a very different place asked me to dinner an hour ago. "If he's Schmuÿle, then you must be—"

He leans forward in a formal bow. "Samuel Goldenberg, at your service."

"How predictable." Schmuÿle looks away. "As always, a pushover for a pretty set of eyes."

Goldenberg smiles wickedly. "I see you noticed them as well."

"I assure you, gentlemen, I am far more than just a pretty set of eyes."

Schmuÿle laughs again. "There's fire in this one, Samuel."

"Behave yourself, Schmuÿle." Goldenberg shows me back into the drawing room with the bizarre monkey wallpaper and the three walls lined with books. "Lady Scheherazade, please make yourself comfortable. Despite the intrusion, I would speak with you."

"Very well." I take a seat on the high-back chair, while Goldenberg and Schmuÿle sit on opposite ends of the couch across the ornately carved coffee table at the center of the room. "And what would you like to discuss?"

He thinks for a moment. "You may start with your presence in my home, though I am far more fascinated by your involvement in the Exhibition and your many rumored interactions with she who waits at the end of the hall."

"You mean Baba—"

Schmuÿle's finger shoots to his lips. "Do not speak her name here. This is one of the few pictures she has yet to enter, and if Samuel and I agree on anything, it is that we would like to keep it that way."

"Though your presence here threatens our long held peace with the witch," Goldenberg adds, "your boldness intrigues me. Tell me, Lady Scheherazade, how it is you came to be here?"

Careful, Mira. "I hail from a place far away and come here with a purpose. The boy from the French garden. He is a captive here in the Exhibition. I have come to free him, if I can."

"The boy?" Schmuÿle shoots a glance at Goldenberg. "He is walled up in the castle and if Modesto knows what's best, he's hidden him in the Catacombs below."

Goldenberg's hand goes to his forehead, his eyes drifting closed. "For such a self-proclaimed skeptic, you're certainly quite free with your tongue today."

"She's been there, Samuel. The Lady has seen the castle, walked its stony hallways. She all but took the boy there herself. It would be insulting to act as if she knew nothing."

Goldenberg fastens his gaze on me, his eyes piercing through to my very soul. "And what business of yours is it what happens to the boy?"

"His mother sent me. Isn't that enough?"

The two Jews share a knowing glance.

"What?" I rise from the chair. "What aren't you telling me?"

Schmuÿle is the first to break. "She may well have sent you for her son, but I question the necessity or even the wisdom of such salvation." His face turns up in a sarcastic smile. "Have you considered that perhaps the boy is safest exactly where he is?"

My own ire continues to rise. "Where I come from, Anthony cannot speak or move, make his own decisions, and can barely wipe his own nose. He is totally dependent on the goodwill of others. Would you wish to live that way?"

"And his previous existence?" Schmuÿle's glare now surpasses Goldenberg's. "Beset with bullies. Misunderstood by everyone. You want him to suffer that life again?"

Goldenberg raises a finger. "She does have a point my friend. All life is a gift, Schmuÿle, and not something to be wasted."

"A gift, you say?" Schmuÿle draws himself up straight, his eyes afire with passion. "Life is no gift. It's an odious, pointless job. A job that occupies your every breath until you take your last. A job that not a single one of us applies for, but rather is thrust upon each of us, quite literally, by two people who don't have the wherewithal to find something to do besides fornicate."

I recoil at the force of Schmuÿle's words. "You can't be serious."

He silences me with a glance. "You spend your first year at the teat of your tormentor, dependent on her for your every need from mouth to anus. Then, once you are old enough to fend for yourself, it's danger after danger as the universe conspires to end the pain of your existence. But do you acquiesce to the inevitable? Of course not. You charge ahead, stay healthy, learn your multiplication tables, study the scribbling of numbers and letters so you can spend your life writing checks to pay for this bucking stallion you never asked to ride."

"That's enough, Schmuÿle," Goldenberg says.

"Enough? I've barely started." He pulls a flask from inside his tattered coat and takes a drag before turning back to me. His high-pitched voice grates at my mind, shattering my concentration even as I strain to take in his every word. "Eventually, you leave behind the perpetrators of your existence and move out into the world. That's where the real cruelty begins. The entire universe pairs off, starting the cycle again, and either you perpetrate the same crime against some poor unattached soul, or all the world stares, wondering what's wrong with you that you are so alone."

In the decade and a half since I first came into my tenuous partnership with my particular set of gifts, I've usually found the ability to read the emotions of others a boon. Manifesting as aromas from my experience or the other person's, this true sixth sense has helped me navigate many an untenable situation. Here in Anthony's Exhibition, other than in the *Tuileries* garden where a lifetime of a troubled boy's emotions swarmed over me like a hive of angry ants, that ability hasn't even come into play, leaving me in many ways deaf to a symphony that in the real world fills my every waking minute.

As the tidal wave of Schmuÿle's pain, anger, and utter despondency threatens to drown me in vitriol, I pray for the deafness to return. The knowledge that the man I'm speaking with is merely another aspect of Anthony Faircloth breaks my heart even as the emotional onslaught pummels me with near physical force.

"You're a failure if you don't find someone to love." Schmuÿle's eyes flare with a cold gleam. "Someone who loves you back. People try to help, insisting you'll find love when you least expect it. When you stop looking. When the time is right. That there is someone out there for everyone. The truth? They don't have the first idea. Then, if you don't sign up to produce your own 2.2 kids to follow you in the same shit job, you're a double failure. And God forbid you get sick of the shitstorm of your life, realize you're in a losing situation, and try to leave the game early."

"Stop it." Racked with agony, I raise my hands before me in surrender. "Please…"

Schmuÿle drives on as if I haven't said a word. "Pull that and the world calls you depressed, bipolar, or psychotic and shoves pills down your throat. Remember, no matter what, you've got to be happy. Happy, happy, happy. Stay alive as long as you can. Be healthy. Exercise. Eat right. Find love. But for God's sake, no matter what, be happy." Schmuÿle hawks a wad of spit into the rich carpet at his feet. "Truth? I think most would rather just stay in the fucking ether than have to put up with this shit of an existence."

The psychic agony wafting off Schmuÿle doubles me over, ripping through me like I've swallowed a cup of tacks. Anthony's great potential has been evident from the start, but to affect me like this from so many miles away is beyond anything I've ever imagined. With power like this, his talent clearly outstrips mine, but it's more than that. More than any of my other visits to his mind, this particular encounter is more visceral and far more personal.

"Now, now, old friend." Goldenberg's silky baritone finally comes back into play. "Your life hasn't been all that bad and I would know. I've listened to your every complaint for years." He turns to me, his every word and emotion soothing the racking pain at my core. "Never shuts up, this one. The glass isn't just half empty with him. Those few swallows of wine have been stolen, and he wants them back."

"Will you never tire of that old jibe?" Schmuÿle leers at me from half-closed eyes.

"Birth and death, my friend. Can't stop either one. As for the in-between, that's up to each one of us every day of our lives."

"Rather gauche, making such a statement considering our current circumstances. Eternal optimism must seem so simple when the whole damn world follows your every notion."

Goldenberg shoots from his end of the rich leather couch and motions to the room around us. "You speak as if all this was handed to me. Like I haven't worked for every inch of this carpet, every stick of furniture, every piece of art. How dare you accept my hospitality for all these many years and then ridicule me as if it's not deserved, and in front of a guest, no less?"

Schmuÿle grins. "Just demonstrating there's anger in you as well, Samuel."

"I've worked and worked to get to this point, and now that I've finally arrived, you should be grateful I continue to tolerate the sour taste you bring to my life."

"Arrived? You've arrived?" Schmuÿle throws his head back and laughs. "No one ever arrives, not until the big arrival that awaits us all. Each and every person gets up each day and repeats the same list of humdrum tasks we did the day before. Brush the gunk from your teeth. Cleanse yourself so you don't offend others with your stink. Force hunks of the dead down your gullet so you may continue to live. You have achieved many things, my friend, but achievements are nothing but mountains along each person's road they either scale or find a way to skirt." He glares at me. "Tell me, Lady Scheherazade, in your experience, are the downhill runs ever worth the climb?"

I raise an eyebrow. "My mother always said for every climb, there's a summit."

Schmuÿle's mouth turns down in a spiteful grimace. "And I would argue for every summit, there's a climb. The view from the mountaintop is always too brief, and the climb longer and longer with each hill."

I gasp at the familiarity of Schmuÿle's answer. "But those were my words, from so long ago. I still remember the hurt in Mom's eyes. How could you possibly know that?"

In a flash, everything is clear. Why everything feels so different. Why Schmuÿle's words hurt me so. Why the characters in Anthony's mind sound more grown up and real than they ever have in the past.

Why he's imagining two people he's never met.

Anthony's mind may be the canvas, but it would seem at least in part, I'm supplying the paint here.

"Mr. Goldenberg, Mr. Schmuÿle. All this arguing. It's for my benefit, isn't it?"

The two of them share a knowing glance and begin to speak as one, the words flowing from one mouth to the other and back again as if they share a mind but only one can speak at a time.

"We are not the only ones in this room who split an identity." The vacillation between Goldenberg's deep baritone and Schmuÿle's squeaking tones jars on my ears. "Mira-Scheherazade, what do you know of chaos theory?"

I start at the mention of my true name. "Not much more than what Jeff Goldblum's character went around spouting in *Jurassic Park*."

"Oh, it's so much more than that," they say in unison, before returning to the back and forth singsong of their opposite tones. "One tenet states that even under otherwise identical conditions, merely changing the set of parameters by which a system is evaluated can drastically alter the outcome."

"All right." Nice to know there's some Anthony inside these two as well. "That makes sense, I suppose."

"A thorough understanding of this concept points to a simple truth."

"And that would be?"

"The closer you attempt to measure a thing, the more likely it is the simple act of measurement will change the result."

"I don't follow you." But I do. I just can't bear to hear it.

"Yes, you do." Goldenberg and Schmuÿle rise from the couch and stand on either side of me. "Do you truly believe you are here in this place? Talking to two strange men? Sitting on a velvet-seated chair in a nineteenth century drawing room?"

"No. I—"

"Where are you? Right now, where do you think you are?"

"In Anthony's mind, I suppose. Trying to—"

"Anthony's 'mind' is merely a hundred billion neurons, each fighting for supremacy, trapped inside three pounds of pink tofu. Do you really believe you reside there?"

"No."

"Then where are you, Mira?" they ask in unison. "Where are you right now?"

I cast my mind back. "In a tub. I'm resting in a tub in my hotel."

"Precisely. This place isn't real. You're not in Anthony's mind, but his mind influences yours just as yours does his."

"The closer you attempt to measure something…" The truth dawns on me.

"Not only has the measured been changed," they say, "but the measurer as well."

"The pair of you. You're not Anthony. You're… me."

"At least in part, Mira. Your thought before, about Anthony providing the canvas but not the paint, was more accurate than you know." As one, they fall back on the couch and in unison say, "It would seem you've visited the Exhibition so often you've become one of the exhibits."

XVIII

Entr'acte

My entire body convulses as I wake, my jerking limbs sending a good portion of the now tepid bathwater onto the tiled floor. After a few choice words I don't use around my mother, I clamber out of the tub, turn on the shower, and spend the next twenty minutes doing my level best to boil the skin from my bones. As the chill from the water leaves my body, another works its way up my back as the words of Goldenberg and Schmuÿle echo through my head.

"It would seem you've visited the Exhibition so often you've become one of the exhibits."

Dammit, they're right. More than anyone, I understand the risks of doing what I do. Still, who would dream the kid would be able to draw me into his crazy mindscape from halfway across the city? An unbidden image of a framed picture of Scheherazade hanging in Anthony's Exhibition fills my mind's eye.

I turn the water even hotter.

An hour later, I'm sprawled out on the bed in my favorite set of pajamas drowning my troubles in a pint of Rocky Road from room service. Staring through bleary eyes at the flat screen on the wall, I flip from station to station, skipping past Headline News and the rest of the 24-hour news channels as quickly as my thumb can punch the button.

One more missing persons story might just put me over the edge.

My thumb dances atop the send button of my phone. I have to talk to somebody about what's happened and I can't think of anyone else to call, though I dread the hint of condescension and even more, the "I told you so" in his tone. He warned me about the risks of proceeding with Anthony, and though we've made serious progress in the last few days, the events of this evening may prove him right.

I press the button. The phone rings six times before going to voicemail.

"Hello. This is Dr. Thomas Archer at Metrolina Counseling. If this is a medical emergency, please hang up and dial 9-1-1. If you have reached this number after hours, please hang up and call our answering service at 704-555-2112. Otherwise, leave a message and I will get back to you at my earliest convenience."

"Hello, Thomas…" As with every other trip through the Exhibition, my voice comes out like sandpaper over wool. "I mean, Dr. Archer. It's Mira. Something's happened and I need to talk to someone. Well, not someone. I need to talk to you. Call me when you have a chance."

I press the end button before I say anything more stupid than I already have.

How does Thomas do it? Day in, day out. Nothing but listening to one person's problems after another. Last thing he needs in the middle of the night is a message from me all freaked out.

A little late for that.

I rest the phone on the nightstand and go to the window. Sliding it open as wide as it will go, I breathe in a lungful of cool evening air and crane my neck to get a view of my favorite building from the Charlotte skyline. Like something out of a different century, the gothic skyscraper looms like a glass-covered casket jutting out of the center of the city. Lit up for the evening, its upper stories alternate between reflected radiance and fleeting shadow.

The shrill tone of my phone plays across my frayed nerves like a rough bow across an out-of-tune violin. I grab the phone and put it to my ear.

"Hello?" My voice cracks, half from my recent sojourn and half with relief at the name displayed on phone's screen.

"Mira?" Archer manages to keep that characteristic calm in his voice, though there's an undercurrent of fear there I haven't heard before.

"What's wrong? You sound terrible."

"I'm fine." The sharpness of my tone surprises even me. Why I suddenly care that I sound "terrible" eludes me, but it doesn't change the simple fact. With as even a tone as I can manage, I add, "Thanks for calling back so fast. I hope I'm not… interrupting anything."

"No, nothing like that. I was just heading for bed. It's been a long day. Didn't quite make it to the phone in time."

"Sorry to bother you so late, but I'm kind of freaked. Do you have a minute?"

"Sure." He does his best to suppress a yawn. "What's going on?"

"I don't know. Something's happened. Something strange."

A barely concealed chuckle comes through the receiver. "Coming from you, that means something." Before I can beg him not to laugh, he slides into his therapist persona as if putting on a well-worn pair of jeans. "Go ahead, Mira. Tell me what happened."

Archer listens for twenty minutes as I relate the events of the evening. To his credit, he doesn't interrupt me once, though a part of me wonders if this is out of courtesy, because I sound like a complete mental case, or worst of all, that Archer has dozed off.

"Hello? Dr. Archer?"

"I'm right here, Mira."

"Tell me. Am I going crazy?" Not a rhetorical question.

"I don't think so, but I do have a question."

"Hit me."

He pauses, taking in a deep breath. "How can you be sure what happened was a trip to the Exhibition? You've never seen these two men on any other trip through Anthony's mind. Is it possible you were just having a vivid dream?"

My face grows warm, flushing with angry heat. "This was no dream."

"Sorry," he says. "I'm trying to help, but this whole thing is a bit out of my league."

"No." I pull myself up straight on the bed. "I'm the one who should apologize. I didn't mean to snap. I just feel so violated. And the worst part? It's all my fault."

"No, Mira. None of this is your fault. We're all of us traveling without a map on this one." He waits for a moment before continuing.

"Assuming this was some sort of 'long distance call' from Anthony, how did he do it? What does it mean?"

"There's more. Goldenberg and Schmuÿle. I don't think they're aspects of Anthony, at least not completely. Anthony has never met either of the detectives working the Julianna Wagner case." I swallow, a part of me afraid to admit the next part out loud. "I believe Goldenberg and Schmuÿle are pieces of *me*, each dancing on the stage in Anthony's mind."

"But you're already represented there, right? You're Scheherazade, the storyteller."

"From what I've seen, you can be in the Exhibition more than once, even simultaneously. I mean, look at all the different aspects of Anthony I've encountered. Tunny and Modesto argue constantly. How is that any different from me as Scheherazade arguing with the two detectives in yarmulkes?"

"But why would you manifest as the two officers investigating the Wagner case?" Archer's tone, not to mention the accompanying aroma of fermenting apples, reeks of jealousy. "You've only met them a couple of times."

"Have you heard the piece?" The melody from the CD Caroline lent me echoes in my mind. "Like two voices arguing, the woodwinds and trumpet grow closer and closer until they merge into one melody. Sterling and Bolger may bicker like an old married couple, but in the end, they're partners with a common purpose." I rub at my brow as pain flares to life behind my left eye. Am I picking up on Archer's migraine? "Anthony casts the various characters in his mind from people in his life and matches them as best he can to the music. Maybe I've become so much a part of his Exhibition that he now draws from my life as well."

"And that's the part I don't understand. If you're just a tourist in his mind, how is it you've become a part of his bizarre art gallery? Shouldn't those characters have already been present when you arrived?" Before I can answer, he adds, "Unless…"

"Unless what?"

"We've always gone with the assumption the Exhibition is a self-imposed prison Anthony created for himself to avoid dealing with whatever trauma started this whole cascade of events."

"Right. You're thinking something different?"

"Do you remember what you told us? As you first entered Anthony's mind last Friday?"

My first day in Charlotte. Anthony's head in my lap, his tousled hair, his crooked glasses. The run of notes I now know as "Promenade" pounding at me like fists. My mind drowning in the prismatic tidal wave of color.

In a flash, it comes to me. "I told you Anthony was stuck."

"Think about it, Mira. What if before you came along, he simply recycled those thirteen notes, over and over into infinity? What if before Scheherazade, there was no Tunny or Modesto, no Baba Yaga…"

"No Exhibition." This latest epiphany takes my breath. "The Exhibition isn't a prison at all. It's the only way Anthony has of talking to me. To us."

"And perhaps the reason you've been cast as Scheherazade, the storyteller, isn't so much to tell stories to the characters there…"

"But to relate Anthony's stories to the outside world. To Caroline." I fall back on the bed, my chest tight with the responsibility of it all. "Without me, there's no point to the Exhibition." A revelation washes over me. "I have to go back."

"I'm not sure if Caroline will allow it. She called me this afternoon. She was pretty upset after your little… encounter with Jason."

My cheeks grow even warmer. "You know about that?"

"Caroline feels badly about how she behaved, but she's made up her mind, and a part of me can't blame her. One child near comatose and another sick, at least indirectly, from your involvement. She can't risk anymore pain right now."

"But she's the one that called me here in the first place. I still want to help." I suck in a lungful of air. "I'm the only one that can."

Archer's sigh comes across the line loud and clear. "As much as it pains me to admit it, you're right, and Caroline knows that. Still, it doesn't change anything."

"What do I do, then?"

"Give her some time. She'll come around. I'd be lying if I told you I haven't been in the exact same spot with Caroline in the past." He pauses. "You know, if you're free, we could get together tomorrow after work and try to come up with a way to get you back in her good graces. Maybe grab a cup of coffee near your hotel?"

"Sounds good. Maybe around—"

Wait. I'm an idiot. Tomorrow night. Sterling.

"Mira?"

"Sorry. I can't make it tomorrow evening. I already have plans."

"Friends in Charlotte?" The hopeful inflection in his voice says it all.

"Not exactly." My heart sinks. How old do we have to be to finally outgrow all this crap?

"Oh. In that case, I may be able to squeeze you in tomorrow afternoon." The energy drained from his voice, he's back to the man who spewed Freud and cynicism at me at our first meeting. "Can you be at the clinic around two?"

"Two o'clock." I try not to stutter. "I'll be there."

My phone beeps twice as he disconnects. The silence that follows draws the knot in my already pretzeled intestines even tighter. I didn't come to Charlotte to hurt anybody, and yet in the space of eight hours I've managed to alienate myself from almost everyone I know in this town.

At least tomorrow can't be any worse.

XIX

Breaks

Today is worse.

Last night, I set my phone to wake me around seven in case Sterling called to discuss any developments with the Glenn Hartman lead. His call beat the alarm by almost an hour.

The clock on my dashboard reads a quarter to seven as I pull up to the Faircloth home. The suburban ranch surrounded in police cars, half a dozen sets of flashing blue lights blind me from every direction. A dozen or so officers are standing around, not to mention half the neighborhood, many still in bathrobes and slippers. From my parking place along the curb a few houses down, a flurry of activity around one of the patrol cars catches my eye. I step out of my car and head for the Faircloth house, making a point to walk past the cruiser in question. Despite the dim morning light, a glance through the windshield reveals a lone man seated in the back. Much like the déjà vu I experienced in Veronica Sayles' classroom, my scalp tingles as I find familiar a face I've never seen with my own eyes.

Glenn Hartman, his right eye set off by a large purple bruise, glares at me, though I doubt he has the slightest idea who I am.

Just past the police cruiser, I catch a glimpse of Detective Bolger in the early morning light, his emaciated form casting a thin shadow as the sun crests the horizon to the east. Next to him, Sterling takes a sip from a travel coffee cup. A whiff of dark roast flirts with my taste buds though better than thirty yards separates us. He looks up and catches my eye. The warmth of his smile hits me a second before the corners of his mouth turn up. The moment is perfect until Bolger registers my presence as well. The stink of freshly shoveled manure overpowers the pleasant coffee aroma in less time than it takes to blink.

Sterling finishes his conversation with the patrolman and heads over to join me.

"Thanks for coming out at this hour, Mira." He motions to the car where they're holding Glenn Hartman. "I know it's early, but I figured you'd want to be here for this."

"Hartman came here?" I glance over at the patrol car. "What the hell was he thinking?"

"Wait. You recognized him?"

"Either that, or I'm a pretty good guesser."

"You're saying he's the man you saw in Anthony's mind?"

"Jason's too. I know it sounds crazy, but that's Hartmann the Cart Man, live and in color out in the real world. Minus the upside down chalet and field of dead girls, of course." A chill courses through my body. "The way he looked at me. So angry."

"You've got nothing to worry about. We've got more than enough cause to keep him in custody for the foreseeable future."

"What happened?"

Sterling shrugs. "He showed up on the Faircloths' front porch around six and refused to leave until he got to speak with Jason. It's not exactly clear what he wanted to talk about, but as you can probably guess with the Faircloth kid involved, there was a fight."

"Oh no. Is Jason in more trouble?"

"Not this time. Hartman entered their home uninvited and as far as we're concerned, Jason was well within his rights to defend himself. Hartman, on the other hand, is under arrest for trespassing and assault. With all the previous circumstantial evidence, we'll have no trouble keeping him under wraps for a few days. We're hoping if we turn up the heat a bit, he may get careless and let something slip about the real question at hand." He pulls in close. "Between you and me, any help you can lend in that arena would be most appreciated."

Ice water fills my veins. "And what do you mean by that?"

"You know exactly what I mean." He inclines his head toward the squad car. "Take a look inside Hartman's mind. See what's swimming around inside that bruised head of his. Find out what we need to know to put him away." His voice drops to a whisper. "Like where he hid the body."

"Sorry, but it doesn't work like that." I try to keep the exasperation from my face. "Most of the time, what I get is impressions, scents, hints of emotion. Occasionally, I get images from the past, but those may or may not be mixed with dreams, fantasy, or even lies."

Sterling's eyes glaze over. "I don't know, Mira. You were confident enough in what you picked up from your trips into the Faircloth boys' heads to notify the police. Hell, you're out here before sunrise following up on one of your hunches. A hunch, I might add, that was right."

As one, we glance over at the patrol car. Hartman glares through the window at us with his one good eye.

"Anthony is a special case. I've never tried anything like what I'm doing with him before, and truth be told, I hope I never have to again." I rub at my brow. "You have no idea what it's like to have such an intimate connection with someone."

"Intimate?" Sterling's brow furrows.

"To be inside someone's mind, to see their innermost thoughts, to meet parts of their soul that have never seen the light of day." My eyes slide closed. Even now, miles away, Anthony's thoughts tiptoe around the periphery of my consciousness like a skittering mouse in an empty room. "You can't imagine what it's like."

Sterling waits for me to open my eyes before letting out a measured breath. "You didn't have any problem peeking inside the Faircloth kid's brain yesterday."

"And you see how that turned out." I shiver, the chill running through me having little to do with the early morning hour. "Jason begged me to help him, and even then, I'm not certain it was the right thing to do. Mucking with people's minds without their express consent, however, is unethical and wrong." My headache from the night before makes a brief return to the stage for an encore performance. "Not to mention, if you have to fight your way in, the effort leaves you with the queen of all migraines."

Sterling's eyes brighten. "So, you *have* done something like this before."

"Drop it." My arms instinctively cross as the part of me looking forward to dinner with the good-looking detective dies a quick yet painful death.

"Okay. Sorry." Sterling's thoughts drop into full backpedal. "Not trying to push."

"Actually, you're pushing pretty hard." Unable to look Sterling in the eye any longer, my gaze drops to the asphalt at my feet. "I know you're desperate to bust this guy and could really use some help, but it's not a won't. It's a can't. "

"In that case, Detective Bolger and I have a lot of work to do." He turns to leave, but shoots a quick glance back at me before walking away. "I guess tonight is off, then?"

And there it is. Dammit. "We've both got our work cut out for us. You've got your man and I've got some things to straighten out with Caroline before I can continue my work with Anthony."

"Got it." He swallows, his thoughts a whirlwind as he searches for something to say. "Thank you for your help, Ms. Tejedor."

His words leave me cold.

Sterling heads back over to the congregation of cops after allowing me past the police tape. Already sick to my stomach, I stand at the Faircloths' front door for the better part of five minutes before I get up the nerve to knock. Another minute passes before the lock turns. The door cracks and Caroline peers out, her bloodshot eyes too tired to mount the derisive glare from yesterday.

"Mira?" She rubs at her neck and tries to suppress a yawn. "What are you doing here?"

"The cops called and I came. Detective Sterling filled me in on what happened, or at least the basics."

"Can you believe this?" she asks. "I don't know how much more I'm supposed to take."

My forehead breaks out in a cold sweat as the potent mix of rage and fear wafting off Caroline hits me like a wave of jalapeño.

"May I come in?"

"Of course." She undoes the chain, pulls the door open wide, and beckons me inside. "I just put on a pot of coffee."

The rich aroma of the brewing dark roast fills the room and tickles my nose, much as it tickled my mind minutes before. Caroline and I stand there in silence, neither knowing where to begin. No matter how much her words from yesterday still sting, nothing has changed for me. I'm all in. Caroline, on the other hand, is more than a bit conflicted. Her emotions reach out for me even as an undercurrent of fear and anger screams that part of her still wants to turn me away.

"How is everyone holding up?" I finally ask.

"How do you expect? Rachel's up in her room trembling and Jason punched a hole in the drywall before taking off to God knows where." A sarcastic chuckle passes her lips. "Is it pathetic a part of me is glad Anthony's too oblivious to know what's going on?"

A coffee maker sputters through the open doorway. Caroline leads me into the kitchen and pulls an old Ziggy mug from the cabinet. The rich aroma makes my mouth water.

"Sugar's in the bowl and there's some hazelnut creamer in the fridge."

We sit at the kitchen bar for a couple minutes before Caroline speaks again.

"Look, Mira. I owe you an apology for yesterday. The stress has been more than I can handle. The thing is, at the end of the day, it's just me. Rachel's too young to understand, Jason's so wrapped up in the whole thing he can barely help himself, and Anthony…"

I take Caroline's hand. "I get it. My little one just turned six, a couple years younger than Rachel. I don't know what I'd do if I had to deal with a quarter of the stuff you've had on your plate."

"I haven't slept well in weeks," Caroline says. "Dealing with Anthony's turn would have been enough, but this mess with Jason and Julianna's disappearance. It's just too much."

"And I'm sure the episode with Rachel yesterday didn't help a bit."

Caroline nods. "I was finally nodding off an hour or so before sunrise this morning when I heard someone trying to beat down the front door."

"Sterling told me."

"Did he tell you who it was?" Caroline asks. "You won't believe it."

My toes curl inside my shoes. "Try me."

"It was one of the teachers from Jason's school. He was talking out of his head, demanding to see Jason, like he was on drugs or something."

"Do you know why?"

"Oh, yes." Caroline's voice grows quiet. "Though I still can't believe it."

"Well? What was it? Why was he here?"

She glances at the front door. "Are you working with them?"

"The cops?" A bitter laugh escapes my lips before I can stop it. "Not as of ten minutes ago."

"Then I need to show you something." She goes to a drawer across the room and pulls out a manila envelope. "Mr. Hartman brought this."

I unwind the red twine holding the envelope closed and pull out a collection of 8 X 10 photographs, the subject of each picture a blue Honda parked behind a dumpster. The focus is a little off, but there's no doubt about the identities of the car's occupants. Reclining in the driver's seat, Glenn Hartman appears more than content. Next to him, not quite in the passenger seat and more visible in some of the photos than others, Julianna Wagner is clearly occupied.

As I flip through the photographs, the air fills with the odor of fermenting apples. The scent of jealousy, roiling off a stack of 8 X 10 glossies. Unmistakable.

An index card fastened to the bottom of the last photo contains a scrawled message.

I know.
J.F.

"My God." I rest the photograph on the table. "Did Jason take these pictures?"

"I don't know." Caroline rests her cup of coffee on the table and rubs at her eyes. "I don't know anything anymore. All I can tell you is Jason became very upset when he saw these. That's when the fight broke out. Don't tell anyone, but I'm a little proud of the shiner my son left under Hartman's eye." A wicked smile spreads across her face. "The Faircloth left hook is one thing he gets honest from his father."

"You didn't give these pictures to the police?"

Caroline's eyes grow cold. "My son has already been brought in for questioning twice over the last three weeks. You don't seriously think I'm going to hand the police photos that suddenly give him motive, do you?"

"You're obstructing justice, Caroline."

"I know. I just didn't know what else to do."

"Call Sterling. Tell him what happened. He'll understand." I pray my advice doesn't get Caroline thrown in jail, or Jason for that matter, but holding on to those photos is like sitting on a burning powder keg. It's not a question of if it's going to blow. It's a matter of when.

"Thanks, Mira." She raises an eyebrow. "Can I ask you something that's been on my mind all morning?"

"Hit me."

"Do you think any of what's happened this morning has to do with what Jason asked you to do yesterday?"

I bite my lip. "Actually, I think it has everything to do with it. Do you remember the session with Anthony where I met Hartmann the Cart Man?"

Her face blanches. "The visit where you saw Julianna's body plowed out of the field?" Her gaze darts to the door and then back to mine. "It was him, wasn't it? Mr. Hartman, or some psychotic version of him, living in Anthony's mind. Like Jason, Rachel, and the others."

"It's more than that, Caroline. One of the reflections I picked up from Jason's mind yesterday was a memory of a party. Jason was there, as were Julianna and Mr. Hartman, who I understand is her teacher as well as her music tutor. He and Julianna seemed… close." I gesture to the photo of the two of them in what I'm guessing is Hartman's car. "Looks like my suspicions yesterday weren't too far off the mark."

"You exonerated my son, even after I kicked you out of the house." Caroline's cheeks go crimson. "I'm so sorry."

"No apologies. It's all water under the bridge and we still have Anthony to take care of."

Caroline brightens. "You'd still work with Anthony after all the things I said?"

"It would seem I don't have any choice in the matter."

"What do you mean?"

I relate my experience from the night before, at least the parts I can remember. I make a point to leave out my suspicion as to the true origins of *Samuel Goldenberg and Schmuÿle.*

"You think Anthony touched your mind from all the way out here in the suburbs?"

"Not intentionally, but yes." I glance down at my watch and yawn as the adrenaline of the morning begins to fade. "For better or worse, it seems my multiple visits to the Exhibition have linked us somehow." I squeeze Caroline's hand. "I may need his help now as much as he needs mine."

Caroline's incredulous expression fades into a disheartened scowl. "If that's the case, God help us all."

I spend most of the morning with Caroline, taking a few minutes early in the day to arrange a meeting with Veronica for lunch. Now that Caroline has invited me to work with Anthony again, I need every advantage in figuring out the younger of the Faircloth boys. Other than Anthony's family and Dr. Archer, she's the only person I've met who has the first insight into what he was like before the Big Event.

My desperation for answers goes well beyond my wish to see Anthony back among the land of the living. This Pandora's box I've opened will never shut again until Anthony is whole. Even if I left Charlotte and never looked back—and that thought has crossed my mind more than once—the Exhibition would follow me. Tunny's appearance in my car. Goldenberg and Schmuÿle coming for me from all the way across town. Isabella's screams as I fall seizing in our home in Georgetown a week from now, my mind fighting an invisible battle with an imagined witch who lives only inside the mind of a comatose little boy.

I have to finish this. I have no other choice.

I pull into Anthony's school and sprint for the sheltered walkway to get out of the light mist falling from the slate-gray sky. Veronica waits for me on a bench in the designated smoking area.

"Nasty habit, I know." She takes one last drag off her cigarette and flicks the butt in the trash. "Trying to quit, but on days like today, the nicotine is all that gets me through."

"No judgment here. I had to give them up when I found out I was pregnant with my little girl. Not sure how I've managed to stay quit. Six years plus, though, and I still wake up some days wanting a smoke with my morning coffee."

Veronica shakes her head. "I had pretty much given them up till this past summer."

"What happened?"

"Oh, I was seeing this guy. You know how it goes." Her eyes roll almost imperceptibly. "Things didn't end so well, and I ended up falling back in with my old boyfriend, Mr. Marlboro." She smiles and offers a subtle shrug. "Once something's got its hooks in you, right?"

"I get that." My mind flashes on an image of Anthony Faircloth, so innocent and helpless, and yet all the while his Exhibition grows in both our minds like some kind of psychic cancer.

"Shall we?" I rise from the bench and motion in the direction of my car. "Maybe we can beat the lunch crowd if we leave now."

As we head for the parking lot, a strange heat breaks on my neck as if I were an antelope being stalked on an open plain. A glance back at the school's front entrance reveals the janitor I met on my last stop at the school standing atop a ladder. He's working on one of the gutters and though he appears to be paying me no mind, at least one of his eyes seems to follow me all the way to the parking lot.

Mental note, Mira. Pay closer attention to your surroundings in the future.

We reach the car and I pop the locks with my keychain fob. Veronica drops into the passenger seat.

"Thoughts on lunch?" I ask.

"Don't know what you're in the mood for, but there's a diner just down the road that serves a mean BLT."

Veronica and I exchange pleasantries over a checkered tablecloth and wait for our food to arrive. The chlorine scent I picked up from her the last time we met has developed a pungent edge.

"Is everything okay?" I ask.

"Is it that obvious?" She takes a sip of tea, leaving a crimson crescent on the rim of her glass. "It's been quite a morning."

A quiet chuckle escapes my lips. "You have no idea."

"No, seriously. Before classes today, the principal called us all into the teacher's lounge for an emergency meeting to let us know one of our teachers was arrested this morning."

I work to keep any expression from my face.

"It's Glenn Hartman, one of our music faculty. Well liked by the other teachers. Popular with the students. Hell, he won Teacher of the Year two years back."

"Did your principal say what happened?"

"Not outright, but there were whispers after the meeting it has something to do with the Julianna Wagner case." Her gaze grows quizzical. "You knew, didn't you?"

"Between you and me?"

"Of course."

"I was called to the Faircloth house early this morning. Glenn Hartman and Anthony's older brother apparently had a bit of a disagreement. Sounds like it wasn't pretty."

"Oh no." She says. "Is Jason okay?"

"How do you know Jason?"

"He used to come by the classroom every afternoon and pick up his brother. Anthony doesn't do well on buses, as you can probably imagine." She puts down her glass. "How is Anthony, by the way?"

"I've been working with him for just under a week." My fingers find my fork and nervously tap at the blade of my knife. The rhythm, strangely, follows the "Tuileries" melody. "I thought I was helping him. Turns out, he may be worse off now than when I got here."

"What do you mean?"

Veronica barely says a word as I spend the next twenty minutes trying to explain my experiences with Anthony and his bizarre Exhibition. I leave out some of the more intimate details, though I do opt to tell her about her doppelganger in the *Tuileries* garden. She takes it all in stride, though her eyes flick toward the door more than once during our conversation.

"You're serious?" she asks when I'm finished.

"Deadly serious."

"This isn't some kind of gag. You're a psychic. An honest-to-god psychic."

"Since I was eleven."

She glances down at the table and then locks gazes with me. "Do you know what I'm thinking right now?"

"It doesn't work like that, at least not most of the time. Impressions. Feelings. Emotions. Those are my stock in trade. Visual images or any sort of concrete answers are normally the exception, not the rule. This thing with Anthony is different, and so far in my life, unique."

And if I make it through this, it damn well better stay that way.

Veronica takes the last sip of her tea and leans across the table. "What can I do to help?"

"I was hoping you could join us tomorrow. Anthony wrote that story for you. It's clear he's not afraid of letting you in. I'm hoping if we maximize the positive energy in the room, we can finally break through and free him from this cage he's created in his mind."

"And you really think I can help?"

"Can't hurt having you there." I finish my sandwich and gulp down my last couple swallows of tea. "I'll talk with Caroline and make sure she's fine with you coming."

"Count me in, then." Her lips pull back in a cautious smile. "Whatever it takes."

XX

The Marketplace at Limoges

Archer's one o'clock slinks past me on her way out of the office. Well into her third trimester, the girl is maybe fourteen and reeks of abandonment and loneliness. The twin aromas of mold and rotting leaves threaten to turn my stomach until she is well out of sight. I'm not certain why it should seem so strange, but a part of me balks at the notion Archer has patients other than Anthony. Not when Anthony's own need is so great.

A moment later, Archer appears at the front desk and whispers in Agnes' ear. He's had a haircut since the last time I saw him and the two-day-old stubble he's sporting works for him.

The mood in the room shifts. The client and mother sitting across from me smile for the first time since my arrival thirty minutes ago. Nothing but fear and anxiety for half an hour, but just a glimpse of Dr. Thomas Archer and the room fills with calm, even confidence. Regardless of his opinions about things they don't teach you in grad school, Archer is good at what he does.

As he finishes talking with Agnes at reception, he glances out across the waiting room and our eyes meet. He catches himself mid-smile and instead shoots me a curt nod before disappearing back into the office. A moment later, Agnes calls back the two o'clock patient and her mother. Once they've passed out of sight, she motions me up to the desk.

"Good afternoon, Ms. Tejedor. Dr. Archer asked me to let you know he had a last minute add on. If you can wait another hour, he should be free at three."

Like I have anywhere else to be. "Three o'clock will be fine. I'll just wait out here."

Agnes appears grateful when the phone rings a second later and somehow manages to stretch out the call and avoid my gaze till I return to my seat. More times than not, people experience some level of disquiet around me when they know who and what I am, but even after all these years, it still stings when someone is scared of me simply because of what I can do.

On the other hand, I did come to her office, wander the mind of one her clients, and fall out in a grand mal seizure right in front of her. Two hundred years ago, they'd already be building a bonfire at the center of town. Perhaps I should count my blessings.

I spend the next hour perusing the stack of magazines arranged on the table. An issue of *Men's Health* with the latest Bond actor posing shirtless, a recent issue of *Us Weekly* with some reality show bimbo explaining how she's not still hung up on her ex, some other rag plugging the fall movie lineup. Just when my brains feel poised to leak out my ears, the girl and her mother emerge, schedule a follow-up appointment, and leave. Soon after, Archer appears and waves me back. I follow him to his office and take a seat in the armchair by the bookcase. He sits opposite me, his plateau of dark cherry between us, and retrieves a pair of bottled waters from the mini-fridge in the corner.

"Thirsty?"

"Sure." I unscrew the cap and take a sip. "Glad you could squeeze me in today."

"Sorry you had to wait, but we had a last minute add-on who needed to be seen today." The mix of pepper and vinegar wafting off him betrays his placid expression. "I hope keeping you here another hour hasn't messed up your evening plans."

"Nothing to worry about there, apparently." I punctuate my comment with a quiet sigh, and immediately regret it.

"Oh." Archer's face doesn't move a muscle, though the peppery smell shifts a bit more toward the floral end of the spectrum. "Sorry to hear that."

"On the other hand, I got a chance to clear the air with Caroline. Things with us look like they're going to be all right."

He chuckles. "Glad you took my advice on giving her some space."

I coil like a snake. "It wasn't exactly my choice. The police called me to the Faircloth house a little after six this morning."

Archer coughs with surprise. "The police? What happened?"

I catch Archer up on the events of the day, detailing everything I can remember about my near encounter with Glenn Hartman and carefully avoiding any further reference to my falling out with Sterling.

"Sounds like the police have their man," Archer says. "Once Jason's name has been cleared, Caroline can focus on Anthony again. Maybe we can finally make some headway with him, if you'll pardon the pun."

"You're worse than my ex."

Archer cracks a smile and I answer in kind.

"Last I heard, though, Jason hadn't come home or even checked in since taking off this morning. Caroline has no idea where he could be."

Archer raises an eyebrow. "That's odd. You'd think he'd be ecstatic about being cleared."

I let out a bitter chuckle. "I don't think Jason does ecstatic."

My phone rings. It's Caroline's home number.

"Hello?"

"Mira?" It's Caroline. She sounds terrified.

"I'm here." I do my best to keep an even tone. "What is it?"

"I… I need you. Can you come over?"

"What's happened? Is it Jason?"

"No. He hasn't come home yet."

I shoot a worried glance at Archer. "What is it, then?"

"It's Anthony. He's… humming."

"Humming? Another song from the Mussorgsky piece?"

"Not exactly. Listen to this."

A static squelch fills my ear as Caroline holds the receiver up to Anthony. At first I can't hear anything, but as the line grows quiet, I can just make out the boy's squeaking voice. The tune he's humming is indeed familiar, though it's not Mussorgsky but Rimsky-Korsakov.

A melody I know all too well.

Scheherazade's theme.

The sound of Anthony attempting to duplicate the high-pitched whine of a violin sets my nerves on end. Over and over again he repeats the few bars that depict the wife of Sultan Shahriyar begging for her life. With each repetition, my heartbeat grows faster.

"There's no doubt about it. He's calling for you." Archer leans over Anthony and raises one of his closed eyelids. "But in this state, I'm not even sure he knows you're here."

"Oh, he knows." I draw closer a few inches and the volume of Anthony's caterwauling rises. "He always knows."

"He's been doing this for hours." Caroline paces the room. "It was so quiet when he started, I couldn't make it out."

I wince as Anthony hits the high note for the hundredth time since Archer and I arrived at the house. "It's not quiet anymore."

"What do you think he wants?" Archer asks.

"Isn't it obvious?" I wipe a bead of cool sweat from my brow. "He wants me back in there. Back in his Exhibition."

"Out of the question," Archer says. "This 'controlled' experiment of yours has gone off the rails. In case you've forgotten, he's already proven he can find you all the way across town."

"And if I don't return willingly, what makes you think he won't come find me again?"

"She's right, Thomas. She has to go back, and this time I'm pretty sure I know what she should expect." Caroline rests a hand on her son's forehead and looks me dead in the eye. "Unless I miss my guess, your next stop is a marketplace."

Archer and I turn to Caroline and together ask, "What?"

"Anthony is taking you through *Pictures at an Exhibition*, movement by movement as best I can tell. Don't ever forget, I've heard the thing a thousand times. You just met 'Samuel Goldenberg and Schmuÿle' so 'The Marketplace at Limoges' is next."

"And what do you think Anthony has waiting for me there?" I turn to Archer. The determination on his face would be almost cute under any other set of circumstances. "It's a French Market. You want me to bring you back a baguette and some Brie?"

Archer doesn't appear amused. "Have you considered it might be a trap?"

"A trap?" Caroline asks.

"Anthony's 'Art Gallery of the Damned' reaches all the way across town to get Mira's attention last night and now the boy is literally singing her song. Mira may have friends inside your boy's head—"

"But I have enemies as well." My eyes slide closed. "You're right, Dr. Archer. For all we know, it's the witch calling out to me, luring me back so she can get rid of me once and for all."

"That's my boy you're talking about." Caroline turns to me. "He needs you, Mira. Can't you hear him?"

Of course I can. The fact that the neighbors haven't called to complain about the screeching is a miracle.

"You're certain you want me to do this? After everything with Jason?"

"Forget what I said. I was upset. Wasn't thinking straight." Caroline buries her face in her hands. "Help my boy, Mira. Please. You're the only one who can."

I shoot Archer a glance. "Any other ideas?"

"You already know my thoughts on the matter." Archer rubs at his eye and sighs. "But it's your neck on the line. Do what you have to do."

I brush the hair away from Anthony's face. "Like I have a choice."

Two melodies compete for supremacy as I descend through the prismatic torrent of Anthony's thoughts. Mussorgsky's "Promenade" on thundering piano clashes against the high-pitched vibrato of the violin playing Scheherazade's theme, the divergent melodies threatening to deafen me or drive me insane.

"I'm here, Anthony," I shout. "You can cut the soundtrack." The ear-splitting music continues to pound at me like invisible fists, as if the invisible orchestra is mocking me. "I know you can hear me. Now cut it out, or I'll turn around and you can play in here by yourself."

The music stops immediately and the sensation of falling ceases. As with each trip before, the maelstrom of color around me fades into the all too familiar gallery of Anthony's vision of Mussorgsky's Exhibition. Though the herringbone pattern in the wood at my feet remains the same as always, the fresco across the ceiling appears, as always, quite different. No mythological characters this time, no comic book heroes, no horrifying images of crimes against humanity. This time the picture is very simple.

Me, in Scheherazade garb, sprinting down the hall toward one of the open alcoves.

Anthony may not be the subtlest of creatures, but this screams of desperation.

In an attempt to prepare for this particular sojourn through Anthony's mind, Archer and I did some research. An online encyclopedia revealed a couple of interesting facts. The original picture by Hartmann that inspired "The Marketplace at Limoges" was also known as either "The Great News" or "French women quarreling violently in the market." What that means for me remains to be seen. A more surprising discovery was learning the sister city of Limoges is, of all places, Charlotte, North Carolina.

Mom always taught me coincidences are just the signposts of fate, a lesson made evident as the frescoed ceiling above my head shifts again. Freed from the Exhibition, the sprinting Scheherazade there now runs toward a nightmare version of the Charlotte skyline.

A shiver travels up my spine. Even as I walk through Anthony's mind, some small part of him is clearly walking through mine as well.

I creep down the open hallway and come to the alcove where I first encountered Tunny. The *Gnomus* placard hangs askew, singed at the bottom corner. The painting, once a lush forest of oil strokes now portrays only a burned-out husk, the canvas charred at the edges as if the fire was more than just represented in the painting. The smell of burnt pine and smoke fills the space and a bitter tear trickles down my cheek.

I continue down the hallway past *The Old Castle*, now barricaded with its drawbridge up. The destroyed canvas that was once the *Tuileries* painting hangs in tatters from its frame. The fields of *Bydło* lie fallow with any evidence of Julianna's body hidden beneath the newly and neatly plowed parallel rows. The stage of *Ballet of the Unhatched Chicks* remains empty while the dueling voices of the still arguing *Samuel Goldenberg and Schmuÿle* echo from their alcove, their rich baritone and high-pitched nasal voices playing off each other in syncopated rhythm.

The next alcove opens on a painting of four women in fine French garb from the turn of the twentieth century. As Caroline guessed and the

Exhibition's frescoed ceiling confirmed, the sign above the painting contains four words written in elegant script.

THE MARKETPLACE AT LIMOGES

Rendered in the short thick strokes of an impressionist's oils, the quartet of women stand in the shade of a tea merchant's awning exchanging pleasantries. I take a step closer, my heart pounding. A tea stand surrounded by French socialites is anything but terrifying, but neither is a crowd of children standing in a garden. As I debate what to do, the women all turn to face me, bristling with impatience as if they've known I was there all along.

As one, they beckon me to enter.

With a skipped heartbeat and a silent prayer, I leap into the painting.

My feet land on the cobblestone walkway, my silk sarong brushing against my ankles like rose petals. An energetic tune leads with a muted trumpet fanfare before launching into alternating strings and woodwinds and brass. Despite my circumstances, the song fills me with a strange joy as I move to join the quartet of women. A fine parasol appears in one hand and a lace fan in the other as my attire shifts to fit my new surroundings. Admiring the fine green dress that now falls from Scheherazade's form, I open the parasol and rest it across my shoulder to block the impression of sunlight on my back and draw closer to the women. Three of them are unknown to me, other aspects of Anthony's fractured consciousness, but even from behind and through a fishnet veil, the identity of the fourth woman to my left is irrefutable.

"Madame Versailles. After our encounter in *Tuileries*, I never dreamed I'd see you again." I cock my head to one side, surprised to hear my words coming out in French. "It seemed you'd rather die than leave your precious garden."

"Life and death work a little different around here." Versailles turns to face me. "Not to mention a lot of things have changed since your first walk along the Exhibition."

"What are you doing here in Limoges?" I ask.

"I closed my eyes as *Tuileries* imploded around me and awoke here in *The Marketplace*." One shoulder rises in a half-shrug. "Apparently, there is more of my story left to tell." Her lips turn up in a subtle snarl. "And speaking of people who have worn out their welcome, I've caught wind of your continued encounters with our delightful friend from the end of the hall."

"Have you?" I sidestep her subtle inquiry. "Who are your friends?"

"These are the women of *The Marketplace*. They come here to talk. I used to visit from time to time, but since the garden at *Tuileries* is no more, I spend my days here." She shrugs. "Not to mention my nights." She leans in conspiratorially and whispers, "I've learned a few things since we last spoke. Brigitte here was the first to find me. She is quite the gossip."

"Do tell."

Madame Versailles and I both glance in the direction of a plump woman across the circle, her hair a long cascade of blonde ringlets. She blushes and offers me a polite *bonjour*.

"Brigitte," Versailles says. "Please tell the Lady Scheherazade what you were just saying about the girl, Juliet."

"We miss her so," Brigitte says. "It hasn't been the same around here since she went away."

"Enough sentiment," Versailles hisses. "Tell her what you know."

"About the girl?" Brigitte leans in. "Or the baby?"

"Baby?" My gaze darts back and forth from Brigitte's blushing face and Madame Versailles' self-satisfied smirk. "What's she talking about?"

"The girl, Juliet." Versailles studies the ground at her feet. "She was with child."

"Was?"

"You saw her." Versailles points out of the painting. "In Hartmann's field."

The story from Anthony's classroom. The picture. "Juliet is Julianna."

"Inasmuch as you are Scheherazade in this place, so is she Juliet. Do you understand?"

"I'm not sure." I bite at my lower lip. "I understand both more and less with every new jaunt through the Exhibition."

Versailles throws her head back and laughs. "Now there's an honest answer."

I turn to Brigitte. "This Juliet. She was pregnant, you say?" The French flows off my tongue as if I were a native.

Brigitte crinkles her nose in disgust. "A vulgar word, but yes."

"And the father?"

"You're a bit slow today, Lady Scheherazade." Versailles places a hand on her hip and raises an eyebrow. "Answer me this. In whose field did you find the girl's body?"

"Hartmann's." A connection forms in my mind even as my heart goes cold. "Hartman."

Madame Versailles gazes at me, her eyes triumphant. "At last, you see. A child of *Tuileries* with the Cart Man from the fields. Until her demise, Juliet served as the fourth of *The Marketplace*, a position I was more than happy to fill after my own home was ruined."

Her eyes stab at me as she speaks that last word.

"Did Hartmann know?"

"Oh, Scheherazade. Surely you are not so unschooled in the ways of men. Why do you think he put her in the ground?"

My mind floats back to Glenn Hartman's baleful glare from the police car, his left eye slowly swelling shut from its encounter with Jason Faircloth's fist. My hand goes to the hilt of my dagger. "That bastard."

Brigitte stares at me aghast. "Madame Versailles, your friend has quite the devil's tongue."

Versailles lets out a chuckle. "The Lady is not from here and therefore isn't bound by most of the social constraints imposed on the rest of us."

"Constraints?" The fear in their eyes answers my unasked question. "The witch."

Another of the women steps closer to me and whispers. "Silence, Scheherazade. Would you bring her down upon our home like you did when you stood within Madame Versailles' frame? *Tuileries* is no more. If *The Marketplace* is destroyed, where would you have us go?"

"Sophie." Versailles interposes herself between us. "Stop."

"I'm sorry." I step back from the circle of women. "I had no idea."

Sophie steps around Versailles and continues her rant. "You come here time and again demanding answers to questions that should be left unasked and leave nothing but havoc in your wake. Tunny's forest and *Tuileries* have been destroyed, the *Ballet* is empty save Trilby's occasional performance, and the bridge at the castle is drawn against us all, friend or otherwise. The Exhibition was never the happiest of homes, but at least everyone knew their place in the scheme of things."

I step forward, bringing my nose close to Sophie's. "Apparently, at least one person's place was six feet below the ground. My questions may be stirring the pot around here, but at least I'm doing something while the rest of you stand around gossiping over tea."

Versailles steps between us again and raises her hands in a placating gesture to both sides. "Please excuse her reckless words. Lady Scheherazade is a visitor here, and though she doesn't understand the rules, she was careful to avoid mentioning *her* name."

"But I will." I push Madame Versailles out of my way and step to the center of the circle. "Tell me what I need to know or I will bring her down on all of you. Mortar, pestle and all."

The fourth woman, who had remained silent throughout the interchange, steps forward. "Please forgive Sophie and Brigitte. They do so relish their place here."

"And you are?"

"I am called Antoinette."

I fight back a sigh. "Of course you are."

She offers me a polite curtsy. "Tell me, Lady Scheherazade. What is it you wish to know?"

"How did it happen?" I work to formulate a more appropriate question. "I mean, did Hartmann come here and take her?"

Antoinette shakes her head. "No. Juliet was ever a free spirit. The three of us were always more than happy with our position here, but with Juliet, the wanderlust claimed her body and soul. In the end, it was her undoing."

"What do you mean?"

"She was the only one among us to have visited all the other places, barring the Russian wood where 'you know who' and her house on chicken legs resides, of course. She amused us with tales of the Gnome's forest, captivated us with descriptions of the tower view from the castle, even entertained us once with a dance she learned from Trilby. Then, one day, she didn't come back."

"We never knew what happened to her, until the day when you found her in Hartmann's field." Brigitte blushes and looks away.

"But you knew she was preg—" I stop myself at Versailles' stern glance. "I mean, with child." I raise an eyebrow. "How could you know such things in a place like this?"

Versailles' eyes narrow. "A woman knows these things."

"Indeed she does." A sixth voice comes from across my shoulder, the harsh Russian accent made all the more ominous by the intermittent snapping of iron on iron.

I turn to face the witch. She rests atop her mortar, her pestle pointed at my head like a judge's gavel, while the ever-swishing broom undulates back and forth behind her, appearing to hold her aloft.

"It is as I said," Sophie whispers. "Scheherazade has doomed us all."

Brigitte steps forward. "Please, Mistress. Do not destroy *The Marketplace.* This square is all we have, one of the few places left for us to go."

Baba Yaga shrugs and offers what passes for a smile. The metal-toothed grimace will haunt my dreams for the rest of my days. The broom stops and the witch deposits both it and her pestle into the mortar bowl before climbing down and making our circle six.

"I have no intention of destroying this place." Rancid spittle flies from her mouth. "Is it not a place where women meet? Am I not a woman?"

My body assumes a defensive posture, though the witch appears unarmed. "Have you come here for me? To eject me yet again from your precious Exhibition?"

Yaga laughs, the rhythmic wheeze sending a shiver to my core. "Lady Scheherazade, how many times have I sent you from this place? Yet you return and return and return. Persistence may be a virtue wherever you call home, but here, it is little more than an annoyance. How many times must we do this dance? You are no closer now than when you first saw the gnome, and you are quickly running out of places to stick your oh-so-pretty nose."

"I may be closer than you think, witch. I've learned much on this particular visit, and dare I say I am eager to see what hides in the Catacombs. I'm guessing a conversation with the dead in a dead tongue might be rather enlightening."

Baba Yaga recoils at my words. "You will never see the Catacombs. I have blocked the portal and even I cannot breach the seal."

"Perhaps." Modesto's knowing smile flashes across my mind's eye. "Perhaps not."

"You think yourself quite clever, do you not, my dear? Do not make the mistake of overestimating your position. Remember in whose realm you now walk."

"This is Anthony's mind, you old hag. You are no more real than Brigitte or Sophie or even the lovely Madame Versailles."

"Yet I have sent you from this place time and again with no more than a waggle of my finger. Have you learned no respect?"

"What I've learned is while you may have the power to remove me from what you perceive as your own private Exhibition, you cannot keep me out. I will keep coming and coming until I have learned what I need to know to free Anthony from this prison."

"And why would you wish to free the boy?" Yaga pulls so close her fetid breath sends my stomach into spasm. "To face a world that will never understand him? He has so much to offer so many, and all the world does is stand and mock." She turns away. "He is safer here."

"Safer with you who keeps his mind in chains?"

"Have you never considered the wisdom behind the concept of 'necessary evil,' fair Scheherazade?" She offers a subtle bow, before gnashing her iron teeth together yet again.

The sound threatens to stop my heart.

Banishing the fear from my face, I step closer to the witch. "There is nothing necessary about any of this. Mark my words. I will free Anthony."

"You assume he wishes to be free, and therein lies the flaw in your theory." She climbs back into her mortar and turns her baleful glare back on me. "You are the one who keeps reminding everyone this is the boy's mind, but would that not by extension mean when you speak to me, you speak to Anthony himself?"

"Yes." It's the opportunity I've been waiting for. "Anthony. Speak to me. Not as her, not through her wrinkled lips and metal teeth. Speak to me as yourself."

Yaga's face twists briefly into a mask of stark terror that eventually resolves into a smug grin. "The boy cannot hear you. He has chosen his proxy. Now, Scheherazade, begone from this place." Her eyes close and I am surrounded in color and sound. "And do not return."

XXI

VERISMO

"Mira?" Caroline's voice is distant, as if she's shouting from the far end of a tunnel. "Can you hear me? Mira?"

I force open my eyes and bring a hand to my face. Drenched in sweat, I awake on the floor of the Faircloth living room. Archer looks down on me, his upside down features melting from concern to relief.

"I take it you ran afoul of the witch," he says.

"What was your first clue?" As always, my sojourn through the Exhibition in Anthony's mind has left my voice a bit raspy, but not nearly to the degree of previous trips. I pull my sleeve across my brow and try to sit up. I fail.

"She booted me." My eyes attempt to focus on the lighting fixture above me. "But not before one of the women of *The Marketplace* revealed something. Something big."

Caroline returns to the room, a wet washcloth in her hand. "What did you learn?"

"Understand I'm basing all of this on the testimony of a woman who only exists in Anthony's imagination, but," I glance back and forth from Archer to Caroline, "it appears Julianna was pregnant."

"Pregnant?" All color leaves Caroline's face. "And the father? Did you learn that?"

Shit. I was so focused on Glenn Hartman, it didn't occur to me Jason is just as likely a possibility on that one. No telling how far around the baseball diamond those two had run. Not to mention the pregnancy itself is no more than a rumor told to me by a fictional character in a comatose boy's mind.

"I'm sorry, Caroline. That's all I can say at this point." I massage my temples as yet another headache tries to start behind my right eye. "Does Anthony even know what the word pregnant means?"

"He was always an astute boy," Caroline says. "I never lied to him or put him off regarding matters of birds and bees."

"And even if he didn't quite get all the details, understanding Julianna was carrying a baby is not out of bounds?"

"The kid's created his own internal reality, complete with multiple sets and supporting cast, all within his own mind," Archer says. "I don't think understanding where babies come from is too much of a stretch."

"Two points to the only doctor in the room." I try a second time to sit up, and meeting with more success, rest the back of my head on the cool fabric of Caroline's couch. "The real question is, did Hartman know?"

"Would explain a lot," Archer says. "We've already seen him get irrational and violent trying to keep a secret under wraps. Who's to say what he'd do if there was a chance it could come out he knocked up one of his students?"

"We'll never know till we ask." The spinning room slows down a notch. I push myself up out of the floor and sink into the cushions behind me. "Give me a few minutes to collect myself and we'll head down to the police station and see if Glenn Hartman is up for a chat."

"It's posted right there on the wall." Looking for all the world like a bulldog with a close shave, the cop manning the desk has on his game face. "I'm sorry, ma'am, but evening visiting hours don't start till eight. Plus, I'm not sure they're even done processing Mr. Hartman just yet."

"Pardon me, Officer Bryce, but what part of 'emergency' do you not understand?"

"Emergency." Bryce picks up the clipboard from his desk and motions around the room. "See this list? I've got at least a dozen 'emergency' visitors waiting to come back and see their people, and more on the way. Your guy was picked up this morning for assault on a minor, not to mention possible charges in another case, so pardon my lack of enthusiasm."

"It's all right, Mira. It's just another hour."

"Are you two family?" Bryce raises an eyebrow. "Or lawyers, maybe?"

Archer steps in before I can jam my toes farther down my throat. "We have urgent business to discuss with Mr. Hartman involving the health of a child. Trust me. He'll want to see us."

"Fill out this form, then, and we'll see what happens."

Archer and I grab a couple of seats, and I drop into mine with a huff. I don't like waiting, and I've spent the majority of the day in one waiting room or another.

"What's got you so riled up all of a sudden?" Archer asks. "You've always taken this business with Anthony seriously, but you've been different since your last 'walk' through the Exhibition. Is everything okay?"

Isabella's mischievous grin flashes across my thoughts.

"Let's just say if my suspicions are accurate, I will do everything in my power to make sure Glenn Hartman never sees the outside of a prison for the rest of his life."

Forty-five minutes later, Officer Bryce shows us through a locked door and back to a large room with four sets of tables and benches, all bolted to the concrete floor. Archer and I wait at the table in the corner for several minutes before one of the doors on the opposite wall opens, allowing in a small gaggle of men all dressed in day-glow orange.

At the back of the crowd, Glenn Hartman looks around the room as if in a daze. He glances in our direction, his expression going immediately cold when his eyes meet mine. He pauses by the doorway, most likely considering whether to talk to us or not, but eventually joins us at the table.

"Hmm." He sits with a huff. "I figured it'd be someone from the school."

"Hello, Mr. Hartman." I slip into my best approximation of a smile. "My name is Mira Tejedor."

"You were at the Faircloth house this morning." His eyes drill through me like twin lasers. "What do you want?" The pungent vinegar of anger fills my senses and I have to suppress a cough.

"We'd like to talk to you for a few minutes, if you'll allow it."

"Are you cops?"

"Wouldn't be stuck in the visitor's area if we were cops."

"I've already got representation, if that's why you're here."

"We're not lawyers either." I glance down at the table before again meeting his gaze. "We're friends of the Faircloth family."

His nostrils flare as he gets up from the table. "In that case, I'm out of here."

"Wait." I shoot out of my seat as he turns to leave. "You'll want to hear what I have to say. It's about… J."

A chemical tang cuts the vinegar odor filling my senses. I've got his attention.

He sits back down. "I'm listening."

"There's a lot going on here, and I may be able to help you, Mr. Hartman. First things first, though. Can you tell me why you were at the Faircloth home this morning?"

"You're not cops, but you're going to sit here and interrogate me?"

"Just giving you a chance to explain yourself. Any particular reason you dropped by the Faircloth's and tried to beat the snot out of a high school senior before sunrise?"

"Like you don't know." Hartman leans in, whispering. "You've seen the pictures. I can see it in your eyes. What would you have done?"

I draw close, keeping my voice down. "You're admitting you were having an affair with Julianna Wagner?"

"I didn't say that." Hartman's cheeks grow a shade more crimson.

I take a deep breath. "You went to their house at six in the morning and tried to knock the front door down. Something got you pretty worked up."

"I was heading out for my morning jog. Found an envelope sticking out of my mailbox and took a look inside. I wasn't thinking too straight after that."

"And you assumed Jason Faircloth left those pictures for you to find?"

Hartman glances around the room before turning his attention back on me. "The kid's always acted real strange around me. Nosing around after school, getting in my business." His voice drops to an angry whisper. "Not to mention the fact his initials were written at the bottom of the note."

"Way I see it, he had good cause." I cock my head to one side. "You were sleeping with his girlfriend, after all."

Hartman's eyes grow wide. "We're done here."

He shoots up from the table a second time and turns to walk away. Archer glances at me sidelong, but keeps his cool. A moment later Hartman deflates and sits back down.

"Look, I know this looks bad, but I didn't touch her."

I drop my chin and give him a blink or two. "Really?"

He gives me a look that says "Go to hell" more than any three words ever could. "You know what I mean."

"Mr. Hartman, if you were caught sleeping with one of your students, your career would be pretty much over, wouldn't it?"

His hands ball into fists atop the table. "*If* such a scenario were the case, I suppose losing my job would be a possibility."

"And if she disappeared, and you didn't come forward, what do you think that suggests?"

"I told you. I didn't touch her."

"Was it when you found out she was pregnant? Is that what tipped you over the edge?"

Hartman's eyes grow wide. "What did you say? Pregnant?"

"Come on, Glenn." I cross my arms before me. "You're not seriously going to try to pull the blissful ignorance card, are you?"

"But we were careful. She said she was…" Hartman's gaze falls to his lap. "You're sure?" The vinegar and chemical smells vanish, replaced by the unmistakable aroma of old scotch.

I glance over at Archer, who appears as surprised as I feel, then back at Hartman.

"You… didn't know."

"Does it look like I knew?" Only the tremor in Hartman's lower lip betrays his stoic facade. "Wait. How the hell could *you* know? Have they found her? Where is she?"

"That's all for today." I rise and head for the door leading out, my heart pounding in my chest. I half expect Hartman to come after me, but as I look back at his pitifully angry face, it's clear he realizes he's in it deep enough as it is.

The guard opens the door and I step out of the room with Archer close behind.

"That was pretty abrupt," he says. "What are you thinking?"

"I don't believe it." I fall back against the wall. "He really didn't know."

Archer and I return to the Faircloth house. Caroline's eyes are swollen from crying. Rachel's upstairs in bed and Anthony lies resting on the couch, his head in his mother's lap. As she strokes his dark brown hair, it occurs to me it's the calmest I've seen the boy in some time. No humming, no agonized grimace marring his innocent face, as if he's merely sleeping instead of being trapped within the labyrinth of his own mind. And for once, he's accepting his mother's touch without drawing away.

"And you believed him?" Caroline asks.

I tap at my temple. "I'd never claim a hundred percent accuracy on this kind of stuff, but it's kind of hard to lie to me."

"This begs a bigger question." Archer sits in the chair opposite Caroline. "Maybe two."

I crash into Caroline's well worn loveseat. "And those would be?"

"If Hartman didn't know about the pregnancy, he doesn't have nearly as much of a motive for murder." Archer leans forward. "Who did?"

"They were sleeping together." I bite my lip as I try to put it all together. "She could have threatened to expose him."

"Did you see his face when he found out she was pregnant?" Archer's lips pull to one side. "It was more than surprise. He seemed, I don't know, sad."

"You think he wanted the baby?"

"I think he had real feelings for the girl."

"Whoa," Caroline interjects. "Tell me we're not all jumping on the 'Free Glenn Hartman' bandwagon here."

"No, Caroline, but I have to tell you, if he's hiding something, he's good. He may be angry and feeling a bit guilty, but that's all I got today. Either he's so smooth he's fooling my psychic bullshit sensor or there's still more to this story."

Caroline turns to Archer. "And the other one, Thomas? You said there were two questions."

Archer scratches his chin, a subconscious tic I've caught him doing most when he's in a quandary. "The reason we're all here. Me, you, Mira. Regardless of what happened between Glenn Hartman and Julianna Wagner, how does any of it relate to Anthony or his condition?" He rises from the chair and kneels beside Anthony, the boy's placid face showing no evidence he's heard a word we've said. "Anthony's current state, the Exhibition, the witch, the ties to everyone involved. There's a link there. I'm sure of it."

The click of the front door brings all three of us to our feet. A moment later, Jason strides past all of us heading for his room.

"Jason," Caroline says. "Where have you been?"

"Out." Jason does his best to avoid his mother's gaze. "Needed to think."

"You needed to think." Caroline's hand goes to her hip. "You could've called me or just answered your stupid cell phone one of the last fifty times I called you today. Do you know how many people I've had hunting for you? I've been worried sick."

A flicker of contrition passes Jason's features. "Sorry, Mom."

"You're home now. Go start dinner. We'll be finished in a few minutes."

"That's okay," he says. "I'm not hungry."

"You're not hungry." Caroline motions to Anthony's still form. "I've been stuck in this house all day taking care of your brother and waiting for a call back since you ran off this morning. I've barely eaten two bites today. Now, drop all this macho crap and help me put together something to eat before I start gnawing on your leg."

Jason barely succeeds in keeping his eyes from rolling, a move that probably saves him a slap across the face. "Can I go clean up first?"

"Actually, I have a question for Jason." I rise from the chair.

"There's a shocker." Jason speaks just loud enough to ensure I can hear.

"Can't it wait, Mira?" Caroline asks. "He just got back."

"It's a simple thing, really." I motion to the manila package resting on the dining room table. "Mr. Hartman drove all the way over here before sunrise and tried to beat down your door over the pictures in that envelope. The note is signed with your initials."

"Mira, please," Caroline says.

"You think I did this." Jason glares back and forth from his mother to me. "Sent those pictures." His face grows red. "And now you think I killed Julianna too." He storms out of the room and down the hall. The force of the slamming door nearly pops my eardrums.

Caroline shoots me a withering glance. "Thank you, Mira."

"You can't hang on to those photos forever. What do you think the police are going to do?"

"I just wanted one night of peace. Is that so much to ask?"

Archer joins us by the foyer. "Mira's right. As awful as it is, we need to know if Jason took those pictures, and more importantly, if he knew."

"Knew what?" Caroline's frantic gaze passes from Archer to me.

My hand goes to my hip. "That his missing ex-girlfriend was carrying a baby."

"You're going to tell him?" Caroline begins to pace. "What if he doesn't know?" She wrings her hands. "That kind of news will kill him."

"I think he can take it," Archer says. "He's tough."

"That's what he shows the world." Caroline rejoins Anthony on the couch and strokes his mussed hair. "Jason may seem like he's all rough and tumble, but he's one of the more sensitive people I know. You should have seen the way he and Julianna were when they were together."

"Which would make it all the more painful if he found out she was sleeping with someone else, especially one of her teachers."

Caroline turns from us. "Jason didn't hurt anyone."

I rest a hand on Caroline's shoulder. "That's what we all want to believe, but there were two people involved with Julianna."

"And just because Glenn Hartman didn't set off your little psychic lie detector today, Jason moves to the top of your list?" She shrugs away my hand. "I'm so glad you both have so much faith in my son."

"It's not like that, Caroline." I stoop in an attempt to catch her gaze. "It's—"

"Now, Caroline," Archer says. "You know as well as I do those photos aren't all you're hiding. I've admired how well you've held it together through this entire thing, but if you're going to stand here and argue with us, perhaps you owe Mira the courtesy of the whole truth."

The pungent stench of sulfur fills my mind as Caroline's eyes grow wide. "What are you—"

"What you told me on the phone earlier today." Archer's lips narrow into a thin line.

"Thomas," Caroline says, refusing to meet my gaze. "Don't."

"What is it, Caroline?" Her sudden fear hits me like a hurricane of sulfur. "What haven't you told me?"

Caroline lets out a weary sigh. "The night Julianna disappeared. We were all sick, you know. Some kind of stomach bug."

"I've heard this story. The four of you were holed up here all night."

"Anthony started throwing up a couple hours after dinner and wouldn't stop. I spoke to the doctor on call who phoned him in some medicine." Caroline bites her lip. "I had to drive to the pharmacy around eight and pick up the prescription. Left Jason in charge. I was only gone for half an hour, but the truth is I didn't see him again till the next morning."

"You didn't check on him?"

"I figured he was asleep and didn't want to wake him. I was up half the night taking care of Anthony and Rachel and truth be told, I was sort of glad at least one of my kids survived the evening without Dr. Mom. That is, till everything hit the fan the next morning."

"But his alibi." I glance in the direction of the hallway. "It's all a lie."

"I know." Caroline's pale cheeks continue their progression toward bright pink. "No one is putting a child of mine in jail." She turns toward the hall. "Jason? Can you come out here, please?"

No answer.

"Jason?" Archer shouts.

"Oh no." Caroline sprints down the hall only to return seconds later with slumped shoulders and defeat written across her face.

"His window is open. He's gone." Her hands tremble at her sides. "What more can possibly happen?"

Her question is answered a moment later as Anthony again begins to hum. Gone are the high pitches of Scheherazade's theme, the quick notes of a woman pleading for her life replaced by the low notes of a dirge that only Anthony can hear. Caroline runs to his side.

"I recognize this." She strokes Anthony's mussed hair. "It's from the Mussorgsky piece."

Though I've heard it only once, I don't need to guess which movement. "The Catacombs." My stomach knots at the name. "I'm sorry, Caroline. I can't go back right now. I'm exhausted. Can I have a night to think and prepare?"

"I understand," she says. "I'm sorry I didn't tell you about Jason till now."

"It's all right. I'd probably have done the same if Isabella was the one under the gun. No matter what, though, I'm in this for the long run. You know that, right?"

"That goes for both of us," Archer adds.

"Thank you." Kneeling on the floor beside her son, Caroline cradles Anthony's head in her hands. "Thank you, both."

She spares a second to glance up at me, before returning her attention to Anthony. I catch Archer's eye and incline my head toward the door.

"Drop me off at the Blake? My car is all the way back at your office and I already feel like I'm about to pass out. I can catch a cab tomorrow, but right now I just need to crash."

"Sure. It's been a long day." He fights back a yawn. "For all of us."

"Agreed." I follow Archer onto the porch and pull the door closed behind us. "And I have a sneaking suspicion tomorrow's not going to be any better."

XXII

Bruscamente

"Look's like there's a wreck up ahead." Between swipes of the windshield wipers, Archer stares with tired eyes at the line of cars creeping along the bypass toward the next exit. "There's nothing to do but wait it out." He chuckles. "Unless you want to walk."

"It's not even ten yet." Despite my best efforts, a yawn from the depths of my soul escapes me. "I'll be all right."

"You're not fooling anyone, you know." Archer shoots me a wink. "A few minutes ago, you catnapped straight through a fascinating story about my summer in Ecuador two years back."

"Sorry. Unguided tours of catatonic children's minds take it out of me every time."

"I can only imagine." His eyes flick in my direction. "I hate to admit it, but I owe you an apology."

"For what? I get why you didn't tell me about Jason. Doctor-patient privilege, right?"

"I think Caroline's been trying to confess everything about that night to me for weeks but today's the day she finally did it."

"Glenn Hartman showing up on her porch this morning must have really shook her up."

"I thought it best if you heard it from Caroline. If I'd told you, that truly would have been a breach of confidence, but that doesn't change the fact that you needed to know." He clears his throat. "I mean, you can't help Anthony if you don't have all the facts, right?"

"Every bit helps. Still, you don't owe me an apology for doing the right thing."

"Of course not." Archer taps the brake. "But that wasn't what I was talking about."

"Oh?" A swarm of butterflies threatens to burst from my chest. "Do tell."

"I just wanted to let you know I'm sorry for doubting your intentions in the beginning." He chances another glance. "You're a good person, Mira."

"Says the therapist who spent his entire evening helping a patient for free and is now providing taxi service to an exhausted psychic with a migraine."

"But with all you've put yourself through trying to help Anthony…"

"You'd do the same, if you could." My cheeks grow warmer by the second and I'm suddenly grateful for the muted lighting inside Archer's car. "A little secret? You're not the first person in your profession to start measuring me for either a straitjacket or a jail cell within seconds of shaking my hand. Soul-crushing professional ridicule comes with the territory." Our eyes meet. "And to be fair, I imagine most people you meet claiming they can read minds probably could use a short stint in a rubber room."

"From your lips to God's ears." Archer laughs. "You know? I envy you a bit. The things you can do. The progress you've made with Anthony. It's a miracle."

"It's not all sunshine and puppies. I have a gift, but it's not necessarily one I asked for. As for Anthony, Dr. Archer, don't count your miracles before they hatch."

"Thomas." He offers me a half-smile. "With all we've been through together this past week, I believe we can leave the titles at work."

My breath catches. Just a little. "All right, Thomas." The smell of baking bread fills my senses. It's comfortable. Warm. "I wanted to ask you something. A question that's been on my mind since I made my way out of the Exhibition the first time. Was it true what you said a few days back? About dreams not being able to kill you?"

Thomas considers for a moment. Would be nice if the answer to this particular question rested a bit closer to the tip of his tongue.

"There are a few cases in the literature of people with near death experiences coinciding with them dying in a dream. Most people, however, either wake up before they die or continue to sleep and dream after the death event occurs. That opens up a different question, though."

A weary smile touches my lips. "And that would be?"

"Can you truly consider what you and Anthony do as dreaming?"

"And now we're back to uncharted territory." We lock gazes and a hint of lilac filters across the warm bread scent.

"Hey. Check it out." Thomas points through the windshield. The blue lights at the top of the hill stop flashing and the line of cars in front of us starts to move. "Looks like we won't be stuck out here all night after all."

A couple minutes later, we exit the highway and navigate the city streets in silence as the gentle rain makes the road and sidewalks glisten in the mercury lights of Uptown Charlotte. As we pull up to the Blake's main entrance, Thomas puts the car in park.

"Door to door service," he says with a smile.

"Thanks for the ride. I hate driving in the rain at night. Gives me chills."

"Says the woman who wanders unguided through the minds of catatonic children."

"Touché." I pause, my hand on the door handle.

"You forget something?"

"No." My cheeks go hot. "It's just, umm, I was feeling my second wind kicking in and was wondering if you'd like to come in for a drink. We're finally getting somewhere with Anthony, but like Caroline said, the next stop along the Exhibition is *The Catacombs*."

"More chills?"

"Sort of. The witch has made it more than clear she'll stop at nothing to keep me from ever setting foot in that place. As Scheherazade, my main weapons are words, and if anyone would know how to talk their way past an old hag with a mortar and pestle, it's a board certified psychologist." I level an even gaze at Thomas. "Drinks are on me."

His eyes slide closed and a quiet breath escapes his lips. I already know his answer.

"Any other night, I'd say yes, but I've got a six a.m. meeting tomorrow morning I have to be conscious for and a full load of patients tomorrow." He looks over at me. "I hope you understand."

"No problem." The warm scent of bread and the hint of lilac both vanish, leaving the mental air between us stale and uncomfortable. "Best I get on to bed anyway. Been a long day."

Thomas clears his throat. "We're meeting at Caroline's tomorrow afternoon at four, right?"

"Yeah." I fake a wide grin. "Don't be late."

He shakes his head. "I'll do what I can. Like I said, I have a full docket tomorrow. As much as I want to be there for Anthony, my other patients need me too."

"Of course." His words echo in my mind. "Good night, then."

I shut the door gently behind me, refusing to look back as Thomas pulls away. Once he's out of sight, I hurry for the door, the nagging headache at the edge of my consciousness all but crying out for a glass of wine before bed. I venture into the hotel bar and grab a stool.

"Evening." The bartender, an older man that reminds me a bit of my dad, wipes down the section of bar before me and flips the towel across his shoulder. "What are you having this evening?"

"A glass of red will be fine."

"Coming up."

Half a glass and my eyelids are already heavy as I flirt with that in-between state of not quite awake and not quite dream. The witch's face fills my mind.

"*You will never see the Catacombs. I have blocked the portal and even I cannot breach the seal.*"

At least in that particular arena, I have something of an ace up my sleeve. Her previous claim, however, is the one that echoes in my mind, the one that has awakened me at least nightly since I first heard the words, "*Still I will deny you the one answer you seek.*" Her skin like parchment, even now she stares at me with those yellow eyes, grinning her iron smile. "*That revelation rests in my realm, and you dare not go there.*" The thought of facing Baba Yaga on her own turf makes my head swim.

Or is it the wine?

Someone taps my shoulder.

"Ms. Tejedor." The rumbling bass is familiar, and after our last encounter, so is the tone.

I turn in the barstool and try to expunge the utter exhaustion from my face.

"Why, Detective Sterling, if you weren't a cop, I'd swear you were stalking me."

"Don't worry. I'm here on business."

The bartender heads to my end of the bar. He must have seen me tense up.

"This guy bothering you?" he asks.

"This 'guy' is a detective with Charlotte PD." Sterling flashes his badge. "I just need to discuss a couple things with Ms. Tejedor here, if that's all right with you."

"Chill, man," the bartender says, backing away. "Just looking out for the pretty lady."

"That makes two of us," Sterling says, taking the stool next to mine. "You look beat, Mira. Where've you been all night, besides stirring up trouble with my suspect?"

My chest tightens. "I kind of figured you'd hear about that."

"What were you thinking? Glenn Hartman is the lead suspect in the biggest missing persons case in the state and instead of doing me a little favor and finding something to help me put him away, you go down to the jail and get him all riled up."

"My apologies. I just needed to get some information."

"And what's this fascinating bit of information that earned one of my buddies a black eye?"

"There was a fight?"

"You left Glenn Hartman in a pretty agitated state. He had to be restrained and things got a little rough."

"Sorry." I look away, the disappointment in Sterling's eyes more than I can handle at the moment. "I didn't mean for anyone to get hurt."

"Look, it's clear you know something we don't. Hartman was a little on the nervous side before you showed up, but after…" His fingers shake with rage as he combs them across his close-cropped scalp. "You know, I don't get you. I'm working my ass off trying to find this girl and you go interrogating the prime suspect without giving me so much as a warning. Whose side are you on, anyway?"

"I'm on Anthony's side, Jason's, the whole Faircloth family." For the second time since arriving back at the hotel, the heat rises in my cheeks.

This time is far less pleasant. "I don't work for you and I sure as hell don't work for Hartman. I had a theory and needed to see his reaction."

"And?"

"To be honest, I was surprised."

"I hope it was worth it. Hartman seemed ready to crack earlier today, but thanks to you, he's even more withdrawn than before. We've got him in solitary for now, but he says he's done till he sees a lawyer." His eyes focus on something past my head and his expression, if possible, grows colder. "Oh yeah. I forgot the best part. Someone at the station recognized you."

"What?"

"Look." Sterling points to a television at the far end of the bar. A photograph of Thomas and me leaving the station fills the screen. The closed captioning across the bottom reads, "Psychic Mira Tejedor, who helped in last year's investigation of the Sarah Goode abduction, along with an unidentified man, left the station earlier today…"

"Oh no." It's starting again. "This wasn't supposed to happen."

"The Wagner home was already besieged with reporters. This bucket of blood you just dumped in the water has already doubled the number of news vans and cameras around their house, so thanks for that."

My chest grows tight. "I was just trying to help."

"No. You were trying to advance your own agenda with not a single thought about the repercussions." He looks away. "Something you're pretty good at."

"Now hold on. You can get all pissed off at me for screwing up your investigation, but leave you and me out of this." Though a part of me recognizes the truth in what he's saying, it doesn't rile me any less.

"This conversation isn't going anywhere." A sharp tang of copper fills my senses as Sterling stands to leave. "We'll be talking again soon, Ms. Tejedor. For now, though, stay away from my suspect. I'd hate to have to charge you with obstruction of justice. Are we clear?"

"Crystal."

"Good night, then." He turns to leave. "I'm really sorry it ended up this way."

Sterling is already halfway across the room as a quiet "Me too" falls from my lips.

The bartender reappears across the bar, the bottle of wine in his hand. "That cop sure left in a huff. Everything all right?"

"None of this is all right." I tap the top of my glass. "None of this."

An hour later, I'm lying in bed staring at my half-asleep daughter via a fuzzy Skype connection.

"When are you coming home, Mami?" Her voice comes through the speakers with a strange vibrato.

"It won't be much longer. I promise." Another little piece of my heart breaks at the flicker of disappointment in her drowsy eyes. "Are you having fun with Nana?"

"It's fun, but I miss you."

"I miss you too, sweetie." Anthony's catatonic face flashes across my subconscious. "More than you can possibly know." We share a yawn. "Can I talk to Nana for a minute?"

"I'll get her." Isabella climbs off the bed out of range of the camera and calls for my mother. A few moments later, she appears on the screen.

"I have to say, Mira. I know you're in the middle of a complicated case, but this is the longest 'couple of days' I've ever seen."

"Sorry, Mom. This thing with the Faircloth family is taking a lot longer than I imagined." I stretch and try to massage away the knot below my neck that's been tying itself tighter and tighter since Sterling's call woke me up fifteen hours before. "Still working both sides of the case. Was making some headway with local law enforcement, though I'm pretty sure that's all flown out the window at this point."

"You think so?" she asks. "Word is you're officially on the case now."

My heart freezes. "Where did you hear that?"

"It's everywhere. Julianna Wagner is national news, honey. Young, pretty, blonde, rich girl goes missing for weeks. What do you think happens when the psychic who helped find Sarah Goode shows up at the police station to chat with the lead suspect in the case?" She taps some keys on her computer. "Here. Check this out."

A few seconds later, my computer sounds off as a link appears at the bottom of the screen.

I open up the article in my browser.

Virginia Psychic Called In on Wagner Case
Visits Missing Student's Teacher in Jail

"Crap." My stomach does a somersault. "That just happened a couple hours ago."

"I've told you a hundred times, Mira. You can't do what you do and fly under the radar."

"You did, back in the day."

"A different time, dear, and even I made the tabloids a couple of times. Not to mention, I can't do a tenth of what you can."

My heart sinks in the way it always does before I ask for my mother's advice. "What would you do?"

"Much as I want you home, you need to do what you promised. Stay there in Charlotte till you've helped that boy or you've done all you can do."

"And the Julianna Wagner case? I'm here to help Anthony, but I keep getting sucked back into hunting for a girl I'm pretty sure is already dead."

"I know you swore you'd never work another case like that after the whole thing with Sarah Goode, but look what you did there. You keep telling me the two cases seem intertwined. Maybe you're there in Charlotte for a reason."

I stifle a groan. "You know what I think about the whole 'God has a plan' thing, Mom."

"Look at it this way. There's a hallway in a little boy's mind only you can walk and a missing girl no one else seems able to find. Sounds like *someone's* got a plan." She pauses for a moment. "Still, based on everything you've told me and what I've seen on the news, there's something about this whole thing that doesn't quite add up. Be careful down there, Mira."

"Got it, Mom. If there's one thing I've learned over the years, it's to trust your intuition." I stretch and yawn. "Can I say good night to Isabella?"

Mom looks away from her webcam. "She's conked out on the couch. Do you want me to wake her?"

"Let her sleep. I'll call again tomorrow."

"Take care, Mira. Love you."

"Love you too, Mom."

As I close down my laptop for the night, my mind continues to work overtime trying to put together the jigsaw puzzle the Wagner case has become. If my instincts are right, Glenn Hartman is telling the truth, which means whoever is responsible for Julianna's disappearance is still on the loose. Though I try to drive the thoughts from my mind, I can't stop thinking about Jason's reaction from earlier and Caroline's big revelation about his alibi. Missing for hours, evading everyone, angry at the world. His mind may have given up Glenn Hartman's secret, but what if Jason is hiding a secret of his own?

XXIII

The Catacombs

I pull into Caroline's driveway a little before four in the afternoon. After losing most of the morning sleeping off the previous night's chain of disasters and what ended up being most of a bottle of wine, I woke up with a well-deserved hangover. A couple hours walking around Uptown Charlotte helped to clear my head, as did a half hour in my room's whirlpool tub. As ready as I expect I'll be to face whatever Anthony has waiting for me in the Catacombs, I shift the car into park and step on to the concrete driveway. Archer's car is nowhere in sight, but an unfamiliar vehicle with a parking sticker from Jason's high school is parked in front of the Faircloth house.

"At least Veronica made it." I hold onto that, even as I cringe at the thought of entering the Exhibition without Archer here to back me up. Regardless of the fact he can do little to help me there, knowing Anthony's Kalendar Prince is just a few feet away has always helped keep me calm. I shake off the image of the colossal doors at the end of the Exhibition hallway and knock on Caroline's. After a few seconds, the door cracks. The circles under Caroline's eyes appear a shade darker than yesterday.

"Good afternoon, Mira." She forces a smile, though she appears so exhausted, I imagine a stiff breeze would blow her over. "Did you eat? I have some sandwiches left over from lunch."

"I got a little something on the way." I tilt my head to one side. "Are you feeling all right?"

"A friend of mine always says a mother is only doing as well as her least happy child." She shows me to the living room where Rachel sits stroking Anthony's hair. Jason, on the other hand, is nowhere in sight. "Take your pick."

"I saw another car out front. I take it Veronica beat me here."

"In here." Ms. Sayles appears from the hall. "I've only been here a few minutes. Caroline and I have been catching up."

"Would you two like some tea?" Caroline asks.

"That would be great." Veronica smiles.

"Thanks, Caroline." I turn to Veronica as our exhausted hostess steps into the kitchen. "And thank you, Veronica, for coming out this afternoon. I know it's probably the last place you want to be after a long day at work, but I believe having you here is really going to help. From what I've seen traveling Anthony's Exhibition thus far, you've made quite an impression on him."

She raises an eyebrow. "I hope it was a good impression."

"It seems that way. On my third encounter with him, when *Tuileries* was destroyed, he sent you someplace else in his mind. Someplace safe. I think that says a lot."

"This all still sounds so crazy." Veronica looks back and forth from me to Caroline. "I know he loved my class, but I have no idea why he would've singled me out the way you're describing."

"He used to talk about you all the time," Caroline shouts from the kitchen. "You were his favorite."

"It's funny. I rarely did anything special for him. Tried to treat him like the rest of the kids in the class, except in situations where extra attention was required."

I glance over at Anthony. "Maybe you were the only one who gave him that. A sense of normalcy."

"Maybe." She bites at her lip, and a hint of chlorine anxiety wafts across my senses. "So, I'm here. What do you need me to do?"

"For now, just be here. I'm hoping having another person who is close with Anthony in the room will be enough to help us break down this wall he's built in his mind."

"But how will he even know I'm here?"

I shake my head as a laugh escapes me. "Anthony may be the next thing to catatonic, but there's no question he knows when I'm around. His mother and sister too."

"Especially Rachel." Caroline returns from the kitchen with a tray of iced tea and sets it on the coffee table. "Her mere presence has always calmed him, and even more so since the incident." She joins Rachel on the couch and gently wraps an arm around her daughter. "Honey. Why don't you go play in your room while we talk?"

"But I want to stay here with Anthony."

"Please, Rachel," Caroline says. "Go play in your room. Ms. Mira is here and she needs some privacy to work with your brother."

"But Anthony needs me." Rachel begins to cry. "He told me so."

"Don't be silly, Rachel. Anthony hasn't spoken in days."

"He did. He told me he needed me. Not to leave. Don't send me away, Mommy. Please."

"It's okay, Rachel." I kneel beside Anthony and stroke Rachel's knee. "You can stay if you want to. Just be real quiet while I'm working."

"Mira," Caroline says, "can I talk to you?" She rises from the couch and leads me to the foyer. "All is forgiven from the other day, but it doesn't change the fact I don't want Rachel to have any part of this."

I rest a hand on her shoulder. "I know it's scary, but I don't think sending Rachel to her room is going to make much of a difference. The last time she got caught up in Anthony's mental crossfire, she was all the way across town. And remember, she's tough. The *Ballet* is one of the few aspects of the Exhibition that survived an encounter with the witch unscathed."

Caroline rubs at the bridge of her nose. "I suppose you're right."

Heading back into the living room, Caroline kneels beside her daughter and takes her hands. "You can stay, but like Ms. Mira said, you have to stay quiet and out of the way so she can work. Is it a deal?"

At Rachel's silent nod, I pull a chair over and take my position above Anthony's head.

"Let's begin." Caroline and Veronica draw close and the three of us link hands. "Stay with me, ladies. I have a nasty feeling this one's going to be rough."

My eyes slip shut even as my mind opens. My first time into the Exhibition, I had to push my way in. This time, I feel pulled—no—dragged in. The prismatic torrent I always face as I fall into Anthony's mind this time lasts no more than a second. In a blink, I stand again in the grand Exhibition hall of Anthony's splintered mind. Behind me, the body of artwork I've already explored and for the most part left in ruin rests in silence while before me await two remaining alcoves. The first is directly to my right and the second rests at the far end of the hall. Two alcoves, two remaining pictures with which to solve the mystery that is Anthony Faircloth.

Barring one small complication.

The alcove to my right has been completely bricked over.

What do you know? In addition to classical music, the kid is a fan of Poe.

I rush to the doorway and press my shoulder against the burnt orange masonry. The wall doesn't budge, nor does Scheherazade's dagger do any more than scratch the brick surface. Frustrated, I glance up at the ever-shifting fresco above my head and nearly have a heart attack. Filling the entire space, an image of Baba Yaga stares down and points her pestle at me from atop her enormous stone mortar.

"Bitch," I curse under my breath, even as a smile spreads across my face. I point the bejeweled dagger at her cackling image and shout, "Laugh as you like, witch. This time, you're the one who's underestimated their enemy."

I spin on my heels and sprint back up the hallway for the second alcove where I hope to find Modesto waiting within his castle. Stepping into the alcove, I study the painting within. The stone walls of Modesto's home still stand, secured against invasion. The bridge is drawn and the windows are covered so even light cannot escape. A blue and white flag at the highest parapet flaps in the wind at half-mast.

"I wonder who they're trying to keep out." A bitter chuckle wells up from within. "The witch or me?"

I step into the frame and marvel yet again as my form takes on the properties of the painting. My arms, legs, and torso, all clothed in Scheherazade's ornate sarong, are suddenly rendered in meticulous oil.

"No time like the present, I suppose." I walk across the rocky landscape to the castle in the distance and examine the churning waters below the closed drawbridge. Though it crosses my mind to try, I don't dare attempt the swim. God only knows what creatures Anthony's imagination has summoned to fill the black waters around one of its sole remaining refuges.

"Modesto." My shout echoes off the granite walls of the ancient edifice before me. "It is Scheherazade. Let down the bridge."

Several seconds of silence broken only by the whistle of the buffeting wind lets me know either the castle's guardian can't hear me, or worse, is ignoring me.

Maybe a different approach. "Tunny, are you here?" I retrieve a stone from the ground and hurl it at the raised drawbridge, followed by another, and another. A small cairn forms below the enormous wooden barrier before a familiar groan finally answers my call.

"Go away," Tunny's voice calls down from above. "You have brought enough trouble down upon our heads for a lifetime."

"That's not you, Tunny. That's Modesto telling you what to say. Ask him please to lower the drawbridge. I need to speak with him. It's a matter of life and death."

"Modesto, Modesto. It's always Modesto. Was I not the first you met here? Did I not save you from the burning forest? The children in the garden? Do I no longer matter?"

Fantastic. Anthony's inner gnome has gone and got his feelings hurt.

"I'm sorry, Tunny. I don't mean to upset you. Of course you still matter to me. All of you do. Why else do you think I returned?"

A muted harrumph echoes across the moat. "Go on."

"I have business with Modesto. This is still his castle, is it not?"

Wind whistles through the parapets above.

"It is," Tunny whispers.

"Go and convince him to let me back inside. I have information he will no doubt find quite interesting."

"You have brought the witch's anger down upon picture after picture." Modesto's crisp British accent cuts through the space as if he were standing next to me. "The castle is the last stronghold remaining, save the place of the dead and the realm of the witch herself. Why would any sane person allow you into their home a second time?"

"Because she's here to save us."

The voice comes from behind me. I turn to find a wistful Trilby staring at me in wonder, just as a certain little girl watched me from a waiting room a few days earlier. Still dressed in the ruby and black lace costume from the *Ballet*, she looks so grown up for one so young.

She glances up at the castle. "Listen to her, Modesto. For all our sakes."

A moment passes before Modesto's voice echoes down from above. "Very well. Speak, Scheherazade."

I mouth a quick "thank you" to Trilby and then gaze up at the castle's stone wall. "I believe I have found a way to defeat the witch, or at least placate her, so all of you can be free. But you must let me in or my hard won knowledge is worthless."

"And if I don't?" The mocking tone in Modesto's voice stabs at me even as a faraway boom sets my heart racing. In the distance, the alternating crash and thud of Baba Yaga's mortar and pestle begins anew. The back and forth of the twin sounds grows in volume with each repetition, even as the witch's boisterous theme competes with Modesto's mellow saxophone.

"Then the old witch might just have me for dinner. You've read the stories, seen what she can do, know what she's capable of. Would you leave me out here to face her mortar and pestle? Her iron teeth?"

Modesto appears at the castle's highest parapet. "What makes you think I care one whit about your fate?"

"The answer to that is very simple." I keep my voice calm and quiet. "Because you do."

"She'll be here any moment," Trilby shouts. "Let us in."

I glance across my shoulder. Past Trilby's trembling form, the bounding shadow of the witch atop her mortar appears, just visible through the hole in space left by the floating picture frame.

"The Exhibition's mistress has dismissed me from this place oh so many times. She may not be so merciful this time." Though my voice becomes a harsh whisper, it echoes through the space as if amplified. "Would you have that on your conscience?"

Even from this distance, the crimson in Modesto's cheeks stands out like a beacon.

"We can't just leave them out there." Tunny's croaking groan becomes a ray of hope as the crashing of the witch's pestle begins to shake the trees. Exasperated, Modesto stares down at me for another second before disappearing from view.

"No." Panic rises in my throat. "It can't end like this."

The thud of the stone mortar, so close my eardrums pop with every strike, causes my teeth to shake.

"Please, Modesto." I pull Trilby close to my side. "If not for me, then for your sister."

Silence reigns for a long moment before the clank of chains and a squealing creak fill the air. The drawbridge begins a far too slow descent, even as the witch's music crescendoes to ear-splitting volume. My pulse roars in my ears as my heart tries to tear its way out of my chest.

"Hurry," I shout.

"She's almost here," Trilby pleads.

The drawbridge freezes two thirds of the way down, its rough wood-and-iron edge still several feet from the tips of my outstretched fingers. I glance back and find the witch peering at me through the framed portal.

"When will you learn, Scheherazade, that you are not welcome here?" Her clashing iron teeth ring like hammer strikes on an anvil. "I had hoped you would honor my polite requests to leave, but perhaps a visit to my home is in order. Are you available… for dinner?"

"Let the bridge down," I scream. "She's coming for us."

"It's stuck. God help us, it's stuck." Modesto's crisp accent cuts through the space even as the sound of brisk steps like wooden mallets reverberate through the bridge.

"Scheherazade." Tunny peers down at me frantically from the bridge above. "Hand me the girl." He stretches down his stump-like arms. Without a second thought, I scoop up Trilby's squirming form and hold the girl above my head.

"No, Scheherazade." She bucks in my grasp. "I won't leave you."

"Take her, Tunny."

The gnome pulls Trilby up and over the lip of the bridge. Then, the longest thirty seconds in history pass before he returns for me. Though we both stretch for all we're worth, his gnarled root fingers remain more than a foot out of reach.

"I'm sorry, Tunny. It's too far."

"Then take a leap of faith, Scheherazade." Tunny waggles the stubby fingers of his outstretched arm. "As we have with you."

"Yes, fair Scheherazade. Leap to your death." Her mortar and pestle left behind in the gallery, Baba Yaga strides toward me armed with only her broom, the grass and weeds at her feet wilting as she passes. "See how you fare against the creatures that stir the murky waters surrounding this ancient castle."

I glance down at the churning water mere inches from my toes and make a decision. I tear the sarong from my body and throw the length of cloth into the air. The delicate silk catches on one of Tunny's splintered fingernails.

"Pull me up," I shout.

"The gnome cannot save you," the witch hisses as she closes the distance between us. "No more dismissals. No more reprieves. This ends now."

"No." Tunny spins the sarong like a bullwhip, transforming the fine green fabric into a silk rope. "Grab the end, Scheherazade."

I leap from the witch's outstretched claws and grab the end of the makeshift rope. Though the beadwork cuts into my fingers, the hundred little barbs give me something to cling to as my toes dangle inches above the seething black water of the moat. My weight nearly pulls the silk from Tunny's wooden fingers.

"Don't let go, Tunny."

"I'm trying," he shouts between grunts. "I'm trying."

"Don't worry." Trilby's face appears next to Tunny's. She grabs the rope with her graceful hands and pulls. "We won't let you fall."

I adjust my grasp in an attempt to get a better hold on the rope and instead slide another few inches. The icy water steals the warmth from my feet as my toes dip below the turbid surface. And there's more than mere water below me. My foot brushes against something hard and rough. I glance down and immediately wish I hadn't.

A pair of antennae longer than my body emerges from the churning water, followed by a giant claw that reaches for my dangling legs. My breath catches in my throat as a terror from a child's darkest imagination rears from the moat's muddied surface. A nightmare combination of lobster and squid, the thing levels its two eyestalks in my direction, its monstrous pincer unhinging as bile-colored water runs off its muddy green exoskeleton.

Hand over hand, I pull myself up the quickly unwinding silk, the creature's slime-covered claw snapping at the air where my leg was a split second before. With a roar, the monster erupts from the water, its beak-like maw gaping as it hurtles at my midsection.

"Pull, you two," I scream. "Pull." The sound of rending silk fills the air, only to be swallowed by the creature's bellowing even as the witch's staccato laughter echoes in my head. I squeeze my eyes shut, imagining myself falling toward the creature's mouth, when two very different sets of hands grasp my wrists. One like tree bark, the other as supple as a lover's touch, the two hands jerk me up and over the lip of the drawbridge. I open my eyes to find Modesto and Tunny hauling me across the lip of the drawbridge as Trilby holds what's left of my sarong.

The four of us tumble down the other side and land at the base of the bridge in a tangle of bodies. The monster's roar and the witch's frantic screams fill the air. Before I can take another breath, the drawbridge shudders at the force of a monstrous blow.

"She's still coming for you." Modesto extricates himself from our twisted knot of arms and legs and runs to a large barrel-shaped device wrapped in chain. "The windlass got stuck as I tried to lower the bridge. I'm not sure I'll be able to get it back up."

Tunny and I scramble to our feet and rush to Modesto's side. Our efforts to get the windlass working are futile. Dark movement catches my eye. Trilby screams as the monster's enormous claw clamps down on the base of the bridge. The wood groans like an old tree in a hurricane.

I grab Modesto's sleeve and point to the giant pincer. "Isn't that monstrosity supposed to protect your castle?"

"Once." Modesto strains at the unmoving crank. "The witch controls it now."

Though better than a foot thick, the section of timber deepest in the creature's claw snaps like a twig as the bridge continues to splinter in its monstrous grasp. Trilby squeals and runs to my side.

"It's getting through." Tunny grabs the other handle of the windlass crank. "Pull, Scheherazade, with all you've got."

In a flash, the answer comes to me. "Modesto. Tunny. Stop."

"What?" Modesto says. I can't decide which of the three appears the most shocked.

"The witch. She runs everything here. She controls the creature. Who's to say she's not in control of the bridge as well?"

"But the bridge is meant to protect us." Trilby runs to my side. "Isn't it?"

Another timber snaps in two as I drop to one knee and take Trilby by the shoulders. "The bridge didn't keep her out before and that was before she had a bus-sized lobster at her command."

"What would you have us do, then?" Modesto throws his hands up. "Lie down and die?"

"No. The opposite, in fact. I'm here for a reason, and she knows it."

Tunny turns and looks at me. "And what purpose is that?"

I rise and take Modesto's hands, more to get him to abandon the useless windlass than any other reason. "Remember when I was here before and we were running from the witch?"

A lone eyebrow rises. "How could I forget?"

"You showed me a stairwell before, one that leads to the Catacombs."

At the sound of the word, half the drawbridge tears clear, revealing the witch riding atop the monster's armored carapace.

I pull Modesto toward the hall. "Take me there, now, before it's too late."

We sprint from the windlass room across the courtyard and back to the keep, slamming the ten-foot double doors behind us for all the good that will do. The witch, mounted atop the clawed nightmare, has already covered half the distance from the front gate, and the doors to the keep are no more substantial than the two-foot thick timbers the monster splintered moments before.

"Quickly," I whisper to Modesto. "The stairwell."

"It's this way." Modesto grabs my hand and pulls me down the same grand hallway as before. "Just a little farther."

"Wait." Tunny jerks his thumb in the opposite direction. "We can't leave him in here with the witch and that monster."

"Leave who?" Trilby asks. "Who are you talking about, Tunny?"

It takes a moment for my mind to make the connection. "Of course."

Tunny leads us down the hallway to the left as the monster's first blow lands upon the door to the keep. The corridors twist and turn more like an amusement park ride than any structure a sane person would design. Finally, at the end of a narrow section of hallway, we come to another stairwell, this one leading upwards. We rush single file up three flights of winding stone and step off into a room decorated with rich tapestries and fine carvings.

"He's here?" I ask.

Tunny nods as he steps past me and pulls back a tapestry decorated with lion and unicorn, revealing an arched doorway similar to the alcoves of the Exhibition. There, in the hidden room seated on a satin pillow and eating some sort of porridge, Antoine glances up at the four of us and lets out a gasp.

"Lady Scheherazade," he stammers, his *Tuileries* accent even more pronounced than before. "You came back for me."

"Yes, Antoine, I came back for you." I offer him a hand and help him to his feet. As he joins the others by the door, I lower my gaze to meet Tunny's sad eyes. "For all of you."

In the distance, the series of blows against the door to the keep grows faster, louder. The crack of splintering wood fills the air.

I turn to Modesto, his face frozen in a rictus of fear. "The Catacombs. Take us there. Now."

For once, Modesto remains quiet and does as he's told. The five of us sprint back down the stairwell leading to Antoine's tower and back out into the main hall.

"This way," Modesto shouts. "Hurry."

As we rush past the intersection, I chance a glance to my left and find the doors to the keep demolished. Atop the monster, Yaga barrels down the corridor at us, the floor fracturing beneath the thing's clawed feet.

"Move, Modesto." I slide the dagger from its sheath, for all the good it will do against such a beast. "She's inside."

"I noticed," he grunts as he picks up his pace for the far end of the hall.

Seconds later, the five of us arrive at the doorway Modesto says leads to the Catacombs. Cool humidity and the musty scent of damp earth float up from below as if from a waiting grave. One by one, we take the spiral stone staircase that leads down into darkness, a series of flickering torches all that lights our way. I take some comfort in knowing the narrow staircase may allow the witch to follow but not her monstrous steed.

As if the laws of physics matter in a place made of dream.

At the end of what seems an eternity of descent, we come to a stone landing and a small, round door.

"Shall we?" Modesto asks.

He opens the studded door and steps through, beckoning me to follow. I stoop as I pass the circular portal and sheathe the dagger as my eyes adjust to the dim. The unsteady incandescence of eight torches barely illuminates this octagonal room that appears hewn from solid granite. Across the way, at the center of the far wall, another door of similar dimensions rests slightly ajar.

"The Catacombs, Lady Scheherazade, as requested."

"Fantastic," I sprint for the other door. "Let's go."

I'm halfway across the room before I realize I'm alone. I look back. Tunny, Modesto, Antoine, and Trilby all stand staring at me in the dim light at the bottom of the stairs.

"What are you all waiting for? We've got to get out of here."

As one, their gazes drop to the floor.

"What is it?"

Modesto steps forward. "We may bring you to the Catacombs, Scheherazade, but none of us may enter."

"It is forbidden," Tunny adds.

Antoine, so happy just moments before, stands sullen and silent while Trilby bites at her lip and refuses to meet my gaze as she fidgets with her hair.

"Forbidden?" I ask. "By who? The witch?"

"Who else, dearie?" Yaga's voice echoes through the space as she steps through the door behind the others and closes it behind her. "For all your bluster, these four still know who runs the show around here." Trembling, Modesto and Tunny part, allowing the witch to pass between them. She looks me up and down before turning her attention to the dimly lit room. "I should have imploded this place the last time I was here. Would have saved us all a lot of trouble."

"But you can't." I continue to back toward the opposite side of the room. "You talk a good game, but destroying the Catacombs is beyond even your power."

The witch glares at me, even as her lips pull back to reveal her iron smile. "And why exactly is that, Lady Scheherazade?"

"Because the truth lies here. Despite your best efforts to keep me out of your Exhibition and away from this place, here I stand on the precipice of discovering whatever it is you're so desperate to hide." I echo her smile. "The truth, it seems, cannot be bricked up."

"So very clever," Yaga says, "but as always, your knowledge is incomplete. You think a visit to the Catacombs will give you the answers you seek, but beyond that doorway lies only death and pain. Pain for you, for me, for all who call the Exhibition home. You've seen what I can do in this place, but I assure you my influence pales in comparison to what you will unleash if you go through that door."

"More empty threats, Baba Yaga? More scare tactics?"

Unlike the last time, she doesn't even blink at the utterance of her name. "I speak only the truth. Pass through that door if you must, but be warned. What you learn there may prove your undoing and that of us all."

I retreat the last few steps, never taking my eyes off the witch's bent form, and rest my hand on the door handle. "I'm willing to take that chance."

"Farewell then, Scheherazade. Pass the portal and face your destiny, but forget not that you were warned."

I weigh the witch's words even as the despondent gazes of the four I am forced to leave in her foul presence bore into my soul. Riddled with indecision, the tear coursing down Antoine's face reminds me of where and who I am. I spin and jerk the door open and the musty dampness of death fills the room. I glance back to wish the others well and find the room empty.

"Dammit." Simultaneously defeated and victorious, I turn back to the door. Etched into the wood with what appears to have been someone's fingernails, three words are barely visible in the dim light.

CATACOMBÆ SEPULCRUM ROMANUM

Before I can even mouth the words, gravity shifts sideways and I fall through the open doorway. The door slams shut above me. I tumble through utter blackness and land on smooth, cool stone. All around me, murmurs fill the air, just below the threshold of understanding. In pain but uninjured, I rise from the floor and strain my eyes, trying to pierce the veil of darkness. To my left, I spot a flicker of yellow incandescence down what appears to be a long passageway. I move toward the light, the whispered voices around me growing louder with every step.

I walk for what seems a mile in the gloomy hallway, finding my way by touch as much as sight. Water drips down on my head from above, each chilling rivulet like a dead man's finger tracing the line of my scalp. At times smooth and at others jagged, the walls feel as if they are constructed of thousands of individual stones, all placed with such care it makes following the passage relatively easy. Only as the light in the room increases do I discover what I'm feeling aren't stones at all, but human skulls.

As I approach the flickering light, the whispering grows louder. The language sounds foreign, but as before in *Tuileries* and *The Marketplace at Limoges*, I can somehow understand what the voices are saying.

"*Sounds and ideas are hanging in the air. I am devouring them and stuffing myself.*"

The words are Latin, though I hear them in my head in English complemented by of all things, a Russian accent.

"*The creative spirit of the dead Hartmann leads me toward the skulls, invokes them. The skulls begin to glow softly from within.*"

"The dead Hartmann?" I whisper. "What does this place have to do with him?" Answered only with the sound of dripping water, I add, "Or Anthony for that matter?"

"Everything, I'm afraid." The voice deep and resonant, the Russian accent comes across as almost comical despite the gruesome surroundings. A stout man with a thick black beard and unkempt hair steps from the shadow of a column to my left. "I can only assume you are the Lady Scheherazade that has been causing all the uproar along the Exhibition."

"That would be me." In this place of the dead, I had assumed I would finally meet the lovely young woman whose secrets rest at the center of this mystery. Why I thought anything in this madhouse would occur according to my expectations is beyond me.

The man's face is nothing like the pictures I've seen on Anthony's records. Still, I know his identity immediately. Tailored black suit. Formal manner. Wise eyes that have seen everything. "And you must be—"

"Your instincts speak true, Lady Scheherazade. They have led you to this moment and you now speak with the composer of this Exhibition." He takes a slight bow. "As you have no doubt guessed, I am Modest Mussorgsky."

XXIV

Cum Mortuis in Lingua Mortua

Mussorgsky gazes upon me with an even mix of curiosity and amusement. Though I understand I am merely meeting another aspect of Anthony Faircloth, the true composer of this symphony of pain, I take a step back, not out of fear but a strange reverence.

"Why are you hiding down here in the dark?" I ask. "The Exhibition is your place, your creation. You should be out in it, enjoying it, living it."

"Ah, dear child, would that I could. Once I roamed the hallways and alcoves above, admiring the various pieces, reveling in the harmonies that poured from each framed canvas. Music and tranquility ruled the Exhibition, that is, until the Dark Day."

"The Dark Day?"

"The day everything changed. The day the pictures came to life, left their canvases and walked the halls alongside their creator. The day *she* assumed control and banished me to the one place in the Exhibition she dare not go."

"You speak of Baba Yaga?"

Mussorgsky winces. "You say that name so freely. She cannot come here, and still I will not speak her name. You are brave, storyteller, though more than a bit foolhardy."

"I've faced the witch more than once and survived, yet everyone in this place is terrified of her. Is she truly deserving of such awe and fear?"

"You, perhaps, can saunter around unaffected by the witch's influence, but you are an outsider and not subject to her whims. Those of us who call the Exhibition home don't enjoy such freedom." He takes a hesitant step toward me, the shadows across his face briefly hiding the sadness in his eyes. "I've not seen it myself, obviously, but I've heard through various channels about the destruction left in the wake of her many encounters with you. Other than the witch's own, do any of the pictures remain untouched?"

"The last one, I believe." Without understanding why, I hang my head in shame. "I have yet to see *The Bogatyr Gates*."

"Then all is lost." Mussorgsky slinks past me and rests his forearm and head against one of the skulls. "As best I know, the Gates no longer exist."

"They don't exist?"

"There are whispers, particularly down here among the skulls, that *The Bogatyr Gates* once rested at the end of the hall, past *The Hut on Fowl's Legs* where the witch resides. However, no one along the gallery, including me, has ever come upon the final canvas of the Exhibition."

"But you're the composer." I fix Mussorgsky with a confused stare. "Didn't you create everything here?"

"I'm afraid I don't follow your question."

Magical landscapes. Odd friends. A witch all that stands in the way of going home. And the man who supposedly has all the answers as clueless everyone else.

"This must have been how Dorothy felt."

Mussorgsky's brow furrows. "Who is this Dorothy of whom you speak?"

I ponder how it's possible Anthony, who has apparently seen every movie under the sun, doesn't know what I'm talking about. Then, in a flash, it becomes clear. Mussorgsky died years before L. Frank Baum put pen to paper on his most famous work, and over half a century before the movie hit the silver screen.

If there's one thing I've learned about Anthony Faircloth, it's that the boy is a stickler for detail.

"Another time, oh great and powerful Oz." I offer a devilish smile, taking some comfort in knowing at least one thing the composer doesn't.

He levels an even gaze at me, his lips turning up in a slight smirk. "So, Scheherazade. I have explained why I hide in the Paris Catacombs, but you have not explained your own presence down here amid the darkness and skulls of the long dead."

The answer is on my tongue in a second, though the over-arching "why" behind my actions eludes even me. "*The Catacombs* picture was blocked from the Exhibition proper. I figured anything the witch was so eager to keep hidden was something that needed to be brought into the light."

Mussorgsky's robust laugh echoes through the space. "Other than the last and only refuge of a once great composer, I'm not certain what you hope to find here."

"Maybe nothing." I jump as a skull falls from the wall and shatters on impact with the stone floor. "There is one thing you can answer for me, however, if you will."

Mussorgsky strokes his beard. "And what might that be, my child?"

"This Dark Day. What happened to cause such a calamity to your Exhibition?"

The composer's piercing stare freezes me to the spot. "Why would you care about that?"

"I wander your Exhibition for more than merely the fine art and music. I seek a boy hidden among the pictures. I've found evidence of him more than once since coming here, but each time it's been no more than an echo. A shadow, if you will. I believe the circumstances of your Dark Day and his whereabouts are somehow intertwined."

"What is this boy's name?"

"Anthony Faircloth."

A flicker of recognition twinkles in Mussorgsky's eyes. "Anthony. A strong name. Derived from the Latin, I believe, as would befit this place. A name shared by generals and artists alike."

I stare at the composer sidelong, studying his eyes. "Do you know where I might find him?"

"You already have the answer to that question." He circles me like a curious lion, his unkempt mane and dark beard adding to the illusion. "Or at least knowledge of where you must go to find the answer." At my baffled stare, he adds, "Tell me. Who seeks to keep you from learning what events transpired on this Anthony's Darkest of Days?"

"Baba–" At Mussorgsky's grimace, I stop mid-name. "The witch."

"You know where you must go, then."

I curse myself for ignoring a simple fact that's been staring me in the face since my first walk down the Exhibition hall. "I must enter her picture." I think back to the album I studied at the Faircloth house. "*The Hut on Fowl's Legs*, as you called it before."

"You will find your answers there." His eyes take on a sad cast. "Both to questions you have asked and others you have yet to consider."

"I'm not so sure about that. I can consider quite a bit."

"From your lips, Lady Scheherazade." He glances about. "Is that all you require?"

I raise an eyebrow. "And what could I possibly be keeping you from in your little dungeon of skulls?"

"Oh, I have nowhere to be. It's just that I had a notion your instincts led you here for a bigger purpose than to obtain answers you already possess." He cocks his head to one side. "Tell me, Scheherazade, what is it you really wish to know?"

He's right. I've been holding back, half afraid of what I'd find if I probed further. "Why this place, Mussorgsky? Why the Exhibition? Do you and the others know where you are? What you are? Hell, who you are?"

Mussorgsky looks away, his face turning up into a furtive smile. Before I can ask another question, a strangely familiar sound fills the space.

Humming.

Like a certain boy in a place very far from here.

Scheherazade's theme.

"On some level," he says, "everyone knows their true nature. Some hide it well, and some even delude themselves into believing they're something they're not. In the end, however, everyone knows." His piercing gaze sends a chill to my core. "Everyone."

"Another question I already had the answer to."

"Sometimes the answers we already know are the hardest ones for us to see."

A grim smile blossoms on my face. "If cryptic is the order of the day, I'm not certain there's any reason to continue this conversation. Do you?"

"You could stay and keep an old man company." He spreads his arms wide in a sweeping gesture. "The skulls do an awful lot of whispering but their ears are long gone and they don't tend to listen much anymore."

"As tempting as that sounds, I'm afraid I must be going." I glance back the way I came. "Any thoughts of how to get back to the main hall of the Exhibition? I came via the castle, but Modesto's home is no longer safe. I left a rather angry witch there when I joined you here and don't relish the thought of another encounter with her. At least not till I'm ready."

"That is wise, fair lady, and I may indeed be able to help you." He brings his hands together before his chest and cracks his knuckles. "This Exhibition, as you said upon our meeting, is my creation, but a piece of it is more you than me. Do you remember? Other than this place, what is the one picture the witch has yet to invade?"

It comes to me in a second. "The home of the two Jews. She's never set foot in Goldenberg and Schmuÿle's place that I'm aware of."

"Go on." Mussorgsky cocks his head to one side and gives me a smiling nod.

"Anthony's never met Sterling or Bolger as far as I know, so how would he—" My mouth turns up in a bemused smile. "I get it. That little corner of Anthony's brain is my turf."

Mussorgsky makes a conciliatory wave. "That is one way of saying it."

"But I still don't understand. How do I get there?"

Without another word, Mussorgsky raises his hand and a conductor's baton appears in his nimble grasp. He waves the slender length of wood in graceful rhythm and as if in answer, the sound of violins at the high end of their register fills the space. A few seconds later, woodwinds break in, the tune a familiar one. A variation of the "Promenade" theme, this darker, sadder version echoes those same thirteen notes I first heard upon my initial descent into Anthony's mind, a melody that has followed me every step of my sojourn through the Exhibition.

Mussorgsky smiles at me. "You recognize the melody." I'm not certain if some look of recognition on my face brought his compliment or if somehow he read my mind.

"This piece. It serves as a bridge between all the others."

"Precisely. The name of this section, '*Cum mortuis in lingua mortua*,' translates literally as 'with the dead in a dead language' as I believe you already know. More melancholy than its previous incarnations in the suite, this second part of 'The Catacombs' melody is indeed a simple variation of 'Promenade,' the melody I crafted to lead the listener from one piece to the next."

The baton undulates in his hand, the gentle back and forth motion reminding me of the witch's broom. Over the next few seconds, the music filling the space shifts from dark to bright, dismal to cheery. Mussorgsky waves the baton at the wall of skulls to his left like a sorcerer's wand and the grisly bulwark opens into a doorway beyond which rests the rich carpets and lush furniture of Goldenberg's study.

"And just like that, Dorothy is returned to Kansas." I glance down at my sandaled feet and laugh. "And I don't even have to click together any ruby slippers."

"If we meet again, you will have to tell me more of this Dorothy, but for now, I suggest you go quickly. While it's true you are trapped in the Catacombs with this decidedly aged composer, like him, you are also safe from the witch's machinations within their bony walls." He motions toward the open doorway with the baton and takes another bow. "Out there, neither I nor the souls of these thousand skulls can protect you. I suggest you watch your back."

"I will." Stepping to the door, I turn back for one last question. "You do know, don't you? Who you are?"

"Better than you, my dear, though you are indeed insightful." With his free hand he motions to the gloom that surrounds us. "The Catacombs are the only place the witch cannot go and therefore the only place secrets other than hers are safe. Things can be known here, even if they are not shared. Now hurry back to the Exhibition before she discovers you've returned. She's quick, that one, but even she can't be everywhere at once."

"Thank you for everything…" I stumble on the next word. What to call such a man?

He laughs. "You may call me Modest, if you wish."

"Pun intended, I'm guessing."

"Perhaps." He cocks his head to the side and offers me one last smile.

I return his mischievous grin. "Thank you, Modest."

I step through the door and onto the plush carpet of Goldenberg's study. After my time in the Catacombs, the dim lighting of the room appears as bright as noonday sun. The insane monkeys dancing across every square inch of the wallpaper all turn and giggle at my entrance. I turn back to tell Mussorgsky one last goodbye only to find the wall sealed behind me as if the door never existed. The space filled with an ornate full-length mirror, the olive-skinned woman staring back at me is fully clothed again, her green sarong restored and the dagger at her side glinting despite the room's muted light.

I turn and suppress a laugh at the scene before me. Asleep in their respective chairs, Samuel Goldenberg and Schmuÿle seem hell-bent on deciding who can snore the loudest. Goldenberg's dark features bring flashes of my recent falling out with Sterling, and I decide it best to leave without waking them.

Creeping past the two sleeping men and into the next room, I close the door to the study with a quiet click. I search the place for a way out and fail, every door leading to yet another room of opulent extravagance. Then it occurs to me. I'm looking for the wrong type of door.

I scour the house again, going from one of Goldenberg's paintings to the next, brushing my fingertips across each canvas, and still nothing. I'm somewhere along the Exhibition, but I have no way to get to the hall, and there is no composer here to point me in the right direction. Frustrated, I kick the wall, leaving an ugly crack in the previously perfect plaster.

"Why so angry, Lady Scheherazade?" Startling at first, Goldenberg's deep voice summons conflicting emotions from deep within. "Is it such a terrible fate to visit my home a second time?"

I turn to face the master of the house. Not surprisingly, he isn't alone.

"Can't you see, Samuel? She can't figure it out." Schmuÿle's leering grin and nasal tones raise the hairs on my neck. "So simple, and yet she can't see it."

"Can't see what?" I ask. "Will one person in this place please speak in something other than riddles?"

"Behave yourself, Schmuÿle." Goldenberg leads Schmuÿle and me back into the study. He offers me a high-backed chair in the corner before he and Schmuÿle retire to their respective ends of the couch opposite. "Now, fair lady, how may we assist you?"

"You speak for both of us now, do you?" Schmuÿle says.

"Quiet." Goldenberg's eyes flare with barely kept anger. "Lady Scheherazade, it is clear you're upset. What can I do to help?"

"I've been to the Catacombs and met who resides there. With many questions answered, I seek to return to the Exhibition, but cannot find the way."

"I told you, Samuel. She's lost. Lost in this maze of a house you've built."

Goldenberg ignores his erstwhile roommate. "You seek to return to the main hall, then?"

"The others. I left them with the witch. I need to find out if they're okay."

"Always putting others ahead of yourself. That is why you are the storyteller and we merely the stories."

"Can you help me?"

"We can." Schmuÿle winks at me. "Whether or not we will is another matter entirely."

Goldenberg plants his palm on his forehead. "Once more, Schmuÿle, and *you* can go stay with the witch in the Russian wood."

With a huff, Schmuÿle crosses his arms and looks away, though he does keep his silence. Goldenberg turns back to me. "I met the composer once. A gentle, wise man. What did you learn from him?"

I think for a moment. "Everything I asked him, I already knew."

"I would argue you already know the way out of your current predicament as well."

"But how? None of the doors go anywhere but another room and unlike the Exhibition, your paintings are nothing but that."

"Ah, but when you look at the paintings, you look at another." Goldenberg wears the same mischievous grin Mussorgsky wore minutes before. "Perhaps you are looking for the wrong thing."

"Or *at* the wrong thing," Schmuÿle says.

Goldenberg's words from before return to my mind.

"*It would seem you've visited the Exhibition so often you've become one of the exhibits.*"

"This place. It's me."

"Precisely." Goldenberg leans in. "And if one wishes to look upon oneself?"

Without a word, I stand and go to the mirror. The woman looking back is confident, though her eyes betray a hint of fear. "To return to the hall, I have to go through the looking glass?"

"Indeed," Goldenberg and Schmuÿle say in unison.

Fascinating. First Dorothy. Now Alice.

Goldenberg rises and joins me at the mirror. The image of Sterling and me standing together sends my heart racing.

Dammit.

I meet his reflected gaze. "I suppose this is goodbye, then."

"Fear not, Scheherazade. We may yet meet again."

I glance across my shoulder. "Farewell, Schmuÿle. Thanks for the delightful conversation."

"How… amusing." Schmuÿle rises from the couch, pulls his threadbare coat about his gaunt midsection, and slinks out of the room. "Have fun storming the castle," he mutters before slamming the door shut behind him.

I turn back to Goldenberg. "I do hope we meet again someday."

He touches his fingertip to my forehead. "A part of me will always be here. Like you said, this place is as much you as anyone else." He smiles and gestures to the mirror. "Now, go."

As I step through the mirror's polished surface, the various characters I've met on the Exhibition rush through my mind. Witch, gnome, troubadour, schoolmarm, farmer, ballerina, the oddest couple imaginable, the four women of the market, and now the composer himself. All so real, and yet all just a figment of a boy's vibrant imagination.

Mussorgsky's words echo in my mind.

"*On some level, everyone knows their true nature. Some hide it well, and some even delude themselves into believing they're something they're not. In the end, however, everyone knows.*"

My foot comes to rest on the parquet floor of the Exhibition hallway. The space is unusually quiet and the lights even dimmer than I remember. The fresco above my head for the first time is blank with no mythological beings or comic book heroes there to keep me company. The stale odor of smoke wafts from the *Gnomus* alcove up the way. The sound of falling stones echoes from the alcove of *The Old Castle* and I sneak up the hall to take a peek. There, framed for anyone to see, Modesto's castle lies in ruin. The splintered drawbridge hangs crooked, half-devoured by the monstrous lobster-thing from the moat, while all that remains of the main wall and its fine battlements is a pile of rubble.

The last bastion of sanity along the hall and I've destroyed it. Only the realm of the witch remains, the last place I want to go and the only one that will provide the answers I seek.

"Satisfied, are you?" The metallic bite to the words sends an icicle through my heart. I turn to find Baba Yaga staring at me. No mortar. No pestle. No broom. Just her and that wiry body, foul iron teeth, and grungy hair. Her eyes, always full of such venom, appear sad. Almost regretful.

"He was right." I feel my lips turn up at the corners and hope my face is more smile than snarl. "You are fast."

"I know everything that happens in my Exhibition." She pulls air through her nostrils with a loud snort. "Your scent carries far, storyteller."

"What have you done with the others?"

"I assure you they are safe. My quarrel is not with them, as well you know."

"Then what is it you want?"

The witch's eyes narrow. "Now you ask, now that every place but the Russian wood where I reside has been spoiled beyond repair. Now you deign to ask what it is the old witch wants."

"You didn't have to destroy those places. You've had every opportunity to talk with me."

The sadness in the witch's face shifts to exasperation. "And if a thief enters your home in the night, you would offer her a drink and a blanket? Forget not which of us is the intruder."

"And I will keep intruding until I find Anthony. You could have ended this long before now, but you have chosen to dismiss and ignore my every effort to find and free him."

"The boy is safer this way." She covers her mouth, realizing she's said too much. "We are all safer this way. None of us in pain, none of us suffering, none of us in danger." She points a long, crooked finger at me. "Except from you."

"But don't you see? All of you were suffering even as I walked the Exhibition the first time. Tunny, all alone and lonely in his abandoned forest. Modesto, his beautiful music unappreciated in his empty castle. Antoine, alone despite the sea of children surrounding him. Hartmann, his entire existence literally turned upside down. Trilby, forced to dance at the whim of any passerby. Goldenberg and Schmuÿle, perpetually arguing over nothing. Even you, Baba Yaga, are forced to rule here by mortar and pestle. The rest all fear and hate you."

"Fear? Yes. Hate? That is a matter of perspective." She peers off into the distance. "I provide order to this place. Keep the various exhibits in line. Discipline them when needed."

"When needed? You've destroyed nearly every canvas but your own."

"And whose fault is that?" Foul spittle flies from her iron teeth. "Each of the exhibits was quite satisfied with their lot until you came along. I could argue you are as much responsible for the destruction as I am. Perhaps more so. Hate me if you will, Lady Scheherazade, but you cannot argue the fact I am needed."

"In this realm, perhaps, but for every moment this realm exists, the boy I seek remains a prisoner in his own body and no one can help him or even reach him but me."

Baba Yaga opens her mouth to respond but holds her tongue, stroking the misshapen mole at the tip of her chin as she considers her next words.

"I take it you spoke to the composer," she eventually whispers, her voice no louder than the wind whispering through the ruins of Modesto's castle.

"I found him in the Catacombs. Or at least, he found me."

"What did he tell you?" she asks. "Lies, no doubt. Lies about me."

"He told me you hold the answers. That they rest in your realm and within your hut." I take a breath. "He told me of the Dark Day."

Her flesh, already the color of dead fish, grows a shade paler at my words.

"We do not speak of that day." The witch turns and heads for the alcove where her painting awaits. "None of us."

"And that's the problem. The whole lot of you ignore the real issue at hand, living your sham lives as if any of you even exist, while the boy whose mind you occupy suffers in silence. And you're the worst of all. The warden of this prison."

"This place is a thing of beauty." The witch's eyes burn through me. "Or at least it was."

I return her glare. "A beautiful prison is still a prison."

"You're no prisoner here." She motions to the walls surrounding us and snarls. "More like a rat that keeps popping back in for a bite of cheese. Now, begone from this place."

"Begone, begone, begone. Is that all you can do? All the fearful reverence the people in this place give you and all you can do with the one thorn in your side is send me away time and again?"

"Dare set foot in the picture at the end of the hall and you'll wish you had stayed away." She raises a hand to banish me from the Exhibition, but before she can utter a word, I turn my back on her and head for the enormous chained door at the end of the hallway.

"Where do you think you're going, storyteller? I haven't dismissed you."

"I've heard quite enough of your metal mouth for one day, but don't worry. I'll be back."

"But you can't go that way. The door is barred and the Kalendar Prince's magic word, already spoken once, cannot help you again."

I ignore her protests and continue walking for the door. At my simple wave, the body of the colossal padlock holding the door closed slides from its shackle. The square of iron crashes to the floor with a thud that shakes the entire structure. I chance a single glance back and catch the witch's astonished stare.

"As you so politely pointed out, I'm no prisoner here." A musical quality colors my words. "If it's all the same to you, I'll show myself out."

XXV

Doloroso

For once, I return from a trip through Anthony's private gallery of insanity with some semblance of control over my body. This time it's like waking from a nap instead of coming out of a seizure. As always, my eyes need a moment to adjust to reality. Caroline and Veronica stand on either side of me, both looking on with concern, while Rachel sits on the couch staring at me. It's the first time she's borne witness to my work with her brother. I'm impressed by her lack of tears, though her trembling lips betray her true emotions.

"Don't worry, Rachel." I sit up, my head spinning with a hint of vertigo, and squeeze her knee. "I'm fine. So is Anthony."

"You were gone a long time." She bites her lip to still its quivering. "Where did you go?"

I caress Anthony's forehead. "I was in here. With your brother."

She tries to smile, but the fear in her visage steals any warmth from her expression.

I glance over at Caroline. "How long this time?"

"A couple of hours." She offers me some ice water and I take it greedily. "You made it to the Catacombs, didn't you? You and Anthony were humming together just a few minutes ago. You've never done that before."

"Humming? What did it sound like?"

"The quiet section at the end of *Pictures at an Exhibition*, right before the part with the witch."

"*Cum mortuis in lingua mortua.*" The hairs on my neck stand at attention, both at the invocation of the movement's title and at the realization everything before has led to this, an inevitable confrontation between Baba Yaga and Lady Scheherazade. "Speaking with the dead in the tongue of the dead."

"Dead." Caroline's face blanches. "Was it…?"

"No. Not Julianna."

"Anthony?"

"No, he's very much alive."

"What about the witch?" Caroline asks. "Did you see her?"

"More than once, though this time I left of my own accord." My quiet laugh brings on a fit of coughing. "I don't think that went over too well."

"Hold on, you two." Veronica, who has held her tongue since I awoke, looks from me to Caroline, her gaze incredulous. "I know what I just saw, but you two can't seriously expect me to believe Mira actually went into Anthony's mind. That's impossible."

"I know it's hard to swallow," I whisper, "but it's the truth."

"That's an understatement." She brings her attention back to me. "These characters you say you keep meeting. They're all pieces of Anthony, right?"

"As best I can tell."

"And you're working to put him back together, like some kind of puzzle?"

"It's the only thing that makes sense."

"*All the king's horses and all the king's men…*" Veronica's eyes grow distant. "What could have done something like that to him?"

"If and when we find that out, then the real work can begin." I turn to Caroline. "I met a new character today. There, in the Catacombs. He called himself Mussorgsky. Said he was the composer of the whole thing and the creator of the Exhibition."

"The composer stays hidden below while his various works run amok?"

"He told me he was banished there by Baba Yaga and claims it's the only place in the Exhibition truly safe from her." I turn back to Veronica. "As to your question, Mussorgsky spoke of a Dark Day, after which the various paintings of the Exhibition came to life. I have no doubt that's the same day Anthony fell silent."

"Are we really having this conversation?" Veronica rises from the couch. "I thought when you said 'psychic' you were talking about hypnosis or some new age psychotherapy. What you're talking about is impossible."

"But, this is exactly what I explained to you." I wonder why she's having so much trouble with this, until I remember I'm the only one in the room that's been sensing other people's emotions since puberty. "Isn't it?"

"I'm sorry. It's just a lot more real when you see it with your own eyes." She paces the room. "Did my being here… help?"

"It's hard to know for sure, but I've always found the more positive energy in the room, the better for all involved."

"Then I'll be back tomorrow." The color rises in her cheeks. "As long as you promise not to take me along for the ride." The usual cool chlorine smell I get off Veronica evens out as she takes a deep breath and attempts to smile.

I shake her hand. "It's a deal."

Caroline shows Veronica to the door and upon her return sits on the couch between her two youngest. Rachel cuddles up close to her mother while Anthony, as with almost every encounter, shudders at her slightest touch.

"Anthony's still not loving the physical contact, I see."

"I don't know." Caroline looks away. "He never seems too upset when you're around."

My toes curl in my shoes. "I'm sorry, Caroline. I'm guessing that's because I'm the only one he can truly communicate with right now.

"That's all fine and good, Mira, but other than one particularly nasty piece of Anthony's subconscious, he seems to welcome you into his mind every time. Rachel as well." She motions to her daughter who has reached across her lap to stroke Anthony's leg. "Meanwhile, he won't even let me touch him without breaking into a sweat."

"He's been traumatized. No matter how much it hurts, it's nothing but a part of how he's dealing with whatever's happened to him."

Caroline pierces me with her despondent gaze. "And how would you feel if your child curled into the fetal position every time you got close?"

"Don't worry, Mommy." Rachel wraps her scrawny arms around her mother's neck and squeezes her tight. "Anthony may be sick, but we both still love you."

"I know, honey." Caroline wipes away the tear coursing down her cheek. "I know."

Caroline offers to take me back to the Blake, but for once I actually feel well enough to drive myself. This particular walk through the Exhibition left me nowhere near as drained as the others, though my decision is more about Caroline than it is about me. Her life has been an emotional tilt-a-whirl for a month and even though I'm here at her invitation, it's clear my involvement has taken its toll. She could most likely use a little time apart from the weirdo psychic that keeps playing in her kid's imaginary sandbox. Not to mention I need some alone time to mentally prepare if I'm to face Baba Yaga on her own turf in the morning. The witch may be nothing but a boy wearing a Halloween mask, but what happened to Rachel before was very real. There's not a doubt in my mind it could get a whole lot worse if Anthony's subconscious decides expelling me is no longer the best means of getting rid of a certain problematic storyteller.

The ring of my phone startles me back to reality. It's Mom.

"Hi, Mom. Everything okay?"

"Just checking in. How are things?"

"Coming along but I'm a little tired. Left the Faircloth house a few minutes ago and I'm headed back to my hotel."

"Any progress?"

"Yes and no." I take the exit for Uptown. "Though I have a feeling tomorrow morning will be quite telling."

The beep of another caller sounds in my ear. It's a Charlotte number.

"Sorry, Mom. Need to run."

"What is it?"

"Another call. Probably work. Talk to you tonight?"

"Sure." She sighs. "Just don't forget, there's a child here in Virginia who needs you too."

"Thanks, Mom." Her dig leaves a gaping hole where my heart should be. "Exactly what I needed to hear."

"I'm just saying—"

I press the end button and take the other call before Mom can finish her sentence.

Woman doesn't just know how to push my buttons. She's got them on speed dial.

"Hello? This is Mira Tejedor."

"Hi, Mira. It's Sterling."

A flood of emotion washes over me. Annoyance. Anger. Disappointment. I'm glad I don't sense the static coming out of my own head. I'd probably have to pull over and vomit.

"How may I help you, Detective?"

The pause that follows speaks volumes.

"I guess I deserve that," he answers eventually.

"You guess?"

"All right. I admit it. I was a jerk. I'm sorry." He clears his throat. "Do you have a minute?"

"One minute. I don't have to be a psychic to know you wouldn't be calling if you didn't need something from me."

Another pause. He's picking his words carefully. "You know, I really do feel bad about how things went yesterday. I kind of hoped you'd let me apologize for—"

"Apology accepted." My cheeks get hotter by the second. "Now, what is it you need?"

"Fine. If that's how you want it, here it is. Glenn Hartman is demanding you come back to the station. He's refusing to talk to anyone else until he speaks to you."

He must be kidding. "I'm sorry, Detective. Someone made it very clear yesterday I was to stay away from your prime suspect. I'd be glad to help out with the investigation, but I'm afraid I'd be charged with obstruction of justice."

A quiet sigh comes across the line. "All right, Mira. You win. I hate to admit it, but we're getting nowhere fast here. We need your help. What will it take to get you to come talk to this guy?"

I take a long moment formulating my answer. "A public apology would be a nice start. Official consultant status on the case as well, though I want my involvement kept quiet this time. No more little news leaks."

"Yes. Now—"

"That's not all. Listen. My rules are my rules, and they're there for a reason. If you so much as think about pushing me again like you did yesterday, I'm out."

"Understood." Then with barely a beat, he asks, "Can you come in now?"

"I'm on my way." A satisfied smirk blossoms across my lips. "Save me a donut."

I pull into the parking lot fifteen minutes later. A police cruiser nearly hits me as it rockets past, its tires squalling as they bite into the main road.

"Can't believe I agreed to do this," I mutter under my breath as I pull into a parking spot. I keep telling myself I'm here for Anthony, the Faircloths, the Wagners, and not for Sterling.

I almost convince myself.

Officer Bryce at the front desk has been replaced with a squat balding man about ten years my senior and a good hundred pounds heavier than is good for him.

"Well, hello there." His gaze focused about a foot lower than I'd like, my stomach turns as a heavy musk fills my mind. "Anything I can help you with?"

I turn on the spot and head for the exit. "I am not putting up with this shit tonight." I'm halfway to the door when Sterling's voice stops me in my tracks.

"Mira."

I wish I didn't like the way my name sounds coming off his lips so much. Every fiber of my being wants to keep moving, but I slow my steps and let him catch me. The circles under his eyes speak volumes. He's had a rough couple of days. I fight to squelch any sympathy and shift my expression to business casual.

"You may want to retrain your front desk help in regards to appropriate interactions with members of the opposite sex."

He glances over at the desk sergeant and sighs. "Johnson? Don't worry about him. He's harmless. An idiot, but harmless."

"We can discuss the 'harmlessness' of sexual harassment later." I cock my head to one side as my hand finds my hip. "Well? Here I am, as requested."

His gaze wanders, refusing to meet mine. "I wasn't sure you'd come."

"Neither was I." After a moment of awkward silence, I clear my throat. "Can we dispense with the not-so-pleasantries and get to work?"

He steps back as if struck. "Of course."

Good. Just the right amount of contrition. At least everyone knows where they stand now.

Sterling motions for me to follow him back into the holding area. I eye Sergeant Johnson at the front desk as we pass. He wisely keeps his head down and studies the sign-in list until we pass.

Once we're through the secure door, Sterling stops and turns to face me.

"I don't know what you said to Hartman yesterday, but he's a different guy. He was evasive before, but now he says he wants to talk as long as he gets to talk to you first." He smiles nervously. "Don't know what it is with you and men, but I'm hoping it pays off today."

"Wow." I make certain he sees the roll of my eyes. "That was nearly a compliment."

"You going to break my balls all day, Mira? I told you I was sorry."

"And the fact I'm the only one in this whole city that can help you get what you want has nothing to do with your apology, right?" My lip trembles slightly. It takes all my willpower to make it stop. "Look, I may have overstepped a bit."

"A bit?" Sterling's chin drops as he works to keep any exasperation from his tone.

"Okay, a lot, but I was only trying to help." I put my finger in his chest and try not to notice the firmness of the muscles beneath his starched shirt. "From here on in, you treat me like a partner in this, or I'm out. My priority is the Faircloth family. If I can help you along the way, so be it. Otherwise, this is your case to puzzle out. Are we clear?"

"Crystal."

The tables turned, Sterling's expression shifts to business mode and the turbulent emotions wafting off him dissipate. A part of me is disappointed.

"Now that we've got all that behind us, can we get started? Whatever you said to Hartman seems to have brought out his inner songbird. Any idea why he wants to talk to you again?"

I stop my fingers from fidgeting with my watch. "I have a pretty good guess."

"May I at least ask where you got your information?"

I close my eyes and, despite my better judgment, tell Sterling the truth. "It was Anthony."

Sterling raises an eyebrow. "I don't understand. I know you were helping him, but how could he—"

"He knows more than most give him credit for and he's actually pretty talkative once you get him started. You just have to know how to… listen."

"And he somehow knew something about Julianna?"

"Maybe. That's what I'm working out. Sure got Hartman's attention, though." I catch the glint in those investigator eyes of his. Good. I've got Sterling's attention as well. "Shall we?"

Sterling buzzes us back. We take seats at the table where I left Hartman the day before. We sit in tense silence for a couple minutes waiting for them to bring out the prisoner.

"What do you plan to tell Hartman today?" Sterling asks.

"Whatever he needs to hear to find out what we need to know."

Sterling laughs. "You sure you're not a cop?"

The door at the far end of the room springs open and a pair of officers directs Glenn Hartman in our direction. He appears exhausted.

Looks like nobody is getting any sleep these days.

"Good afternoon, Mr. Hartman." I try to keep any trace of contempt from my voice, at least in part because I'm no longer sure it's warranted.

"Don't 'good afternoon' me." Hartman's glare could melt glass. "You waltz in here yesterday, barely identify yourself, drop a bomb like that, and walk away without another word? What kind of person does that?"

My heart races at the question. Yesterday, I felt vindicated leaving him as I did. If he is proven innocent in the end, my actions will have been nothing but cruel.

Fantastic. Another black mark on my karmic wheel.

"In case you've forgotten, Mr. Hartman," I answer, trying not to stammer, "you're the one locked up for assault and battery of a high school senior."

Hartman leans across the table. "You know exactly what led to that."

Sterling puffs up as if he's about to leap to my defense, but before he can say a word, Hartman inclines his head in the detective's direction.

"If you want to talk, Ms. Tejedor, get him out of here."

"I'm not going anywhere," Sterling says. "Don't forget who's in charge here, Mr. Hartman."

"What part of 'I'm only talking to her' do you not understand?"

"Detective Sterling." I rest a hand on his shoulder. "If you'll give us a few minutes alone to discuss some things, I suspect Mr. Hartman will be more than glad to answer whatever other questions you might have." I glance at Hartman. "Isn't that right, Glenn?"

After a long moment, Hartman gives a grudging nod. The smell of cayenne wafting off Sterling abates as he stands and walks toward the door.

"I'm trusting you on this one, 'partner.' Don't let me down."

Hartman is silent till Sterling disappears behind the door.

"I thought you weren't working with the cops," he says.

"I'm not, though we both have a vested interest in finding out what happened to Julianna Wagner." I lean forward and rest my chin on interlaced knuckles. "As do you, Mr. Hartman."

He looks away. "Look. Whatever happened to Julianna, I didn't do it. I swear."

"I'm not here to prove you did."

His gaze returns to mine. "Then what do you want? Who the hell are you, anyway?"

"I'm a consultant. I'm working with Jason Faircloth's brother, Anthony."

"Wait." I can see the wheels spinning behind his eyes. "The special needs kid?"

A grim smile crosses my face. "That's the one."

For a moment, Glenn Hartman isn't a prisoner or a murder suspect, but a teacher. The calm that crosses his face echoes in his thoughts. Even in this place, a part of him cares. The smile worn by the kind Cart Man who offered me tea in an upside down house flashes across my memory. Perhaps Anthony's instincts about the man aren't so far off the mark after all.

"What does he have to do with me, or Julianna for that matter?"

"Anthony started having issues the day Julianna went missing. Serious issues. Pretty big coincidence, wouldn't you agree?"

Hartman leans back in his chair and studies me. "You're hoping if you can figure out what happened to her, you'll have your answer about what happened to him."

"More or less."

"You really aren't here for me." His eyes well with emotion. "Help me, Ms. Tejedor. They've got the wrong guy."

"I don't know, Mr. Hartman. The only two things I know for sure about you outside your resume are that you sleep with your students from time to time and have a history of assaulting teenage boys in their homes. Why should I help you or believe anything you say?"

"I loved her, dammit." He rubs the sleeve of his orange jumpsuit across his eyes. "The rest of society may see what I did as wrong, but that doesn't change a thing."

"You're referring to Julianna in the past tense." My words come out crueler than I intend, but I can't seem to stop myself. "Any reason for that?"

He glowers at me through squinted bloodshot eyes. "You know as well as I do how these things turn out."

Not the first time I've heard those words.

"Still, you seem pretty confident—"

"I didn't hurt her," he shouts, pounding the table with a white-knuckled fist. An officer from the opposite corner of the room takes a step in our direction. The cool smell of mint, however, lets me know Hartman's already starting to calm and I motion for the guard to stay back and let him be. Once Hartman regains his composure, we begin anew.

"You're in love with Julianna Wagner."

"I am. Was. Whatever." He looks away. "She said she felt the same way. More than once."

"But she was dating Jason Faircloth."

A sad grin overtakes Hartman's face. "She broke up with him to be with me."

My arms cross before me. "Must've been pretty thrilling, bedding a seventeen-year-old girl. Nothing tastes quite as good as forbidden fruit, does it?"

"It wasn't like that. It wasn't like that at all." Grief contorts his already miserable face. "A question, Ms. Tejedor. Do you actually know anything about Julianna Wagner?"

"Only what her parents and the Faircloths have said and what I've picked up from the news. Honor student, cheerleader, athlete." I raise an eyebrow. "And 'talented' enough to score the lead in the school play."

"She was the most beautiful girl I'd ever seen." Hartman's eyes drift closed. "Crystal blue eyes. Flawless skin. The voice of an angel."

I'm filled with Hartman's sense of Julianna. The scent of roses and fresh-cut grass and rain compete in my head for supremacy.

"She sounds perfect. Couldn't leave her alone, could you?"

"The truth?" he asks. "At the beginning, she was the one that put the moves on me."

"Really?"

He answers my deadpan question with a simple shrug. "Do I seem like the kind of guy who would put his entire career in jeopardy over a girl?"

"Foregone conclusion. You *did* put your entire career in jeopardy over a girl."

A bitter smile invades the grimace occupying his face. "She was worth it."

"Worth jail time? Julianna is a minor, Mr. Hartman."

"For four more months." Hartman lets out an overwrought sigh. "I've watched more than my share of great women walk out of my life. I wasn't letting another one go, especially one who said I was her everything."

Roses. Cinnamon. He really loved her, or at least he thought he did. Frustration, anger, and guilt all emanate off him like heat off a radiator, but no hint of anything that would lead me to think he would harm her in any way.

"And you honestly didn't know she was pregnant."

For the first time, he seems embarrassed. His gaze cast downward, he mutters, "We'd only been... intimate a few times. She was on birth control. Even showed me the pills. Still, we were careful." He clears his throat. "At least most of the time."

"But not every time."

"No," he whispers. "Not every time."

"Any others? Anybody she mentioned?"

"She told me she and the Faircloth kid had fooled around some, but things hadn't gotten much past a little fumbling in the dark." The earnest teacher makes a brief reappearance on Hartman's face as he meets my gaze for the first time in almost a minute. "Everything considered, Jason's a pretty good kid. I'm sorry things have ended up like this."

"You mean you're sorry you went to his house and tried to kick in his teeth."

"I'll admit, I went a little crazy when I saw those pictures. I don't know about you, but I don't take well to being blackmailed."

"I'm going to level with you, Mr. Hartman. I'm not the biggest fan of most of the decisions you've made in the last few months, but strange as it sounds, I believe you. I'll talk to the good detective out in the hall and see what I can do."

"Thank you."

"No promises."

"Right. But that's not all." He glances in the direction of the guards in the corner. "There's something else on your mind, isn't there?"

A pretty good kid.

A twinge of pain forms above my right eyebrow as Jason Faircloth's angry stare fills my mind. For the first time, I entertain a thought that chills my blood. The main clue that led us to Glenn Hartman in the first place was an image I gleaned from Jason's memories.

What if what I saw was nothing but exactly what Jason wanted me to see?

XXVI

Echoes

"I still can't believe you got Hartman to admit he was sleeping with the girl." Thomas checks his mirror before passing a VW bug that's been creeping up the highway in front of us. "How'd you manage that one, Mira?"

"Not much left to lose when you're already in jail and people are dropping off photographic evidence of your illicit activities at your house." I roll down the window to let in a bit of fresh air. "Besides, I think he kind of wants people to know."

"Because he 'loved' her so much?"

"Maybe."

"And you don't think all that talk is just a ploy to make himself look sympathetic?"

"I'm sure that's part of it, but like I said before, it's hard to lie to me. My particular skill set makes me a pretty good emotion detector."

"Emotion detector." Thomas chuckles and shakes his head. "Clever."

"It's not mine, but thanks."

Thomas taps the brake and slides his car back into the right lane. "One more time. Our visit with the Wagners this evening is supposed to accomplish exactly what?"

Though he sounded less than enthused when he took my call an hour ago, Mr. Wagner all but jumped through the phone when I told him I had news about his daughter's case. I didn't have the heart to tell him my every instinct says I'm three weeks too late for this story to have a happy ending. All he and his wife have is hope and I have no desire whatsoever to take that from them.

"I need to see her space, where she lived, ate, slept. Hopefully, there's something I can glean from her things. Impressions. Images. Feelings. Julianna and her disappearance rest at the center of all of this and I've pretty much ignored her till now. Her room may give us some answers we can't get anywhere else."

Thomas exits the highway and in less than a minute, we're into the suburbs of Charlotte. I chafe a bit as we pass house after house bigger than my entire apartment building. He slips off his shades as the sun disappears behind the trees lining the road to the west.

"According to the GPS, it's only a mile or so now," he says. "What are you going to tell them? You can't let on anything about the pregnancy and if you tell them what Hartman said, you'll just make things worse. They're looking for anyone or anything to get their daughter back and you and I both know that's looking pretty damn unlikely."

"God knows I don't want to make anything worse for them, but I need to find out what happened to Julianna if I'm going to have any hope of discovering what happened to Anthony. I'm hoping something of hers will at least corroborate the pregnancy. All I'm going on now is the offhanded comment of a dreamed up character in a near-comatose boy's mind."

Thomas laughs. "And you think some psychic impression off a teenager's jacket will hold up better in court?"

"Careful, Dr. Archer. The cynic in you is peeking through."

"Cut me some slack, Mira. In just over a week, I've had to learn to accept the existence of telepathy, astral projection, and the weirdest case of multiple personality disorder anyone's ever heard of. I'm doing my best to keep an open mind, but give me a break."

I smile for the first time in an hour. "You have been playing nice, I suppose."

"So." Thomas turns onto a tree-lined two-lane avenue. "You plan to get inside, see if they'll let us inspect her room, and wing it from there?"

"You have a better plan?"

We round another corner and Thomas' GPS announces we've arrived. Directly ahead, a media circus, complete with tents and no doubt a few clowns, fills the street and the adjoining front yards. Several news vans, each adorned with its own two-story satellite dish, form a four-wheeled phalanx before the three-story brick home. A dozen or so reporters and cameramen have various territories staked out in the yard. Another shrine to Julianna at the corner of the sidewalk looms even larger than the one at her school. Even now, as the day approaches twilight, a small crowd stands by to pay their respects, or perhaps watch the spectacle.

"It's a madhouse." I glance over at Thomas. "Just like Mr. Wagner said."

Thomas passes the clot of news vans and makes a right, pulling his car to the curb one block behind the Wagners' home. Grateful this neighborhood isn't too keen on fences, we sneak across the lawn of an old bungalow and into the Wagners' backyard like Mr. Wagner suggested. As we pass an old wooden swing set, the image of a little blonde girl flying down the sliding board floats across my mind. My heart grows cold when the imagined child's hair goes black and her features flow into Isabella's.

Thomas steps onto the Wagners' back porch. "Shall we?"

He knocks at the door, and after a few seconds, cautious footsteps sound from within.

"Who is it?" The voice is Mrs. Wagner's, though fatigue has taken any life from her words. A scent reminiscent of old socks fills my senses.

"It's Mira Tejedor."

The door opens a crack and Margaret Wagner peers out at me from below a brass chain before opening the door.

"Come in, before they see you."

She leads Thomas and me into their living room and seats us on their leather couch before dropping into an oversized recliner and grabbing a half-empty martini.

"Stuart will be down in a moment."

A few seconds later, Mr. Wagner steps into the room. "Good evening, Ms. Tejedor." He shoots a puzzled glance at Thomas. "I see you've brought a friend."

Thomas rises and shakes Mr. Wagner's hand. "Thomas Archer. I suppose you could say I'm here for moral support."

I rise from my chair and shake Stuart Wagner's hand. "Thanks for agreeing to see me."

"Frankly," he says, "we were surprised to get your call. Detective Sterling told us yesterday you were no longer working on the case."

I catch Thomas' concerned gaze and carefully choose my next words. "I'm afraid Detective Sterling and I had a bit of a disagreement yesterday regarding how I was handling certain aspects of the investigation."

"And?" Hope and fear battle in Mrs. Wagner's eyes as she joins us.

"We were able to come to an understanding earlier today. Let's leave it at that."

"Has there been a break in the case?" Mr. Wagner asks. "We saw on the news you interviewed Glenn Hartman yesterday. Did he say anything about Julianna?"

"I don't care a whit about Glenn Hartman," Mrs. Wagner says. "Have you or the police found out something about our daughter?"

Thomas and I share another quick glance, his admonition from the car echoing in my mind.

"Nothing yet." As the words leave my lips, I can't help but imagine how it would feel if the child were Isabella and I were on the other end of the conversation. The guilt coursing through my mind is only made worse by the double dose of sorrow and frustration that washes over me from two parents who deserve better than a pack of half-truths. "At least nothing substantial. I do have a favor to ask, though. Is that all right, Mrs. Wagner?"

"Please. Call me Margaret." She glances down at her nearly empty glass. "Can I get either of you a drink?"

Thomas and I both request ice water. As Margaret disappears into the kitchen, Mr. Wagner leans in close and lowers his voice to a conspiratorial whisper.

"Listen to me. I'm only allowing you in my home because it's what Margaret wants. Whatever you do, don't go getting her hopes up. You know as well as I do how this is most likely going to turn out, but my Margaret hasn't given up hope yet. I'm afraid when she finally accepts Julianna is gone, it's going to destroy her."

"We're not here to cause you or your wife any more pain. We're just here to help."

Mr. Wagner lets out a forceful exhalation through his nose. "Unless you can bring our daughter back to us safe and sound, I'm afraid there's not much you can do."

"Let her try," Thomas says. "She's doing all she can."

"Two ice waters." Margaret reenters the room and sets two glasses down on stone coasters on the wood and glass coffee table. "If I can't interest the two of you in something a little stronger."

I glance over at her nearly finished martini, the staked olive abandoned in the almost empty glass. "Not today, but thank you."

"Ditto." Thomas smiles. "Water's fine."

Margaret goes to the bar, pours herself a glass of wine, and rejoins us around the glass table. The four of us sit and stare at each other for what feels like forever until Mr. Wagner finally breaks the silence.

"I'm confused, Ms. Tejedor. You've gone out of your way to meet with us but don't seem to have any new information. What exactly is it you need?"

"I was hoping I could see Julianna's room, maybe go through some of her things, see if anything gives me an impression that might shed some light as to what's happened to her."

"Her room." Mr. Wagner glances over at the stairs peeking through from the foyer.

"Is there a problem?" Thomas asks in the same practiced "avoiding confrontation" voice I've heard him use with me more than once.

"No," Mr. Wagner says. "It's just—"

Mrs. Wagner cuts in. "We haven't set foot in there since the police searched the room three weeks ago. It's too painful. Too many memories."

"You don't have to come," I say. "In fact, it may be better if I can do my work there alone."

"Very well." Mr. Wagner rises from his seat and directs me toward the stairs. "Come with me."

I raise an eyebrow at Thomas. "Coming, Dr. Archer?"

"No," he says. "I think I'll stay here with Mrs. Wagner. See if I can help on this end."

"All right. See you in a few."

Mr. Wagner leads me up the hardwood stairway, the wrought iron bannister beneath my hand cool to the touch. At the top of the stairs, he pauses for a moment before leading me down the hall to a door covered in purple and pink hearts. He rests his hand on the doorknob as his gaze drops to the floor.

"The police have already scoured the hard drive on her computer and the forensics people have been here more times than I can count. Not sure what you hope to find in there, but take all the time you need." As I step past him into the room, Mr. Wagner grasps my wrist, not hard, but insistent. "Find her, please. Dead, alive, just so we know. Anything is better than this."

"I'll do what I can." Closing the door behind me, I walk over to Julianna Wagner's bed and lie back on the pastel comforter. A stuffed black and white tiger smells of sweat and faint perfume and exudes the essence of a thousand nights of deep slumber. The sensation nearly renders me unconscious. I catch myself mid-yawn and force my eyes open.

"Can't let that happen, Mira." I slap myself on the cheek hard enough to sting. "You've got work to do."

Julianna's closet is packed tight, and going through her clothing piece by piece is like a roller coaster of emotion as images from almost two decades of experience filter through my head. The first day jitters from Julianna's college prep calculus class that left their mark on a silky green blouse. A tray full of spaghetti dumped in the lap of a yellow and red flowered sundress as the entire cafeteria looks on in shocked laughter. Jason Faircloth waiting for her at her locker and helping her into a burgundy jacket.

An image of Glenn Hartman helping her out of the same jacket.

At the back of the closet, I find a pair of jeans a size larger than the rest, tag still in place and hung inside an old raggedy sweatshirt. As evidence of pregnancy, it's far from irrefutable, but it's something. Holding the midnight blue denim to my chest brings flashes of a department store to my mind's eye. Julianna stands at a cash register, but she's not paying. Someone else is there with her. I can almost see their face.

My phone rings, shattering the moment.

I fumble pulling the phone from my pocket, catching it before it hits the hardwood floor.

"Hello?" I whisper, mindful of where I am.

"Hi, Mami. How are you?" As I sit in the room of a girl who has almost certainly been dead the better part of a month, the sound of my own daughter's voice sets my heart racing.

"I'm good, sweetie. And you?"

"I'm fine."

"How's Nana?"

"She's fine too." She pauses for a couple seconds. "Mami?"

I don't like the sound of this. "Yes?"

"Is it okay if I go stay with Daddy for a couple of days?"

"Maybe." The lump in my throat threatens to choke off my next words. "What does he have planned?"

"He and his friend, Autumn, are going to the mountains this weekend and they want me to come along. He says there's a horse stable near where they're staying."

"Isabella, is your father there now?"

"Yeah. He's right here."

I take a deep breath. "I need to speak with him."

"He's talking to Nana. Wait a minute." She shouts for her father, leaving me to wait for an interminable thirty seconds for a voice that for eighteen months has brought equal parts bitterness and longing every time I've heard it.

"Hello, Mira."

"Dominic."

"How are things?"

"How are things? Seriously?"

"What? Isabella said you wanted to talk to me, and here I am, as requested."

Dammit. Is it too much to ask for once in our relationship he be the one that comes across as a little bit crazy?"

I swallow hard as I consider my next words. "I hear you have news."

"Oh. Rosa must have told you."

"She's *my* mother, remember?"

"You're upset Autumn and I are finally making it official? Is that what this is?"

"No. I'm upset you and the woman you slept with for the last months of our marriage are making plans to take my daughter away for a 'fun-filled weekend in the mountains' while I'm down here working my ass off trying to keep a roof over our heads."

"She's *our* daughter, Mira, in case you've forgotten."

"Was she *our* daughter for the last year and a half where you've barely showed your face?"

"You made it pretty clear I was anything but welcome in *your* home. Check your facts, Mira."

My breath catches in my throat. "And what makes you think I'd be cool with Isabella spending time with *her*?"

"I called a few days back. Rosa said you were away on a case. Thought it might be fun to drop in and see Izzy and maybe free your mom up for a day or two."

"I'll be home in a day or two." The heat rises in my cheeks and I'm strangely relieved to be several hundred miles away. "Mom can keep Isabella till then."

"Your mother tells me you've been saying that for over a week now." Dominic's quiet chuckle sparks a twinge of pain behind my left eye as I remember simultaneously why I married him and why I divorced his ass. "I'm in town for a few days. Why won't you let me help out? I'd love to spend some time with her."

"Where have you been the last eighteen months when I needed your help? Off to God-knows-where photographing penguins in Antarctica or wildebeests on the Serengeti instead of watching your daughter grow up."

"Funny, Mira. I didn't hear you complaining about those photographs when you were spending the money they brought in. I've had some good months and some lean months, but if you check your records, you'll find I haven't missed a single month of child support."

"Yes, Dominic. The automatic payments from your bank have come on the sixteenth of every month for the last year. I'll call the Vatican and have you put in for sainthood as soon as we get off the phone."

"Come on. Is the idea of Isabella spending some time with her father that horrible?"

"You don't call for almost four months, and now you waltz in with expensive presents and that whore on your arm and expect me to just roll over and be happy about it?"

Dominic doesn't speak for a moment. I've made him mad. I don't know whether to celebrate or hang up immediately.

"Look, Mira," Dominic says, his voice barely above a whisper. "Last time I checked, you were the one who started sleeping in the guest bedroom after the whole thing with Sarah Goode last year. Scream at me all you want, but we both know what and who got in the way of us."

Eighteen months. Eighteen months and he finally said it. I prepare to strike back and fill the phone line with all the things I've waited a year and a half to say, but in the end all that comes out is, "Put Isabella on."

"Wait, Mira. I'm sorry."

"Put. Her. On."

A bit of static hits my ear, followed by Isabella's quiet whisper.

"Mami?"

"Isabella." As I search for just the right words to forbid my daughter from so much as setting foot in the car with Autumn, I look around the room. Julianna's room. The room of a girl who will likely never see either of her parents ever again. Tears well at the corners of my eyes. "You know what? If your dad wants to take you to the mountains, that's fine with me. Just be careful and call me every night."

"Thank you, Mami. Thank you, thank you." She whispers my answer to Dominic and Mom and comes back on the line, her voice even brighter than before. "Daddy changed his mind. Says we'll only be gone for a day. He thinks I'll sleep better in my own bed."

"That's nice, honey. Tell him I said thank you." I bite my lip till it hurts. "Now, you listen to your father and be safe, you hear me? I'll be home as soon as I can, sweetheart. I love you."

"I love you too, Mami."

Despite my best efforts, emotion chokes my last words. "Good night, Isabella."

I sit staring through unbidden tears at the phone in my hand for several minutes until a knock at the door brings me around.

"Yes?"

"Mira?" Thomas' baritone reverberates through the door. "You okay in there?"

Already calmer, I take a breath and answer. "I'm all right."

"I thought I heard you call out. Anything going on in there?"

"Everything's fine." My intestines continue to unwind. "Had to take a phone call."

"Making any progress?"

"Yes, but I need a few more minutes, please."

"I'll go update the Wagners." He pauses. "Let me know if I can help with anything."

"Will do."

Thomas' footsteps echo as he heads back down the hall and it occurs to me I didn't hear him approach. The fact Dom still has such a hold over me makes my blood boil.

Okay. Half an hour, and not much to show other than a pair of jeans I can't mention to the Wagners without causing them more pain. I've turned the place upside down. No diary, nothing but class notes in any of her folders and notebooks except the cute little heart on the cover inscribed with "JW + JF." I refuse to leave until I have something to show for this. Surely she left some clue, picture, wrote something down…

Wrote.

I rummage through the main drawer of her desk and find a small collection of pens and markers, most chewed to within an inch of being unusable. One in particular, however, remains immaculate. In its own special corner rests an ornate silver Cross pen with gold flourishes, its only flaw a tarnished spot at the business end from hours of writing.

Clearly Julianna's favorite pen.

I take a deep breath and grasp the pen in both hands, allowing my eyes to slide shut even as my mind opens. For several seconds, all I see are blue-green flashes on the back of my eyelids.

"Come on, Julianna. Show me what you've got."

The cool metal of the pen warms in my hand.

"You haven't left me anything else. Come on."

Barely noticeable at first, a compulsion to write builds in my mind, my arm, my hand. Even stranger, it's my left hand that itches to churn out a few paragraphs.

Before the sensation can fade, I tear open the top notebook in the stack, flip to an open page, and let my fingers go to work.

At first, the pen produces only the most basic doodles. Stars, cubes, smiley faces.

Then, the number 8, followed by the number 1. Again and again. 818181818181818181.

"What the hell is 81?" I half expect a voice to answer me, and am strangely disappointed at the silence.

My hand is still for a moment before starting again with the doodles. A pair of eyes. Flowers. A checkerboard formation stretching into infinity. Then more numbers. And a pair of words.

4:15 - Parking Lot.

She's meeting someone. But who?

The pen continues to make its way across the page as an antiseptic stench wafts across my senses.

421 North Reginald Road. Friday.

Friday. The day she disappeared.

Or one of the hundreds of other Fridays in her lifetime.

Great thing about this particular talent? The specificity.

My off hand continues to etch out a set of doodles I don't recall ever putting on paper before, but no more words come.

Tearing out the page from the spiral bound notebook, I fold it up and slide it into my pocket before making one last pass through the room. I get a few last impressions of Julianna, but no further clues as to her fate.

I head back down the stairs to rejoin Thomas and the Wagners. Mr. Wagner stands as I enter the room.

"You've been up in Julianna's room for almost an hour. Anything you'd care to share?"

"Nothing definitive. I picked up some impressions of your daughter. People and things that were important to her. A few specifics."

Wagner's eyes flash with fire anew. "And?"

"Nothing I'd hang hopes on." I fight to keep the emotion from my face. "I'm sorry."

He lowers his head rubs at his temples even as Julianna's mother deflates like a balloon on a hot summer afternoon. Thomas steals over to my side, the mere strength of his presence bolstering me even as the emotion wafting off the Wagners threatens to pull me headlong into their maelstrom of grief.

"There's really nothing more you can tell them?" He's only trying to help, but the words still sting. "Nothing?"

"Dammit, Thomas. I'm not going to lie to them."

Hearing me despite my whisper, Margaret Wagner leaves the room crying while her husband falls into his recliner and stares out the window. A gentle breeze works its way through the willow in the backyard, the lithe branches waving in lamentation for the little girl that no doubt used to sprint around their broad trunk. For the hundredth time that day, an image of Isabella's face with her devilish grin and her all-too-wise eyes floods unbidden into my mind.

"Mr. Wagner?"

He looks up at me, his tired eyes red and swollen. "Yes?"

"Julianna. She's left-handed, isn't she?"

He nods. "Why do you ask?"

"Just curious." I take Thomas by the arm. "I'll be in touch."

"What now?" Thomas asks as I lead him to the door.

"It's not much, but I've got something." I glance back at Mr. Wagner in his dark leather recliner, his stoic facade crumbling like a sand castle at high tide. "We're going to need the GPS in your car."

I don't say a word as Thomas sits in the driver seat staring at the folded piece of paper resting in his hand. Turning it this way and that, he glances at me, his eyebrow forming a sideways question mark.

"You wrote this?" he asks.

"Sort of." I take the paper back and study the scrawled pen strokes there. I remember writing the words, though it's not my handwriting and the address is no place I've ever been or even heard of. "I picked up the only one of Julianna's pens that didn't look like a dog's chew toy and my hand just started writing."

"From what you asked Mr. Wagner, I'm assuming it was your left hand."

"Yes."

His eyes fall to my lap where my hands rest. "But you're right-handed."

Impressed he remembered this little detail, I grin, offering only a subtle nod.

"Has anything like this happened before?" he asks.

I shake my head. "Nothing quite like this, though if I made a list of all the things I've experienced in the last week and a half that are new to me, I'd have to buy a ream of paper."

"Wait." He takes back the piece of paper and studies it anew. "Have you ever heard of unconscious writing?"

"My college English Comp professor used to have us do exercises along those lines once a week. We would write as fast as humanly possible for fifteen minutes, not stopping for anything, trying to get at our subconscious thoughts. Some pretty awesome stuff came out of those exercises." A quiet chuckle escapes my lips. "Some pretty weird stuff, too."

"And?"

"This is nothing like that."

"I can't believe I'm going to ask this, but do you think it was Julianna's ghost talking with you?" He stares at me quizzically. "Or maybe, through you?"

"Why, Dr. Archer, how far we've come in a week."

His knuckles blanch as he grips the gear shift. "Just trying to keep an open mind."

I give his arm a playful swat. "And I'm just yanking your chain."

The exasperation in his stare strongly suggests he prefers his chain unyanked. Noted.

"Truth is, if I focus, I can sometimes pick up on psychic impressions left on objects. Learn stuff about their owners or people who handled the particular item. Emotions they felt, things they saw." I gesture to the paper in his hand. "I guess it's not that big a stretch to get an address."

"I guess not," he says, "though a week ago, my answer would have been quite different." Thomas studies the scribbles on the page. "So, this address…"

"Was a place that caused Julianna great fear." I cast my thoughts back to when I held the well-used Cross pen. "And sadness. Overwhelming sadness."

"No time like the present." Thomas presses a button at the center of the console, shifting the screen to GPS, and taps in the address. "Let's see where this takes us."

"421 North Reginald Road, Charlotte, NC." A few seconds pass before a location appears on the map. Some sort of office park, the arrow is fixed atop the large building at its center.

"Reginald Medical Plaza." My hands come to my mouth out of instinct. "Can we take a closer look?"

Thomas taps the touchscreen and the picture zooms in, dividing the building into its various practices. I note a dentist office, OB/GYN, internal medicine, and mental health. As Thomas shifts the screen so we can see what's in the south corner of the building, however, the answer to our question comes into view.

"That's what we're looking for." I point to the screen. "Charlotte Center for Women's Health."

Thomas drops his head. "Poor girl. She was planning to have an abortion."

"Or had one." The emotions that overtook me as my hand scrawled the address in Julianna's room rush back. Fear, trepidation, self-revulsion, and perhaps even a small bit of relief. "If she did, I'm betting she didn't go alone. You're seventeen, scared, ashamed. I don't imagine many young women would even visit an abortion clinic without taking someone along for emotional support. Not to mention, if any procedure was done, she'd need to have someone there to take her home."

"That's all fine and good," Thomas says, "but I can't imagine Jason could keep such a thing from his mother and we both saw Glenn Hartman's reaction when he heard about the baby."

"And that leaves only one question." I massage my right eye where yet another headache is threatening to bloom. "Who else knew Julianna Wagner was pregnant?"

XXVII

MORENDO

When I pull up to the Faircloth house the next morning, I'm half-surprised to see Veronica's car in the driveway. After her response to our psychic freak show yesterday, I half expected she'd find somewhere else to spend her Saturday morning. On the flip side, she's shown nothing but devotion to Anthony since we first met. And then there's always the show itself. Whether we admit it or not, we all rubberneck at wrecked cars on the highway and the rescue crews trying to save lives and clean up the mess. If there's a worse wreck than this thing with Anthony, I hope never to see it.

I ring the doorbell and wait over a minute before Caroline opens the door. As exhausted as I've seen her, she looks like a gust of wind would knock her over, which is unfortunate because it appears another Charlotte thunderstorm is rolling in.

"Good morning, Mira," Caroline says. "Thanks for coming on a Saturday."

"No problem." I hand her the trio of coffees I brought from the hotel coffee shop. "Your cappuccino is the large cup."

She takes her coffee from the cardboard container and looks past me out the door. "Is Thomas with you?"

"He had an errand to run." Though it took some convincing, Thomas agreed to go by the Charlotte Center for Women's Health this morning and pursue that lead while I continued the work with Anthony. "He'll be by later this morning." I peer across Caroline's shoulder, my pulse accelerating. "Did Jason come home yet?"

"No sign of him. I know he's mad, but he could at least call."

"At least." I step into the foyer as Caroline closes and locks the door behind us and crane my neck to peer into the next room. "I saw Veronica's car out front. Is she—"

"In here." There's an edge to Veronica's voice and with each passing moment the anxiety buffeting me from both Veronica and Caroline mounts. Something is wrong.

I head into the Faircloth living room and find Veronica hunched over Anthony on the couch. The strain in the teacher's voice and the fatigue and pain etched in Caroline's features become instantly clear.

Anthony's every muscle is contracted, his body contorted like a scene from one of those exorcist movies. His skin is cool and clammy and his neck is so stiff his shoulders don't touch the couch.

"My God, what's happened to him?" I rush to his side and apply one of the cool washcloths on the coffee table to his brow.

"It all started about fifteen minutes ago," Caroline says. "Anthony had a rough night, but nothing like this. Thank God Veronica got here just after it started. We've been able to calm him down a bit, but he's not getting any better."

"Did you call 9-1-1?"

Caroline lowers her head. "Do you have any idea how many times I've called them in the last month?"

"Then what are we going to do?" I run my hand down Anthony's cheek. He immediately relaxes.

"I was right," Caroline says. "See how he responds to you?" She wipes the sweat from her upper lip.

"Right about what?"

"Anthony doesn't need any more doctors or hospitals or scans. He needs you. Please, Mira, whatever it takes, help my son."

Caroline's desperate eyes make one fact imminently clear.

This has gone on long enough.

I'm not leaving the Exhibition this time without Anthony, witches be damned.

"All right, then." I crack my neck and prepared to settle into my usual spot. "Once more, with feeling?"

My attempt at levity is cut off by a single word.

"Mom?" A quiet voice calls out.

Caroline glances across my shoulder and her eyes grow wide with terror. "Rachel?"

"I don't... feel so... good," the tiny voice squeaks.

Caroline nearly bowls me over as she sprints past me and catches Rachel's head a split-second before it impacts the hardwood floor.

"Rachel?" Caroline lowers her daughter to the floor. "Speak to me. Please."

Rachel's eyes roll up into her head and she begins to convulse.

"That's it." Veronica pushes a pillow beneath Anthony's neck and shoulders and grabs the phone. "I'm calling 9-1-1 like I should've done when I got here."

"Don't bother," Caroline says. "I can have her to the ER before they're halfway here."

"Let her call." I rest a hand on Caroline's shoulder. "A lot could happen between here and the hospital."

Caroline agrees to let us make the call, though she won't meet my or Veronica's gaze. I help her roll Rachel onto her side, something I learned in a first aid class an eternity ago, and sit with Anthony while we wait for the ambulance. Despite whatever is happening with Rachel, my presence seems to calm him. His body becomes progressively less tense with each passing minute, so much so that when the paramedics arrive, he doesn't appear appreciably different from the day I first laid eyes on him.

One of the paramedics works to stabilize Rachel, who fortunately stopped seizing a few minutes after we called, while the other examines Anthony. Caroline knows each by their first name, and flits back and forth between her two children. The fear and anxiety filling the room nearly makes me vomit more than once.

Once they've declared her safe for transport, the paramedics load Rachel onto a stretcher, complete with neck brace and straps. A part of me is glad she's not conscious. The poor girl would be terrified.

The head paramedic eyeballs Anthony and pulls Caroline aside.

"We've got Rachel all loaded up and ready to go. I assume you'll want to ride in the back with her."

"You know me well."

"We've checked Anthony out as well. He's looking pretty good. Better than some of the other times we've seen him."

The other paramedic nods. "Compared to our first visit a few weeks back, he's practically ship shape."

Any semblance of good humor leaves Caroline's face. "You didn't see him an hour ago."

"Do you want us to take him on to the hospital?" I can almost hear the unspoken "again" at the end of the paramedic's question.

"No. That won't be necessary." Caroline motions for me to come over and join the conversation. "Mira…"

"You don't even have to ask." I sit on the couch and brush the hair out of Anthony's face. "I'll stay with Anthony till you get back."

"Actually, we'll both keep an eye on him." Veronica sits at his head, his body tensing again as she applies a cool rag to his forehead. "If Mira doesn't mind a little company."

Caroline's shoulders relax a bit. "I'll call from the ER in an hour or so and check in."

I offer her a quick smile. "And we'll call if there's any change."

"And please let me know if you hear from Jason."

My stomach ties itself in a square knot. "We'll call the second he comes around."

"Jason's a big boy, Caroline," Veronica says. "Probably cooling it at a friend's house."

"You're probably right." Caroline turns to face the pair of EMT's. "Did you save my favorite seat?"

"Right this way, Ms. Faircloth," the paramedic says with a quick bow of his head.

The door clicks closed behind them, leaving Veronica and me alone with Anthony. His scrawny body trembles like he's freezing even as beads of sweat again break out on his forehead.

"Here he goes again." Veronica dips a washcloth into a bowl of ice water on the coffee table and rings it out. "I certainly hope we don't have to call the paramedics back."

"Let me see if I can help." I take a seat just above Anthony's head. Veronica hands me the cool washcloth and I drape it across the boy's brow. "There now, Anthony. Everything is going to be all right." As before, he calms at my touch.

"I hope Rachel is going to be okay," Veronica says.

"She had a similar spell the other day. She made it through that one all right." I keep quiet my suspicions about Anthony's connection to Rachel's seizures. "Still, I honestly don't know how much more Caroline is supposed to take."

"I know you came to work with Anthony today. I suppose we could try again tomorrow, assuming Caroline can get away from the hospital, though unless I miss my guess, they'll keep Rachel for a couple of days." She glances down at Anthony. "Poor little guy didn't come home from the hospital for a week when all this started. I don't know how Caroline stood it, having her son poked and prodded for six days. Watching that happen to someone I love would've driven me nuts." She strokes his cheek and Anthony pulls away from her as if burned.

"It's amazing the connection you have with Anthony, Mira. Your mere presence calms him while the rest of us seem to do nothing but make him want to climb out of his skin."

"We've grown pretty tight in our own way the last few days, though if he woke up right now, I don't think he'd recognize me."

She waves her hand in front of his face. "His eyes are open, but he doesn't see. There's a poem in there somewhere."

"Or a rock opera." Dominic was always a big fan of The Who. Couldn't stand them myself, but I've heard *Tommy* enough times to have the whole thing memorized. "I bet Anthony plays a mean pinball."

Veronica's face goes somber. "How much longer do you think he can go on like this?"

I stroke Anthony's hair. "No idea. This whole experience is a first for me."

"You said his entire self has been splintered. How does a person recover from that?"

"It's odd. Every time I've gone into the Exhibition and encountered some facet of Anthony's psyche, they've all been for the most part friendly, apart from the witch, of course. At worst, the others were indifferent, though every part of Anthony I've met has reached out to me in one way or another."

Veronica shoots me a knowing glance. "You realize you're the savior figure in his story."

"If only the part of him riding around on a mortar and pestle would let me stay long enough, I'm pretty sure I could bring him out of this state. On the other hand, I've already been through nearly the entire gallery. There are only two pictures left I haven't seen."

"If I remember right, you just visited the... Catacombs? What's left?"

Rolling thunder rumbles in the distance. "The witch's realm."

I've only caught the briefest glimpse of Baba Yaga's alcove and the painting that hangs there. Though her and Tunny's pictures both depict woodland scenes, any similarity ends there. *Gnomus* opens on an idyllic forest, a place of joy and happiness, or at least it did until the witch came. *The Hut on Fowl's Legs*, on the other hand, depicts a nightmare wood, the trees dark, gnarled, and naked of leaves. Even the thought of entering such desolation fills me with dread.

"Hers was the first voice I heard on my initial walk in the Exhibition. She rules the place and unless I can persuade her to come to my side or somehow defeat her on her own turf, I think Anthony is lost to us."

"But if you can do it. If you can stop her..."

"I believe I can bring Anthony's mind back together. Already many of the characters along the Exhibition, previously all solo, are spending time together. Tunny the Gnome, Modesto the Troubadour, Antoine from the garden, Trilby the Ballerina. If I can get all of them talking..."

"Then maybe we get our boy back," Veronica says. "That is if the witch doesn't interfere."

"It's a long shot, but I've got to try."

"What are you waiting for, then?"

"What do you mean?"

"No time like the present." Veronica looks down on Anthony's sleeping form. "He's not getting any more broken than he already is."

"I'm not certain how Caroline would feel about me going into Anthony's mind without her here. I agreed to help Jason without her consent and she all but fired me on the spot."

"Come on, Mira. Caroline brought you here today to help her son. I can stay and keep watch, just like yesterday."

"We are making progress." A rush of pride hits me as my rout of the witch from yesterday and her slack-jawed expression as I walked out of her Exhibition replays in my mind. "Maybe we should strike while the iron is hot."

"Agreed." Veronica sits in the chair opposite the couch. "What do you need me to do?"

"Stay with Anthony. Make sure he keeps breathing and soothe him as best you can if he gets agitated." I hand her my phone. "If things go haywire, call Dr. Thomas Archer and tell him what's happening, okay?"

"That takes care of Anthony." Veronica's eyes narrow. "What do *you* need from me?"

"Just make sure I don't hit my head. From what Caroline and Thomas have told me, my body pretty much goes limp once I'm in."

"Done."

"Well, all right, then." I feel strange proceeding without Caroline present, but a big part of me wants to see the look on her face when she walks in the door and finds her boy wide awake and waiting for dinner. "You ready?"

Veronica cracks her neck and shoots me a grin. "More than I was yesterday."

Rain begins to pound the roof as Veronica and I lower Anthony onto the floor and make him as comfortable as possible. Once he's ready, I take my usual position at his head, resting my fingers at his temples.

"Keep him safe," I say, "and remember, positive energy."

Veronica offers me a faux salute as I turn my attention back to Anthony's pained gaze. His eyes no longer vacant, he stares up at me, through me, into me.

"Hold on, kiddo. Ready or not, here I come."

As I adjust to the near darkness of the Exhibition, one truth becomes immediately apparent.

Things have changed.

At my left foot lays the body of Schmuÿle and at my right, Samuel Goldenberg. The bludgeoning wounds covering their barely recognizable corpses seem the work of a blunt object like a club or mace.

Or perhaps a witch's pestle.

As Goldenberg pointed out, he and Schmuÿle were the two entities along the Exhibition who sprang more from my mind than Anthony's. It's no coincidence theirs are the two bodies left for me to find. Someone is leaving me a message and I have little doubt about the messenger.

"Hello?" My shout echoes through the strangely silent chamber. The frescoed ceiling I've always counted on for a quick look into Anthony's mood remains blank. "Is anyone there?"

With continued silence my only answer, I step across the pair of disparately dressed men. My revulsion at seeing even Sterling's doppelganger so maimed speaks volumes.

I proceed down the hall, taking care not to fall as the previously level floor has been rent from one end to the other. Jagged rock and splintered wood hinder my every step as I head for the first alcove. Tunny's alcove.

Hoping I will somehow find my diminutive friend within, I instead find only the remnants of his painting. The singed wooden frame mirrors the devastated forest depicted within. The *Gnomus* sign rests askew on the floor. Similarly, Modesto's castle still bears the marks of Baba Yaga's assault, the entire front wall of the structure now a pile of rubble. There in the moat, the clawed monstrosity rests just above water level, staring at me as if daring me to enter the painting and face it again.

I barely take notice of the *Tuileries* alcove as I pass, the crumpled canvas resting untouched at the door's lower corner. A brief glimpse into the *Bydło* alcove, however, shows Hartmann the Cart Man has been busy. Just inside the frame, an intricate barricade of wood and iron rests, some of the sharp edges protruding from the surface of the canvas. I enter and brush my finger across the tip of one of the nails, only to draw it away in agony.

I'd like to think the barricade is there to keep out the witch, though I have no trouble imagining a sign proclaiming "Storytellers Not Welcome" hanging from one of the nails.

The stage of the *Ballet of the Unhatched Chicks* as empty as before, I purposely keep my eyes focused straight ahead as I pass the home of *Samuel Goldenberg and Schmuÿle.* I can't decide which bothers me more, the image of their bodies or the fear I might share their fate.

I head for the alcove containing *The Marketplace at Limoges*, hoping the gossips there can tell me what tragedy has befallen the Exhibition.

Hopping from one intact section of floor to the next, I eventually reach the alcove. Glancing around to see if I'm being watched, I step from the darkened gallery into midday France. Much like the Exhibition, it's clear things here have changed.

The temperature indicative of spring or summer during my last visit, winter has fallen on Anthony's Limoges. The marketplace is deserted, the music absent, the tea merchant's stand where I met with Madame Versailles and the others now an empty table beneath a torn awning. I pull my sarong around my chilled form for all the good it does. As I fight to stop my teeth from chattering, I tell myself again and again I'm inside a boy's mind and the wind isn't real.

It changes nothing.

"Hello?" Answered again with silence, I turn back for the gallery where at least it's warm.

"Scheherazade." The voice, barely a whisper and thick with death, hits my chilled eardrums and fills me with dread. I peer into the alley between the buildings before me. A wisp of blonde hair plays above a pile of refuse in bags. I rush over and find Madame Versailles lying atop the mangled remains of the other three women. Their gruesome injuries echo the pulverized forms of Goldenberg and Schmuÿle.

"Baba Yaga."

"You see their bodies," Versailles grunts, "and still you dare speak her name?"

"What happened here?" I kneel by her side and pull my head close to her blood-covered lips. "Why did she come back for you?"

"Why indeed, Lady Scheherazade?" She glares at me from her one good eye. "You now see the harvest of the seeds you've sown."

I run my finger along the edge of the crater that used to be Brigitte's face. "I'm not the one who flies around this place toting a huge club of wood and brass."

"You brought her down on all of us with your talk of rebellion and freedom. The witch was quite content before you came. You ruined everything."

"This isn't how it's supposed to be. I came here to free you all so a boy could tell his mother he loves her again. Even with all I've seen today, I'd do it all again."

"You should join the others, then. They still believe in you and your stories, those insidious little tales of freedom."

"The others." I glance around. "Where are they?"

"Where do you think? You've inspired a rebellion, Scheherazade, and rebels do what rebels do."

"They've gone to face the witch."

"On her own territory." Versailles spits out a tooth. "God help them."

"How long?"

"You know as well as I time has no meaning here. An hour, a day, a year. The only question is does the battle rage on, or have the others all faced the same fate as Brigitte, Antoinette, and Sophie?"

"Your friends are all dead, Madame Versailles. How, may I ask, did you survive?"

"You are privy to many secrets, storyteller, but as I am the only one who did survive, that secret will remain mine, if you please."

"As you will." Perhaps a different tack. "The composer. Is he with them?"

"Go and see for yourself. Perhaps your arrival will make a difference." Her good eye rolls back in her head for a moment before focusing on me anew. "Or perhaps you will find their maimed corpses lying about the witch's hut."

A pang of guilt pierces me as I turn to leave. "I didn't mean for it to happen this way."

"Some secrets would prefer to stay buried, Mira."

Spinning on my heels, I peer back at the teacher from *Tuileries*. "What did you call me?"

"Hurry, Scheherazade. Though a second may take a day here, so can a day pass in a second."

Turning to run for the frame hanging in midair at the end of the street, I look back one last time. "We'll return for you."

"No, you won't, but I appreciate the sentiment. Farewell, Scheherazade."

The full import of her words still blossoming in my mind, I sprint for the frame hung in space and dive back into the gallery, the light even dimmer than before. The walls have begun to follow the fractured floor's lead, crumbling from the bottom up.

I've taken a single step in the direction of the last alcove along the hall when groan of metal on masonry fills the air. Above my head, the chandelier at the center of the white stucco ceiling rocks as if struck. Cracks proceed along the plaster in every direction like the strands of some colossal spider's web. Before I can so much as take a breath, the enormous mass of wrought iron and crystal tears free from its moorings and falls straight for me. I sprint to the side and dive behind a pile of rubble that until recently had been the brick wall blocking the passage to *The Catacombs.*

I wait to see if a second shoe drops before standing and brushing myself off.

"Surprise, surprise," I mutter with a bitter chuckle. "Anthony's seen *Phantom.*"

My smile fades as I force my feet along the last few steps to the end of the Exhibition hall and stand before the darkened alcove I've dreaded since first entering Anthony's mind. Though my every step has led to this moment, my instincts still say to run, hide, anything but enter *her* realm.

As if I have any choice in the matter.

My fingers white on the hilt of the dagger at my side, I step into the dim alcove and for the first time look upon the home of the witch.

XXVIII

The Hut on Fowl's Legs

I gaze at the painting I've only seen glimpses of during my previous visits to the Exhibition. Though no placard proclaims the name of this particular piece, I know it well. The subject of the painting has haunted my nightmares for days.

A log cabin with a steeply pitched and doubly gabled roof crowned by a jagged stone chimney, Baba Yaga's hut rests atop a pair of gigantic chicken legs. At the uppermost reach of the front gable, a bloodshot eye the size of my head stares out from beneath a slate roof into the surrounding forest. The yellow and green iris contracts as the hideous eye focuses on the small army laying siege to the witch's bizarre home.

Scattered around the structure and just out of reach of the hut's cruel talons, the remaining residents of Anthony's Exhibition stand gathered to fight. To one side of the hut's octagonal wooden base, Modesto works the keys of his silver saxophone, producing a triumphant tune I've never heard before. Hiding behind the trunk of a tree a few feet away, Antoine looks on, the boy's face an odd mix of fear and pride as the troubadour stands his ground with music his only weapon. On the opposite side of the clearing, Tunny works at the base of a dead tree with a hand axe, no doubt in an effort to send its colossal mass careening into the hut's cedar plank roof. To the hut's rear, Hartmann the Cart Man stands atop his oxcart brandishing an old wine bottle stuffed with a flaming rag.

Everyone is accounted for, save one. As I scan the battlefield for any sign of Trilby, the significance of Rachel's most recent seizure dawns on me. I leap into the painting and rush to Modesto's side.

"About time you showed up," he shouts at me between strains of his newest melody. "This rebellion is, after all, your doing."

No point in arguing. "Where's Trilby?"

"The ballerina?" Modesto asks. "She's–" His hesitation speaks volumes.

"She's there." Antoine points to the octagonal shadow formed by the witch's hut. I strain my eyes for any sign of Trilby in the darkness there, but it's not until one of Hartmann's cocktails misses and spills liquid fire beneath the hut's wooden foundation that I see her. Still dressed in her deep red bodice and black lace, her tiny form squirms beneath the hut's taloned left foot. As the flames draw ever closer, she tries to scream, though the sound comes out more like a gargled hiss.

"Stop it, Yaga." My shout shatters the silence of the forest. The eye at the hut's front gable halts its roving gaze to focus on me and me alone. "Leave Trilby alone, you ugly old hag."

"And so the battle is joined." The craggy voice booms down from the hut's upper reaches, the thick Russian accent punctuated by the metallic clack of tooth on tooth. "The storyteller, friend to all but Baba Yaga and fomenter of this little rebellion, has finally deigned to show her face."

"Come down here and I'll show you a lot more than my face, witch."

A window just beneath the eye opens, revealing the witch's baleful sneer. Her gaze shifts first from me to Modesto and Antoine and then to Tunny who despite his valiant efforts has barely made a dent in the ancient tree's massive trunk. Yaga shakes her head in mock disappointment even as her smirk widens into a full, iron-toothed smile.

"Mind that sharp tongue of yours, Scheherazade. You fared well against me in other frames along the great hall but today you face me in my own wood."

"Let the girl go," I shout. "I'm the one you want."

"But I have you already. You've stepped through my frame and into the Dark Forest, a jaunt from which few ever return. No one looks upon my home without paying a price, and you, my dear, will pay the highest price of all."

The entire hut shudders as the right fowl's leg rises from the ground, placing the full weight of the structure on the left and consequently onto Trilby's tiny form. The shrill scream that accompanies the crunch of snapping bones lasts but a second, followed by an orchestral hit from the end of the Mussorgsky suite.

"No!"

"Yes, Scheherazade. See now the devastation you have wrought with your poisoned words?"

"And yet it's you they fight, witch." I take a step forward. "Baba Yaga, strongest and wisest of all, should strive to protect the others along the hall, not try to destroy them."

"And around and around we go, Scheherazade. Once, I did protect them. Before you came, those gathered against me today were more than content to remain within their frames and live the lives to which they were destined. You and your mad talk of freedom and change, however, rained destruction down upon each and every picture and indeed the Exhibition as a whole, their collective ruin wrapped in the smile of one they considered friend."

"And you think your way was better? Not one of them followed you out of respect or admiration, but out of fear. The Exhibition may have been safe under your iron grip, but even Trilby, lying dead there below the foot of your cruel hut is more alive than any of them were before."

The momentary silence fills me with hope I've gotten through to the witch, a hope dashed by her next words.

"If they choose to disobey, then they're better off dead."

The hut begins to dance as the penultimate movement of Mussorgsky's suite blasts through the darkened wood. More than any other part of *Pictures at an Exhibition*, "The Hut on Fowl's Legs" evoked an intense visceral reaction when I heard it the first time sitting in the Faircloth living room. Mussorgsky somehow captured the sound of an impossible structure dashing madly through a murky forest, a sound that echoes through my mind as a pair of booming orchestral hits signal the beginning of the hut's onslaught.

Hartmann is the first to fall. The hut's right leg returns to the ground even as the left rises from Trilby's mangled form. Then, as if in tribute to the crushed ballerina, the entire structure performs a pirouette, the slashing talons of the hut's outstretched foot lopping the heads off both oxen from Hartmann's cart even as the Cart Man himself is sent flailing into a dark tree trunk.

"Clumsy house." The hut spins around again and the witch stares down at me triumphant. "I meant to take all three heads at once." She cranes her neck out the window to see Hartmann's body lying at the forest edge. "Still, decapitated or crushed, the Cart Man is done."

"Stop it," I scream. "If you kill them all, you kill yourself."

"Don't you think I know that, storyteller?"

"But…"

"Would you want to live this way? Betrayed by everyone in your life, forced into hiding by those to whom you have devoted your all, only to watch those selfsame ungrateful souls rail against the walls of your last refuge?"

My heart races. Am I speaking to the witch, or to Anthony himself?

"Now only three remain. Who shall be next, Scheherazade? The grotesque gnome, the charming musician, or the all too innocent boy from the garden?"

"Leave them alone. Your quarrel is with me."

The witch laughs. "Ah. The gnome you say."

Baba Yaga and Tunny meet each other's gaze and an image of a cobra staring down at a helpless mouse flashes through my mind. Terrified, Tunny begins to flail away at the tree trunk as quickly as his short limbs will allow. Yaga waves a hand and one of Hartmann's unlit Molotov cocktails rises from the cart and flies into her grasp. With a snap of her fingers, the cloth ignites.

"Dangerous, I suppose, to have skin of wood." She hurls the cocktail at Tunny, his scream engulfed by the exploding ball of orange flame that surrounds his form. "Dangerous indeed."

I rush to Tunny's side and rip off my sarong to beat out the flames blackening his face and torso.

"Don't die, Tunny."

"Just let me go." Tears of blue flame rush down the rough wooden grain of his face. Why he isn't screaming in agony is beyond anything I can understand. "Have I not suffered enough?" he groans. "Being as I am, maybe this is for the best."

"There's nothing wrong with the way you are, Tunny. There never was."

My every attempt to extinguish the flames scorching his face seems only to make the fire burn hotter. My fingers blister, the aroma of burnt flesh joining the smell of charred hickory filling the air. As real as any pain I've felt in either world, a part of me wonders if my inert body resting a universe away burns as well.

"Leave me, Scheherazade," Tunny whispers as he pushes away my scorched hands. "Save the others."

"Fear not, little gnome." The witch cackles from her window vantage. "I will ensure you do not suffer alone."

As I continue to beat at the blaze engulfing Tunny's form, Yaga turns her attention on Modesto and Antoine. She raises her arms, and like some colossal marionette, the hut rises to its full height. At a wave of her left hand, the corresponding leg of the hut comes off the ground. The witch winks at me, a sparkle in her eye as she brings her hand down to her thigh in a swooping gesture, the movement echoed in the hut's raised leg. The scaly foot strikes the forest floor with a resounding thump, its black talons missing Modesto's form by no more than an inch.

"Funny." She raises her right hand above her head and the hut's other leg rises. "Never developed a fondness for saxophone."

"Run." My shrill scream even hurts my ears. "Both of you. Before it's too late."

"It's already too late," the witch cackles.

My sarong, the only tool I have to put out the flames surrounding Tunny catches fire. I leap back from the blackening cloth and watch helpless as the hut's right foot slashes the air between Modesto and Antoine and plants itself between them. Terrified, Antoine backpedals and falls across a raised root. Staring through his broken glasses, the boy lies frozen to the spot as the hut's other foot comes off the ground and hovers above his trembling form.

"No!" Even as my body launches in Antoine's direction, there's no doubt I'm too late. I steel myself for the inevitable, dreading the inescapable moment where this reflection of Anthony suffers the same fate as his sister's doppelganger.

A burst of silver light flashes from the forest. An unseen force pulls

Antoine to safety as the hut's foot, a taloned pile-driver, impales the ground where he lay a second before.

As one, my gaze and Yaga's shoot to the wood line. From across the clearing, the composer stares at both of us, a grim smile across his face.

"How dare you enter my realm?" The rest of us forgotten, Yaga stares down at Mussorgsky, her eyes filled with a hatred tempered by sadness and perhaps a hint of longing. "All this time, and now you come." She spits a foul gob of phlegm in the composer's direction. "Where were you when everything fell apart?"

"Oh, my dear Yaga. That is precisely why I have come. I understand, as does the Lady Scheherazade, that in your mind all you do is for the good of the boy, however misguided your methods. To your credit, your efforts until recently kept safe one who could not care for himself, but you know as well as I that she and the others are right this day."

"I know no such thing." She raises a hand and one of the hut's feet rises from the dank forest earth.

"Yaga," the composer says. "Stop this now, of your own accord, or we will be forced to bring you down."

"I'd like to see you try." The witch's teeth clang like a blacksmith's hammer striking an anvil. "All you have remaining is a musician with a broken instrument, a walking campfire log, and a frightened little boy.

"And the storyteller." He motions to me. "Do not make the mistake of underestimating her."

"She is nothing. Perhaps elsewhere in the Exhibition she had influence, but here–"

"Enough." Mussorgsky silences the witch with a raised hand and turns to me. "Lady Scheherazade, despite your many trips to my Exhibition, it seems one of its truths has escaped you."

"Silence, you old fool." Disappearing from the window, the witch raises quite the racket making her way to the ground floor, where I suspect awaits her mortar and pestle.

We don't have much time.

"This truth," I ask Mussorgsky. "What is it?"

"It's quite simple actually. Did you not notice each of those gathered possesses a certain talent?"

Tunny and his way with the woods. Modesto and his music. Trilby and her dance. Even the witch and her perverse wisdom.

"Their defining characteristic." I glance around the wooded battlefield. "The thing that makes them who they are."

"And did you not hear what the arguing Jews told you?"

I consider for a moment. "That I've become one of the exhibits?"

"Gnome, Troubadour, Teacher, Farmer, Ballerina, Gossip, Composer, Witch…"

"And Storyteller."

"Exactly, but if that were all you represented, you would still be at the mercy of the witch."

"What do you mean?"

"Every work of art needs two things to exist." The composer smiles. "The art itself…"

"And someone to experience it."

"Without you, Scheherazade, there is no Exhibition. Not only are you the storyteller, but this, all of this, is your story."

The door of the witch's hut slams open and the witch flies out atop her stone mortar, her pestle brandished like a knight's lance while the broom behind her continues its unceasing back and forth motion.

I look up into the darkening sky. "A violent rain began to fall, dousing anyone and everyone in the witch's forest." My voice rolls like thunder and a second later, a bolt of lightning splits the sky. Clouds roll in and before I can say another word, a deluge begins to fall.

"What have you done?" the witch screams.

"What you should have been doing all along." The smoke roiling off Tunny's body turns to steam as the downpour quenches the flames surrounding his wooden form.

"No matter." Yaga raises the massive club of wood above her head. "I have more than enough strength in these old limbs to pound the rest of you into nothing." Her gaze focuses on me. "Less than nothing."

"Nothing, you say?" I glance at the composer, and at his subtle nod, issue another proclamation to the sky. "Then, just when all seemed lost, the witch lost her balance and her mighty pestle slipped from her grasp."

Yaga glares at me for half a second before her arms begin to flap. The swooshing broom flies from her hand and wedges itself in the crook of a nearby gum tree. The pestle is the next to fall, its wooden head cracking as it wedges between two half buried boulders. Yaga manages to maintain her balance a few seconds longer, but ultimately tumbles from her stony perch, her angular head missing the tip of her pestle by no more than an inch.

"You'll pay for this, you—"

"And then, the witch fell strangely silent." My lips curl into a wicked grin as the words are literally taken from the witch's mouth. "Now, Baba Yaga, *you* will listen to what *I* have to say for a change."

My heart drops as instead of anger, the witch's eyes fill with amusement. I glance over at Mussorgsky, his puzzled expression mirrored in the eyes of Tunny, Modesto, and Anthony who have all gathered close. As one, we all look back at the witch.

"What is it?" I ask.

She points to her throat and shrugs, a mischievous smile playing across her features.

"Fine." I wave my hand before her face as if I'm erasing something from an invisible chalkboard. "Speak."

She rises from the ground and clears her throat, the sound reminiscent of a half-drowned cat clearing a hairball.

"Well?" I bring my face close to Yaga's despite my revulsion at the hag's rank breath.

"For what do you need me, storyteller? You're the one who seems to have all the answers." She glances around at the remnant of the Exhibition. "You've gathered everyone together, attacked the mean old witch in her own realm, and somehow managed to emerge victorious. What could I possibly add?"

I grunt in frustration. "I don't understand. You've always insisted your role, your sole purpose, is to protect the other pictures, and yet here lie Trilby and Hartmann, not to mention you burned poor Tunny within an inch of his life."

"I was merely defending my own space. They did, after all, attack me."

"After you went into the Exhibition and slaughtered Goldenberg, Schmuÿle, and the women of *The Marketplace*."

"The women of the Market?" Yaga's voice trails off. "Ahhh. It all makes sense now."

"What makes sense?" I ask. "There's something you're not telling us. Something important."

"Perhaps." She strides over to Antoine and brushes her rough fingers through his already mussed hair. "Perhaps not."

"Tell me."

"Or what?" Despite the fact the witch is at my mercy, the clang of her teeth gnashing together still sets my heart aflutter.

"I could make you tell me with but a simple declaration."

"You could indeed make me talk, but could you truly make me tell you anything I didn't want you to know? That is for you to decide."

"Fine." I walk over and kneel next to Antoine. "If you won't help me, help him. According to the composer, this boy is the only thing that truly matters to you. Please, Baba Yaga, Mistress of the Exhibition, help him. Help us all."

"I would argue that title no longer belongs to me, but at this point, it simply doesn't matter anymore." All hint of amusement disappears from her face. "I wasn't posturing before when I told you it was already too late."

"What is that supposed to mean?" Mussorgsky draws close, his gaze dancing back and forth between Baba Yaga and me.

"Have all of you not noticed? The sky growing darker? The air growing colder?" She exhales, her fetid breath steaming the air. "Our world is dying."

Mussorgsky and the others all look up as the already dim sky fades toward twilight.

"She's right." Mussorgsky clutches the witch by her frayed collar. "What have you done?"

"I've done nothing, composer. Your storyteller holds me under her spell, does she not?"

"Then what is causing this?" Mussorgsky begins to pace the quickly darkening clearing. "Why is this happening?"

"Ask the Lady Scheherazade." She crinkles her nose at me. "She's the one that brought her back into our midst." Her gaze shoots down at Antoine. "Both in this world and others."

"Brought who into our midst?" My mind races through every encounter since I first entered Anthony's mind, searching for any clue as to what the witch is talking about.

In a flash, it comes to me. Madame Versailles' final words. That we wouldn't return for her. She knew. Or at least the part of Anthony's mind she represents knew. Knew I would put it together. Knew I would discover the truth.

The wind whispers a single name that answers a thousand questions.

Veronica Sayles.

XXIX

INCALZANDO

My heart begins to race anew. "She's out there with Anthony."

"And with you as well, my dear." The witch studies me, contempt dancing in her yellow eyes. "In your zeal to save the boy, it would appear you have instead doomed him to an early grave. Too late to save the Wagner girl and too trusting to save him or yourself."

"But she's his teacher."

"Are you blind, woman?" The witch spits a brown wad of spittle to the ground at my feet. "Did you not see how he reacted to her touch?"

Anthony drew away from Veronica's touch as if he were terrified. "But she was with us yesterday and Anthony was fine."

The witch sighs. "She wasn't planning to kill all of us yesterday."

"He responds the same way to his mother. How was I to know?"

"The boy may withdraw from her touch," the witch grumbles, "but it's not the same. So perceptive are you, Scheherazade, and yet the most important details seem to elude you."

"She doesn't know?" Mussorgsky asks Yaga. "You haven't told her?"

"No time for that now. The teacher could be ending the boy as we speak, and any revelations made here will then matter for nothing."

"You believe she plans to kill Anthony. She wouldn't. He's her student. He's…" My voice trails off as the full impact of the situation hits me. "He's helpless."

"And who left him that way? You may disagree with my methods, but I trust you'll agree my actions never brought danger to the boy." The witch glances to one side, then the other. "Be warned, Scheherazade. She wastes no time. Look around you. The sky has fallen to night, the air is freezing, and our very world is falling apart."

I take my eyes off the witch long enough to study the forest surrounding us. All around the trees disappear one by one, like candles being snuffed. Before I can utter another word, Antoine falls to the ground, too weak to even moan, followed in rapid succession by Tunny and Modesto. Despite the dim light, I can still appreciate the color leaving Mussorgsky's face. Even Baba Yaga appears unsteady on her feet.

"You must hurry." Her voice grows weaker with each word. "There isn't much time."

Puzzled at the witch's words, I dive forward to catch her as she lists to one side.

"I don't understand." My voice comes out as a grunt as I struggle to hold up the witch's wiry form. "Why are you helping me?"

Despite her weakened state, Yaga still skewers me to the spot with her exasperated glare. "No matter what you may think you understand about our relationship, Scheherazade, one thing has remained ever true. We both want nothing but the best for…" She pauses, as if afraid to speak the name. "For Anthony."

As if in answer, Antoine lets out one last whimper and fades from view while Tunny and Modesto continue to writhe in agony on the forest floor. Mussorgsky falls to one knee.

Yaga's contemptuous smirk melts into an expression I've rarely seen on her face.

A rictus of fear.

"If the composer falls," she whispers, "know that I will not be far behind."

"She's doing it now, isn't she?" I feel a cold numbness creep into my limbs. "Even as we speak. She's killing Anthony."

"If you don't stop her, the boy will die."

"Send me from here then." I glance at the opening in space left by the frame of *The Hut on Fowl's Legs*. "I have to save him."

Yaga snorts. "As you demonstrated so well during your last sojourn through our Exhibition, you have passed beyond my ability to send you anywhere."

"I'm trapped here."

"Not so," she says. "Just yesterday, you left my presence under your own power and brought this doom upon us all."

I focus, willing myself to wake from this strange dream world Anthony Faircloth and I share, but nothing happens.

"Nothing," I mutter in frustration. "It's like my very breath has been taken from me."

With one pathetic groan, Tunny reaches up from the ground for me before slowly fading from view. Modesto cries out in anger and frustration at his diminutive friend's disappearance before vanishing himself. A strange tingling fills my entire body and I gasp as my own form begins to grow transparent.

"It's too late," I whisper.

"No, storyteller," the witch whispers. "There may still be a way."

My heart sinks as the composer falls prostrate to the forest floor. "What do I do?"

"Take the mortar, pestle, and broom and go. If fortune smiles your way, you may get to the door in time."

"But what about all of you?"

"In another few seconds, none of us will exist. Now, go."

I ruminate on the witch's words as I lower her to the ground. "I'll be back for you."

"Whatever Fate allows, Lady Scheherazade." Yaga's mouth turns up into the kindest smile the old crone likely can muster. "Do what you can."

I sprint to Yaga's overturned mortar. The pestle lies wedged between two boulders and a glance up reveals the broom stuck in one of the few trees remaining in the quickly fading forest. I struggle to right the enormous stone bowl, and failing that, attempt to wrest the lodged pestle from its stony prison.

"It won't budge. Pestle, mortar, none of it."

Yaga's gaze shoots to Mussorgsky. "She doesn't understand. Help her."

"Remember, Scheherazade." The composer pushes himself up onto an elbow and waves his hand at the witch's implements. "Remember how you disarmed the witch before."

"I spoke what I wished to happen."

"Then speak again, storyteller, for time has almost caught us."

I stare down at the pestle, its massive wooden head pinned between the twin hunks of granite.

"Pestle, to my hand."

A grinding sound fills the air as the massive club attempts to pull free.

"You must believe," Mussorgsky shouts.

The witch's reluctant nod spurs me to action. I return my attention to the witch's pestle, focusing on its smooth surface, the grain of the wood, each intricate carving along the tool's handle. "To my hand, pestle. Now."

Unleashing a shower of rocky shards, the pestle rips itself free from its mooring and lands feather-light in my hand. Holding the giant cudgel before me, I climb across the lip of the witch's stone bowl.

"Rise, mortar." Without hesitation, the witch's vessel obeys my command, rising from the ground and coming to rest upright with me inside. Only one thing remains.

"Broom, to me." Just before the tree holding it fades from sight, the witch's spindly broom rockets from the tangle of branches and lands in my outstretched hand.

"Now," I shout as the hut and its mistress fade into nothingness. "Take me to the door of the Exhibition."

The witch's theme begins in earnest, the swishing broom and pounding pestle sending the mortar with me inside hurtling toward the wooden frame hovering in the air. I can't fathom how the stone cup will possibly fit through such a tiny portal, but I continue the forward charge regardless. I squeeze my eyes shut as we come upon the frame, only to open them a moment later and find myself sailing through the ruined Exhibition hall. I fly across the destroyed hardwood floor at the colossal double door that waits at the end of the hall. Still barred, chained and locked to prevent my comings and goings, I focus my attention on the center of the door and speak.

"With no more than seconds to spare, the Lady Scheherazade flung the pestle at the door, shattering the barrier between this realm and the next."

With a strength only possible in the world of dream, I hurl the witch's club. Flipping end over end, the head hits the pair of doors like an oaken thunderbolt and splinters the barrier from top to bottom. The bars and chains fall to the floor, followed by the demolished remains of the doors themselves, until all that remains is a massive arch surrounding the cyclone of color I traverse every time I enter Anthony's mind. Then, with one final whisk of the witch's broom I dive into the kaleidoscope whirlwind and offer a silent prayer I get to Anthony in time.

My fingers tingle like they're covered in ants. I try to move my hands and realize they're bound beneath me. Feet too. Feels like duct tape. There's something in my mouth as well. I let one eye slide open a crack and find a dishtowel shoved past my teeth. I can get in just enough air through my nose not to suffocate, but even a scream would be little louder than a whisper.

She's planned this well.

Laid out on the floor, my head is tilted away from the couch where I left Anthony. The sounds of a struggle fill the room. With all the kicking and thrashing, I can only imagine what Veronica is doing to the poor boy.

Pulling as deep a breath as I can through my nostrils, I turn my head slowly to the right and find Veronica hunched over Anthony's struggling form. She holds a pillow across his face, even as her own grows redder by the second.

"Just die, you stupid brat," she grunts through clenched teeth.

I don't know which chills me more, that Anthony has seconds left to live or that Veronica is almost certainly coming for me next. Certain I'll only have one shot at stopping her, I send up a quick prayer she doesn't see me coming. Rolling to one side, I pull my knees to my chest and strike out with both feet like a coiled snake. Veronica catches the movement from the corner of her eye and tries to dodge, but she's too involved with Anthony to avoid my attack. My stiletto heels hit her full in the ribs with an audible crack and the impact sends her sprawling across the low-backed couch and out of sight. Only down for a couple seconds, Veronica is back on her feet before I can so much as right myself.

"You stupid bitch." She steps around the couch and stands over me. "That hurt." She buries the pointed tip of her boot in my side. The pain nearly renders me unconscious, though the air forced from my lungs does send the rag flying from my mouth.

"Stop this, Veronica." My voice little better than a grunt, I fight to catch my air. "You're already guilty of one murder. Don't make it any worse for yourself."

"You have it all figured out, do you?" Her lips turn up in a snarl. "I had a feeling today was going to be the day. Made damn sure I was here just in case."

"To do what? Murder all of us? Caroline and Rachel too?"

"If I had to. Fortunate for Caroline that Rachel had that seizure." Her snarl fades into a smile. "But not as fortunate as me."

"They'll never believe you, you know."

"Oh really?" Veronica folds her hands before her waist and puts on her most innocent face. "I'm the boy's teacher for God's sake, invited by his mother to supervise him while she rode with her sick little girl to the hospital. Is it my fault the loose cannon psychic she hired to figure out his Swiss cheese brain couldn't wait for her to return? I stepped out of the room to get some water, and when I got back, you had gone crazy, suffocated the boy, and were waiting for me."

"You're planning to pin Anthony's death on me?"

"More than planning, my dear. In case you haven't noticed, your little surprise attack was the last card in your hand. Now lie there like a good girl, or I'll finish you first. And trust me, it will be anything but painless."

She rounds the couch, retrieves the pillow, and resumes her position over Anthony's unmoving form. "Still breathing." Her angry whisper chills my blood. Holding the pillow to her chest, she looks over at me, her manic gaze colored for a moment with something akin to sadness. "I know you have no reason to believe me, but I take no joy in any of this. Anthony was one of my favorites. A pleasure to teach. Unfortunately, he has a few too many secrets floating around in that head of his for me to let him live."

"And the fact I'm all taped up. How are you going to explain that?"

"We fought. I won. I wanted to make sure you wouldn't come after me again if you came to. Unfortunately, I had no idea how bad off you really were."

Her sickening grin chills me to the core.

"There's still one thing I don't get." I scramble for anything that might keep her from finishing Anthony. "Why Julianna Wagner? As best I can tell, she trusted you with the biggest secret of her life, and you killed her for it."

Veronica's lips draw tight across her teeth. "The great Mira Tejedor doesn't have all the answers after all. Will wonders never cease?"

"If you're going to kill me anyway, I deserve an answer."

"You deserve shit."

I replay every conversation I ever had with the crazed woman straddling Anthony Faircloth. Then, a flash of inspiration.

"Wait. Your breakup from back in the summer. This is about Glenn Hartman, isn't it? He dumped you for Julianna Wagner, didn't he?"

She doesn't say a word, her eyes narrowing as she pushes the pillow into Anthony's face.

"Answer me."

Her gaze drops to the floor, and for a moment, a flash of humanity peeks through.

"That bastard flirted with me for months. Finally got me to meet him out for drinks a week after finals last year and we wound up back at his place. After that, he was at my door three or four nights a week, all summer long, sniffing around like a fucking dog in heat. Wasn't good enough for going out in public, but if little Glenn needed his back scratched, he was all hearts and flowers. Then the new school year started and he stopped returning my calls. Didn't take long to figure out why." Her face turns up in a disgusted snarl. "They were none too discreet, I assure you."

"So you killed her."

"Not right away. Figured he'd eventually get tired of the tramp and come crawling back."

"Until you found out she was pregnant."

A single laugh breaks the momentary silence. "Julianna came to pick up Anthony at school one afternoon. Didn't need to be a psychic to figure out she was upset. Took about five minutes to get her to fess up."

Revelation hits me like a wave. "You went with her to the abortion clinic."

Veronica's gaze drops to her feet. "She hadn't decided what to do about the baby and asked me to go along for emotional support. She made it easy for me to get close." She glances up at me. "Almost as easy as you did, Mira."

I rack my brain for anything to keep her talking. "And the text from Jason's phone?"

She makes a dismissive wave. "Ah, the jealous ex. That was the easiest part of this whole thing. Boy needs to lock up his stuff up better during football practice."

"It was you." My heart swells at the deep voice that echoes from the foyer. "You killed Julianna." Jason Faircloth steps into the room, soaked to the bone from the torrential downpour outside.

"Jason," Veronica says. "This isn't what it looks like." I follow Veronica's stare and note the size of the puddle at Jason's feet. He's been here more than long enough to hear it all.

"I swear to God." Jason takes another step forward. "You're going down for this."

"Dammit." Veronica leaps for the chair by my feet, pulls a snub-nosed pistol from her purse, and levels it at Jason's chest. "And this was all going to be so clean."

The gun roars and Jason flies backward into the arched doorway before crumpling to the ground.

"Don't worry, Mira." She sneers down at me as she steps across my body. "I won't keep you waiting long."

XXX

TUTTI

Jason clutches his left shoulder, bright crimson filling the spaces between his fingers as he struggles to come to his feet. "You bitch. You shot me."

"I'd watch the names, kid. Don't forget who's holding the gun."

Veronica fires a second round and narrowly misses Jason as he charges down the hall for the bedrooms. She races after him, the sound of pounding steps and slamming doors and gunfire setting my heart racing. Despite the ringing in my ears from the first pair of gunshots, I can just perceive the sound of Anthony's labored breathing. Though raspy and intermittent, the sound means he's alive. We can sort out the rest later.

If there is a later.

I strain against the duct tape cutting into my wrists and kick my legs like alternating pistons in an attempt to loosen the bindings at my ankles. I'm just beginning to make headway, as evidenced by the sensation of a swarm of spiders crawling across my feet, when a noise captures my attention.

No. A voice.

Anthony's voice.

Strange. Though I've interacted with Anthony on almost every level through his various aspects along the Exhibition and explored the most unfathomable depths of his shattered psyche, I've never heard the boy speak, much less sing, until this moment.

So quiet I can barely hear him at first, Anthony begins the last few bars of *Pictures at an Exhibition.* From a low humming, he eventually breaks into full on song. The lyrics he sings, of fire and fate, endings and beginnings, life and death, threaten to break my heart.

"Anthony?" I keep my voice low. "What is it? What are you trying to tell me?"

Then three words, sung with all the triumph and glory of a chorus of angels.

"Death… is… life."

Though Anthony's face is hidden by the couch edge, I can imagine the concentration etched on his features, the strain in his voice doubling with each grunted word.

"I'm here, Anthony." Despite the pain from my bruised ribs, I pull myself into a seated position. "Tell me what to do."

Anthony's answer is simple. He begins to hum Scheherazade's theme.

"No, Anthony. I can't come back right now." For the first time since our initial meeting at Thomas' office, I begin to cry. "The danger's out here in the real world and there's not a damn thing I can do about it."

"Isn't there, Scheherazade?" The voice coming from Anthony's mouth has shifted. He speaks with the inflection and diction of the composer.

"Mussorgsky?"

"I'm a bit disappointed, storyteller." Hearing the deep Russian accent coming from Anthony's barely moving lips is as surreal as anything I've experienced along the Exhibition. "Have you already forgotten all you've learned?"

"With all due respect, Mr. Composer, anything I learned in your musical madhouse doesn't exactly apply out here in the real world." I struggle anew against the restraints at my wrists. One of the bones pops out of joint, the sound turning my stomach even as pain and dull heat work their way up my arm. "I can't talk my way out of duct tape, now can I?"

"Can't you?" The composer's voice takes on a mocking tone as it shifts into Modesto's charming British baritone. I do my best to hear what he's saying over the back-and-forth screaming from the hallway. As best I can tell, Jason has barricaded himself in one of the bedrooms and Veronica isn't handling it well at all.

"Telling a story is much like performing a piece of music," the troubadour continues. "If you don't like the arrangement of a section, you rewrite until the sequence has a more pleasing sound."

"You want me to rearrange my way out of being tied up?"

A crisp laugh. "You're making a relatively simple situation rather complicated."

"Listen, Modesto, or whoever in there is running things at the moment. You all may have had the option to retreat to a nice, safe place when things got rough, but I'm stuck out here in the real world and we're all going to die unless I get free."

"You still wish to save us, then?" Antoine's voice takes over, the hint of French in his intonation coming through loud and clear.

"Yes, Antoine."

"And yourself?"

"Of course."

"Then come back to us," comes a voice like creaking limbs. How Anthony's little mouth creates Tunny's voice is beyond me. "It's the only way."

"You've got to be kidding. If I return, Anthony and I will both be vulnerable again. I can't stop her from in there."

"I would argue your current plan isn't meeting with much success either." Modesto's tone borders on mocking. "If you wish to survive this day and keep this woman from killing us all, then return to the Exhibition and finish what you started."

"You don't understand. Regardless of what I do in there, it won't mean a thing when she comes back."

"No," comes the composer's rolling Russian. "It is you who does not understand. What do your instincts tell you? You may believe our realm is separate from yours, but is not the boy's sister in the hospital as we speak, suffering from injuries her other self acquired in my Exhibition? Have you not seen the gnome in what you consider the 'real' world? Been pulled into the Exhibition from half a city away?" For the first time, Anthony Faircloth turns his head and stares directly into my eyes. "Are you not conversing with the composer, Mussorgsky, at this very moment?"

A chill works its way up my spine as I struggle to formulate a response.

"Come back to us," the composer says. "Come back to us and make this right."

I close my eyes and shake my head. "She'll kill us all. Me, you, Jason, maybe even Caroline when she returns."

"Perhaps. As Mira Tejedor, you are powerless to save the boy, but as the Lady Scheherazade, your potential is limitless. You've brought us all so far, yet one task remains."

"One task." I bite back a mouthful of foul words. "And what would that be, oh great Mussorgsky?"

"Simple," the composer's voice says. "Unite us."

"Unite? What do you think I've been trying to do? The witch won't let me so much as—"

"Return, Scheherazade." From Anthony's lips comes the first voice I ever heard along the Exhibition. "Return and unite us." Anthony gnashes his teeth together, and though his aren't made of iron, I have no doubt I'm speaking with the witch. "It is time."

Teetering on the verge of panic, a kernel of an idea sprouts inside my mind.

"All right, Anthony," I whisper as another gunshot sounds from the hall. "You want me, you've got me."

My first trip into Anthony's mind required a supreme effort of will, as if the price of admission to the funhouse existing between the boy's ears was no less than turning my soul inside out. This entrance feels as easy as stepping into a warm bath. Surrounded again in the prismatic whirlwind, I'm buffeted by the disparate melodies of "Promenade" and *Scheherazade*, but where before the two tunes were dissonant and harsh, they now articulate with each other as if written to be played as one. The back and forth between the two melodies reminds me strangely of the interplay between Samuel Goldenberg and Schmuÿle. I dread seeing their mutilated forms at the center of the devastated hall, though I have little doubt the body count will continue to climb if I turn back now.

Seconds, minutes, hours pass in the maelstrom of color. Then, in a blink, I'm standing alone in a pristine version of Anthony's Exhibition. The floor restored to its original state, the herringbone pattern of wood beneath my feet stretches to the nine alcoves of the various pictures. No bodies clutter the well-lit space and the frescoed ceiling lives again, the dark thunderstorm there mirroring the actual sky above the Faircloth house. At the far end of the hall, the wall-eyed janitor from the school performs one last sweep with a long-handled broom before raising his head to smile at me.

"Now you're here as well?" I ask.

"You left the Exhibition quite a wreck, Lady Scheherazade." He motions to the vast hallway. "But I was able to get nearly everything back to its original state."

"Who are you?"

"Just the Janitor, milady. Once, I was known as the Sage, but this is the shape I now possess." He peers across his shoulder at the long hall of empty alcoves. "Wish I could stay and chat, but time is of the essence and your business with the others is far more important." He kisses my hand. "How truly unfortunate we had no more than a moment, Scheherazade. I would have liked to have known you." Before I can answer, he shoots me a mischievous wink and disappears in a scintillating flash of silver. As my eyes readjust to the muted light, I find myself alone.

"Hello?" My voice a rough whisper, the words still echo in the perfect acoustics of the space. "Is anyone there?"

A single breath passes before the characters step as one from their various alcoves to greet me. To my right, I find Tunny's mossy countenance grinning out at me from the *Gnomus* alcove, Antoine staring off into space at the entrance to the *Tuileries* garden, and Trilby's graceful form framed *en pointe* in the doorway leading to the *Ballet of the Unhatched Chicks.* To my left, Modesto works his saxophone from the alcove leading to *The Old Castle.* Farther down the hallway, Hartmann stands at his station appearing disgruntled but content, the women from *The Marketplace at Limoges* stop their gossiping to point and stare, and even Goldenberg and Schmuÿle cease arguing long enough to each bow to me before turning on each other anew. At the far end of the hall, Baba Yaga sits atop her mortar, her switch broom swishing back and forth behind her like a dog's wagging tail. Mussorgsky watches from beneath the witch's perch, his arms crossed and expression impassive. Yaga points her wooden pestle at me, but where I've always found derision in her baleful sneer, I now find a strange warmth.

"Come, Scheherazade. Our time is short."

"But how is this possible? Trilby, Goldenberg, Schmuÿle, Hartmann, the women from the market. They're all dead."

Yaga's nose wrinkles. "As you never fail to remind us, this is a realm of imagination. I have personally dispatched you from this place more times than I can remember and yet here you are again. Is it so hard to imagine others could do the same?"

I walk the restored Exhibition hallway and meet the expectant gazes of each of the various characters from the pictures. All, that is, save one.

"The women of *The Marketplace*," I ask. "There are only the three." My voice goes quiet. "Where is Madame Versailles?"

Mussorgsky steps forward. "We hoped you would know. Despite all she has done, she is still a part of us after all."

"A part of us." Yaga hawks a green wad of spittle onto the pristine floor. "Once, perhaps."

"Regardless of your feelings, we're going to need her if we are to survive this day." I raise my head and gaze at the ceiling. "Exhibition, I wish to see Madame Versailles."

The thunderstorm above our head parts to reveal an image of Versailles limping through the darkened streets of *The Marketplace at Limoges*.

"Ah." A vindicated smile spreads across my face. "There she is."

I motion for all present to hold their position and raise my voice to the ceiling. "Madame Versailles, come forth. I demand your presence." The image in the fresco shifts. Versailles glances across her shoulder, her eyes frightened and desperate.

"Madame Versailles." My whispered words fill the space. "I will not repeat myself again. Come forth."

A shimmering ball of silver light blossoms before the alcove of *The Marketplace at Limoges*. The scintillating sphere grows brighter with each breath, eventually exploding into a million dazzling sparkles, leaving a bedraggled Madame Versailles standing amid the others of the Exhibition.

"Quick," Tunny shouts. "Bind her before she can escape."

"Bind her?" Baba Yaga gnashes her iron teeth. "We should tear her limb from limb for all the suffering she has caused."

Versailles screams as the characters of the Exhibition converge on her frail form.

"No." My whisper echoes through the place like a peal of thunder. "I didn't bring her here to meet her end this way, no matter how much she deserves it." I raise a fist and as one the various characters that make up Anthony's fractured psyche freeze in place. "Now, bring Versailles to me." I lower my hand. "I would speak with her."

Tunny and Modesto flank Madame Versailles and escort her to my side with Antoine and the others trailing not far behind. Crumpled on the floor at my feet, much like her canvas in the *Tuileries* alcove, she glares up at me.

"What could you possibly want with me?" she mutters.

I consider for a moment. "A confession, perhaps?"

"A confession? And to what exactly would I be confessing?"

"The truth." I stare into her squinted eyes, the hate in her gaze mirroring the emotion found in Veronica's face moments before. "You know of what I speak."

"Please," Versailles says. "Enlighten me."

"Juliet. You said Hartmann was responsible for her disappearance and I believed you. Then you took her position in *The Marketplace* and convinced everyone you simply needed a new home after the destruction of *Tuileries*. I no longer believe your stories represent the truth."

"Quiet, Scheherazade," she says. "You know not of what you speak."

"Don't I? You desired Hartmann for yourself, and when he preferred someone younger, more talented, more beautiful than you…"

"Stop it," she hisses.

"You killed her and took her place." I draw close. "And later, when things didn't go your way, you attacked the others. Goldenberg. Schmuÿle. The women of *The Marketplace*. You crushed their bodies to ensure the witch would be blamed."

"You're the one that ended Juliet?" Hartmann lowers his chin, his eyes filling with hate. "And put her in my field?" The Cart Man rushes to my side to stand over the kneeling Versailles. "I'm with the witch," he says. "She dies now."

"No, Hartmann. No more death. Madame Versailles is as much a part of the boy as any of you. I will not risk harming him any further than has already been done."

"A part of the boy." Goldenberg and Schmuÿle speak as one, their respective ruddy and sallow faces each turned in my direction. "And look at us. All of us. Together." Each of their gazes drift to the other, both of them simultaneously comforted and terrified.

"Yes. As hard as it may be for some of you to understand, there is another place where all of you are but pieces of a wonderful boy, like the different facets of a cut stone. I believe he needs all of you if he is to survive."

"Wait." Versailles raises a confused eyebrow. "You came here to save me?"

"I didn't say that." As the remainder of the Exhibition gathers close, I gesture around the circle. "Gathered here stand a composer, a musician, a dancer, a storyteller. We each weave together disparate parts of our individual abilities to create a functional whole. You are many, but in truth, you are one. Something inside of Anthony called me back to the Exhibition to bring you all together. I'm ready to try, but I have no idea how to begin."

"Lady Scheherazade." Mussorgsky smiles. "Or perhaps we should call you... Mira?"

My heart quickens at the mention of my true name. "Perhaps you should."

"As before, Mira, you already have the answer. There, in your mind."

"The answer."

"A lesson you learned long ago in a happier time." The composer's eyes clench shut in concentration. "Think back on a favorite teacher. Not the tallest man you've met. Thick brown mustache. Blue eyes."

My mind seizes upon a name I haven't thought of in years. "Mr... Hatley?"

"The same."

"What about him?"

"The banner above his blackboard. He quoted it constantly. What did it say?"

"I don't remember."

"But you do." The witch speaks, her voice strangely kind, though the metallic clang of her teeth still leaves me weak in the knees. "Just as you have been in the boy's mind, so has he been in yours. Even I can see it there among your memories. Now tell me, Mira Tejedor, what did the banner say?"

"I don't know." My fingers ball into fists, and somewhere a world away, I feel my wrists strain against the tight duct tape binding my hands together. "I can't remember. I… Wait…"

Mr. Hatley. Eighth grade. Earth Science. Played the bagpipes at our eighth grade graduation. Served as chess club coach for one of my junior high boyfriends. In a blink, I'm thirteen again, walking into his classroom, taking a seat at my desk in the third row. There above the board, a favorite saying, blazoned in our school colors of black, white and orange.

"The whole is greater than the sum of its parts." The words fall from my mouth, as if another person speaks through me. "Aristotle."

"A truism that serves doubly in our situation." In an instant, the composer is by my side. "Each of us represents some aspect of this boy Anthony you seek, and your instinct since first coming here has been to bring us together and sort out this puzzle the boy has become." He glances at Baba Yaga, smirking. "Despite, evidently, the best efforts of some of the pieces."

Yaga raises her nose. "Laugh all you want, composer, but I did more to keep the boy safe than you ever did from your sepulcher of skulls."

"Bygones, Yaga." He turns back to me. "There is something about the situation, however, you're missing."

"And that would be?"

"Your own role in this drama." Mussorgsky takes my hand. "You've always perceived your visits to our Exhibition as you leaving your mind and entering Anthony's, and yet, the two of us established when we first met that without you, the Exhibition doesn't exist." Mussorgsky gestures around the room. "Art without someone to perceive it is nothing. Anthony's mind may provide the canvas, the substrate, the raw imagination, but without your thoughts, ideas, emotions, perceptions, understand there would be no Exhibition."

"No pictures," mutters the witch.

Tunny tugs at my sleeve, realization dawning on his gnarled face. "No us."

"This fractured state," I whisper. "It's not the problem."

"No, dearie." The witch floats over and climbs down from her mortar. She takes my hands and places them in Mussorgsky's. "The Exhibition has never been the problem, but the solution."

"What do we do then?"

"If what you speak is true," Mussorgsky says, "then we are the boy you call Anthony. You and he created this place, so if it is to end, it will take all of us."

"But how?"

"There is one picture you have yet to visit." The witch stretches out her wiry arm toward the far end of the gallery. "A place I believe holds the answers all of us seek."

I rack my brain, working through the various movements in Mussorgsky's magnum opus. I study each of the gathered characters in turn, my gaze meeting the witch's as I come to "The Hut on Fowl's Legs." the penultimate piece of the suite. Then it comes to me. The album cover from Anthony's favorite version of *Pictures at an Exhibition.* The trio of arches below the Russian double-headed eagle.

"I remember. The last movement of the suite, the last picture." Glancing down, Antoine's innocent smile fills me with hope. "We must find *The Bogatyr Gates.*"

XXXI

The Bogatyr Gates

"*The Bogatyr Gates*, the legendary Russian 'Gate of Heroes.' How fitting as we gather here at the end." Mussorgsky's wistful grin melts into a befuddled frown. "Still, I don't believe the myth of the Exhibition's missing picture is going to help us very much."

"Like this whole place isn't something out of myth." I wander from one end of the hall to the other, counting the alcoves as I pass to assure myself I've visited them all. "You're right, though. There are no more alcoves. No more paintings."

If possible, the composer's frown deepens. "Thus, the word myth."

"But it must be somewhere in the Exhibition. Anthony has recreated the entirety of your–I mean Mussorgsky's–magnum opus down to the last detail. There's no way he would have missed an entire movement, especially not the big finale."

"Apologies, dearie, but even I know nothing of the Gates beyond the legends." Baba Yaga climbs down from her mortar and creeps toward me, her wicked grin cold as she kicks the prostrate form at my feet. "What about you, Versailles? Do you know where it's hidden? You seem to be the one keeping all the secrets these days."

She glares up at the witch, defiant. "I haven't the first idea where it would be, hag."

"Hag, you say?" Yaga drops to one knee and leans close to Versailles' ear. "Give me half a minute with that pretty face of yours and no man alive will ever give you a second glance again."

"Stop it, you two." I step between the two women before Versailles can throw any more gas on the fire. "There's no time for this." I help the schoolmarm to her feet and pull her away from the others. "Every moment that passes is a chance for Madame Versailles' counterpart on the other side to put a bag over Anthony's head and finish him. Do any of you want a repeat of what happened in the witch's wood?"

I search the eyes of Anthony Faircloth's many faces for a spark of hope.

"Modest," I ask. "Your conductor's baton. Can it help?"

Mussorgsky smiles and holds up the implement of his station. "This simple foot of maple and mahogany may weave spells of melody and harmony, but it is no magic wand."

I turn to Modesto. "What about your castle? One door led to the Catacombs. Perhaps another of the doors there, or one of the tapestries."

"I know every inch of my abode." Modesto crosses his arms. "The Gates are not there."

Goldenberg and Schmuÿle stare at me as one.

"Maybe one of the paintings in your home, Samuel?" I ask.

Bizarre in their silence, Goldenberg shakes his head while Schmuÿle looks away, doing his best to ignore the question, if not the questioner.

In the opposite corner, Antoine stands sobbing. Despite all that has happened, Madame Versailles moves to comfort him, or at least I hope that's her intent. Regardless, I block her path with an outstretched arm.

"Sorry. The kid is off limits."

Versailles tries to conceal a baleful glare as she steps back. "Of course."

Hartmann steps forward. "Then it's over. All of it. First Juliet, and now the rest of us."

"I will not allow that to happen." I rest a hand on Hartmann's shoulder. "There must be a way."

"Excuse me." The quiet voice all but lost in the creaking of nearly two dozen feet on the parquet floor, I almost miss it. "There is one thing you haven't considered."

As one, we all turn and look into Tunny's muddy brown eyes.

I kneel by the trembling gnome. "What did you say, Tunny?"

"There is something you haven't thought of," he says. "Something simple."

"Spit it out, gnome." The witch pushes past me and grabs Tunny's collar before I can stop her. "Let's hear it."

"Get off him," I shout as I pull them apart. "Give him some space." I glare around at the crowd as they draw close around Tunny and me. "All of you."

Modesto steps up behind me. "You heard the Lady, everyone. Back off." His crisp British accent replaced with Jason Faircloth's mild Southern twang, the troubadour glances across his shoulder at Tunny. "Let's hear what the little guy has to say."

A tear of sap begins a long sojourn down Tunny's cheek.

I take the gnome's hands, his tree bark skin rough against my fingers. "What is it, Tunny? What do you know?"

"It's just, when you first came here, there weren't pictures or halls or anything. If what you say is true, and each of us is nothing more than a tune playing in a boy's head, then maybe you don't look for the Gates along this hallway, but—"

"In the music itself." I turn to Mussorgsky. "Modest, what can you tell me about the last movement of *Pictures at an Exhibition*?"

"The final movement opens with fire and thunder." The composer strokes his beard, his eyes glassing over as if in deep thought. "A royal fanfare. Maestoso in tempo. Forte in volume."

"And just before that?"

Mussorgsky's gaze shoots to Baba Yaga.

The witch cranes her neck around to stare back at her alcove. "My hut sprints one last time across the listener's imagination."

I step to the witch's side and study her in profile. "It's up to you now, Baba Yaga. Help me. Help us. Help… Anthony."

"As if I have any choice in the matter." The witch's lips curl into a half-smile, half-sneer as she raises her arms to the ceiling. She claps her hands in rhythm, a couplet followed by two triplets and a quick succession of six. Bowing her head, she begins humming the menacing tune that has accompanied her every appearance along the Exhibition. In answer, music fills the space, an entire symphony of unseen instruments mirroring the odd sequence of claps and the unintelligible syllables rolling off the witch's tongue. Then, overpowering the invisible orchestra, the sound of the hut's legs ripping through the forest underbrush as it races toward us fills the air. As the sound grows closer and closer, a pair of terrifying realizations crosses my mind.

The size of the witch's hut.

The size of Yaga's alcove.

Though the witch's mortar and I passed the aperture of her painting before with ease, my heart fills with a strange certainty this time will be different.

"Everybody, down!" I leap at Antoine and force him to the ground, covering his fragile form with mine as Baba Yaga's hut explodes through the gallery wall. The storm of shattered brick, mortar and plaster flies at us and then… nothing.

Peering out from behind my clenched fists, I find the entire assemblage untouched by the ton of shattered masonry.

"But… how?"

Yaga laughs. "My alcove. My hut. My rules." She taps her temple. "As you remind us at every turn, the Exhibition is all up here." The witch's strange home lowers itself to the ground and Baba Yaga bends at the waist in a humble bow, her outstretched arms gesturing toward the hut's open door. "Lady Scheherazade, your chariot awaits."

"Thank you." My gaze passes across the assembled pieces of Anthony Faircloth's psyche. "But, this chariot isn't for me."

Before I can utter another word, a voice rips through the hall. The inflection reminiscent of Madame Versailles sans the French accent, the words echo from somewhere far away.

"*Damn him. Everything's a mess.*" The metallic click of a gun being locked and loaded fills the air. "*Nothing to do now but finish this.*"

The witch's eyes grow wide. "We must hurry. It would seem your friend has returned to finish the job."

I peer inside the hut, confirming there's room, and step away from the door. "Everyone inside. Now."

One by one, the various characters that populate Anthony's Exhibition step into the witch's home. I give each a solemn nod as they pass, thankful they obey me without question. If what I am planning is to work, it must be all of them.

All of them, that is, save one.

I step into Madame Versailles' path as she moves for the door. More than one gasp sounds behind me, but I know better than to take my eyes off the teacher from *Tuileries* for even a second.

"So, Mira. You plan to leave me here to suffer alone?" Versailles turns her head to one side, the glint in her eye identical to that of a woman no doubt standing over my body in a place a million miles from here. "An eternity with no one to talk to save myself?"

"If you think you have eternity, Versailles, you are sorely mistaken."

Yaga stands in the door of her crouching home, watching my every move. "What now?"

A revelation hits me. "Lock your door, Yaga, and take the hut into the maelstrom."

"The maelstrom?" For only the second time in our many encounters, fear invades the old witch's eyes. "But we cannot go there. The door is locked. More, it is forbidden."

"Forbidden? By whom? You? Anthony? By the very trauma that birthed all of you?"

"That way leads to death." Mussorgsky stares down at me from a triangular window in the side of the house. "For all of us."

"Death."

Lyrics flit through my mind, the same strange anthem Anthony sang as he lay on the couch. I can only remember the ending, and pray it will be enough.

I lock gazes with Versailles. "A boy I know recently shared with me a truth."

"Don't," Versailles whispers, her eyes wide with fear.

The invisible orchestra from before swells, filling the room with piercing brass and booming drums.

"Death…"

"Stop it." Her eyes grow wide in fear.

"Is…"

"You'll destroy everything!" Versailles leaps at me and we go to ground in a tangle of arms and legs.

Despite her claws at my throat, I belt out the last word, the others within the witch's hut all joining me in a chorus Mussorgsky himself heard only in his wildest dreams.

"Life…"

Before she can utter another word, a mighty wind pulls Madame

Versailles from my body and hurls her into the nearest wall. I half expect her to leap back to her feet and charge again, but instead her crumpled form lies there beneath the fractured plaster, bent and still.

A single moment of silence passes before the sound of tumblers echoes in the hall. As one, the various fragments of Anthony Faircloth's mind, already ensconced in the witch's home on taloned feet, scream out in terror.

"The door," Modesto shouts above the others. "It's opening."

The lock falls to the floor, the thunderous crash of metal on wood pummeling me with physical force. Then, as if I've angered the Exhibition itself, a hurricane wind fills the hall and blows the doors off their hinges. Beyond, the spectral whirlwind of color awaits.

No.

Beckons.

"Death." Tunny's voice squeaks with panic. "The maelstrom means death for us all."

"Congratulations, Schmuÿle." Goldenberg's first words in what seems like years have an edge I've never heard before. "It seems, here at the end, you were right." His despondent gaze bores into me. "About everything."

"Do not despair, Samuel," Schmuÿle says to the surprise of all present, his grating tone almost tolerable for once. "Perhaps there is still hope."

"Of course there is hope." From atop the crouched hut, Baba Yaga looks down from her mortar as if she were the captain of a ship. Or in this case, it would appear, an ark. "Now, storyteller. You would have me take all of them into the unknown based on nothing but your word?"

"Yes, oh trusted storyteller." Versailles rises from the floor, her broken form somehow restored and her eyes full of hate. "What would you have them do now?"

"Go." I motion to the doorway filled with light. "All of you."

"Come with us, Scheherazade," Tunny shouts from a window. "Don't leave us to face the maelstrom alone."

"You are not alone." I catch the composer's gaze in one of the hut's windows and give him a quick nod. "None of you are. Not anymore."

"Thank you, Mira." Mussorgsky returns my nod and grins. "For all you have done and all you're about to do."

"Keep them well, Modest." I glance up at Baba Yaga and gesture to the end of the hall. "Get moving. I'll catch up."

The witch's lips grow wide in an iron smile as she raises her arms anew. She claps but once, the sound augmented by a single orchestral hit that brings the hut to its feet. Two more claps and the hut takes two steps, the pair of footfalls accompanied by a deafening symphonic couplet. Then, the rushing music begins anew and the pair of enormous chicken legs propels the strangest piece of architecture I've ever seen toward the swirling whirlpool of light and color.

"No!" Versailles hurls herself after the rushing house on chicken legs. "You can't leave me alone like this."

I again step into her path. "Their fate is not yours, Versailles."

"Out of my way, Mira." In a flash, a gleaming rapier appears in her hand and she wastes no time thrusting its razor point at my heart. I dodge to one side and slide the bejeweled dagger from the sash at my waist.

"You will call me Scheherazade." I hold the gleaming blade before me. "And even if it kills me, I swear you will never leave this place."

Her eyes narrow. "You believe that name gives you power, don't you? Your little stories may serve to sway the others and may have even allowed you to best the witch, but you'll find your words have no effect on me. Surely you have guessed by now I am not like the others."

"Guessed, you say?" I raise an eyebrow. "I'm counting on it."

"Don't you realize?" The bluster in her voice is replaced with uncertainty. "The boy needs me too. I'm as much a part of him as the others."

"Oh, he needs you, all right." The dagger pulses in my grip, ready. "Here. Now."

The witch's bizarre home continues its slow progress as the invisible orchestra playing "The Hut on Fowl's Legs" grows louder and faster. Trumpets sound from every corner. The sound of French horns oscillates high and low. Screaming violins alternate with blasting tuba. Then at the end of a long run that weaves together strings, woodwinds, and snare, the witch's tune transitions into a different piece of music altogether.

Rich and brazen, the fanfare sends Versailles into convulsions. Screaming as if her very soul has been set aflame, she stares past me with bleary eyes. I spin on my heels and nearly drop the dagger in awe as the swirling light takes shape. At the edges of the billowing color, a giant frame forms, though this one stands as wide and tall as the hall itself. Within the frame, the spinning maelstrom of light grows slower and more muted until the radiance resolves into a surface. This last canvas depicts an enormous triple arch of stone and brick.

The Bogatyr Gates.

The hut slows its pace, marching in time with the new melody and stepping with every other beat like a bride promenading down the aisle. With each step, the painting of the massive triple gate grows more defined even as the Exhibition around me begins to dissolve into random bits of light and darkness. Six stories high and just as wide, the enormous structure stands open on a landscape of slate and pine. Neither man nor beast guards these arches, and for the briefest of moments, I let myself believe the way is clear and the surprises at an end.

Yaga sends the hut through the shimmering canvas and onto the path leading to the Gates. I wave after them, though my fond goodbye comes out as a scream as a searing pain rips through my shoulder. I fall to the ground in agony.

Versailles stands over me, crimson blood dripping from the tip of her rapier.

"Forget about me, did you?" The smile occupying her face somehow makes Yaga's seem almost pleasant. "As if some silly piece of music could so much as slow me down. Confidence may be a virtue, Scheherazade, but overconfidence leads only to failure." Versailles leaves me writhing on the floor and races at the shimmering canvas.

The composer's final lesson echoes through my mind.

"*Speak again, storyteller, for time has almost caught us.*"

And three more words that fill me with fire.

"*You must believe.*"

I grip the hilt of my weapon and touch the tip to my wounded shoulder. "Just when all seemed lost, the magic of the Sultan's dagger closed Scheherazade's wound." Before I can finish the sentence, the pain in my shoulder dissipates as the skin knits itself back together. I launch myself from the ground and sprint after Madame Versailles. As fast as I run, though, I'm still a good thirty paces behind her when she looks back with a vicious grin and steps through the frame of the final picture of the Exhibition.

"Farewell, Scheherazade," she shouts across her shoulder as she reappears on the winter landscape and rushes after the witch's hut, the bizarre structure continuing its jaunt atop its pair of massive chicken legs. I arrive seconds later and dive after Versailles into the painting. Driving snow falls from an undulating prismatic sky, yet the air is warm and smells of tea and vanilla. The hut continues its slow progress and nears the Gates with Versailles close behind. The witch glances back from her perch atop the roof and levels the pestle at Versailles.

"What now, Scheherazade?" Yaga shouts. "She is almost upon us."

It occurs to me that just days before, I used those same words about the witch. "Through the Gates," I scream. "Hurry."

"Too late." Versailles hurls her rapier to one side and leaps. Her fingers find a chain dangling from the hut's foundation. "Where they go, now I go as well. Your move, storyteller."

I clench the dagger between my teeth and leap at Versailles' swinging form, catching her about the waist and nearly ripping the yellow and teal dress from her body. She kicks at my thighs and torso, but I hold on, clawing my way up her body inch by inch until we hang eye to eye from the chain. I grab the weapon from my teeth and beat at her hands with the pommel, though it takes everything I have simply to hold fast to the chain.

"Let go, Versailles," I grunt. "If you pass the Gates, Anthony dies."

"Like I give a whit about the boy. Don't you understand? I am not him and he isn't me."

"But some part of you is Veronica Sayles. She's his teacher for God's sake."

"Then perhaps it's time for one final lesson." Her lips draw down to a tight line. "Trust no one."

I look past her shoulder. "A lesson you could stand to learn yourself."

"What are you talking—" Before she can complete her thought, one of the hut's clawed feet grabs her from behind and pulls the two of us from the chain like grapes from a vine. Hurled into the surrounding woods, Versailles lands in a copse of saplings while my body takes the full force of an ancient poplar.

Despite the pain, my lips turn up in a grin. "As you so eloquently put it, Madame Versailles, overconfidence leads only to failure." With supreme effort, I turn my head in the direction of the witch's hut. "It's all right, Yaga. I'll be fine." I cough blood onto my clenched fist. "Just take them through and don't look back."

The witch looks upon me with an admiring smile.

"Thank you, Mira." Yaga's voice changes, the rough timbre replaced with a pleasant, if not familiar, Southern inflection as her features shift like quicksilver into the face of Caroline Faircloth. She raises her hands, clapping them together one last time. The hut steps through the Gates and vanishes in a flash of silver light.

"No," Versailles screams. "If they leave, this place and everything in it ceases to be."

"Then so be it," I mutter.

Versailles and I brace ourselves for our imminent destruction, but the feared cataclysm never comes. The landscape grows placid while the sky above remains gray and foreboding. The snow stops, and everything in sight takes on the appearance of a paused movie. Everything, that is, but the Gates which continue to pulse in time to a silent rhythm I suspect represents a boy's heart a universe away. Versailles leers at me, triumph blossoming through the bruises forming along her high cheekbones.

"Your final gambit has failed, Scheherazade. There stand the Gates, open for me to walk through and you cannot stop me." She pushes herself up from the ground and shambles toward the pulsating arch of stone.

"An interesting choice of words, Madame Versailles."

She glances back. "More games, storyteller?"

"You are a teacher of language, are you not?"

"What of it?"

"The word gambit. It means an action with a significant risk, but to a chess player, it means something quite different."

"A sacrifice." She turns to face me. "Helpless, you lie there, and yet you still believe you can sacrifice me to save the boy?"

"It's far more than that." I prop myself up one elbow. "You see, the composer shared with me a truth."

"And you think this truth will save you?"

"Where do you think you are, Versailles? What do you think lies beyond the Gates?"

"We exist in the confines of a boy's mind. Beyond the Gates lies freedom."

"But that's where you're wrong. This place is not Anthony alone, but a reality borne out of a harmony of minds. His." My gaze locks with hers. "And mine."

Something akin to fear reappears in her eyes. "So?"

"A wise friend told me no matter what happens, a dream can't kill you." I retrieve the dagger from the snow-covered ground at my side. "But if this entire Exhibition is nothing but another canvas and Anthony and I the frame that holds it together…"

"No." Versailles eyes grow wide as she finally comprehends my plan. "You can't." She spins as fast as she can in her full-length dress and dives for the Gates, but not before I pull the dagger to my chest and slide its gleaming blade between my ribs.

Versailles screams in defeat as the stony arch crumbles to the snow-covered ground. The sky darkens. The forest around us disappears, then the rubble, then the ground itself. Surrounded in nothing but ever-darkening gray, Versailles fades into oblivion. Left floating alone in the dim void, I look on dispassionately as my body—no—the body of Lady Scheherazade, the storyteller, begins to fade as well.

Somewhere far away, the thunder of gunfire splits the sky just before everything fades to black.

XXXII

Coda

I awake with the great-grandmother of all headaches, my head throbbing in time with a beeping somewhere to my left. I open my eyes to find my shivering form nestled safely between a set of overly starched white sheets. An IV line protrudes from my hand, the fluids sending a chill up my arm and into my chest. Though the pastel blue curtains surrounding me block my view, the sounds and smells make it a safe bet I'm in a hospital somewhere. The rhythmic beeping of the machine next to me captures my attention again and I find strange reassurance seeing the rhythm of my heart play out as a squiggly green line on the screen.

I try to sit up. As I have many times before in the last week, I fail miserably.

"Hello?" My voice comes out as an all too familiar croak. "Is anyone there?"

A nurse pops around the curtain, notices I'm awake, and rushes over to check on me.

"Good evening, Ms. Tejedor. How are you feeling?"

"Like I got hit by a runaway train. Where am I?"

"The Emergency Department. Carolinas Medical Center. If you'll wait a moment, I'll go get the doctor."

"Hold on a minute." My words are barely a whisper. "You said evening. How long have I been out?"

"Let me get the doctor." The nurse disappears behind the curtain, leaving me alone with my thoughts and the monotonous beeping of the heart monitor by my left ear. Fortunately, I don't have long to wait.

"She's awake and talking?" comes a male voice from beyond the curtain. A doctor who looks like he just graduated high school pulls back the curtain and strides over to the bed.

"Ms. Tejedor. It's good to see you awake. I'm Dr. Holst. I've been taking care of you for the last few hours." He pulls a pen light from the pocket of his white coat and checks my eyes. "Are you in any pain?" The combination of the bright light and his excited words sends a twinge straight through to the back of my skull.

"I've got one killer of a headache." I turn my lips up in a weak smile. "Think you can turn down the volume just a bit?"

"Sorry." His voice drops a few decibels. "I'm just surprised you've recovered so quickly."

"Recovered? What happened to me?"

"From everything we were able to put together from the EMT report and your head scan, it appears you suffered a serious concussion. I was just finishing up the paperwork to send you upstairs to our neurology floor."

"Concussion? But what in the world would…" A flood of images comes rushing back. The Exhibition. The Gates. Madame Versailles. Jason. Veronica.

Anthony.

"Last thing I remember, I was at the home of Caroline Faircloth working with her youngest son, Anthony." I inhale, afraid to ask the next question. "Is he… okay?"

"Anthony? Why don't you see for yourself?" He pulls back the curtain separating me from the next bay. There, lying on his side facing me, Anthony Faircloth plays with a toy truck. He looks up at me, offers an absent wave reminiscent of Antoine from the *Tuileries* garden, and returns to his toy. "Normally, we would have sent him to the Pediatric ER, but he was stable and his mother was adamant we keep the two of you together."

"He's… awake?"

"Awake? According to all the records I reviewed, he hasn't looked this good in weeks. It's clear he's been through some trauma, but the boy barely has a scratch on him. You and the other patient, however, are a different story."

"Veronica Sayles."

"Um… yes." After a quick glance across his shoulder, Holst draws in close. "The EMTs found both you and Ms. Sayles unconscious on the floor, you bound with duct tape and she crumpled on the floor next to you, apparently holding a spent pistol. The bruises around your neck suggest she went down with her hand at your throat."

I bring my free hand to my neck. The skin and muscles there are tender to the touch.

"Where is she?" I try in vain again to sit up. "Veronica. Is she—"

"I'm very sorry, Ms. Tejedor." Holst massages the bridge of his nose and stares down at the chart in his hand. "I've already told you more than I should have."

"Look. That woman tied me up, threatened to kill me and Anthony." I grab the sleeve of his white coat with my free hand. "Can't you at least tell me if she's still alive?"

Holst takes all of two seconds to consider my question before pulling the curtain closed and taking a seat next to me on the gurney.

"We never had this conversation, right?"

"What conversation?" I raise an eyebrow and offer him an exhausted smile. "I've got a concussion, remember?"

"Right." He lets out an impassioned sigh. "From what I understand, she isn't doing well. They've got her upstairs in the OR as we speak. When they found her, she was bleeding from her ears and nose. Neurosurgery is working to evacuate a pretty significant head bleed and they're not sure she's going to make it."

"But she's alive."

He looks away. "For now."

Though Veronica likely lies dying in an operating room several floors away, the mere memory of her icy glare chills me more than the bag of IV fluids running into my veins.

Holst meets my gaze, his brow furrowed. "Is it true she's the boy's teacher?"

I nod. The effort sends a new twinge of pain from my neck up into the back of my skull.

"You're voice is pretty rough." Holst takes a yellow pitcher and pours some ice water into a styrofoam cup. "You must be thirsty."

Holst is still adjusting my bed so I can sit up and sip my water when Detectives Sterling and Bolger round the corner. Bolger, even more surly than usual, hangs back while Sterling's earnest expression suggests he's forgotten the tone of our last couple of conversations.

"Mira." Standing at the foot of my bed, his hands tremble. "Thank God you're all right."

"Good news, Detective." I rub at the shooting pain above my eye and flash an ironic grin. "I think I found your murderer."

Bolger snorts into his coffee as Sterling's eyes drop.

"I'm sorry, Mira." His shoulders slump as his gaze wanders across the various pieces of medical equipment. "I should've been there for you."

"Don't beat yourself up too much. I didn't suspect Sayles either. Call me crazy, but I don't make it standard practice to delve into deep psychic trances with a homicidal maniac standing watch over me."

Sterling glances in the doctor's direction. "Is she well enough to talk for a minute?"

Holst catches my subtle nod. "Make it quick, Detective. Ms. Tejedor has had a rough day." Bolger follows Holst out into the ER, leaving me alone with Sterling.

"How are you feeling?" The contrition in Sterling's eyes cut with genuine concern, the baked bread scent is the first emotion my mind has registered since I woke up.

"About as well as can be expected. Doc Holst says I've got a pretty good concussion and the railroad worker hammering spikes into the back of my skull would tend to agree."

"But you're going to be okay?"

"I've had worse. Believe me." I pray he doesn't see past my bold-faced lie. "Anyway, I'm a lot more worried about Jason. Last thing I remember, Veronica shot him. Is he all right?"

"We took his statement earlier. He looked pretty pale, but the doctors say he should pull through." Sterling leans in and his voice takes on a conspiratorial tone. "Kid saved your life, you know. Took one in the shoulder leading Sayles away from you and Anthony."

"But from what I understand, they found her lying on the floor next to me."

"Jason's a conditioned athlete. Even down a pint or two, he led Sayles for quite the chase. He climbed out his window before she blew the door off its hinges and ran a few blocks before holing up in a neighbor's garage. He made a quick 9-1-1 call on his cell and then hunkered down and kept pressure on his wound till the EMTs and cops arrived. Best I can tell, after Sayles lost him, she circled back to the Faircloth house." Sterling looks around and his voice goes even a shade quieter. "What the hell happened, Mira? It's like someone clubbed her… from inside her skull."

"I'm not sure what you're insinuating. Anthony was all but comatose and I was bound and gagged on the floor."

"Bound and gagged, maybe, but helpless? Forget about the A negative blood we found on those four-inch heels of yours." He taps his temple twice and raises an eyebrow. "You're telling me it wasn't you?"

"I'm afraid anything like that is a bit beyond my capabilities, Detective Sterling, but I appreciate your open-mindedness about who I am and what I can do."

Sterling clears his throat. "One of our guys found five different bottles of psychiatric medicine at Sayles' townhouse and her blood tests here popped positive for amphetamines. Working theory between medical and law enforcement is she stroked out from all the drugs ratcheting up her heart and blood pressure. What's your take?"

"Sounds plausible to me." I offer him a coy smile. "And I can all but guarantee your report will be easier to write if I remain a helpless victim in all of this, wouldn't you agree?"

A grim smile overtakes Sterling's lips. "I suppose it would."

A thought flashes across my memory. "What about Glenn Hartman? You held him for his assault on Jason, but you and I both know the real reason you kept him as long as you did."

"Jason Faircloth has already dropped all charges against Hartman, though there's still the matter of the pictures." Sterling takes in my shocked expression. "Caroline showed me. At least I finally understand what Hartman was doing at the Faircloth house that morning. Can't say I'm too happy those pictures were withheld, though I can understand why you all did it."

"The last thing Caroline or Jason needed at that moment was to get dragged down to the police station again. And Jason didn't take those pictures. Veronica did."

"A fact you didn't know at the time, I might add." Sterling checks his watch. "So, Veronica steals Jason's phone and makes it look like he's the one that texted Julianna. Meanwhile, Glenn Hartman thinks it's Jason blackmailing him with pictures of him and the Wagner girl. God, what a piece of work."

"You have no idea." I rub at my ribs where Veronica kicked me. "What happens to Hartman now?"

"Once it gets out he was sleeping with a student, his career will likely be over, but truth is, the age of consent in North Carolina is sixteen."

"He goes free? Wow." I try to read Sterling's expression, as my sixth sense is still a little hit-or-miss. "The only question remaining then is… what happened to Julianna Wagner?"

"We've redoubled our efforts on the case since finding out about Sayles' involvement. I'll let you know if and when we find out anything." He pushes the blanket back from the edge of the bed and takes a seat. "So, are we good? You and me?"

"I'd say so. You've got your murderer, if she survives the night. We've helped exonerate an innocent man, well, sort of innocent. Anthony appears to be back to something resembling normal and to top it all off, I made it through with nothing but a splitting headache, some bruised ribs, and a few tape burns. The good guys won."

"No," he says. "You know what I mean. I was wondering if—"

"She's awake?" A welcome voice sounds from beyond the curtain. A moment later, Thomas pokes his head inside my corner of the ER. His face breaks into a broad grin when our eyes meet. "Thank God, Mira. I've been out of my head."

"Hm." I give him the best grin I can manage. "And I thought that was my job."

He steps around Sterling and joins me at the head of the bed. "Are you all right?"

"Getting better every minute."

"Good evening, Doc." Sterling rises from the bed.

"Detective." Thomas returns his attention to me. "You need anything?"

"The doctor is off getting me something for the quartet of Clydesdales tap dancing on my skull. Otherwise, I'm doing just fine."

Thomas' voice grows quiet. "They weren't sure you'd wake up."

I gesture around the room with my free hand. "And miss all this?"

"If you'll excuse me, it seems you two have some catching up to do." Sterling grasps the edge of the curtain. "We'll be in touch sometime in the next few days to get a statement, Ms. Tejedor, when you're feeling up to it, of course."

"Thank you, Detective. I'll be glad to help in any way I can."

Sterling pauses at the edge of the room as if about to say something else, but opts instead to keep his silence. He pulls the curtain closed as he leaves.

"Did I interrupt something?" Thomas looks down on me, his expression somewhere between curious and hurt. Jalapeno burns my senses.

"Just business." I stretch my arms above my head and wince as the IV line connecting me to the hanging bag of fluids pinches the skin at my wrist. "How are you doing, Thomas?"

"How am I?" he asks. "You're the one laid up in a hospital bed."

It's good to see the smile in his eyes, and I take a bit of comfort as the sharp pepper scent shifts to fresh-baked apple pie. "The women's clinic," I ask. "Did you find out anything?"

"I suppose it's a foregone conclusion at this point, but it was Veronica. She didn't go in with Julianna, but they've got footage of her dropping our missing teenager at the door on the Friday before her disappearance."

"You're not a cop. How did you get them to show you the security video?"

"More than a decade of training in the field of psychology." He raises an eyebrow, his lips curling into a subtle smirk. "I can be pretty persuasive when I need to be."

"I imagine so." The fingers of my free hand ball into a fist. "Something's rotten. Julianna was at the clinic less than a week before her face hit CNN and they didn't come forward?"

"I thought the same thing," Thomas says. "Apparently, their usual doctor was on vacation that week and the locum doctor that was filling in is now out of state. As for the staff, they claim they didn't put together that Julianna was the one who had visited their clinic, but if you want my opinion, they were just scared."

"Too scared to help find a missing girl?"

"They're an abortion clinic, Mira. I drove past a small army of protesters just to get to the parking lot today. If I were in their shoes, I'm not sure I'd advertise if a client went missing."

"I suppose. Still, don't they have some responsibility to look out for their patients after such a traumatic procedure?"

"That's the thing." Thomas sits where Sterling sat moments before. "Unless I'm way off base, I don't believe Julianna went through with it."

"She didn't?"

"The nurse didn't come right out and say as much, but I could read between the lines."

"What did she say?"

Thomas looks away, his body tensing as he searches for the words. "Eight weeks is the cut off for the pill, what they call a medical abortion at the clinic. Even a day over, though, and you're looking at a surgical procedure. She told me a lot of young women change their minds when they hear that. Ring any bells?"

"Eight weeks, one day." The meaning of Thomas' words sinks in, as do the meaning of the scribbled numbers that flowed from my hand in Julianna Wagner's bedroom. "Veronica killed a pregnant woman in cold blood, and all over a man."

"Not the first crazy thing I've seen a person do in the throes of infatuation." Thomas clears his throat, the emotional air shifting as he changes the subject. "Anthony's in the next bed. Have you seen him?"

"The doctor pulled back the curtain a few minutes ago so I could see him. He looks great."

"I'm not sure what you did, but it's a miracle. He's back to normal, well, whatever passes for normal when it comes to Anthony."

"What can I say? I always was good at putting together jigsaw puzzles."

Thomas' eyes drop to the starched sheets covering my legs. "Now that Anthony's better, I guess you'll be heading back to Virginia."

"As soon as possible. I need to get home to my little girl."

"Isabella, right?"

I laugh. "Good memory. Izzy's been missing her Mami, and I can't wait to get back to her." Before I can stop myself, my free hand grasps

Thomas'. His palm is warm on my cold fingers. "That's not to say there aren't things in Charlotte I'll miss."

Thomas stares down at our interlaced fingers, but doesn't say a word. A few seconds pass before I let go and fold my hands back in my lap.

"How's Caroline?" I ask, as my turn to change the subject comes around.

"Outside getting some air. I'll go let her know you're awake. She's been waiting hours to talk to you." He rises from the bed.

"Wait, Thomas." I grasp his arm, and suddenly I'm the one having trouble finding words. "Rachel. Just before everything went down, she had another episode. How is she doing?"

He sits back on the bed. "Rachel is doing surprisingly well, actually. She woke up right around the same time Anthony did." The concern in Thomas' eyes shifts to a look of curiosity. "I was going to wait till you were a bit further out, but I've just got to know. What happened this morning? Anthony's awake, Rachel seems good as new, and Veronica… well…"

"That's a long story." I do my best to fill Thomas in on everything that went down that morning, though reliving it is harder than I would have guessed. The roller coaster of emotions, both his and mine, leaves me even more exhausted than before. Still, it's worth it to see his eyes light up like a child's at Christmas when I describe the Gates.

"The last piece. A door." His fingers shake with excitement. "The whole time, and all he had to do was walk through."

"He had to get himself together first. Don't forget that."

"With a little help from you." His face relaxes for a moment before resuming the furrowed brow and narrowed eyes he's held for the last several minutes. "Still, I don't get how you kept Veronica from killing you both. From what Caroline told me, the official theory is she stroked out on the cocktail of drugs circulating through her system, but I don't buy that for a second. What really happened?"

"Truth?" At Thomas' subtle nod, I answer. "Anthony and I escaped the Exhibition just before it collapsed upon itself and… we didn't bring her along."

Thomas and I share a long silence, neither knowing what to say for what seems an eternity. More than once, I nearly open up about the last moments of the Exhibition, the dagger, and exactly what I dared do to bring this whole thing to an end, but think better of it.

"That leaves the final riddle, then," he says. "The Exhibition itself." Thomas strokes his chin. "The coincidence of Anthony's troubles with Julianna's disappearance is uncanny, but how could one have possibly caused the other?"

"Anthony is a special boy, Thomas. More than any of us ever knew. His talent, the way he connects with people, is unique in my experience and in many ways far beyond anything I can even think about doing."

"I'm listening."

"Imagine this. You're thirteen, brilliant, awkward. There are two women in your life other than your mother that mean everything to you. The first, a devoted teacher and trusted confidant. The other, your most hopeless crush and someone who's dating the person you look up to most in the world."

"Jason."

"What would happen if you were forced to watch one murder the other? What acrobatics might your mind put itself through to forget such a thing ever happened?"

"Dissociative episodes have been documented on more than one occasion in people who have witnessed traumatic events. But Anthony didn't see the murder. He couldn't have. He was home that night with a stomach virus."

"Oh, he saw it. Anthony saw it in a way most will never understand."

"He didn't just see it happen." Thomas' eyes grow wide with comprehension. "He experienced it."

"Through both the eyes of the murderer and the murdered. A unique perspective."

"That's one way of describing it." Thomas lets out a long sigh. "I believe such an experience would send most of us over the edge."

Eighteen months ago, little Sarah Goode told me of the subtle psychic link she shared with her kidnapper, the horror of seeing what he saw and feeling what he felt. After seeing what happened to Anthony, I'm more in awe over the girl's resilience than ever.

"Anthony's world was shattered when someone he trusted did the unthinkable. All I had to do was prove to him there were still people he could believe in. People who would do anything for him and wouldn't let him down, no matter what." My vision goes out of focus as Baba Yaga's visage fills my mind's eye. "You know what's funny? For all the trouble she caused, I never would have won without the witch. Once I had her, the rest all fell into line." The image of Yaga's sneer melting into Caroline's pleasant smile warms me from within. "In some strange way, it's like she was on my side all along."

"You risked it all going back into his mind there at the end." Thomas stares at me, incredulous. "How did you know it would work?"

"I didn't." A shiver starts in my neck and works its way toward my toes. "I suppose you could say I made an… educated guess."

"A guess." Thomas takes a deep breath. "And that was?"

"We saw time and again what happened to my body in the real world when Scheherazade had a difficult encounter on the Exhibition. The same with Rachel."

"Right. But you and Rachel are both… different, right?"

"True, but if my theory is correct and the Exhibition was created by Veronica's murder of Julianna followed by my intrusion into Anthony's mind…"

"Then maybe she was close enough to it Anthony's mind could do the same to her through Madame Versailles."

"Boy's powerful enough to reach my mind clear across town." I shake my head sadly. "Veronica was right on top of him. I suspect it was like stepping on a landmine."

"But you made it out basically okay." Thomas' brow furrows with concern. "Right?"

I take Thomas' hand. "Once I learned Anthony had hidden the Gates in the maelstrom, I realized I'd been unknowingly using them to travel to and from the Exhibition since the beginning. In the end, I gambled my mind knew its way out better than hers did."

"A dangerous roll of the dice, Mira," Thomas says. "You were lucky."

"Luck had nothing to do with it." I lower my head so he can't see the tears forming at the corners of my eyes.

"How so?"

I glance up into that steel blue gaze of his. "Let's just say I remembered the words of a wise friend and took a leap of faith." Apple pie and lavender fill my senses as Thomas pulls me into a tight embrace. "I'm just glad I got to see that friend again," I whisper. "Thank you, Thomas."

"Are you sure you won't stay a couple more days?"

I accept the warm mug of coffee and take a sip. "I appreciate the offer, Caroline, but Isabella has started calling every hour on the hour, asking when I'm getting on the road."

Caroline sits opposite me in her living room. The space seems somehow brighter than the previous week. Anthony and Rachel play in the corner, their end of the room littered with more toys than the average daycare. It's fascinating to watch Anthony interact with his sister. With everyone else, including his mother and me, he acts stilted and aloof. I can understand why entire teams of doctors have tried to diagnose the kid with autism or Asperger's or whatever disease of the day is getting press on daytime television. With her, however, he seems almost normal.

"You feel up for the drive?" Caroline asks.

"Surprisingly, yes. Your hospitality and the pillow-top mattress upstairs have worked wonders on me. I'm practically back to normal."

"At least finish your coffee before you go." She looks down into her own mug, then up into my eyes. "I don't mean to sound like a broken record, but I can't thank you enough for all you've done."

I raise a hand to stop her. "You've already thanked me more than enough, Caroline. You hired me to do a job and it's done."

She shakes her head and smiles as tears well in her eyes. "This was more than a job for you, Mira Tejedor, and you know it. You stepped in where no one else could and saved my entire family. I'll never know what you went through to bring my Anthony back to me, but I know I'll never be able to repay you."

I start to tear up as well. "Just look after your boy. Like you've always said, he's special. I can't wait to see what kind of man he grows up to be."

"Will you at least come with me to pick up Jason? He's supposed to be discharged from the hospital this afternoon. He'll want to see you before you go."

As if summoned, the front door opens and Jason Faircloth saunters into the room. His left arm hangs across his chest in a blue and white sling.

"Jason." Caroline shoots out of the couch and wraps her son in a tight embrace.

"Ow," Jason grunts. "Careful with the shoulder, Mom." Jason's eyes flicker over to the hole left in the drywall by the door. "I just took a bullet, remember?"

"Sorry," Caroline says. "What are you doing here? The doctor said he wasn't going to let you go till this afternoon."

"My surgeon's first case this morning got cancelled, so he made rounds early. Let me go about an hour ago. Brendan and the guys were up visiting, so I signed myself out and they dropped me off." He glances across his mother's shoulder and catches my eye. "Didn't know if you'd still be around."

"Just a couple more minutes." I join them in the foyer. "Good to see you up and about."

"You too," Jason says without a trace of his usual ironic tone as he turns to his mother. "Mom, can I talk to Mira alone for a second?"

Caroline's gaze wanders back and forth from me to Jason. "Of course." She swirls her coffee cup and takes a sip. "You want some rocket fuel?"

"No, thanks. Grabbed a triple shot latte on the way home. Water would be great, though."

"Water it is, then."

As Caroline heads for the kitchen, Jason lowers his voice. "I was hoping I'd catch you before you left."

"You doing okay?" I ask.

"Shoulder hurts like hell, but the pain meds are helping. Doc says with a few weeks of physical therapy I should be good as new."

"That's not what I meant."

The police found Julianna's body yesterday. Between the insight I gained from the Exhibition and Glenn Hartman's full cooperation, it didn't take long to find the shallow grave in the field adjoining Hartman's couple of acres in the outskirts of south Charlotte. Her skull bludgeoned repeatedly by an unknown blunt object, Julianna's body was mummified, a result of the chlorinated lime surrounding her shriveled form.

I'd never tell a soul, but I'm pretty sure I know exactly how the grave must have smelled.

Jason's testimony, along with Hartman's, has firmly pinned the blame on Veronica Sayles, which is a good thing, as the Charlotte Police Department likely won't be calling on this particular psychic for any further information. My involvement in the case relegated to little more than footnote status, Veronica's face is now the one in the upper right corner of every newscast. Despite everything from before, I owe Sterling big for keeping the exact circumstances of her capture under wraps. The Faircloths as well have agreed to keep my part in all of this quiet, and barring a miracle, Veronica Sayles won't be giving interviews anytime soon. Still comatose and on life support, the latest news reports give her even odds on surviving her "stroke" and next to no chance of ever regaining consciousness.

A part of me wishes I cared.

A very small part.

"Mom told me about the baby," Jason says, breaking my runaway train of thought.

"How are you doing with that?"

Jason fidgets with the gauze surrounding his injured shoulder. "I always knew Julianna had a crush on Mr. Hartman, but I had no idea how far they'd gone. Always figured once she got the whole 'idol worship' thing out of her system, she'd come around. Now I'll never find out." He catches my gaze. "We never did it, you know."

"What do you mean?"

"Julianna and I. We never did... it."

I give him an understanding nod. "I kind of guessed."

"Don't know why I'm telling you. It doesn't matter now." He lowers his head and runs a hand through his hair. "I'm such an idiot."

I rest a hand on his good shoulder. "Love makes fools of all of us, Jason."

Caroline returns and hands her son a tall glass of ice water. "You two good?"

"Yeah, we're good." Jason shoves his hands in his pockets and heads for the hall.

"Hey, Jason?"

He turns back to face me. "Yes?"

"Your mom's got my number. If you ever need anything, call. Understand?"

"Thanks," Jason mumbles just before he disappears into his room. I turn for the door and Rachel runs over and flings her arms around my legs.

"Are you leaving, Miss Mira?"

"Yes, Rachel. My little girl misses her Mami and I've got to get back to her."

"You'll come and visit won't you?"

I glance at Caroline, and find warmth there you rarely find outside of family. "Of course." I stoop and return the girl's hug. "I'll see you soon."

On my way to the door, a photograph of a man on one of the built-in shelves in the foyer catches my attention. A grown up version of Anthony, the bearded man in the dark suit is at once familiar and strange. As if pulled from the Catacombs in Anthony's Exhibition, the composer stares out at me from behind the glass.

"Caroline, who is that?"

"That's William," she says, "Anthony's father."

"I've never seen that picture before."

Caroline picks up the framed photograph, her cheeks blossoming crimson. "While Anthony was… away, I couldn't bear to look at it. I felt like I'd let William down. I mean, look at him. Anthony is every bit his father's son." She chokes back a sob. "Like I told you before, he and his father were close. When we got home from the hospital, Anthony dug the picture out of the drawer and returned it to its place on the shelf." Caroline wipes away a tear. "First thing he did."

I rest a hand on her shoulder. "Trust me when I say you both mean more to Anthony than you will ever know."

"Why do you say that?"

I'm lying on a snow-swept landscape, The Bogatyr Gates throbbing with life just a stone's throw away. Baba Yaga's harsh visage melts into Caroline's face as the hut steps into the prismatic radiance beneath the stony arch. Long after the hut disappears into the shimmering light, the composer's devil-may-care grin still hangs in the air like the Cheshire Cat's.

"I've been inside your son's mind. His family means everything to him." I pull her chin up so her gaze meets mine. "And no one more than you."

Caroline returns the picture to its shelf and wipes the tears from her face. "God, I miss Bill as much today as the day he died."

"Unless I miss my guess, Anthony has a lot of his father in him." I pull Caroline into a hug. "And his mother as well."

"If there's ever anything we can do for you, Mira, just call."

I look across Caroline's shoulder. Rachel shoots me a smile and a wave while Anthony continues to run his collection of toy trucks into each other. After being so intimately connected with the boy for so many days, his indifference hits me hard. But I didn't come here to become the kid's new best friend.

I came here to free him.

I pull away from Caroline. "I hate to say it, but we'll stand here saying goodbye for three hours if we're not careful."

"God, I hate goodbyes." She stifles a sad laugh. "Safe travels, Mira."

I rest a hand on the doorknob, the metal orb cool on my fingertips. That's when I hear it.

Quiet, but there.

One last time.

Scheherazade's theme.

Caroline and I turn as one. Seemingly oblivious to the both of us, Anthony continues playing with his sister, the ominous melody the only sound other than the crashing of toy trucks. Perhaps he doesn't want me to leave, or maybe it's just his way of saying goodbye. In any case, it's more than clear he knows I'm walking out the door for good this time.

"Subtle, isn't he?" Caroline laughs. "That's my Anthony. He may not communicate like the rest of the world, but when he wants something, he always finds a way."

"I get that impression."

Wait.

He always finds a way.

"Hold on a second." I bring my hand to my mouth and call down the hall. "Jason?"

A door opens down the hall and a moment later, Jason rejoins us in the foyer.

"Yeah?"

"Something just occurred to me. The day you found Anthony and me with Veronica. You'd been gone for over twenty-four hours. Why did you choose that particular moment to come home? I mean, the rain was coming down so hard I thought we were going to have to build an ark."

Jason rubs at his chin. "I don't know. I was over at my buddy's house and I… just felt like I needed to come home."

I meet Caroline's gaze. "Trilby falls in the Exhibition sending you and Rachel to the hospital, and an hour later Jason drives home through a monsoon just in time to keep Veronica from killing Anthony and me?"

Caroline's eyes grow wide. "From what you've told me, that's the exact moment Anthony chose to speak for the first time in weeks."

As one, we turn and study Anthony. Seemingly oblivious to all of us, the boy plays with his trucks and continues to hum a melody that will likely haunt me till my dying day.

"Is it possible?" Caroline's incredulous gaze passes from Anthony to me. "Could he have orchestrated the whole thing?"

"How could he even do something like that?" Jason kneels next to his brother and rests a hand on his shoulder. "He's just a kid."

"I'm not sure we'll ever know." I shake my head and can't help but laugh. "There's a lot more to your brother than meets the eye, Jason." I turn to Caroline. "And if there's one thing I've learned over the past two weeks, it's that anything is possible."

I cast one last glance at Rachel and her enigmatic brother before stepping onto the front porch and pulling the door closed behind me. Though I can no longer hear Anthony's low hum, Scheherazade's theme echoes across my thoughts as if I stand amid a full orchestra. At one level this terrifies me, but I'd be lying if I denied part of me is going to miss this.

"Goodbye, Anthony."

As I head for my car, Sarah Goode's face flashes across my thoughts for what must be the thousandth time since I hit Charlotte, but this time it's juxtaposed with Julianna Wagner's features. As horrible as the thing with Sarah was, at least she survived. All I could offer the Wagners was some measure of justice and closure. I pray they find some way to heal. Without warning, a third face that I struggle to keep from such trains of thought invades the mental picture. As if in answer, the phone in my pocket rings.

"Hello?"

"Hi, Mami."

Girl must be psychic. Just like her mother. "Hi, sweetheart."

"Have you left yet?"

I check the time. Fifteen seconds past the hour. Right on schedule.

"I'm heading to the car now. I should be home for dinner." I steel myself before asking the next question. "Did you have fun with your dad and Autumn yesterday?"

"It was awesome. We went to the Smithsonian and looked at all the dinosaur bones and then Autumn bought us all sundaes."

The joy in her voice is palpable and in that moment I swear to myself I won't ever be the one to take that from her. Not after everything I've been forced to witness children endure. Sarah Goode. Anthony. Rachel. Hell, even Jason.

My toes curl inside my shoes as I force a pleasant lilt into my voice. "That sounds great, sweetie." I open the car door and toss my bag into the passenger seat. "I'm getting in the car now. Let me get off the phone so I can hit the road."

"Okay." She takes a breath. "I love you, Mami."

"I love you too, Isabella." I suck in one last lungful of Charlotte air and climb into the car. "Tell Nana I'm on my way."

As I pull out of the suburbs and onto the main drag, the sun comes out from behind a cloud and kisses my arm. After two weeks of gray skies and rain, this different side of autumn in North Carolina is a more than welcome change.

Autumn.

The thought of another woman taking my daughter out for sundaes sends my stomach into knots. I'm contemplating how I'll keep myself from encircling my fingers around her slender neck when a certain baritone voice echoes through my subconscious.

"*You're a good person, Mira,*" the voice reminds me.

The smell of fresh-baked apple pie floats across my senses and the tension in my shoulders eases a bit as the memory of Thomas' steely blue gaze fills my mind's eye. I take one of the deep, cleansing breaths I learned in yoga and perfected under the tutelage of the good Dr. Archer and pick up my phone. I dial his number twice, and both times put the phone down before hitting the send button. Before I can make a third attempt, the phone rings. I glance down, fully expecting to see my mother's name across the screen, another call from my intrepid daughter.

I'm wrong.

I scramble to answer the phone before it stops ringing while doing my level best to keep the car on the right side of the road.

"Hello?" Fantastic. I sound like I just ran a lap at the track.

"Good morning, Mira." If the memory of Thomas' voice helped calm me before, the real thing achieves the polar opposite. "Was hoping I might catch you before you headed out of town. There's something I wanted to ask you."

"Okay." I pull into the nearest parking lot, my heart already racing. "And what might that be, Dr. Archer?"

He pauses for a moment. "I was curious about something."

"Curious? About what?"

"If I might talk you into visiting Charlotte again sometime." A slight tremor invades his voice. Good. I'd hate to be the only one hanging off the edge of a cliff here. "I'm… sure the Faircloths would be glad to see you again."

"The Faircloths?" I ask.

"Of course. Anthony's just out of the woods and might need help beyond what I can offer. Caroline could certainly use a friend who understands what went down these past few weeks. Rachel adores you and from what I hear, even Jason's become a pretty big fan."

"Of course. I can probably get back down here in a couple weeks and check in on them."

Thomas clears his throat. "If you have time while you're in town, do you think we could grab dinner? Things have been a little nuts since everything… went down. There's an Asian place just south of Uptown. Maybe we can catch up over some pad Thai?"

I pull the phone away from my face so he doesn't hear my breath catch.

"I'd like that, Thomas."

The conversation goes on for a few more minutes, each of us avoiding what's clearly on both of our minds. As the top of the hour approaches, Thomas tells me he needs to get off the phone and see his next client. Though I have no desire to end the call, I let him go and pull back onto the road. The last few miles as I leave Charlotte in my rearview mirror are bittersweet though I take comfort in Thomas' last words that echo again and again in my mind.

"*Safe travels, Mira. Talk to you soon.*"

Soon.

Come to think of it, Isabella's school has a workday next Friday, I don't have anything resembling a job prospect at the moment, and next weekend is wide open.

A dreamy half-grin breaks across my face.

Wouldn't it be interesting if Dominic wasn't the only one introducing our daughter to someone new this week?

With a quiet laugh, I crank the radio up to eleven on some decidedly non-classical music, punch the accelerator, and head for home.

ACKNOWLEDGMENTS

An old adage states it takes a village to raise a child. Though writing at its base remains a solitary affair, the creation of a book is anything but. The number of people who have in some way helped get Mira and Anthony's tale out of my head and into your hands is staggering. I fully recognize that in my endeavor to remember everyone, I will inevitably leave someone out. The failed neurons responsible for this oversight would like to go ahead and offer their sincerest apologies.

And so, without further ado…

First, to my critique group of J. Matthew Saunders, Jay Requard, Traci Loudin, Rochelle Bryce, and John Hartness. Thank you for your time, advice, insights, and encouragement. Your contributions have proven invaluable in bringing The Mussorgsky Riddle to life. Simply put, this book would not exist without you.

To everyone from Charlotte Writers who have walked through our doors at Morrison Library or sat with me at the big black table at Amelie's French Bakery, and especially those at the Caribou Coffee table discussion of the earliest incarnation of this story's embryonal first chapter, know that you have taught me most of what I know about writing. Thanks for being part of such a great thing. Keep it going.

To Mom, Dad, and Jilly… What can I say? For decades you've shown me nothing but unwavering love, support, and respect, even when I haven't always deserved it. I love you all. Enjoy the book and know that you are on every page.

To Katie and Olivia, I look forward very much to you two being able to read this someday.

To my agent and captain, Stacey Donaghy, thank you for being such a fantastic advocate for me and my writing, and more importantly, for being such a great friend.

To Lisa Gus, thank you for taking a chance on this project and for loving it almost as much as I do.

To Eugene Teplitsky, big thanks for taking my words and making them look so wonderful on the page.

To Sharon Pickrel, many thanks for all your hard work on editing this beast and whipping it into shape. I learned many things from you and will carry the lessons forward on future projects.

To Erika Galpin, many thanks for your diligence in finding the last few weeds (I hope) in my little word garden.

To Polina Sapershteyn, thank you for such beautiful artwork to represent my story. If anyone chooses to judge this book by its cover, I am in good shape.

To the entire team at Curiosity Quills, my deepest gratitude for all the things I know that you did for me, and even more for the things I don't.

To my various teachers and professors over the years, thank you for helping develop me as a writer and a person. And a few special educator shout outs:

To Sue Burgess, for making learning English fun. Glad we've reconnected.

To Carla Robbins, for the A for effort on my travesty of a fantasy short story in ninth grade English.

To John Everhart, for making two consecutive years of science class fun and fresh on a daily basis and for taking us outside on that day in 1987 when the earth was supposed to end so we could experience it first hand. Strangely, we're all still here.

Lastly, to Alan Brumfield, for making sure I didn't leave tenth grade without knowing how to touch type. I don't think any of us knew at the time what an asset that would be in every facet of 21st century life.

And now, if I may be a bit more esoteric…

Clearly, I owe an incredible debt to Modest Mussorgsky, the composer of Pictures at an Exhibition. The various melodies, harmonies, and rhythms he combined to create his masterpiece have captured the imagination of millions for over a century and very clearly created the perfect storm of inspiration in this writer's mind.

Why did I write this book? Why did I feel such a compulsion to bring Pictures at an Exhibition to life? It's very simple.

I love the music.

Every stanza. Every bar. Every note. I could listen to it all day, and have on multiple occasions, often as I wrote many of the words you now hold in your hands.

Where did I get the idea for such a weird story in the first place? Even simpler.

This little experiment of mine all started with a happy accident, as many great things seem to do. Sort of a "You got your chocolate in my peanut butter" phenomenon. It went like this: I flipped over the CD case for Pictures at an Exhibition one fateful evening and after reading the titles of the various movements, all lined up and numbered, one simple thought sprang into my mind.

"These are chapter titles."

The rest is history.

Viktor Hartmann, whose paintings started this avalanche of creation, cannot be overlooked. As Mussorgsky inspired me, so did Hartmann inspire Mussorgsky. Many of his original paintings and other pieces of art have been lost to antiquity, but a few remain that you can find with a simple search of the Internet. Check them out. They're beautiful.

Special thanks to Maurice Ravel, whose masterful orchestration of Mussorgsky's original piano piece is likely the main reason the music is still so well known today. Sorry, Maurice, but Boléro doesn't hold a candle.

Keith Emerson, Greg Lake, and Carl Palmer of Emerson, Lake and Palmer were similarly inspired by Mussorgsky's work and without their various renditions of Pictures at an Exhibition, I might never have been led to the original nor met the symphonic love of my life. The frescoed ceiling of Anthony's Exhibition in one scene is dedicated to those three fine musicians, not to mention the Sage/Janitor may or may not bear a striking resemblance to the lead singer, minus of course the wall-eyed stare. Greg Lake's eyes work just fine, that Lucky, Lucky Man…

Nikolai Rimsky-Korsakov, another outstanding Russian composer, is nearly as integral to this work as Mussorgsky himself. If Pictures is my Mary Jane Watson, then Scheherazade is my Gwen Stacy. I can only hope the words in these pages paint half as vivid a mental picture.

One final thought: A posthumous collection of paintings from the middle of the nineteenth century inspired a piano masterwork which was then arranged to a full orchestral piece that is played worldwide even today. This was in turn transformed into a progressive rock masterwork and now all of the above debut at the beginning of the 21st century, all fused into a novel lying at the intersection of urban fantasy and contemporary mystery.

As Trilby asked Scheherazade along the Exhibition a few pages back, "Where do we go from here?"

About the Author

Darin Kennedy, born and raised in Winston-Salem, North Carolina, is a graduate of Wake Forest University and Bowman Gray School of Medicine. After completing family medicine residency in the mountains of Virginia, he served eight years as a United States Army physician and wrote his first novel in 2003 in the sands of northern Iraq.

His debut novel, The Mussorgsky Riddle, was born from a fusion of two of his lifelong loves: classical music and world mythology. His short stories can be found in various publications and he is currently hard at work on his next novel.

Doctor by day and novelist by night, he writes and practices medicine in Charlotte, North Carolina. When not engaged in either of the above activities, he has been known strum the guitar, enjoy a bite of sushi, and rumor has it he even sleeps on occasion.

THANK YOU FOR READING

Please visit http://curiosityquills.com/reader-survey to share your reading experience with the author of this book!

The Curse Merchant, by J.P. Sloan

Baltimore socialite Dorian Lake makes his living crafting hexes and charms, manipulating karma for those the system has failed. His business has been poached lately by corrupt soul monger Neil Osterhaus, who wouldn't be such a problem were it not for Carmen, Dorian's captivating ex-lover. She has sold her soul to Osterhaus, and needs Dorian's help to find a new soul to take her place. Hoping to win back her affections, Dorian must navigate Baltimore's occult underworld and decide how low he is willing to stoop in order to save Carmen from eternal damnation.

The Department of Magic, by Rod Kierkegaard, Jr.

Magic is nothing like it seems in children's books. It's dark and bloody and sexual—and requires its own semi-mythical branch of the US Federal Government to safeguard citizens against ever present supernatural threats. Join Jasmine Farah and Rocco di Angelo—a pair of wet-behind-the-ears recruits of The Department of Magic—on a nightmare gallop through a world of ghosts, spooks, vampires, and demons, and the minions of South American and Voodoo god shell-bent on destroying all humanity in the year 2012.

Exacting Essence, by James Wymore

Megan's nightmares aren't normal; normal nightmares don't leave cuts and bruises on waking. Desperate, Megan's mother accepts a referral to a new therapist; a doctor dealing with the business of dreams—real dreams. The carnival of terrors that torments Megan nightly is all just a part of the Dreamworld, a separate reality experienced only by those aware enough to realize it. On her quest to destroy the Nightmares feeding from her fear, Megan encounters Intershroud, the governing entity of the Dreamworld, and must work with her new friends to stop the agency from continuing its evil agenda, and to destroy her own Nightmares for good.

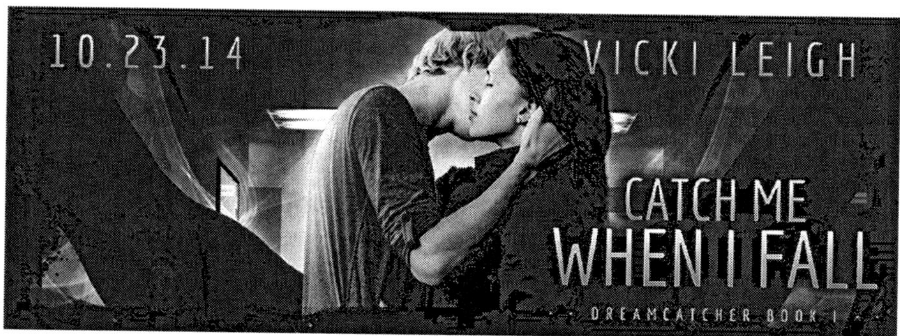

Catch Me When I Fall, by Vicki Leigh

Seventeen-year-old Daniel Graham has spent two-hundred years guarding humans from the Nightmares that feed off people's fears. Then he's given an assignment to watch over sixteen-year-old Kayla Bartlett, a patient in a psychiatric ward. When the Nightmares take an unprecedented interest in her, a vicious attack forces Daniel to whisk her away to Rome where others like him can keep her safe. But when the Protectors are betrayed and Kayla is kidnapped, Daniel will risk everything to save her—even his immortality.

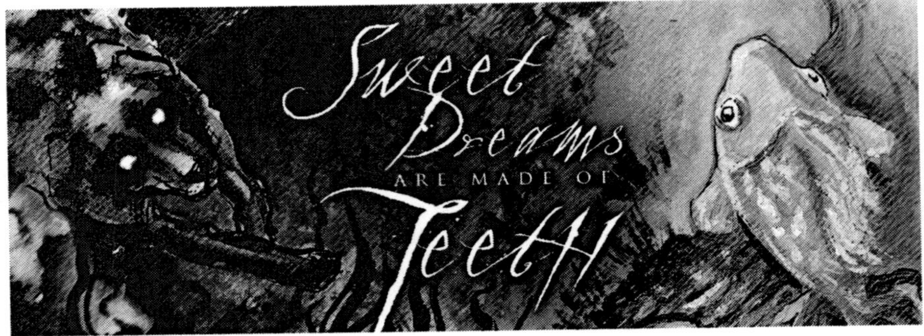

Sweet Dreams are Made of Teeth, by Richard Roberts

How does a nightmare hunt? He tracks your dreams into the Light, and chases them into the Dark. How does a nightmare love? With passion and obsession and lust and amazement. How does a nightmare grow up? With pain and grief and doubt and kindness and learning and dedication and courage.

First Fang hunted, now he loves, and soon he'll have to grow up.

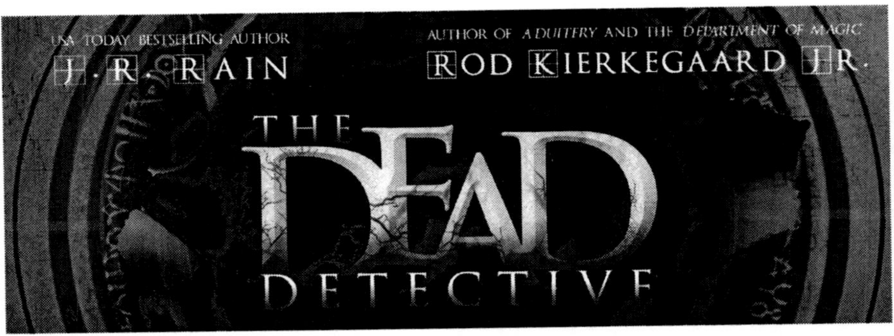

The Dead Detective, by J.R. Rain & Rod Kierkegaard, Jr.

Medical-school-dropout police detective Richelle Dadd is… well, dead. But that won't stop her from trying to hold on to her house in a divorce battle with a bitter husband. Or keep her from digging into her own murder, to discover who put the bullet into her heart. And it certainly won't stand in the way of finding out the reason she's been reanimated as a zombie assassin, no longer in control of her life.

Richelle will face off against Gypsy shamans, double-crossing ghosts, a partner she can't trust, and her own undead nature in a journey into the depths of the occult world and out the other side without losing her sense of humor—or humanity—along the way.

CPSIA information can be obtained
at www.ICGtesting.com
Printed in the USA
FFOW02n1232170816
26786FF

9 781620 078075